I0762092

The Warehouse

By Joyce Crawford

Copyright© 2020 by Joyce Crawford

Hardback Cover

ISBN: 9781733897709

All rights reserved. No part of this book may be reproduced or transmitted in any form or by any means, electronic or mechanical, including photocopying, recording, or by any information storage and retrieval system, without permission in writing from copyright owner.

This is a work of fiction. Names, characters, places, and incidents are either the product of the author's imagination, or are used fictitiously, and any resemblance to any actual persons, living or dead, events, or locales is entirely coincidental.

"He Touched Me"
by permission of Capitol CMG Publishing, October 2020
Non-commercial License 10115781011578

ACKNOWLEDGEMENTS

My sincere appreciation to my friends and family who read and critiqued my book.

Barbara Bockman
Karen Fessenden
Janice Hamilton
Suzanne Olivas
Palma Lee Stephens

Most of all,
My undying love and gratitude to God
for the gifts He has given me

TABLE OF CONTENTS

PART 2

Preface

In The Garden

When God spoke His creation into existence, He flung a fragment of His energy into the darkness to become the Universe. Our galaxy alone, The Milky Way, one of the smaller galaxies, includes four hundred billion stars.

The dust remnants of His creation took the form of beautiful gemstones. Even though they were merely tiny particles of God's immense energy, each speck of dust held specific powers and purpose but was no less precious to The Creator. As we are a part of His creation, we must take care not to give these gems more prestige than He planned for them. Instead, as God's creatures, we are to give praise to only Him.

Since the beginning of creation, there was light in the garden. The light radiated from God's presence, bathing the garden in varying shades of color from His paintbrush. The morning light was a soft yellow glow on the horizon. The afternoon light was more intense, although still pleasing. Soft shades of pink, light blue, and gray adorned the evening light. When God sent the rain, a sweet, refreshing mist veiled the garden in shades of foam green and aquamarine.

As the morning light gently crept over the garden, thousands of flowers turned their faces up to the sun. If you were fortunate enough to be there, you might witness the flower petals transforming into fairies and flying into the sweet morning air. Swishing silk organza in only one color or layers of the most pleasing combinations ruffled the air as soft music. Brilliant gemstones peeping through the organza cast their rays into the air and twinkled over the garden.

Then, without announcement, another spiral of bright color descended as a vortex through the shining mist, piercing the morning. As the spiral came to rest, the colors took on the appearance of daisies or lilacs, daffodils, and baby's breath. With this, the fairy guard changed.

If you looked closer, you might see bits of lichen moving to form the centers of each fairy flower until tiny individual hearts pulsed as one. Just under the flowers, and at the edge of a flowing stream, crickets emerged singing their morning songs. Bits of moss covering rocks in the stream moved, making their hosts appear alive. Dragonflies, with delicately filigreed wings in green and purple hews, kissed lily pads, while smiling fish bubbled their greetings from below. Soon, the whole garden was alive, twinkling in bright colors, as fairies danced and giggled, playing their fairy games.

The smallest of fairies, aptly named Curiosity, was a blur of orange and yellow, oblivious to the hint of the feminine, lavender down peeping through her youthful orange dressing. Because of her youth, she was unaware the power and purpose of the amber gemstones that sparkled through layers of silk organza. Over time, however, she would learn how the gems would enhance her awareness and curiosity. Still, for the present, she was satisfied just to dart between every nook and cranny, searching for anything that might command her attention. Suddenly, she stopped as she sensed a familiar movement in the air. Then her face beamed with a radiant smile. *“He's coming! He's coming! Sir is coming."*

At this announcement, a myriad of fairies gathered in streams of sparkling gems and rustling organza to see The Creator move over His Garden.

"He looks so sad," someone commented, and the fairies' excited smiles fell.

Quickly, Compassion added, *"You would be sad, too, if your dearest friend rejected your love."* The fairy's gown was of pink silk organza accentuated with layers of silvery spider webs. Adorning her gown, tiny rosebuds, and pink gems of morganite, endowed with Divine love and compassion, helped to magnify the fairy's own emotions.

Bedecked in crisp silk organza the color of yellow honeysuckle and enhanced with yellow topaz, Hope’s aura of courage and confidence faded, and she whimpered, *"But, He has us."*

Serenity, always wise and grounded, replied, *"We are not the same as the man."* As the gentle fairy moved, the watermelon tourmaline gems hidden in her turquoise and fuchsia gown gleamed with heart-centering-joy and mind-calming peace. *"The stars in the universe are not the same as the man,"* she added.

Harmony, that sweet fairy dressed in layers of teal and blue silk organza and adorned with sapphires and emeralds, added, *"The animals and trees are not the same as the man."* The sapphires and emeralds gleaming with love and compassion gave evidence of Harmony's heart of wisdom.

Faith's gown, olive green, was not as dynamic as the other colors the fairies wore. It was the tanzanite gemstones that made Faith's gown so special, for the energy embedded in tanzanite gave Faith her passion and the ability to speak the truth from her heart.

The energy from the chrysoberyl gems in Joy's gown helped the fairy to see both sides of any situation with love and generosity. As she moved in her usual humility, the crystal yellow gemstones blazed through her white organza gown. *"I don't understand,"* she lamented, *"Why are we not the same as the man?"* Then she stopped and thought. *"Perhaps it's because God did not actually touch us, as he did the man."*

"I am not sure," replied Serenity. *"I was not here in the beginning."*

"Let's ask Wisdom!" Chirped Curiosity, unable to stand still.

"Good idea, my dear," Agate praised her little friend. *"Wisdom surely will know."* Agate was always reliable and well-grounded, with earthy musk scents radiating from her burgundy gown. The gems of brown tourmaline and jade pulsating from between the layers of silk organza gave Agate an ability to nurture, uplift, and soothe the heart.

The fairies flew off to where they knew the elders gathered. In that place, they found Wisdom resting in a field of lilies of the valley and listening to the white bell-shaped flowers ring. Like the other fairies, her gown was of silk organza in shades of purple and green. The purple color represented her nobility, while the green color noted her generosity and approachability. The greenish-yellow gemstones pulsating in her gown were the beautiful peridot. The peridot gemstone's positive energy was that of sunshine, blessings, abundance, true purpose, and joy.

Since no one wanted to interrupt Wisdom's meditation, Courage stepped forward and whispered, *"Wisdom?"*

Fluttering her eyes open, Wisdom smiled, reassuring Courage. *"What do you seek, my dear?"*

With burgundy, brown, and green organza swishing around her feet, and green tourmaline gemstones emitting their soothing properties to boost her courage and vitality, the brave fairy stepped closer. *"Wisdom, can you tell us, how are we different from the man?"*

"Oh, my dear," began Wisdom. *"You have heard The Creator walking in the garden."*

"Yes, ma'am," replied Courage.

"I will try to tell you. However, it is still a mystery to me," began Wisdom. *"In the beginning, when chaos covered our world, God spoke, and all creation took form. Twinkling embers rained down as insignificant fragments of energy, creating us, your elders. The only creation God touched was the man. God gathered dust in His Hands and formed the man in His image, breathing life into his beloved creation. Then, God dusted off His hands and stepped back to admire His handiwork."*

Curiosity gasped with joy, breaking the silence. *"So that's where WE came from?"*

"Yes, my dear," said Wisdom. *"Fairies are those tiniest bits of energy God dusted off His hands."*

"But, Wisdom," cried Serenity, *"Now the man is gone from the garden, and God seems so sad. Is there anything we can do to help?"*

Wisdom paused, then replied in one word, *"Ask."*

While waiting for God to move over the garden, the fairies discussed who should speak with Him. Serenity whispered to her timid friend, *"Grace, you ask Him. You are so gentle and kind."*

"Oh, no. It should be you, Serenity," Grace almost wailed.

From the back of the crowd, Hematite floated to Grace's side. The most practical of the fairies, Hematite preferred organza, the color of steel gray. However, fire opals, pink baby roses, and layers of silver tulle belied her austere practicality. *"I agree with Serenity, dear. It must be you, Grace."*

"Very well," whispered Grace. She then pleaded, *"Courage, will you come with me?"*

"Of course, I will," said Courage.

"He's coming," squealed Curiosity.

In a flash, the only fairies left were Grace, Courage, and Curiosity; all the other fairies watched from hiding places. Just as God moved over the garden, little Curiosity pushed Grace and Courage forward then flew off to find a place of her own to hide.

Through dry lips, Grace said, *"Sir?"*

God looked down at the trembling fairy, *"Well, good morning, dear. Grace? Isn't it?"*

Grace stood stunned; she had no idea that God knew her name. To Grace's rescue, Courage continued, *"Yes, sir. She is Grace, and I am Courage."* The fairy tried to curtsy.

"Yes, yes, I remember you, Courage." Then God turned to His Son, Jesus, and said, *"You remember Courage, don't you, Son?"*

"I most surely do, Father," replied the Son, Jesus. *"We have often been companions."*

God sat on the cool grass and asked, *"What can I do for you, two lovely fairies?"*

"Oh, nothing for us," Grace said. She quickly continued, *"We want to do something for you."*

For a moment, God was silent, for Grace's proclamation touched His heart. *"That is most unselfish of you, Grace. What would you like to do for me?"*

Grace lost her composure and stammered. Courage quickly said, *"We saw how much you missed visiting with the man in the garden and wondered if we could find you another man to be your friend?"*

God stroked His beard to hide His amusement, then said, *"That is a beautiful gesture. Nevertheless, you see, my dears,* a man or woman, must WANT to be my friend. As much as I would love to, I cannot make a man do anything he does *not want to do."*

"Oh," said a dejected Grace.

"However, there may be one thing I can ask you to do for me."

The fairies stared wide-eyed with anticipation.

God continued, *"Sadly, men do not ask for My gifts or blessings I have to offer, so there is a great need for a storehouse, a place to store the gifts until someone wants to ask for them. Would you like the job of finding a builder for My storehouse?"*

"Yes! Yes!" Courage almost shouted.

"Yes, sir," Grace agreed.

"Very well," said God. *"You can search anywhere on the Earth. However, there are a few restrictions. First, building the storehouse must be man's idea. Second, you may not change the laws of nature to help the man. I am the only one who has dominion over life and death. Third, you may communicate with animals, and although children and the aged may be able to see and hear you, you cannot manipulate them. This job will be a big challenge, even so, I think you will have fun. Report back to me regularly. Now, off you go."* God turned to go, paused, and said, *"By the way, My dears, thank you for your concern."*

When God and His Son moved over the garden, the fairies rushed from their hiding places to congratulate Grace and Courage.

"We must go to Wisdom. She can help us make a plan," said Grace.

Chapter 1

Florida Territory Wilderness, 1817

“One, two, three, nine, ten. Ready or not, here I come!" Cassie peeked between her fingers to see where her siblings were hiding.

The palmetto bushes and sapling trees surrounding the log cabin seemed to twinkle as fairies danced. *"I love this game,"* giggled Curiosity.

“You are not supposed to be playing games. You are supposed to be protecting the children," admonished Hematite.

"Shh," scolded Serenity. "We are supposed to be searching for someone to build God's storehouse."

"Ma! Cassie's cheating again!" one of the children squealed in protest.

Ma, seated on a three-leg stool, held her frayed mending basket in her lap. Her experienced hands worked neat rows of stitches into an assortment of little britches and dresses. To stretch her back, she frequently stood to stir a pot of beans cooking over the open fire.

"Cassie," Ma said to her little nymph with blonde ringlets, "Ya know how to count to ten. Play fair now." Ma did not lift her amused eyes from her mending for fear her lips would betray her.

"Yes, ma'am," a repentant Cassie whispered, twirling ringlets around her four-year-old fingers.

"Start over, Cassie," demanded her older brother, Cody.

Forgetting about twirling her ringlets and about being repentant, Cassie spun around to continue the game. "Can I start at four?"

"I guess so! Just count!"

"Four, five, nine, ten."

Cassie began running from one favorite hiding spot to another, searching for her siblings. As she found each hiding player, giggles erupted, and five happy children squealed. An assortment of fairies and flashing gemstones, seen only by the children, darted from bush to tree to fence rail as the game continued. Clouds of dust from Florida sugar sand swirled under scampering bare feet. "I cain't catch ya, Cody. You got'a slow down," Cassie whined.

"Ya ought to give Cassie a chance, Cody," admonished Caroline, two years his senior. "Yer bigger than she is."

"Cody, slow down!" Cassie cried, sitting flat down in the dirt.

Cody did slow down. In fact, he came to an abrupt stop. All the children stopped and stared opened- mouthed in astonishment at the apparition that had emerged from the denser shadows of the pine thicket. The colorful lights surrounding the children also stopped. Ma dropped her mending basket in the dirt, hugged the two youngest children close to her side, and then pushed them behind her skirt.

When her fear subsided enough for her to find her words, Ma shouted, "What do you want?"

The Indian woman standing at the edge of the cabin's dirt yard said nothing. She just stood there looking through black, lifeless eyes and clutching her dirty bundle. The children had never seen an Indian before, although they heard many stories of Indians slinking into a camp at night and stealing children. A hot Florida breeze blew the woman's long black hair across her face, but she did not move. Her now faded and tattered patchwork skirt clung to her youthful form. Her swollen feet, painfully red and full of prickly pear needles and sand spurs, told a harrowing story.

"Look at yer feet," exclaimed Ma. "Them feet looks painful. Did you walk a long way?"

The young Indian woman said nothing. The fairies with their silk organza and shining gemstones moved to surround her. She noticed the fairies' presence. Still, she did not move.

"Were you running from someone?" asked Ma.

Again, the young Indian woman said nothing.

"I don't know what you want," said Ma. "I wish I knew how I could help you."

"Go to her," Compassion whispered as the fairies encircled Ma.

"Take the bundle," Serenity urged, knowing that Ma could not hear the fairies' pleas.

From her place by the fire, Ma moved slowly and with caution. She held out her hand to the young woman in a gesture of inviting her to sit by the fire. With dead eyes, the young woman held out her dirty bundle toward Ma, who seemed to understand. Ma moved, still slowly, yet with urgency toward the young woman and took the bundle. The children, losing their fear to curiosity, gathered around to look.

"A baby," Coreen, the oldest, said in a whispered gasp. "He's blue! Why is he blue, Ma?"

Ma put her ear to the baby's mouth, then swiftly yet gently, and with wide eyes, tapped on the baby's chest. Nothing. No breath, no heartbeat. Again, Ma tried to revive the child while its mother stood like a dead tree. Finally, Ma took the young woman by a limp arm, led her to the fire, and then laid the lifeless bundle at the young woman's feet.

"*What shall we do*?" Compassion asked as the fairies hovered over the bundle.

"*There is nothing we can do,*" replied Serenity. "*Remember what God said. Only He has power over death.*"

"*I think we should call Him,*" whispered Wisdom. At Wisdom's words, the fairies flew off to tell God.

"*Yes, my dears. I have watched her for some time and was never far away*," said God.

"*Is her baby going to die?*" asked Compassion.

"*The baby is already with Me*," God assured the fairies. "*He is safe and well taken care of. I will give his energy a new purpose*," whispered God.

"*Why did the baby have to die?*" asked little Curiosity.

"*While it is sad that the baby died, I have a special job for this young woman to do*," God said.

Tenderly, Ma reached out to the young woman with both arms open. The young Indian woman fell into Ma's arms and wept.

With great patience and encouragement, Ma was able to spoon hot bean soup between the woman's dry, sun-cracked lips. After nourishment and love filled the strange woman's mind and body, Ma led the weary traveler inside the log cabin and laid her on a pallet near the fireplace, where Ma tended to the strange woman's painful feet. The woman slept fitfully for three days, waking just long enough to take more bean soup and water. While the young woman slept, Ma took the pitiful bundle into the pine forest and, all alone, gave it a Christian burial. The fairies hovered over the tiny body and stayed near until Ma returned to the cabin.

When Pa came home from harvesting resin in the pine forest, Ma told him what had happened over the past three days. At first, he was concerned for the safety of his family. However, Ma put his fears to rest. "Charles, nothing has happened to us since this woman has been here. I don't think we are in any danger."

Eventually, Pa became more concerned for the young woman's plight. After a much-needed, healing rest, the young Seminole woman, though still fearful, became open to communicating with Ma and Pa.

"Lorie," Ma said, pointing to herself. "Lorie." Ma waited. "Charles," Ma said, pointing to her husband. "Charles." Ma then pointed to the young woman and raised her eyebrows inquiringly.

The young Seminole woman's eyes gleamed, albeit dimly, for the first time. She understood. "E-no-la," she said, pointing to herself.

With relaxed, soft laughter, they repeated each other's names. Ma touched E-no-la and said the young woman's name. In return, E-no-la touched her own heart, then touched Ma and said, "Lorie, Got-ti-gah-rah-quast." That last was the Miccosukee word for Good Spirit.

Ma cried.

With signaling and broken English and Miccosukee, one of the Seminole people's languages, E-no-la told Lori and Charles the story of her betrothal to a young Seminole man, Tomochichi, their beautiful wedding ceremony, and later the coming of her child. However, before the child was born, white men came into their village to kill and drive her people out of their homeland. On their forced journey to the new reservation, Tomochichi and E-no-la, along with a few other members of their people, escaped their captures. Before they reached their homeland, however, the white man killed Tomochichi, and E-no-la was alone, lost, and afraid. She told how she had foraged for berries, nuts, and wild fruit to stay alive. She told how the fairies had guided her. She did not know how long she walked and ran, always trying to evade the white men with guns. Soon, her time came to deliver, and she fashioned a birthing place as was the custom of her ancestors. When the baby was born, E-no-la could not feed the baby, yet she refused to leave her child.

Ma and Pa were confused about E-no-la's mention of fairies. Nevertheless, they considered that to be part of the native Indian's culture.

"How did you know to come to the cabin?" Pa asked.

"Children laughing. When children laugh, there is love. I also saw the fairies playing with the children."

Again, Ma and Pa did not understand what E-no-la meant by the reference to fairies. Still, they made no mention of it.

"Where is my son?" E-no-la asked in Seminole stoicism.

Charles and Lori led E-no-la several hundred yards out from the cabin to a stand of sapling pines nestled among wild myrtle and blackberry bushes. In contrast to the somber moment, cardinals, mockingbirds, mourning doves, and wrens filled the myrtle with song. Underneath the sapling pines, needles fallen from seasons past formed a smooth, soft carpet of pine straw. It was under that soft carpet that Lori had buried the tiny, lifeless body of E-no-la's baby boy.

Lori remembered looking upon the boy's lifeless body. She had gazed at him for a moment, thinking that he was a beautiful baby with his black hair, what would have been a tawny complexion, perfect little fingernails, and long feet and toes.

E-no-la knelt beside the tiny grave and sang the Seminole song of sorrow. She rocked back and forth, holding her arms to her breast. She sang for her baby. She sang, remembering her husband. She sang for all members of her tribe forced from their homes.

Ma sat beside E-no-la and shared her tears. Then she held the young Seminole mother, and they rocked back and forth as they cried together. Then it was over. In that stoic Native American spirit, E-no-la wiped away her tears and never returned to the tiny grave. Since she had no other family, Charles and Lori invited E-no-la to make her home with them.

E-no-la enjoyed her new life, and she loved Lori's children as if they were her own. She tenderly watched over them, bathed them, and taught them her native language and customs. It was a beautiful fall and winter, and she cherished the memories she made with Charles and Lorie.

Going about her chores, Lori always had a song in her heart that inevitably spilled over her lips. Over the years, Charles and the children became accustomed to Lori's singing, but E-no-la took great notice, and she was not the only one who noticed. The fairies, who stayed close, also noticed Lori's singing and were eager to report back to God.

One of Lori's favorite songs contained the words, "Blessed be the ties that bind our hearts in Christian love." If she did not sing the words, she hummed the tune as she washed clothes on the scrub board with lye soap or swept the cabin's dirt floor.

Several months passed. They were happy months for E-no-la, filled with children's laughter, singing, and healthy food. Each night after supper, Charles read from the Bible. This was new to E-no-la. Although they had no other knowledge or contact with the spirit, her people believed in The Great Spirit, so E-no-la grew to love the evening worship together before tucking the children into bed.

On one spring day, Lori went outside to deliver another load of dirty clothes and heard E-no-la singing and humming, "Blessed be the ties that bind..." It touched Lori's heart so much that she grabbed E-no-la, spun her around, and hugged her, soapy clothes and all. Although this startled E-no-la, she soon learned to return Lori's spontaneous hugs.

Shortly after that, E-no-la asked Lori what the words meant and why she sang such beautiful songs. Lori was delighted and shared with E-no-la, "My God puts songs of love in my heart, and I sing praise to Him."

"My people believe in a Great Spirit and believe that he lives in all animals, plants, and trees. I have never heard of your God. You speak of Him as if He is a person."

"He is not a person. He is a spirit, like yer Great Spirit. He is my friend, and He lives in me," Lori shared.

The gentle fairy, Serenity, had been hovering about and beamed when she heard Lori's reply to E-no-la. The fairy decided then to start a journal on a stack of fresh leaves and tied them together with a bit of golden straw. God would be so pleased with the report of Lori sharing with E-no-la.

E-no-la pondered Lori's words for many days. As she did, she continued to talk with Lori, and a bond grew between them that changed E-no-la's life forever.

"Peace," whispered Grace, *"let's hurry back to the Garden to tell God that the man teaches God's Word to his children, and the woman sings hymns of joy and praise."*

When the fairies made their report, God said, "*Well done, my dears. I have heard the singing and watched as the man read Scripture to his little ones. It delights my heart.*"

Later in the fall, Charles reluctantly returned to the forest to continue harvesting turpentine. It had become apparent that Lori was to have another child. "Mr. Charles, you go. I will take care of Miss Lori and children," E-no-la told Charles. So, with that encouragement, Charles left for the turpentine fields.

Lori waddled around doing what she could, and E-no-la took great care of Lori, the children and kept a clean home for when Charles came home from the harvest.

When Lori's time to deliver the baby came in March, the weather turned cold and rainy. E-no-la built a fire in the fireplace and assigned chores to the children. The youngest ones who could not do chores played with wooden toys, potatoes, and pot lids in front of the fire.

To the delight of these little ones, the fairies, Serenity, Compassion, and Grace, also played among the potatoes and pot lids. Little Curiosity showed the children wonderful ways to make the potlids spin and sing.

E-no-la was a great organizer, and great mid-wife, and a great friend to Lori. She genuinely cared for her new family. This birth was easy for Lori, who had already borne six children, and she gave Charles another boy. He was healthy and hungry, this Corbin Lewis Bates.

"Miss Lori," E-no-la said, "We must make yer bed clean. Here is a clean gown. Let me help ya put it on." E-no-la cleaned bed linen and fluffed pillows and quilts. She bustled between Lori and baby Corbin, then over to the fireplace where she cooked the evening meal, then over to the youngest children to change cloth diapers, to the washtub to wash loads of diapers, britches, and little dresses, and then back to Lori and the baby. She was so happy. However, when baby Corbin demanded his next feeding, and E-no-la carried the baby to Lori, shock interrupted E-no-la's joy.

"Miss Lori," E-no-la whispered, offering the baby, "here's yer hungry, little Mr. Corbin." E-no-la stopped and looked hard at Lori. "Miss Lori?!" Lori was unresponsive, and blood stained her clean sheets.

E-no-la put baby Corbin down in his cradle and ran back to Lori. She tried desperately to remember the Native American medicine for severe blood loss, yet nothing she did could revive Lori. E-no-la could do no more.

The reliable fairy, Agate, fluttered over Lori, hoping burgundy gemstone dust might give aid. At the same time, Hematite used all her practical austerity and willed her opal dust and rosebuds to provide Lori with comfort. All the while, they fluttered desperately about Lori, the diligent fairies remembered what God said about how only He has dominion over life and death.

E-no-la called Coreen and Caroline from their chores. In her broken Seminole language, she said, "My dear children, yer mother is dead. The baby is alive and well. You must be brave and help me lay yer mother to rest."

Coreen and Caroline turned white. Then tears overwhelmed them, and E-no-la held her precious ones in her arms to comfort them. After the crying, E-no-la, with Coreen's and Caroline's help, rolled her dear friend, Lori, into a quilt. Together they dragged their friend and mother outside and buried her next to where Lori had earlier buried E-no-la's baby. E-no-la and the girls knelt beside the fresh grave and cried. Their soiled dresses and their hair hanging loose in their faces told the story of their ordeal.

Although no one knows for certain if fairies feel sadness, Agate, Hematite, Compassion, and Grace felt the children's pain. With reluctance, Compassion said, "*We need to go back to the garden and tell God that another friend has died.*"

"*Serenity and I would like to stay,*" said Courage.

So, with heavy hearts, Agate and Hematite fled back to tell God of Lori's death.

God met the fairies on the edge of the garden. The saddened fairies were surprised when God said, "*I know, my dears. Be patient, and you will see; all this will work together for good.*"

When Charles came home from the turpentine fields, he stomped into the cabin, knocking mud and manure off his boots. "Lori, honey," he called. There was no answer. He looked in the bedroom. "Cassie? Where's yer Ma? Cory, where's yer Ma and E-no-la?"

Subdued flashes of turquoise and burgundy moved around the children as Serenity and Courage tried to comfort the young ones.

"Here's the baby, Pa," Cory choked then whimpered. Fairies adorned with watermelon colored gems did little to soothe him.

Baby Corbin lay on the bed, snug between two pillows, sucking his fist. Tragic scenes ran through Charles' mind, and fear struck him in the gut. "Lori?" Charles cried out. "Lori?"

E-no-la walked in from outside the cabin. Her steps made no noise. Her mussed hair, soiled dress, and swollen eyes spoke volumes. With an ashen voice, she answered, "Yes, Mr. Charles?"

"Where's Lori?" Charles whispered.

E-no-la was unable to answer. No sound would come from her grief-thickened throat. She just voiced her sadness in a deep Seminole groan.

Intense flashes of burgundy, brown, and green silks radiated as Courage made gallant attempts to intercede without changing the course of nature as God had instructed.

"No!" Charles shouted. "No! No!" He ran outside.

The three older children stood nearby, trying to be brave as E-no-la had instructed. "Braves do not cry. Braves must be strong. Talk softly. Braves wear a strong face to protect their families."

They tried to be brave, though when they saw Pa, they ran to him and fell into his arms. Pa swooped up the younger ones and buried his pain in their soft, baby-sweet necks. They all cried. E-no-la did not cry. It was the Seminole way. Charles retreated to the pine forest to work and to grieve. He stayed there, pouring out his grief to his God and listening for the reason why. All the while he was in the field, the fairies tried in vain to give Charles peace, courage, and understanding. At this dire time in his life, it was only the Spirit of God who could minister to Charles.

Eventually, Charles found strength in prayer. He watched the trees lift their branches as if in praise to God, and Charles, too, raised his weary hands in praise. Then he returned home to his family. His steps were deliberate, his back was straight, and his chin set firm. He hoped his faith was strong enough to take on the challenges of living without Lori. His family needed him, and he needed them in return. It was the beginning of a new life for Charles, his family, and E-no-la.

Charles was only thirty-two when Lori died. His oldest child, sweet Coreen, was ten, and Kyle, the youngest before Corbin was born, was only eighteen months old.

Even three years later, some days were more challenging to his faith, patience, and love than others. With E-no-la's constant help, he did more than survive his pain. He conquered it. He continued working in the pine forest, providing for his family. When he was with them at home, he continued teaching them about God's love while counting his blessings.

He did not know how it happened. It just did. E-no-la already had a sweet bond with the children, and her bond with Charles was more of a partner-in-Christ relationship. It was a bond they each needed. Eventually, he discovered that he needed more.

"Coreen," E-no-la called in her soft Seminole voice, "will you bring in the children from play to wash up for supper? I will prepare the three *yaatooche*."

Coreen herded in an assortment of little blonde, brown, and reddish-brown heads as an assortment of fairies flitted about to help. Trying to get Cody, Cassie, and Cory to stop playing and wash for supper was as much fun and productive as herding cats. E-no-la watched with poised amusement while she fed and changed both the infant Corbin and Kyle.

As the children filed into the cabin, E-no-la stood at the door and inspected little hands and faces. "Cody, you must go back out and wash yer hands and face until there is no dirt. Children, please take yer places at the supper table, and wait for yer Pa." E-no-la insisted that the children be quiet and respectful. That was the Seminole way. That is not to say there were not moments of rowdy storytelling, for that was Pa's way. So, there was much laughter, shining eyes, giggles falling out through missing teeth, and more than a little mischief.

After supper, Pa reached for his Bible, as usual. He chose a passage the children could understand. "Here, children, is a Bible scripture you should know in yer heart, and he read Psalm 139, verse 14: 'I praise you because I am fearfully and wonderfully made; yer works are wonderful, I know that full well.'"

"Cody, please stop kicking Kyle's seat," E-no-la asked with a gentle voice.

Kyle, the toddler, pointed in Pa's direction and said, "Putty," then giggled. Kyle watched as little Curiosity danced around Pa's shoulders, entertaining the children. Her silk organza gown swished in the air, and the amber gemstones sparkle around Pa's head.

"Cody, do you 'member who wrote the Psalms?" asked Pa.

"Uh. Uh."

"I know! I know!" Cory wiggled in his seat with his hand waving enthusiastically in the air.

"Thank ya, Cory. You can git the next question. Cody," Pa asked, trying to hide his smile, "have you 'membered yet that it was David?"

"DAVID!" shouted Cody, barely giving Pa a chance to finish his sentence and pleased with himself that he could answer one of Pa's questions.

"Good boy, Cody. Now, Cory, what do you think David was talkin' about when he wrote this here Psalm?"

"Why do I git the hard questions?" Cory whined.

"This here is not so hard, son. Look at it in pieces. I am wonderfully made. What do you think that means to ya?"

"I am special made?" the nine-year-old mumbled.

"There, that weren't so hard, were it?" Pa encouraged.

"Pa," asked a confused Cory, "how be I special made?"

Curiosity fluttered around Cory, tickling the boy's ear, and whispered, "*Remember the calf.*" Cory giggled out loud and rubbed his ear.

"Well, sir." Pa paused thoughtfully. "The Lord done give each of us special things, like kindness and love. He give to some a talent for growing food. To others, like E-no-la, he give a talent for cooking fine dinners like this here one. I reckon if we like doin' somethi'n and it makes people happy, then we should be practicing it so's we can do it better."

"*Remember the calf,*" Curiosity whispered to Cory again.

"I 'member making that baby cow feel better," said Cory.

"That's right, son," said Pa with a kind smile. "You done a right fine thing stayin' up all night with that calf. I don't rightly know what you done. The next morning, that calf was up and friskin' around buttin' his ma for his breakfast."

"Does that make me special, Pa?" inquired Cory.

"Yes, indeed. I reckon it surely does. If you take care, you can be a right good animal doctor," encouraged Pa.

Cory beamed.

"So, let's pray and thank the Lord that He done made us special. We is each special in different ways, and I am proud ya are my children."

E-no-la delighted in these family scenes. The memories and Bible scripture filled her heart as her love for her family and faith in her new God grew. "Time for bed, yaatooches," she announced. "Kiss yer Pa good night, and I will come tuck ya in."

At that announcement, the romp began. There was the usual pushing, thuds, bumps, and owies associated with six happy children racing to see who could climb the ladder fastest and claim the center of the bed. Because she was thirteen and showing all the signs of becoming a young lady, Coreen slept downstairs with E-no-la.

At last, when everyone was in bed and quiet for the night, the embers in the fireplace burned low and warm, and fairies nestled between children or sat on bedposts keeping watch. Charles crept from his bedroom. A dim shaft of light partially filled the living area where E-no-la and Coreen slept. "E-no-la?" Charles whispered. His stomach dropped to his feet. "E-no-la?"

"Yes, Mr. Charles?" E-no-la whispered back.

"E-no-la, will you share my bed?"

E-no-la lay still, not knowing what she should do. Then, as she had done with her young husband on their honeymoon night, she slipped out of bed and took Charles' hand. He led her inside, and he shut the door.

The fairies, who had been listening all through dinner, now watched over Charles and E-no-la and breathed sighs of joy.

Before he took her to his bed, he gave her his vow. "E-no-la, I want you to be my wife, and I pledge before God that I will love you and cherish you as long as I shall live."

"Mr. Charles, I want to be yer wife and the mother to yer children."

"OUR children," he corrected.

"I want to be the mother to our children. I pledge before our God that I will love and cherish you as long as I shall live."

The fairies fluttered about, covering the room with multi-colored light, energy, and sound from their gemstones. "*Come away*," urged Serenity. "*We must not intrude.*"

Obediently, the fairies slipped out of the warm bedroom, trying not to look back on the love and joy that filled the room, then they rushed to tell God.

Charles caressed E-no-la. Although it was awkward for a moment, their lips found each other. He kissed *E-no-la* deeply. *E-no-la* could not help remembering the gentleness of her first husband's embrace. Still, Charles's embrace was equally as comforting, and she melted into his arms. Their heartbeats and breathing were in sync, and then he touched her. After making love, they slept satisfied in each other's arms. They were now, indeed, a family.

In the spring, E-no-la gave Charles another son, Frederick Tomochichi (Thomas) Bates. Charles called him Fred. Fred was a sturdy little fellow with straight black hair like his mother's, sharp cheekbones, and anything but a quiet Seminole manner, and he thrived.

THREE YEARS LATER

Earth colors of browns and ivory mirrored Agate's reliable character as pulsating gems of brown tourmaline and jade further reflected her stable nature. Her companion fairy, Serenity, wore turquoise organza enhanced with gleaming watermelon-colored tourmaline, radiating heart-centering-joy and mind-calming peace. Joining Agate and Serenity were Hope and Curiosity. Hope was clad in yellow organza with topaz stones shining with courage and confidence, while Curiosity's gown of orange and yellow had a bit of lavender peeking through, enhanced by amber gemstones that magnified her awareness and curiosity. Together, the fairies watched over Charles and E-no-la and their children.

"Pa?"

"Yes, um?"

"Pa, how many acres you reckon you got?" asked sweet Coreen.

"Oh, two or three, I reckon."

"Oh, Pa. I knowed you been buyin' a parcel when each of us kids was borned."

"Well then, I reckon I got about nine acres," Pa said, trying to keep a straight face.

"No, really, Pa. How many you got?" begged Coreen.

"Mr. Charles, don't fret her so," E-no-la said, pulling Coreen close to her side.

"Okay, honey. Well, I reckon, I got 'bout three hundred acres."

"Which 'un is mine, Pa?"

"Well, I reckon it depends on what you want it fer," Pa continued to tease.

Coreen blushed a bright pink. "Jimmy's a-goin' ta ask me to marry him, and…"

"Mr. Charles," E-no-la scolded.

"I knowed it, honey. He came yesterd'y, and we done talked about it. We rode out so's he could look over the parcels. Since you are the oldest, it's only fittin' that you get first choice."

Coreen beamed, trying to control her excitement. "Which one did he choose, Pa?"

"He chose the west twenty. Said he was gon'a run cattle on it. Good land for cattle and babies." Pa opened his arms, and Coreen ran in.

The fairies danced, their silk organza gowns swishing in the air, and their gemstones sparkled in gay profusion. Serenity wrote about this event in her journal.

Right away, Charles started cutting timber for a proper house for Coreen and a barn for Jimmy. On Coreen's sixteenth birthday, she and Jimmy were married, and the same day moved into their new house. Pa gave Jimmy and Coreen the twenty acres and their house, and Jimmy's Pa gave them a good breeding bull and three heifers, one ready to calf.

One by one, Charles' children grew up, claimed their twenty acres, and started their own families. Within a few years, Kyle, Corbin, and Fred were the only ones still at home. However, that's not to say that Charles and E-no-la had a nearly empty nest, for grandbabies, when finally allowed to run through the clear forests by themselves, wore a path to Grandma's and Grandpa's house, always under the watchful, playful attention of fairies.

Noticing how the families grew, Hematite, in her practicality, charged Hope and Curiosity with returning to the garden and asking God to send more fairies. With a feeling of satisfaction, Hope and Curiosity approached God. The naive little fairies were unaware that God had been with them and the families all along. When Hope and Curiosity delivered their most important message, God hid His amusement in His gentle hands, not wanting to crush the fairies' dedication and willing spirits.

In the evenings, as Charles and E-no-la sat on their front porch watching grandchildren running through the fields and pastures, Charles smiled and shook his head. "Praise God from whom all blessings flow," he whispered to E-no-la.

"Yes, dear. The thread still binds us together." Then, from the depths of her heart, E-no-la sang softly, "Blest be the ties that bind our hearts in Christian love…" Her voice trailed off as she remembered Lori.

Just as his siblings did before him, Fred claimed his twenty acres and chose a parcel with tall pines and grassland for farming. Having learned the timber and turpentine business working at Pa's side, Fred felt sure this business would one day provide for his family and allow him to pass on his skills to the next generation. Even though Charles was getting older, he helped Fred cut, mill, and build his house on the twenty acres east of Coreen's farm.

Then Fred set about searching for a wife.

"Fred," Charles said, always training his children in the Lord, "Don't be searchin' for a wife without askin' the Lord about it first off. Let Him find you a good woman who will love you and love Him above all others. You don't want to be yoked with a mismatched partner. You know, like that onry ole mare and that cocky stallion. They don't never work together. You just cain't never git nothing done with them. You want a wife who will share yer love for the Lord."

"Yes, sir, Pa. I already been prayin' about it."

"Good boy," Pa said and relaxed, knowing that his son's faith in God was strong and that his faith would see him through any challenge.

The Lord did send Fred a loving wife, Kari, who gave him six beautiful children and shared a great love for the Lord. Fred understood then what David meant when he wrote Psalm 127:4-5, which says, "Like arrows in the hand of a warrior, so are children born in one's youth. Blessed is the man whose quiver is full of them." Fred also understood what his Pa meant when he said, "The thread still binds us together." It was the thread of faith in God.

Sadly, within the next nineteen years, Charles and E-no-la died, and their children buried their faithful parents in the little patch of pines and myrtle next to Lori and E-no-la's first son.

Fred's oldest son, Leo, now twelve, was chomping at the bit to become a man. Leo tried to walk and talk like his pa, and Fred cherished those things, so he took every opportunity to take walks and talk man to man about anything that came to mind. "Leo, son. Let's go out into the forest," Fred called.

As had become His custom, God also walked with Fred and his son, enjoying the love and faith Fred and Leo shared.

"Comin', Pa. Don't walk so fast, Pa. I cain't keep up," shouted Leo.

Courage, Curiosity, and Serenity darted out of the cabin where they were playing with the babies. Like excited children, the fairies raced and giggled, eager to join in the fun down the dirt road toward the sawmill. Not that Courage and Curiosity needed an invitation to accompany Fred and Leo anywhere. The young fairies were delighted to flutter from bush to bush, sprinkling their fairy dust around the father and son.

"Did I ever tell you about yer Grandma E-no-la and Grandpa Charles, son?" Fred's heart ached as he remembered his ma and pa.

"Yes, sir. Will you tell it to me again? I love to hear yer stories," replied Leo.

"Yer a lot like yer Grandma E-no-la. Her Seminole blood was strong, true, and good. You look a lot like her, too, with yer honey-brown skin and dark hair. I'm proud you look like my ma, Leo. She was a great and wise woman." He smiled and continued, "Yer Grandpa Charles was a tall man with yeller-colored hair. He was a fine man. Pa was loving and kind, an' a hard-workin' man. And he always taught us young'uns how to be fine human bein's. He was also a God-fearin' man who taught us about God's love. I 'member one story he told me about my brother, Cory, and the cat's claw and pine burs."

"Tell me again, Pa," begged Leo.

God also delighted in hearing the story again, for whenever God heard Fred speak to his children, teaching them faith, God's heart swelled with love and pride.

"Pa caught Cody throwin' pinecones at my sister, Cassie, but Pa didn't say nothin' right away. He waited for just the right time..."

"Owie! Pa, help!" Cody stood frozen with briers tangled in his legs.

Pa didn't hurry in a panic, though he did push forward in fear his son was in pain. "There, you go, boy," Pa said, pulling the last of the cat's claw thorny briers out of Cody's britches. "Ya know, Cody, them cat's claw briers is a lot like sin."

Cody looked up at Pa with adoring yet quizzical eyes. "How is they like sin, Pa?"

"Well, sir, just like them cat's claws, sin looks right nice, but if you let it grab a-holt of ya, it will keep ya tied up somethin' awful. And sometimes, just like this here, it can be painful. So, we need to be a-stayin' away from sinful things."

"What be a sinful thing, Pa?" asked the eight-year-old.

"I reckon sin is anything that makes us treat others bad, like throwin' pine burs at yer little sister. That might a started in fun, but when ya seen it hurt her, ya should'a stopped and said ya was sorry. It mightin' be a big deal today, but if ya let it go, yer bound to treat other people bad."

"Oh, I see," Cody said in a subdued voice. "I'll tell her I'm sorry as soon as we git home."

"Good boy," Pa said, hugging his youngster.

Fred followed his pa's example in teaching his own children about God's love and forgiveness. And so, the thread continued, and God was pleased. *ya're*

"Ain't it purty out here, son?" Pa asked Leo as they walked the wagon-worn trail. "The breeze whisperin' in the pine trees is a bit cool, but the sun warms a body up right fast. Look over yonder, Leo. An armadillo is crawlin' out of that gopher hole."

"I didn't know other critters lives in gopher holes, Pa."

"I reckon ya can find just about any small critter taking advantage of a gopher hole for protection and shelter. But beware, Leo, rattlesnakes also like to hide in gopher holes just waitin' for a tasty varmit to drop in. Ya know, son, just like a gopher hole can be deceiving and dangerous, young men must be wise and look to the Lord for wisdom, lest he fall into a trap of worldly pleasures. Do ya know what I mean, son?"

"I think so, Pa." Leo hesitated than asked, "Pa, what are worldly pleasures?"

Fred chuckled. "Ya'll find out soon enough, boy. Ya just walk with Jesus, and ya won't have no problems."

Again, God beamed with love and pride. Walking with Leo and Fred was a delight to God.

As father and son continued their walk together, Pa sang a new song, "Safe in the Arms of Jesus."

Safe in the arms of Jesus,
Safe on His gentle breast;
There by His love o'ershadowed,
Sweetly my soul shall rest.
Hark! 'tis the voice of angels
Borne in a song to me,
Over the fields of glory,
Over the jasper sea.

Upon hearing Fred speak the name of Jesus so sweetly, it touched God's heart with love and joy, and the fairies bowed in reverence.

"Who wrote that song, Pa?"

"A mighty fine woman named Miss Fanny Crosby. She was blind since she was six weeks old, but she wrote some mighty fine hymns. I reckon she could see better'n most people who have two good eyes."

"Looky, Pa. There's some blackberries, all fat, and black."

The fairies fluttered a warning, scattering their fairy dust around Leo, to no avail. They remembered God said only babies, small children, and the dying could see and hear fairies. Still, the fairies were distraught that God was not intervening.

"*Shh. Be still*," whispered God. "*Remember, I have a plan in all things*."

At that moment, a small gray mouse scampered out from under a blackberry bush.

"Guess we interrupted his breakfast," said Pa. "Let's see if these berries is fit to eat." Pa stepped closer to inspect the blackberries. "They look good and ripe and plentiful. Thank ya, Lord, for blackberries. Ain't we blessed, Leo?"

As he said those words, Fred reached out to pick blackberries for his son. From under the blackberry bush, a six-and-a-half-foot rattlesnake with twelve rattles and a button, struck, extending the full length of its body. Although rattlesnakes typically strike and release, this was no typical snake, for the powerful fangs hit Fred's arm, penetrating flesh and bone. Instinctively, Fred knew the snake had delivered its lethal dose of venom. Even though Fred was in great pain, his first thought was for his son. With his free arm, he pushed Leo back out of danger. "Git out of the way, Leo!" Pa yelled in pain.

Leo fell to the ground, unable to utter a word.

"Go git my gun, boy," Fred shouted.

Leo stared in fright, then tried to get up. However, all he could manage was to crawl backward on all fours. His breath felt trapped in his chest. His chest ached. His head ached. The gruesome sight of the snake writhing in hate, fangs lodged deep into his pa's arm, left Leo in a state of shock.

Courage, lighted on Fred's shoulder then fluttered over to Leo. Upon both father and son, Courage sprinkled green tourmaline gemstones, allowing their soothing properties to boost their courage and vitality. Meanwhile, Serenity sprinkled her turquoise gem dust over Fred, hoping the mind-calming peace would help the stricken friend. Curiosity could do little.

Leo's suffering touched the heart of God. In His compassion, God would not allow Fred or his family to suffer long, and at the end, He would greet Fred home in Heaven.

"Run, boy, run," Fred shouted, afraid to dislodge the snake from his bone for fear it would indeed strike again and harm Leo.

When the twelve-year-old boy, yearning to become a man, finally caught his breath and regained his wits, Leo staggered to his feet, turned, stumbled, and then ran to the house calling wildly for help.

Kari was feeding the chickens and stopped, wiping her hands on her apron, when she heard Leo call.

"Ma! Ma! Git Pa's gun quick. Pa's been bit by a snake, and it's bad. Oh, Ma! Ma! Help!"

Meanwhile, gripped in pain and fear, Fred could only pray, "Lord God, give me strength. Give me Your peace and comfort. Oh, God! It hurts." As if gripped by the very hand of God, the snake ceased his fierce struggle, yet was no less alive.

"*I am here, Fred,*" God said. "*Don't be afraid, for I am with you, and I am your God.*"

As if sent by God, Salt Jones, a neighbor, and a customer came by in his wagon to pick up his completed order at the sawmill.

"Oh, my lands!" Salt exclaimed as he jumped down from his wagon with his rifle in his hands. "Lay as still as you can, Fred."

Salt was quick to assess the critical situation. Knowing the danger of his action, Salt fired one shot, blowing the snake in two. He then wrenched the fangs from Fred's arm and threw the remains into the briers.

"This is a-goin' ta hurt, Fred," said Salt, not thinking.

"Cain't hurt no more than it do already," said Fred with a weak chuckle.

"Ya know I gots to git that poison out," warned Salt.

"Go ahead and do it," cried Fred. Sweat ran down Fred's face, mixing with blood and venom, drenching his shirt. "Don't mind me if I do a bit of yellin'."

Salt grabbed his knife. Holding his breath, he opened Fred's wound deeper and sucked the poison out, hoping he was not too late. The venom was bitter in his mouth and seemed to numb Salt's tongue.

Again and again, Fred cried out, "Oh God!"

"*I'm still here, Fred,*" God said to give Fred peace.

"Come on, Fred," Salt said as he picked up his wounded friend and carried him to the waiting wagon. "I'll git you home."

As soon as Salt lay his friend in the wagon bed, Fred lost consciousness. By that time, the rough ride, bouncing over the gopher-hole-pocked wagon trail, was of no consequence to Fred. At last, he experienced God's peace and mumbled, "Thank You, Lord God."

"*You're welcome, My son,*" God replied. "*I am sorry you must suffer so.*"

When Fred said aloud, "Your own Son suffered, so it is an honor to suffer," Salt thought his friend was delirious.

"*Thank you, Fred. Remember, I have a plan for you and your family. All things work together for good for those who love Me. I will take care of your family. Now I must go and prepare your home in Heaven.*"

Before Salt got to the house, he met Leo and Ma, running back with the gun. Salt stopped for them to get on the back of the wagon with Fred.

"Pa! I tried to hurry. I'm sorry, Pa. Don't be mad, Pa." As Leo pleaded, his tears flowed onto Fred's sweat and blood-drenched shirt until it was hard to tell Leo's tears apart from Fred's anguished sweat.

As the racing wagon came to a sudden stop in a cloud of dust, Kari jumped down from the wagon and shouted to Leo, "Leo, dear, fetch some water!"

As soon as Salt had Fred in the cabin and on the corn husk bed, Kari said, "Fred, I'm a-gon-ta wash out yer wound. It looks mighty swoll. Don't want-ta cause you more sufferin', Fred, but the poison is runnin' a black line up yer arm." Kari kept her voice deceivingly calm.

Within hours, Fred's arm swelled to twice its size. The poison-laden vein looked black and menacing as it crawled slowly up Pa's arm, delivering the deadly poison to the rest of his body. Leo winced at the sight. Pa's arm turned blue, then purple, then black. It took three long and painful days for the poison to rot Fred's arm from within and paralyze his nervous system. Fred's bodily functions ceased to the point where he could no longer eliminate the waste in his body. Leo lay in bed in tears and covered his head with a pillow, trying to block out the screams each time his pa vomited.

All through the three days of torture and agony, Fred prayed. "Thank Ya, Lord, for keepin' my son safe. Thank Ya, Lord, for rescuing me." Other times, Fred cried out, "Oh God! It hurts!" And he went into a violent fit of vomiting. Through his pain and suffering, God gave Fred a few moments of strength to talk with Leo. "Don't be angry with God, Leo. Be strong and brave and 'wait patiently on the Lord.' Remember what the Bible said, 'Fear thou not; for I *am* with thee: be not dismayed; for I *am* thy God: I will strengthen thee; yea, I will help thee; yea, I will uphold thee with the right hand of my righteousness.'"

The morning Fred died, he charged Leo in labored breath with the care of his mother, siblings, and the sawmill. "Take good care of yer Ma and the young'uns. Keep the sawmill runnin'."

"No, Pa! No!" Leo cried tears on his Pa's neck.

"Now, Leo, 'member what we talked about. You must be the man now. And be a godly man and love yer family." Fred looked again at his wife. "Ya been a good wife, Kari. I thank ya. Thank ya fer our children. Thank ya fer bein' my best friend. You been a blessin' and a great helpmate to me. I pray the Lord will take care of ya."

With those words and a kiss, Fred exhaled a final breath.

"*Are you ready, Fred?*" God asked.

"*Yes, sir, I am.*"

"*Then take My Hand,*" God said, holding out His nail-scarred hand to Fred.

In realization, Fred gasped then took God's hand. Together, they went Home.

The fairies wept, then said, "*God is good. God is kind. God is full of tender mercies*."

Chapter 2

John, John Wilkins From Missouri

During that same year in Florida that Fred Bates died, John Wilkins began his journey of life in Missouri - his coming of age.

From His garden, God and Jesus watched the cruel and gruesome Civil War. God shook his head and said, "*It is not right to enslave human beings and treat them so cruelly. And it's not right for countrymen to fight against each other, killing and ravaging their neighbors. It breaks My heart to see brothers killing brothers in the name of an economic principle, which goes against all of My teachings.*"

Jesus agreed and then added, "*This John Wilkins is different. He is a brave young man. I did not see that he holds to the principles of slavery. He will make a good friend, Father.*"

"*Yes,*" replied God, "*just as his father, Gil Wilkins, is a good friend. Almost like the man in the garden so long ago, Gil and I have special quiet times together. He is teaching well his boy, John, and that boy will also be a good friend. I have a great plan for the boy's life.*"

A ragtag company lay on their stomachs, tense, waiting. Tattered remnants of their faded, homespun shirts stuck to their backs, and sweat dripped from their grimy hair. The silence was surreal. The company listened intently for any sound of the enemy. They heard nothing. There was no breeze to rustle the leaves in the trees. No squirrels scampered around, gathering nuts. No birds sang. The air was still and hung heavy over their heads.

Out of the menacing silence, a twig snapped.

Their weary muscles tightened, and they each cocked their rifles. The strain of waiting was intense. Then, an armadillo wobbled out from under the wild blueberry bushes, and they all exhaled with relief.

"Hey Will'am," Luke whispered, wiping the sweat from his eyes. "What'd ya be a-doin' right now if you weren't in this here hell hole?"

"I'd be a-plowin' up summer crops, getin' ready to plant fall 'uns. What about ya, Luke?"

"I'd be puttin' on that new roof I been promisin' Betsy."

John's heart jumped when he heard Luke talking about his home and his family. He never imagined that he could miss Ma and Pa so much.

He recalled how the family sat in front of a warm fire after dinner, and the memory dug into his heart, gripping like talons. He remembered Pa reading the night's Bible scripture, Ma nursing baby Beth, while he and his younger brother, Kyle, jousted for a position on their chair. After the Bible reading and prayers, it was time for bed. However, that night, John had shattered the tranquility of the evening.

“Pa, I want to join the war,” announced twelve-year-old John.

Pa's eyes widened, and his pipe fell from his lips, spilling hot tobacco embers down his shirt. Ma froze in the middle of tucking Beth under the patch-work quilt.

“Where did you hear about war?” asked Ma.

“From men talkin' in the churchyard.”

“Well, now, John, shootin' at a man is a far sight differ'nt than shoottin' at a squirrel or a rabbit.”

“But, Pa, I don't want to do no shootin'. I want to be a drummer boy.”

Pa's mind reeled, taking several seconds to recover from this second pronouncement. “I see. Well now, John, let's wait a couple 'o years until you are, well, maybe, this tall.” Pa took a smoldering stick from the fireplace and made a charcoal mark on the doorpost. “When you are this tall, maybe then we can talk about yer goin' on an adventure. But until then, you need to stay close to home and help Ma and me with the farm and do yer schoolin'.”

Pa had hoped by then that the Civil War would be over, and John would lose interest in being a drummer boy. However, the impatient lad could not wait to grow even one inch, so he decided that night he would run away and volunteer for the Civil War.

The next night, he packed a pillowcase with a clean pair of britches and a shirt. At first, he was not sure where he would go. Then, he thought he would go to the churchyard where he had first heard men talking about the War. So, twelve-year-old John stole away from home and headed out to be a drummer boy, not knowing about war or what to expect when he got into the dire straits of battle.

John Wilkins, now twelve years old, choked on the dust. His feet, stuffed into shoes one size too small, screamed with every step. Rocks from the foothills caused further misery to his sore feet.

"Keep a-movin' there drummer boy!" John's lieutenant shouted. "Don't lag behind. Git upfront there!"

Despite the humidity-laden moss hanging from trees like long, green fingers, there was little buffer from the dry dust and pollen swirling between his feet and up to his mouth and nose.

"Them cicadas is a-drivin' me crazy!" one soldier whispered.

The cicadas' ear-splitting mating call only added to the dense air's humid misery, and the Civil War dominated his Missouri summer. He should be jumping into the spring, picking mulberries, or laying on the cabin porch in the heat of the day.

"Wil'iam," Luke whispered.

"Yeah?"

"When the war's over, which gov'ment will control Missouri?"

"Don't know. Confederate, I hope."

"Well, do you think them Yankee boys'll smash our mines and ruin the rivers like they said they would?"

“Nah.” William spat tobacco juice at a passing insect. “They need them rivers and mines just as much as we do. Besides, them rivers is too big to ruin, and them minerals will always be in them hills.”

“Jess is a-fightin' on the Yankee side. Could you shoot him?” asked Luke.

“Don't know. I like Jess and his family, so I 'magine it would be hard to shoot him, knowing that I would have to go back home and help take care of his wife and kids.”

John ducked at the sound of a sniper's fire, and as gunshots tore through the air, a barrage of lead whistled by John's head.

“Charge!” shouted the lieutenant.

John surged to his feet and beat the charge cadence. The troops charged with their bayonets fixed. The noise of battle came fast and fierce as rifles and cannons exploded all around him. Cannons fired, and John ran, losing all sense of time and place.

“Boy!” called out his lieutenant, “keep the cadence! You can't stop! Keep cadence!”

Another cannonball whistled through the air and exploded, filling the air with sulfur. John gasped for breath. Even though his ears rang, and he choked, he still ran and beat cadence. John stumbled and fell over a branch that ripped his drum from his neck. Amid the thick, blinding smoke of spent gunpowder, he searched the ground for his drum. Finding it, he staggered back to his feet.

“Incoming!” the lieutenant yelled. “Take cover!”

“Duck!” a scout yelled.

For some, like Robbie Baker, it was too late.

"Robbie! Where are ya?" coughed James Baker, calling his younger brother.

Robbie never heard the whistle of the incoming mortar. John did. John quickly learned to heed that whistling sound. However, when it came, he was numb with fear. Still, he beat his drum in a charge cadence and ran. Sulfur filled his nose and mouth. The burn was relentless. Tears did nothing to ease the sulfur's burning; they just intensified the burn. Dirt, smoke, and tears streaked his face, blinding him, choking him. He stumbled again.

Another cannon fired, again throwing shards of burning metal through the sulfur-seared air. As the smoke cleared, John saw the horrors of war, and he choked and gagged at the gruesome scene. Everywhere he looked, bloody body parts, ripped off by the blast, littered the blood-soaked ground. Mangled arms and legs, pieces of flesh, unidentifiable except for what could be an eye or an ear, caused his stomach to convulse in painful dry heaves. John squeezed his eyes tight, trying to forget seeing arms that still held their rifles, or parts of legs, some still in their shoes. The injured cried out in agony, reaching up to anyone for help. Frozen in fear, John could only stare until his lieutenant pushed him forward.

"Don't forgit what yer here for, boy! Beat that drum!"

Despite his burning eyes and the overwhelming urge to stop and puke, John kept running, beating the charge cadence to signal the unit's pitiful fragment to keep fighting.

"Beat the drum, boy!" John heard the nightmarish orders over and over in his mind.

Although he wanted to stop, John knew he must follow orders. He was too afraid to stop anyway, so he kept running. Finally, the fury ended, and blessed rain came. However, falling through the sulfur, it was acid rain, not a cleansing, cooling rain.

"Boy, you okay?" his lieutenant asked.

John nodded. "Yes, sir," he mumbled in a weak and wavering voice.

"Thought for a minute, you was a goner, seeing all that blood on yer face."

Instinctively, John wiped his face with his sleeve and licked his burning lips. He had never tasted human blood or human body parts before. It tasted sweet, metallic, and gruesome.

"No time to puke, boy. Beat the cadence."

The rhythm of the drum was surreal. Its repeated sounds consumed John's mind in nightmarish rhythms. It repeatedly pounded in John's head. "Beat the cadence, boy. Don't stop. Run. Run and beat cadence." After what seemed like hours of running or marching, a scout spotted a farmhouse. A farmhouse meant food and water and, hopefully, a bit of rest.

"What year is it?" John whispered through his burning throat.

"1863. Why?"

"If it's June, it's my birthday."

"Well, happy birthday, boy!" Carl, a middle-aged man, slapped John on the back. "How old are ya?"

"Fourteen, sir. I think," answered John. He thought it unbelievable that only a year and a half ago he had left home. It felt as if he had died twice and got up to run each time. "I never did so much runnin' in all my life, not even chasin' rabbits on the farm," John said to Carl. "I used to like to run in the summer, but now, runnin' in the summer is no different than running in the winter, 'cept my feet is colder in the winter."

"Got any more cardboard for inside yer shoes?"

"No, sir. I used that up during the thunderstorm."

"Did you ever hear so much thunder in all yer born days?" Carl howled and spit tobacco juice.

"Sometimes, I couldn't tell the difference from a cannon blast and thunder," lamented John.

"'Know what you mean, son. My hearing ain't come back proper yet. I still think I'm a-hearin' them cannon blasts. When we get home—"

Carl did not finish his sentence before a sniper's bullet caught him in the face, spewing flesh, teeth, and blood through the air.

John screamed and wet his pants. Then he passed out. When he woke, delirium consumed him. John cried, "Home. I want to go home. Ma! Ma! I'm a-comin'." He saw himself running up to the cabin and Ma engulfing him in her soft arms like when he was a boy.

"John! Come to me, son." Ma's arms were open.

He wanted to bury his face in her soft breasts and bathe in her scent.

"Blast them cannons!" the scout cursed, and John's dreams of Ma and home shattered at the volley of a cannon blast.

"Beat the drum, boy! Beat the drum!"

After the rain, the ground was even more of a mire, still soggy and sticky with blood. Painful cries rose from men covered with blood and dirt. The last thing he remembered was falling and losing his drum again. Someone picked him up, and he fainted.

DAYS LATER

"He's been a-sleepin' for four days," a voice whispered.

"Let him sleep," replied another. "It'll do him good."

As John began to awaken, he thought he smelled bacon frying. Still, he did not dare to open his eyes. He was afraid of seeing bloody body parts crawling over his face again.

"Thank Ya, Lord, for bringin' my boy back home safe."

This is not war. What is this, another dream? John thought to himself. As sleep still clouded his mind, he listened. It sounded like Ma praying. As soon as John opened his eyes, Ma grabbed her boy, clinching him close to her heart, and smothered him with kisses. Pa stood stoic, afraid to succumb to his tears.

"Oh John, yer home. Johnny, yer home."

John pressed his face into Ma's breast. He shook and cried until there were no tears or fear left. He never again spoke of going to war.

BACK HOME IN MISSOURI

"Gil is taking his son to the hills again," said God to His Son. "It is good that they have bonding time together. It is a good bonding time for Me, too."

God the Son, walking with God the Father, added, "I enjoy that time with them, as well. Gil and I continue to talk together, and he tells Me his deepest thoughts and concerns. Gil also expresses his gratitude for our many and often simple blessings. I like that."

God the Father called to the fairies. "Faith, Hope, will you go with Gil and his son? John is older now and will not hear you as he could when he was a boy. However, I believe he will be able to sense your special energies. Please, take Passion with you, too. I think it is time. As always, I will be with Gil and John, too."

"Yes, sir," replied the fairies and giggled to each other. "This will be fun."

Over the next several years, John and Pa loaded up the horses, rifles, saws, axes, and headed north to the hills for six months at a time. In no hurry, father and son ambled along side by side, enjoying the quality bonding time.

"Ya know, John, ya've growed up considerable. Ya've become a man, and I'm proud of ya."

"I still got some growin' to do I 'spect," chuckled John.

"Well, let's not rush it too fast. I kinda like it just the way it is. 'Cept I'd like me a little nip now and again."

"Pa!" John was shocked. "Ma would never approve of that."

"Ma ain't here." Pa winked and chuckled at the thought.

"I ain't never heard you talk like that afore, Pa."

"That's because you was never a man afore, son."

Passion giggled and fluttered about Gil and John. Faith and Hope glanced at each other knowingly, for God had told them of Gil's faithful heart.

Gill and John talked man to man as their horses sauntered on up the hill. They laughed and sang, prayed, and gave thanks, for they had much for which to be thankful.

God and His Son exchanged approving glances and enjoyed the communion with their faithful friends. *"Gil is a good friend, Son,"* said God the Father.

God the Son shook His kind head in agreement yet said nothing. No other words were necessary.

On their first trip, Pa gave his horse reign to plod along as if he knew where they were going. Eventually, John and Pa arrived at a logging campsite. The two men moseyed quietly to the campsite until one big barrel-chested man recognized Pa. Big Jake bellowed out to the others, "Looky who's a-comin' here. It's Gil Wilkins!"

"Hey there! It's Wilkins!" declared Frank, an equally burly, though younger logger.

"Good to see you again, Wilkins," Cory hollered, waving his straw hat.

All the loggers dropped their tools and ran to meet their old friend. A pot of coffee quickly bubbled on the fire, and the old friends drank strong coffee and talked. There was a lot of catching up to do, along with a good measure of bragging.

Finally, Big Jake stood from his stump-seat around the campfire and grabbed his tools. "Time to be a-goin' back to work. You workin', Wilkins?" Big Jake asked.

"What I come fer. Me and my boy aim to do our share."

"Why sure. Come on, boy, what's yer name?"

"John Wilkins, sir."

"Good manners, Gil. You done right good," Big Jake complimented Pa.

John thought those were good times being with Pa and learning the logging business. He worked hard, and indeed, he did his fair share of any job that needed doing.

"I'm a-thinkin' it's about dinner time," Frank said.

No sooner did he say the last word than young girls and their mothers came from the tent campsite. Every afternoon, ladyfolk came from the tents carrying baskets filled with "stick-to-yar-ribs" food and lots of it.

"Well, it's about time," Frank laughed, rubbing his empty belly. "Where you girls been? Don't matter. Yer here now, and don't it smell good."

Gil and John did not hesitate, joining the loggers in filling their tin plates.

"Them beans and grits taste mighty good, darlin'," Cory praised his new wife.

"Betsy Lynn, come on over here and give yer ole Pa a drink of water," Frank called to his pretty daughter.

The young girl deliberately sashayed past John, brushing his britches with her homespun skirt. As Betsy Lynn and three other young girls served gallons of cold spring water, their minds and eyes were not on pouring water or the waiting thirsty men.

Faith, Hope, and Passion fluttered about the campsite, acquainting themselves with the loggers and their families. Passion giggled again, watching the young girls notice John.

"Ain't he purty? Look at them arms," crooned Betsy Lynn.

"Don't you just love that wavy brown hair?" another girl said in a dreamy voice.

A third young girl whispered, "I'd love to be squeezed by them arms."

They talked and giggled and surreptitiously watched John. When he looked in their direction, they looked away, laughing. Unaware that the giggles and glances were for him, John considered the girls to be just silly.

One afternoon at the noon-time meal, John and Cory sat together talking about the logging business and other things young men talk about. "Cory, you been around here awhile; when did you start loggin'?" John asked, swatting at what he thought were gnats. "Git!" John yelled, hitting the air.

Unbeknown to John, Miss Anne Marie, a sixteen-year-old beauty with long red hair, soft, velvety skin, and full pink lips, had sidled up to him and gently touched his shoulder and ran her hand down his muscular arm, sending shock waves through his core.

Faith and Passion stayed close to John. *"Passion,"* Faith said, *"we need to encourage John to guard his virtue. You must not merely yearn for something passionate to happen."*

"Hey! What you a-doin'? Get on away!" John bellowed as he brushed her away.

Miss Anne Marie ran off in tears, followed closely by the other girls.

When John was bedding down that night, he told Pa what happened. "Pa, girls sure are strange."

"So yer jest findin' that out?" asked Pa with a sly grin. "Yes, sir, they is, and ya got a lot of findin' out to do, son."

“Well, I don't like it, them a-comin' up beside me, a-rubbin' my arm and such. It gives me a queer feeling, like spiders a-runnin' up and down my arm.”

“Ya'll learn to like them 'spiders,' son. Yer Ma still gives me 'spiders,” Pa said with a wink and a distant gaze.

“Really? You git 'spiders'?”

“Yes, sir, an old man like me. I hope I always git 'spiders.' If you don't git 'spiders,' then somethin's wrong.”

Faith smiled at Gil, then settled on his shoulder, arranging her olive-green silk organza gown. Sapphire gemstones hiding in layers of organza cast their beautiful blue glow of trust, loyalty, and wisdom into the night. Hope spread her yellow organza gown and rested on John's chest. Lights of courage and confidence from her yellow topaz mingled with blue sapphire created an energy of friendship, purity, and happiness. Passion fluttered in the evening air, enjoying the bond shared between father and son.

“Well, I still don't like them 'spiders.' They're creepy.”

However, it did not take John long to figure out that he did, indeed, like 'spiders.' He also learned that he could return the favor by casting stolen glances that sent shock waves down Miss Anne Marie's spine.

One early evening, after supper, the loggers, their wives, and children sat around, enjoying a cool breeze and watching lightning bugs. John sat on a ledge with Miss Anne Marie as close to her as considered decent.

Faith sat on a rock close by with her sapphire gemstones pulsating. The sapphires' energy allowed her to focus on being vigilant and receiving wisdom and insight while taking care not to intrude.

"Oh, John," Anne Marie laughed, "stop that. That tickles."

John grinned, still obediently removed his hand.

"Ain't it purty," Anne Marie breathed. "I love how the sky seems to draw a blanket over the hills. The sun dies down like nighttime embers in a fire pit, and the world goes to sleep."

John gave her a starry-eyed gaze, and then lied, "Ain't never thought of it afore." He paused, "I love how you smell." He caught his breath and choked on his words before he could say anything more.

This time, it was Faith who hid her giggles behind dainty hands. The fairy darted back and forth, from John to Miss Anne Marie, and then back to John.

"Oh, you," Anne Marie said as she turned to look at him with shining brown eyes. It seemed that her red, curly hair floated in the air about her head, filling the warm air with her tantalizing musk. "I smell like sweat and dish soap," she said, licking her pouty lips and blushing.

What's *wrong with me?* Thinkin' *and sayin' them things. There must be something wrong with me.* John thought in agony.

Miss Anne Marie wiggled her toes between the delicate violets growing on rocks on the ledge. "Don't you think them violets is so special?" Miss Anne Marie asked as she dug her toes deep into the moist soil, caressing the violets.

Passion also nestled among the purple flowers and sighed as the scene unfolded.

Gazing at Miss Anne Marie with love-struck eyes, John thought to himself, *"Her arms are so soft and inviting. Kinda like Ma's arms."* At that thought, John panicked. *"Oh. No! No! Not like Ma's."* John shook his head, trying to dislodge that thought. "Looky at that hawk up yonder," John pointed out to divert his attention, though without success. His eyes traveled down Anne Marie's hair that lay over her shoulder, caressing her chest. There, his eyes lingered a while. So that no one would notice, he moved his hungry eyes to her waist and down to her ankles and toes peeping out from under the violets. "Can I touch them?" he asked.

"I wish we could," she purred, still gazing at the stars. "I'd love to just reach out and see how many I could grab."

Puzzled, he blurted out, "Ya only got ten of 'em." He hated himself for saying such a fool thing.

"What are you talkin' about, John?" She giggled and turned half-way around to face him, again brushing the air with her red hair and sweet musk. "I was looking at the stars coming out."

John's face went long and red. *Sure made a mess outa that*, he rebuked himself.

Despite what he considered foolish thoughts and words, that summer turned out to be magical. During the day, John worked hard, and in the evening, he rested on a rock next to Anne Marie. Her sweet fragrance, soft curls, and the "spiders" teased him. Anne Marie counted stars, and John devoured her with his eyes.

"How big around are you in the middle?" Over the years, John heard Pa speak adoringly about Ma's middle. Yet when

John blurted it out, it didn't seem the same. He blushed and swore at himself.

Passion fluttered around John. As she did, the rhodonite gemstones in her gown sparkled in an array of red and deep purple rays over John's head, enhancing his emotions.

"What? Why are you thinking about my middle?"

John said no more. He would never be able to say what he was thinking.

"Hear that whip'o will, John?"

John's thoughts were not on whippoorwills. Instead, he dared to think, *I want to touch her.*

"Did you know whip'o wills mate for life, John?"

He longed for her. Instead, he shook his head to loosen the thought, for he knew he was moving into forbidden territory.

He felt the same "spiders," just like the first time she touched him. His young body moved in an unfamiliar quiver, leaving his mind in a euphoric blur. He wanted to reach out and touch her hair. His hands trembled, for there were too many adult eyes watching, and he knew those eyes would not approve. So, he choked back his desires and searched for safe words to say.

Faith intervened with her depth of stability. Glorious rays from her sapphire gemstones vibrated with energies of trust, loyalty, and wisdom.

"Timber is almost cleared," he said, trying to hide the passion in his voice.

"Uh-huh," she almost hummed her innocent whisper.

"They'll be a-hittin' the river soon."

She nodded and whispered, "And then ya'll be goin' home."

He quivered when he heard her melancholy words, yet he could not find any words to say in response. John just sat there listening to Anne Marie breathe.

Faith encouraged Passion to sit quietly and listen to the dreams of the young couple. *"We should not intrude on their special moments,"* said Faith.

By early fall, cutting the timber was complete.

"Ethan, grab that there ax. Seth, you, and David git the cross-cut saw. We need to strip all the limbs from them trees gettin' them ready to hit the river," Big Jake bellowed instructions. "Wilkins, bring over one of them mule teams. The gray un' is the best. She has enough spunk to pull better'n a two-ton log by herself. Couple her with the brown un'. They make a good team."

The mules followed the logger's whistles and haw-to's and maneuvered the logs to the river's edge. The sturdy mules strained at their harnesses and dug their feet into the mud while the loggers directed the heavy load with their long-handled peavey hooks.

Sensing confusion, Faith and Courage stayed close to John and his pa. A youthful Passion flitted from logger to logger as if investigating the motion and commotion going on.

"Okay, stand back this side of the log, John," Pa warned. "When we unhitch them mules, that tree could slide out of control. I don't want my boy rolled over by no tree. Okay, stand back, John, here she goes!"

Pa did not get the last mule unhitched before the two-and-a-half-ton tree, stripped of its branches and extra weight, started sliding and bucking toward the river.

Instead of slipping sideways into the swift-flowing river, the hundred-foot tree twisted in the mud then crashed head-first into the boiling water. The log submerged then reappeared with an outburst releasing its full weight and fury, dragging the helpless mule along with it. As the log popped up from the boiling river, it crashed broadside into the other logs floating down with the current. Men riding the logs strained every muscle to maintain their balance and to steady the massive log caravan.

Sadly, Faith and Hope had experienced such events, but the young Passion had never faced fear and anxiety, such as was to come.

John stood, staring in terror, hearing Pa's Wellington boots squishing in the mud, logs crashing, and the mule braying, thrashing in fear. The tree's weight finally ripped the reins from the mule's harness, and the severely injured mule struggled, stumbled, and limped out of the water.

It was Jake's unpleasant task to put the mule down with a single bullet. John winced at the sound. Quickly the mule was out of danger and misery, but Jimmy, one of the youngest loggers, was not.

"Look out, Jimmy!" Pa yelled. "That log is a-comin' square at ya! Look out! Use yer peavey rod to move yer log up. Mind yer footin'!"

The fairies did their best to warn the loggers of the coming chaos, then remembered that God had said not to interfere. So, the helpless fairies could do little more than release rays of energy and wait.

The resulting chaos from the furious log and raging river was life-threatening. Again, the wayward log hit the closest log broadside. It was that log that Jimmy Hutchins balanced on.

"Jimmy! Don't get in the water between them logs! Do you want yer guts squeezed out of ya?"

Despite Jimmy's struggle to keep his balance and walk the log, he fell. In the time it took him to bubble back up to the surface, the chain reaction was already in place.

"Over here!" hollered Big Jake as he masterfully jumped from log to log in a panic. "Hurry, Frank! Jimmy's caught!"

Jimmy thrashed furiously to get out of danger and back atop his log before the next five-thousand-pound log crashed into him with enough force to decapitate a man. Logs in the middle of the river turned sideways, jousting for position, creating an ever-growing log jam as the whirling river boiled from between the lethal projectiles. Now, red foam bubbled up, covering the jousting logs as they crashed through the swirling river.

"Jimmy! Jimmy!" Adam, Jimmy's brother, yelled in terror. Unfortunately, no one heard him above the crashing noise of the fury.

Gripped with heart-stopping fear, Big Jake shouted, "Somebody git over there and push them logs out of the way. Push! Don't just stand there! Push ya, loggers!"

Quickly, Frank and Jake made a risky move. They each tied cant hooks to ropes and threw the hooks to the place where Jimmy was trapped. After three stressful and time-consuming attempts, Frank's hook finally found its mark. The two seasoned loggers pulled ropes in a desperate attempt to separate the logs that trapped Jimmy. The rest of the crew controlled the rear logs with their peavey hooks, holding back the violent tonnage. However, nothing could control the angry river and the belligerent logs.

With a sense of urgency, Gil tied a rope around a sturdy rock then to Abe's waist. When Frank and Jake finally did open space between the logs, Abe dived into the river and had to fight the strong current from pulling him down-stream. It seemed he was underwater too long. However, after precious minutes, he came shooting up, gasping for air. “I seen him,” Abe shouted to the other loggers. “A submerged tree has snagged his shirt. Otherwise, he would be injured and carried down-river.” With those hasty words, Abe took a deep breath and went underwater again. Although the entire orchestration by the loggers was indeed a combined heroic effort, was it in time? The last time Abe came out of the water, he was gasping for air and holding Jimmy's limp, bleeding body in a life-saving crawl.

“Is he okay, Abe?” called Frank.

“Come git him.” Abe yelled, choking on a mouthful of bloody river water. “He's bad hurt. Somebody go git his Ma.”

Faith, Hope, and young Passion raced off ahead of the loggers to Jimmy's mother. The fairies desperately hoped that the combined energy of their sapphire, topaz, and rhodonite gemstones might help give the grieving parents comfort.

Logging stopped to pay respect to Jimmy, although the raging river kept pushing the belligerent logs downriver to the mill. Emotionally paralyzed, Mr. and Mrs. Hutchins carried their beloved son home to bury him on the side of the hill that he loved so well.

With the sting of Jimmy's death still fresh, the seasoned loggers continued their battle to try and tame the logs and the mighty river. After what seemed to be a lifetime, and indeed it had been for Jimmy, the river returned to its usual peaceful flow. The loggers eventually charmed the giant logs, and they floated blithely downriver to the mill. Although the loggers and their families tried to return to a normal life, their once quiet evening resting on the ridge would not be the same.

Passion followed John and Miss Anne Marie as they walked together. The young fairy, relieved to have a change from the terror and anxiety, looked forward to being with the teenagers and enjoyed the peace of the evenings.

In late fall, with the logging done, it was time to say goodbye.

“I'll be back next spring,” John promised Miss Anne Marie.

“Oh, I do hope so, Johnny,” she said, gazing into his eyes.

The rhodonite gemstones in Passion's red silk organza gown flashed. Brilliant red and dark purple lights dazzled and danced over the faces of the two teenagers in love.

He sensed she wanted him to kiss her before they said goodbye. He wanted to feel her lips on his, to feel her warm breath on his face. Instead, she handed him a piece of white cloth tied with a ribbon. Puzzled, he took the cloth and opened it. “A lock of yer hair?” Nothing could have pleased him more. “I'm a-goin' ta keep it right here in my wallet,” he assured her.

“I hope it's not too vain.” She blushed as she nodded.

Vain? Her? How could she be vain? She's so beautiful. Still, he could not say those words. Instead, he fumbled and reached deep into his tight britches and took out a small, crumpled, brown paper sack.

“Candy?” she asked with laughing eyes.

“No. I found this at the camp store. It's for you.”

She took the small wad of paper and peeped inside. “Oh! Thank ya, John.” She leaned over and kissed him on his burning cheek. “Will you put it on me? Oh, John, it's beautiful. I will wear it forever. I'll never, never take it off,” she babbled.

It was a beautiful gold locket, tiny, beautiful, just like Anne Marie. “I know it's small, but this here's a real gold locket,” he boasted. “And it opens up so's you can put a picture in it.”

“I don't have no picture, John,” she said with beguiling voice and eyes.

“Well, you can pretend,” he whispered low, touching the locket that lay against her homespun shirtwaist. Leaning forward, John was sure he had the courage right then to kiss her, and he hoped she would return his kiss. His warm body, so close to hers, invited her without words.

“Ya young 'uns bout ready to call it a day?” interrupted big Jake.

A young, disappointed Passion was on her tiptoes, waiting for the kiss to unfurl the teenagers' passion.

Disappointment filled John's heart, and he thought to himself, why couldn't he have waited a minute longer? Why did her Pa have to come up right now? Alas, there was no goodbye kiss.

WINTER AT THE WILKINS'

God and His Son delighted in watching Gil Wilkins teach his family of God's love and read Scripture. God took comfort in having such a good friend as Gil and looked forward to the time when John, too, would be a close friend.

The fairies, Serenity and Grace reveled in the happy activities.

Winter at the Wilkins' cabin was, as usual, joyous, filled with laughter at the dinner table followed by Bible readings and prayers, warm embers in the fireplace, and heavy quilts on the beds. John basked in these magical family moments. All the while, he thought of having magical moments, warm embers, and heavy quilts with Anne Marie.

"Did you hear what I said, John?" Ma asked, piercing the euphoria of his daydream. "Where were ya, son?" Ma smiled, remembering what it was like to be young and in love.

"Sorry, Ma," he apologized, trying not to blush and to push the thoughts of Miss Anne Marie from his mind. "I was just thinkin'…"

"He was just thinkin' about a certain little redhead girl," teased Pa.

Kyle giggled and tormented John, as younger brothers are so oft to do, "Miss Anne Marie, I bet. He don't stop talkin' about her."

He endured their teasing, knowing it was true, and he was so happy. Just the thought of Miss Anne Marie gave him pleasure and filled his heart with warm feelings all winter.

As winter came to an end, spring burst over the meadow and through the forest. The sunrays looked like the first rays of creation. Birds sang, searching for their mates and protecting their territories. Drowsy animals peeped out from their warm hibernating places, and John sprang from his bed and nearly slid down the loft ladder as his heart overflowed with song:

"Anne Marie, Anne Marie
Do you love me?
Do you love me, Anne Marie?
Anne Marie, Anne Marie
I want to touch ya.
I want to kiss ya.
I want to touch you and make you mine.
Oh, my Anne Marie."

John was already at the breakfast table, still singing of Anne Marie, and did not notice when Pa came in. John's heart was too full to allow anything else to interrupt his thoughts of the girl he loved.

Pa gave Ma a good morning kiss and took his seat at the head of the table. He cleared his throat and grinned, saying nothing for a moment, allowing John to bask in his sweet dreams. "Let's pray. Lord, thank You for spring and thoughts of spring. Thank You for a good winter with all Yer blessings. Amen."

After the blessing, John could hardly contain himself. "Pa, are we a-goin' ta the lumber camp?"

"I reckon so."

John's heart leaped at the thought of seeing Miss Anne Marie. He let himself slip back into his daydream and imagined Miss Anne Marie, bringing him a cup of water.

"Good mornin', Anne Marie," John would croon. "Thank ya, my dear," he would say as he reached out to take the water. Their hands would touch. "Yar hands is mighty soft and sweet this mornin', Anne Marie." Then, he would look into her eyes and say, "I would like to make you mine."

John never heard the knock at the door. Pa opened the cabin door and found Big Jake, whose long face and swollen eyes announced the news before he spoke a word. "Just thought ya'd be a-wantin' to know in case one of you don't want to come to the lumber camp. Anne Marie took the fever over the winter and died early March."

John went numb. He could not move. He could not breathe. He could not swallow. His daydream shattered, like shards of glass in his soul.

In the next few weeks, he tried to go about life. Still, nothing was normal. He just moved through the minutes of each day without purpose.

"John, them horses need feedin'," Pa encouraged.

"John, boy, will you collect eggs for me?" Ma prodded, knowing full well she did not need eggs.

"John, gear up. It's a great huntin' day," Pa yelled.

As he and Pa walked, Pa tried to lift John's spirits. "Just look at that new barn. You done a fine job, John. And you were good company."

John looked at the barn. Sure, he had helped build the barn, all the while, he imagined it was her barn. He gathered eggs for Ma, pretending they were for Anne Marie, anticipating the twinkle in her eye and the soft touch of her fingertips as she reached for the eggs in his hands. Now, without Anne Marie, nothing brought him pleasure. Time, slow, painful time in Missouri, crawled, filling his broken heart with the sting of emptiness.

Chapter 3

Leo Bates, Florida Territory

Accepting the responsibility of a man was hard for twelve-year-old Leo Bates. Watching his pa die a horrible death from a rattlesnake bite was his first of many challenges. His strong faith in God made this challenge not easier, merely bearable. This not-yet-seasoned Florida pioneer was determined to make his Pa proud and provide for his mother and five siblings.

The only other fortune Fred left his son, Leo, besides a great faith in God, was a steam-powered sawmill and a strong work ethic.

Like Pa, Ma continued to teach Leo and his siblings for as long as she had breath to love and serve the Lord. Among other verses, the one from Deuteronomy 31:6 stayed in Leo's heart: "Be strong and of good courage, do not fear nor be afraid of them; for the LORD yer God, He is the One who goes with you. He will not leave you nor forsake you."

God's Word gave Leo the courage he needed to continue, and he worked the sawmill for ten years to keep the farm going. God also answered Leo's prayers and gave him a good wife, Susan, who loved Leo and shared his faith in God. His siblings were starting their own families, so Leo cleared timber to build their homes and sold the rest to help support his ma. However, two years later, yellow fever claimed Leo's ma.

With his siblings and their spouses living nearby on the forty acres, Leo buried his mother next to his pa under the whispering pine trees. As he listened to the wind rustling through the pines, he could hear in his mind, Ma singing that old hymn as she washed clothes in a big black wash pot heating over an open fire. He remembered, and it comforted him and gave him peace:

Soft as the voice of an angel,
Breathing a lesson unheard,
Hope with a gentle persuasion
Whispers her comforting word:
Wait till the darkness is over,
Wait till the tempest is done,
Hope for the sunshine tomorrow,
After the shower is gone.
Whispering hope, oh, how welcome thy voice,
Making my heart in its sorrow rejoice.

Leo was pleased when his youngest sister and her husband chose to live on the homestead. Now he could start a new life with Susan and leave the sad memories behind. He hitched up his horse to the flatbed wagon, loaded his wife, the saw, and boiler, a plow, and a few other provisions. Susan took their corn shuck mattress and goose feather pillows and linen, a few pots, flour, salt, lard, coffee, and two tin coffee mugs. On a feminine whim, Susan returned to the house to retrieve two china coffee cups and saucers. With tearful goodbyes, the couple headed south.

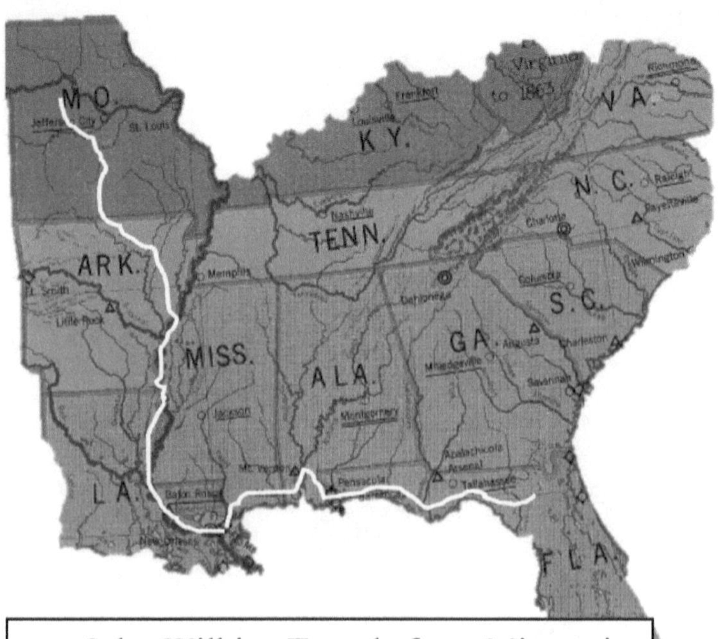

John Wilkins Travels from Missouri

Chapter 4

John Leaves His Home In Missouri

God watched with sorrow as John struggled with losing Miss Anne Marie. Although mere living was difficult, John was beginning to prove himself to be a man who loved and depended on God. For that, God and His Son were indeed pleased.

Again, God called to the fairies, asking them to go with John. "*Faith, John is a fine man; still, he will need encouragement on his journeys. Hope and Courage, he will need watching over. Of course, My Son and I will be with John and with you.*"

In June, the day after his nineteenth birthday, Ma and Pa knew John was planning to leave, so before breakfast, Pa read a special passage from the Bible. "This here passage is from Isaiah 41:10," Pa said in a subdued voice. He sniffed and cleared his throat. "'Fear thou not; for I am with thee: be not dismayed; for I am thy God: I will strengthen thee; yea, I will help thee; yea, I will uphold thee with the right hand of my righteousness.'" Then Pa prayed. "Oh, Lord, our God, Ma and me thank Ya for givin' us this fine son. Now we is a-givin' him back to Ya. We know he will be safe in Yer hands. Give him strength and wisdom for his travels. For this, we give Ya thanks. Amen."

Ma whispered, "Amen." She wiped her eyes on her apron and hopped up from the table to take care of some imaginary thing she might have forgotten.

"Ma," Pa called out, "Can you bring me some more of that fine bacon and biscuits?" However, the biscuits and bacon never came. Breakfast was somber. Pa tried to fill the uncomfortable silence with light talk. "Do you know what trail ya'll be a-takin', John?"

"Yes, sir, Pa. I'll be a-followin' the White River as fer as she goes."

"Good boy. The river will give you food, water, and rest. Do you know where ya'll be a-goin'?"

"No, sir, Pa. I'm just a-goin'."

Ma's troubled heart would not allow her to stay seated. She busied around, wiping the table, getting more coffee, anything to take her mind off John's leaving.

After breakfast, Pa handed John a small package. "Made this for ya, John. I hope it will bring you pleasure."

Unable to speak, John took the package and opened a corner, letting the contents fall to the table. After inspecting the gift, turning it over and over in his hands, John found his voice. "Ya made this for me, Pa? Thank ya, Pa."

Pa nodded; his words stuck in his throat.

"This is my first pipe and tobacco. Thank ya, Pa."

An unmistakable, muffled sound came from the area of the fireplace. Ma was crying. To cover up his own emotions, John set the pipe down on the breakfast table and walked over to comfort her.

"Let me hold you close, John," Ma said before yielding to more tears. "It might be a long time before we hold each other again." John held her and heard her pray, "Our Father, take care of my boy. Keep him from danger. Keep him close to Yer heart." When she loosened her embrace, Ma pushed back John's brown wavy hair and gazed at her son as if trying to memorize his face.

His mind went back to the first time he heard Ma pray for him. It was shortly after the war, he was riding his mare over the next hill alone to help neighbors cut timber. "Don't cry, Ma," he remembered saying. "It ain't like when I was a-goin' ta war. Just a-goin' over the crest of the hill."

Nevertheless, Ma was afraid for him, and she prayed again, "Lord, keep my John safe in Yer hands. Give him strength and wisdom."

When Pa and John got up from the breakfast table, Ma removed the last plate and biscuit crumbs. John dared not speak for fear his emotions would overflow. So, he just went outside to check his gear.

Before he mounted Biddy, his mare, Pa held out the pipe. "Here, John. You forgot this."

John took it, ashamed that he left it on the table. It was so special — Pa's gift. "Sorry, Pa. This here's a great pipe. I will always think of you when I light it up."

Their hands met as John took the pipe and tobacco. They shook hands. Then unable to contain himself any longer, Pa grabbed John in his strong arms. Pa's heart, that gentle, stoic heart, broke, and he cried. John had never seen Pa cry before. It was unsettling and left a pain in the pit of his stomach.

When John mounted the mare, the saddle squeaked, and Biddy whinnied. In the past, a squeaky leather saddle usually indicated a fun adventure ahead, a visit to a friend, or a short ride out to find a new calf. Today, however, for Ma and Pa, that sound was one of sorrow.

"I'm afeared for him, Pa," whispered Ma.

"Now, Ma, you just prayed, puttin' him in God's hands. Don't go a-takin' him back."

"He's the only son I have left," Ma cried, swearing at the horse that had kicked her youngest son, Kyle, and killed him. "That horse should 'a-knowed better 'n to kick a little boy." Ma's clean apron was damp from sweat and tears. Her firstborn was leaving. She reached up, choking back her tears, and handed him a bundle wrapped in a frayed linen dishtowel. "Here, son. Ya'll be a-needin' these."

"Thank ya, Ma. Don't know when I can return yer kitchen towel."

Their hands touched as he reached for the gift of love: biscuits and bacon.

"No need to return it, John. Ya'll be a-needin' a good towel on yer journey."

John reverently placed the biscuits and bacon in his saddlebag.

"Remember, John," Ma added, "God has a mighty job for ya to do."

John understood, remembering the times he stood at Ma's knee as she read the Bible and talked of God. Ma had instilled a strong faith in God in all her family. "I'll remember, Ma," John assured her.

He gently kicked Biddy's flanks and set off for the wilderness, not knowing where he was going or what he might face when he got there. He just knew he had to make a life of his own.

Just before the tall Missouri grass growing in the middle of the trail swallowed him up, he turned and called back, "I love ya, Ma. I love ya, Pa." He wiped his tears away with the back of his hand.

In his saddlebag, John had biscuits and bacon; in his pocket, he carried a dollar twenty-five in silver, and his first pipe Pa made for him—and in his heart, high hopes.

A band of fairies followed John down the trail, taking him away from his ma and pa. Faith, Hope, Courage, Serenity, and Passion became John's loyal companions. As they traveled, Faith called out, *"God are you near?"*

"Yes, dear ones," replied God. *"I have promised to always be with those who love Me."*

The fairies breathed a sigh of relief, for they needed God as much as John did.

"Biddy, if we travel eight hours in a day, I reckon we can make twenty miles a day if we don't stop to play along the way," John told the mare. The friends moseyed along the familiar trail for eleven days until they arrived at the White River just north of the Missouri line.

Pa had told John to follow a river, for the trails, rivers, and streams provided food, water, and rest. Remembering when he was a boy in the army, he recalled how his unit marched south-east to the White River and crossed the Missouri border. Although the river originated south of the Missouri line, it flowed north-east into Missouri, where it made a bend and flowed south back into Arkansas. At that bend, the river, its streams, and tributaries meandered south, flowing until it eventually joined the mighty Mississippi River. John decided to take Pa's advice and follow the river.

After a morning of traveling, John told the mare, "Okay, Biddy, let's take a break." The saddle leather squeaked as John dismounted, and Biddy exhaled. He led the grateful mare to fresh grass and water in the shade of a cottonwood tree.

John took out his pipe and fingered it, thinking of Pa, then packed tobacco in the bowl. With a full bowl of tobacco from home, he sat in the cool grass and lit his pipe, then he drew long, savoring the warm pleasure. Laying back and resting his head against his arms, he exhaled and watched the smoke curl up through the cottonwood leaves into patches of blue sky. His eyes became heavy as the warm sunlight twinkled among the branches, and a breeze stirred the leaves, turning them from green to white and back to green again. He thought if he reached up, he could pluck a fistful of diamonds from the sparkling sunlight in the tree. Instead, he closed his eyes and slipped into a peaceful nap.

Hope and Serenity also enjoyed the green grass and the sound of water. Nearby, Faith, Passion, and Courage lingered with Biddy and spoke with the mare, offering Biddy friendship and encouragement for the trip.

When John awoke, the sun was a little lower in the sky, and he reached for his last biscuit and bacon. The frayed tea towel still smelled like home, and he remembered Ma as he savored her delicious biscuits. He was going to miss those biscuits. He knew he was going to miss Ma even more, and his heart stung.

Not far away, he heard Biddy moving as she cropped grass. He hated to break their tranquility. However, it was time to go. "Time to move on, Biddy," John said. With reluctance, he stretched and tapped out cold tobacco ashes from his pipe in the palm of his hand just like Pa did. "There's still a-plenty 'o daylight to travel by."

After traveling for hours with Biddy as his only companion, John stopped for a late afternoon break under a pecan tree and gathered pecans. Biddy crunched nuts as quickly as John could shell them. She seemed to enjoy eating nuts since John was doing the cracking. When they both had their fill of pecans, John mounted Biddy, and the two friends rode east until the sun began to set, turning the western horizon to a warm apricot color. The breeze turned cooler, and the thought of a warm fire was tantalizing.

"Looky there, Biddy, a deer. Venison would taste mighty good tonight." However, John saw the doe's fawn, just a few days old, creeping out of the bush on wobbly legs. Again, he thought of Ma and let the fawn go to her ma and suckle. "I ain't hungry after all them nuts, anyways."

As Passion looked on, it touched her heart. *"This is a different sort of passion than I have known,"* she said to Serenity. *"It is a gentler passion. I wish more men would have this kind of passion."*

A familiar scurry in the bushes interrupted his melancholy thoughts of home, and John grabbed his rifle from its place on the saddle. The light at dusk was dim, yet he could still make out the form of a rabbit. John did as Pa taught him. He took aim, held his breath, and squeezed. One quick shot, and he had dinner.

"Roast wild rabbit for dinner, Biddy. He'll be a might tough chewin', but dinner on the trail don't get no better than that," John mused with a chuckle.

He threw his right leg over the saddle, jumped off Biddy's back, and ran to retrieve his kill before some greedy scavenger could claim it. The two friends stopped in a clearing, and John gathered dry limbs and hickory nuts for a fire. "Smell them hickory nuts, Biddy?"

The mare nickered.

"Them hickory nuts is a-goin' ta make that wild rabbit taste special good."

Biddy was indifferent as she cropped fresh grass.

"I 'member when Pa and me went huntin'." John paused as if savoring the memory. "Pa's the one who taught me to gather up hickory nuts. I didn't know what fer then, but I found out right quick. Them hickory nuts made dinner cooked over an open fire taste extra good. It was simple, but that's what makes life mighty pleasurable."

Serenity and Faith fluttered about the campfire, savoring the peaceful evening. *"He is a good boy, isn't he, Serenity?"* Faith asked.

"No, Faith. He is a good man," replied Serenity in admiration of John's character.

"He's so young," lamented Faith.

"Have no fear, my dears," responded God. *"As long as young people are open to My Word and direction, I can use them equally as well as adults."*

After a meal of hickory-roasted wild rabbit and sweet reminiscing of home, John drifted off to sleep.

The next morning, Biddy nickered and blew her horse breath in John's ear, waking John out of a sweet dream of Anne Marie. Through thin slits of sleep-heavy eyes, he could see the sun peeping over the Ozark Mountains, casting a soft yellow glow through the cottonwood trees. The leaves twisted in the breeze as if waving to John.

"Mornin', Biddy," John mumbled, rubbing sleep from his eyes. "Sorry, I overslept. We best be a-goin'."

After traveling for some hours and enjoying the warm sun, John stopped to pick berries. He found a place in the river where cool, clear water bubbled and sparkled, singing over rocks, and led Biddy to the edge of the water. "There you go, girl. Take a deep drink." As Pa taught him, John got down on his hands and knees and lapped water right from the river. When he had his fill, he let the water run through his fingers, savoring the refreshing bubbles running over his face.

Returning to Biddy and preparing to travel on, John said in surprise, "Phew, Biddy, you stink! Or is it me? It's been some time since we've had a bath. Let's go! Last one in's a skunk." Biddy was nonplussed.

Without hesitation, John removed his shirt and britches and plunged into a deep spot in the chilling river. As John disappeared into the water, shock waves pulsed through his body, threatening to paralyze him from the ears down. He came bubbling up into the sunshine with diamond-like drops of water covering his youthful form. Streams of water flowed from his head, covering his eyelashes before caressing his lips. He licked his lips, then shook the water from his hair.

"Come on in, Biddy! It's cold, but it's mighty good."

Biddy blew dust from her nose as she cropped grass.

"I'll take that as a no," John laughed and splashed water toward the faithful mare.

After swimming and exercising, the water seemed warmer. Still, John shivered, and his lips felt numb. As soon as he hit the air, the sun warmed his body and blood. Donning his dusty clothes, he lay in the sun, basking in its warmth, and soon realized he was hungry. "I cain't believe we been playin' till late in the afternoon. How's about some dinner, Biddy?"

Biddy was standing under a cottonwood tree dozing. Both front feet and her right hindfoot, planted firmly on the ground, bore all her weight, while the tip of her left hind hoof was touching the ground. She swished her tail in reply.

"Okay, girl, you deserve a nap. I think I'll take forty winks myself." John lay on clean grass, bent his arms, and linked his fingers. "Thank Ya, Lord."

"You are welcome, My son," a loving God replied.

Before John's heavy eyes closed, he remembered words Pa read from the Psalms, and John continued to pray, "Guide me in Your truth and teach me, for You are God, my Savior, and my hope is in You all day long."

"I will be with you always," God assured a grateful John.

Peace covered John like a soft blanket, and he slept.

Chapter 5

"Well, honey, I guess this is where God is a-wantin' us to be."

After traveling thirty miles in the Florida wilderness over Indian trails filled with back-jarring potholes and palmettoes, Leo's wagon hit a deep hole, shattering a wheel. Susan gasped and clung to the rough wooden seat as the crippled wagon leaned to the right, nearly touching the sandy ground, threatening to spill its contents. Leo jumped down to inspect the damage, then reported to Susan. "Five wooden spokes is split on us, Susan, and the rim is bent," breathed Leo in weary frustration. "Seems that God is a-pilin' it on to see just how much we can bear."

Leo never uttered an angry or vain word. Instead, he forced a wry grin onto his face and said, "Well, honey, I guess this is where God is a-wantin' us to be."

God smiled and nodded His mighty head in agreement. "*And I'm always here, Leo, just as I was always with your Pa.*"

Susan simply replied, "Yes, Leo," and breathed a prayer.

"Come on, honey. Let's us unload what we need. It's gittin' to be about suppertime anyways," Leo said as he helped Susan down from the wagon. "We can sleep in the wagon tonight and start fresh in the morn'n."

The couple slept fitfully and awoke to aching muscles and empty bellies. After a sparse breakfast of dry biscuits and greasy bacon, Leo and Susan began the arduous task of making a home. With Susan by his side and his pa's machete in his hand, Leo started hacking down scrub oak saplings and clumps of palmettoes to clear a path.

Susan shaded her eyes and looked up to the sky, her calico bonnet dropped to her back, allowing her long hair to fall free. "What a blue sky," she observed. "Green trees and a blue sky will make a right nice home."

As Susan looked around the area, Leo followed a familiar sound. In the shade of tall ginger, palmetto trees, and elderberry bushes heavy with their white blooms, he discovered a shallow creek that bubbled over moss-covered limestone. On the creek bank grew sparse patches of centipede grass and wild violets in bloom. "Lord, what a beautiful creek. Thank Ya for the cool, refreshin' water. I ain't a-goin' ta tell Susan about the grass and violets right now. I'm a-goin' ta save it as a surprise for her," he prayed.

God replied, "*You are most welcome, Leo. Your wagon breaking a wheel here was no accident. I planned this as a special resting place and home for you and Susan.*"

The land around the creek was flat, so carrying water up to the tent would not be too taxing. Leo joined Susan, where she stood imagining her home. "Oh Leo," Susan sighed, "it's so purty, and just listen to the birds in the trees. What a happy place."

From a distance, Leo pointed out the creek to Susan, and she beamed and admired God's beauty and provision. However, as the smiling couple turned around, their faces fell, for they again faced a menacing thicket of Florida wilderness.

"Well. That there is a challenge," Leo said in a half-hearted chuckle. "Guess we'll be earnin' our supper tonight."

In contrast to the cool, bubbling creek, the area where they stood was a mass of briers, stinging nettles, wild grapevines, palmetto bushes, and roots just waiting to trip up unsuspecting feet.

"Well, Susan, honey, the Lord brought us here, so He'll show us what to do. 'Member the words of Isaiah 41:10: 'Fear not; for I am with ya: be not dismayed; for I am yer God: I will strengthen ya; yea, I will help ya; yea, I will uphold you with the right hand of my righteousness.'"

Again, God smiled upon Leo and said, "*I will always be here to help you, Leo.*"

"Yes, Leo," Susan whispered. "But it's an awful mess."

"Then lets us ask the Lord to help us clear our land and build our home," Leo said. He took off his sweat-drenched hat and grasped Susan's hand as he began to pray, "Lord, we don't know 'xactly why Ya done brought us here to this wilderness, but we believe Yer Word, and know Ya will help us through our toil. For Yer help and protection, we give Ya thanks. Amen."

With renewed spirits, Susan bent down and pulled at a root sticking out of the Florida sugar sand. "Looky, Leo!" she exclaimed. "It come up easy! Thank Ya, Lord."

"*You are most welcome, my dear,*" God said to Susan. "*I will be your fortress and help.*"

With Susan's proclamation, Leo started swinging the machete, cutting a perimeter through the maze of grapevines and briers. Leo looked up from time to time to check on Susan, who was busy pulling roots and vines. He smiled when he heard her singing, "Standing on the promises of Christ our King, through eternal ages let His praises ring; glory in the highest, I will shout and sing, standing on the promises of God…"

As the fairies listened, Harmony said, "*I think God has another new friend.*"

Indeed, God was pleased.

Susan pulled at gooseberry bushes and found that they, too, came up easily, relinquishing their hold on the sugar sand. A few yards farther, she found an area crowded with dense patches of wild myrtle and pine. However, with her keen eye, Susan immediately saw the potential for a home. "Leo! Come see. Looky there, Leo," Susan said, pointing at the wild myrtle bushes. "If ya squint yer eyes a bit, it almost looks like rooms in a proper house. Them pine needles makes a mighty fine carpet for a floor. Can we put the tent there, Leo?"

"I don't see why not. Looks like a fine place for a new home to me."

Using the machete, Leo cleared undergrowth to emphasize the "rooms" as Susan explained them to him. As he hacked down saplings and brush, he made a pile for kindling wood.

"We'll let this here brush dry up," he told Susan, "so's we can have plenty of good fire kindlin'."

Susan was a trooper. She gathered up her skirt from behind and pulled it up between her legs. Using a rope from the wagon as a belt, Susan tied her skirt at her waist and then started in earnest to help clear their land. As Leo cut wild myrtle and pine saplings, she carried the debris to the trash pile. Some of the pieces of debris were bigger than she was, yet she didn't let that stop her. She kept up with Leo despite the Florida heat, swarming mosquitoes, gnats, and wasps.

"Ugh!" Susan groaned.

"What's wrong, honey?" Leo shouted to Susan.

"Oh. I've walked into a spider web, is all," Susan said as she peeled the silken threads from her sweaty face and continued dragging brush.

Her husband beamed with pride.

Leo paced off a few hundred yards north and dug a hole behind a clump of myrtle and palmetto bushes. "This here will be yer fancy privy, Mrs. Bates," Leo teased Susan.

"Why, thank ya, Mr. Bates," Susan said, giggling. "I didn't think about such a thing. Yer so smart." They hugged each other in a tender, sweaty embrace and continued with the clearing.

Indeed, when Leo finished thinning out the wild myrtle, it did look like separate rooms, just as Susan said. "There ya go, honey," smiled Leo as he removed his damp hat and wiped the sweat from his face and neck. "Here ya got yer bedroom. Over yonder ya got yer sitting room, and over there, ya got yer—"

"Nursery?" whispered Susan.

"Susan, honey," exclaimed Leo as he grabbed his wife and swung her around. "When?"

"Not until the spring. That gives us plenty of time to build us a proper lean-to and maybe start a garden."

"Cutting a garden out of this mess is a-goin' ta be mighty hard work, Susan, girl."

"Yes, but ya can do it, Leo. I just know ya can." She gave him a peck on the cheek and returned to pulling gooseberry bushes. "Leo, when ya chop down these here bushes, will ya leave a row of 'em for a little walkway, kind of?"

"Yes, ma'am!" Leo saluted with a silly look on his face.

So, Leo worked cutting out a home for his family. His helpmate, the mother of his child, was right there by his side. He thought she looked ravishing with her cheeks glowing red from physical labor and hair plastered back with sweat.

"A family, Lord," Leo prayed. "Me and Susan was a family afore, but now we's a-goin' ta have a real family. Thank Ya, Lord. Watch over my Susan and the child. I don't rightly care if it's a boy or girl; all I want is a healthy baby. Thank Ya, Lord." He whispered his prayer of thanksgiving.

"*You're welcome, Leo, My friend,*" God said, smiling with pride.

When they finished clearing the area to Susan's satisfaction, Leo returned to the wagon to fetch a tarp and sturdy rope. With Susan's help, Leo stretched the tarp over the myrtle bushes and lashed the corners to pine trees using the rope. As he worked, he whistled, "Leaning on the Everlasting Arms." When finished, he said with a twinkle in his eye, "Okay, my lady, yer tent is all set up and ready for ya. Come over here, wife."

"What's that there twinkle in yer eye fer, Leo?" Susan teased as she sauntered over, swishing her loosened skirt in a flirtatious manner.

As Leo swooped her up in his arms, she squealed. Then he kissed her and said, "I want to do this proper like." With tender kisses, he carried his wife over the imagined threshold of the tent and gently placed her on a soft blanket he had secretly fetched from the wagon. Even though they were both dead tired, it was not difficult to find renewed energy and that special thrill. Leo kissed and caressed Susan as he whispered his love to her. She returned his deep kisses and desperate searching, then together they floated out of their bodies into euphoria.

As the fairy, Passion, stopped to take in the tender scene, Wisdom gently led her away. "*They need their privacy*," Wisdom said.

After making love, they lingered in the tent, pressing their bodies close to each other, glowing in their passion and whispering their hopes and dreams to each other.

"How 'bout a splash in the creek?" Leo teased.

"Right now? I don't have no clothes on," giggled Susan.

"Who's a-goin' ta see us?" Leo laughed. "Besides, there's somethin' I want to show ya."

Playfully, he pulled her up and led her out of the tent. They picked their way through brush, stubble, and pine burs. When they got to the creek, Leo picked Susan up and walked into the cool bubbling water, and when he placed her on a moss-covered rock, she sighed. "Oh, Leo, how wonderful. The water is so cool and blue, and the bubbles make my body feel so good," she purred.

"Yes, yer body does feel good," he teased, and lay down beside her in the water letting the bubbles run cool and succulent between them.

After a luxurious rest, lying together in the cool water and sharing their dreams for their future, Leo said, "There's somethin' I want to show ya, but ya have to come out of the water."

"I don't mind," she replied. "I was gittin' a little cool, anyways."

When they stepped on to the creek bank, Leo pointed out the soft, green centipede grass and the wild violets blooming in sweet purple profusion.

"Oh, Leo," she sighed. "They is beautiful." She ran her toes through the grass.

"Did ya see them violets? Them's yer violets."

"I did. Thank ya, Leo." She pressed her cool body close to his and gave him a soft kiss. "What a beautiful home. Thank ya, Leo. Thank Ya, Lord."

"*You're welcome, my dear ones*," said God.

After they returned to the tent and dressed, they started unloading the wagon and setting up their belongings. Susan hummed, and Leo surreptitiously started thinking of names for baby boys.

"I'm a-goin' ta build a fire, so's ya can make me some supper," Leo teased Susan.

Since this wild Florida territory had very few rocks, he cleared a wide swath of dirt and dug a shallow hole for a firepit. From the wagon, he fetched a cord of split wood and a wrought iron tripod he had brought from the homestead. Soon, the fire began to burn, and the edges of the split wood glowed bright orange. He set the wrought-iron tripod in place so that it straddled the fire.

"I'll fetch some water," offered Susan. "Where'd ya put the bucket?"

"Be careful, honey. Ya know how snakes and varmints like creek water," warned Leo.

While Susan was at the creek, Leo unpacked the cast-iron kettle, a pot, and a frying pan.

"That's right fine," he congratulated himself. "But what we a-goin' ta put in that frypan?" Leo went back to the wagon. Before they had left the homestead, Susan had packed a tub of lard, a small crock of flour, baking powder, salt, bacon, dry beans, and coffee. "Bless her heart," Leo smiled. Then he heard Susan scream. It was not a playful scream. It was a scream of fear.

"Help! Leo! Come quick! Leo! Help!" Susan screamed again, and Leo sprinted.

The memory of his pa's encounter with the vicious rattlesnake invaded his mind. He recalled how the snake had writhed on Pa's body, trying to recoil enough to strike again.

"Oh, Lord! No. Not Susan," Leo prayed as he ran.

He expected to find Susan gripped in death's fangs. Instead, he found his petite wife tiptoeing on a stump, afraid to move. Leo laughed.

"Don't ya laugh, Leo Bates," she scolded. "This here is serious. I'm afraid to move. I don't want to be sprayed by no skunk!"

Leo's big belly laugh was cleansing, and his heartbeat returned to normal. "Shoo! Go! Git! Git on and git yer water or fish or whatever yer after," Leo instructed, waving his hat in the air. "Okay, honey, she's gone." Leo swung Susan down from the stump and hugged her tight, and then kissed her forehead.

"How'd ya know it was a she?"

"Easy. See them little 'uns follerin' her? That's a dead give-a-way."

"Oh, go on with ya," Susan giggled, returning Leo's hug.

"Let's git our water."

Leo picked up the bucket from where Susan had flung it and stepped down to the creek's edge. "I'm glad yer safe, honey."

Leo knelt to fill the bucket, then turned around to find Susan in a heap on the ground where she had fainted. Leo dropped the bucket. Forgetting about the water, he reached for the bandana he always carried in his back pocket. Leo soaked it in cool creek water and placed it on Susan's head. When her eyes fluttered, he picked up his wife in his arms and carried her back to the tent.

After Susan recovered, Leo said with heavy emotion in his voice, "Don't know what I'd ever do if somethin' bad happened to ya. Yer a good wife, Mrs. Bates. And yer a-goin' ta make a good ma, too." Leo hugged his wife close and tight. "Thank Ya, Lord, for keepin' Susan safe," he prayed.

"*I am always with you, Leo*," God said.

"Yer a good husband, Leo. I'm mighty proud to be yer wife. Now fix us some of yer good coffee," she said with a good-natured push.

"Yes, ma'am."

As Leo fixed a pot of coffee, Susan mixed up a pan of biscuits. After a busy day's work, they sat beside the open fire sipping coffee and savoring warm biscuits. What a delightful way to end the day.

Chapter 6

John Wilkins In Arkansas

After traveling eleven days, the White River led John Wilkins into Arkansas, where he stopped at Yellville, a small town just across the state lines. Slowly, he rode through the dusty streets of the small burg, searching for a place to purchase fresh supplies, listening, and watching. Not far away, he heard a familiar, rhythmic sound—ting-ting….ting-ting…sh-sh-sh-sh. He followed the sound down the road and around the corner, knowing he would find a blacksmith's shop.

"Howdy," called John, not wanting to startle the blacksmith. John realized, one misstep and the blacksmith's hand could lose its grip on the tongs holding a chunk of red-hot iron. However, the blacksmith was unconcerned as he looked up with a pearly smile. He thrust the red-hot iron and searing tongs into a barrel of cold water, which hissed in protest and spewed steam into the already hot, saturated air. Hot water droplets spat at the smith from the barrel and onto his blue work shirt, now grey with sweat and soot. "How do," called the burly, Arkansas man, turning from his work and wiping his blackened face on his short thick arm, adding more soot to his rolled-up shirt sleeve. When he removed his right glove, sweat poured out. Copious amounts of sweat mixed with dirt from the hot iron and sawdust ran in black streams drawing lines of mud through his course, thick hair and dripped from his elbow.

"Do ya have any wagons fer sale?" John inquired. "I have this here mare, so I don't need no horse."

"I reckon I do. The name's Carter. Jack Carter," the blacksmith said, extending his burly hand to John. "Didn't catch yourn."

"I'm John. John Wilkins from Missouri."

"How do, John. Come on back to the corral, and ya can see what I got."

There in the corral, baking in the blazing sun was a forlorn-looking empty wagon. Subtle hints of the wagon's condition alarmed John. New hickory planks flashed in random places, revealing extensive repair to the sides and flatbed. Although aged by the weather, the original hickory boards were solid. The iron-rimmed oak wheels, though once strong and resilient, also needed repair.

"This all ya got?" John inquired, trying to act disinterested.

"Yep. Most folks around these parts keeps what they got till it falls apart. Had an unfortunate shootin' last month. That's why I got this un."

John walked around the wagon, trying to remember what Pa had taught him about dickering. He picked up the tongue to judge if it was straight and true and considered the iron connection to be adequate. He hopped up on the bare wooden seat and kicked the break. He bounced on the bench to detect any broken springs. “She looks okay. Them rims needs repairin’, though. How much?”

“Six bits.”

“How ‘bout four bits, and ya teach me to repair them rims?”

Jack thought a minute, calculating materials and time, then thrust his big hand out. “It’s a deal. When can ya start?”

“Right now, if it’s convenient.”

The master blacksmith and his new apprentice spent the better part of four days hammering and fitting iron onto the wagon wheels. John considered Mr. Carter’s training to be a valuable in-kind trade, and the blacksmith considered it time saved. What sweetened the deal was the home-cooked meals that Jack’s wife made each night and the leftovers she wrapped up for John.

When the blacksmith and John completed the job, John reached into the pocket of his buckskins for a silver fifty-cent piece and handed it to the blacksmith. He still had seventy-five cents for food, fresh tobacco, and a tent. “Mighty glad I met up with ya, Mr. Carter. Thanks for the learnin’.” John waved goodbye.

As John backed Biddy up to the wagon, Jack asked, “Where you aimin’ on goin’?”

“Don’t rightly know, Mr. Carter,” replied John securing the last tack to the harness. “Just lookin’ to start my own life somewheres.”

“If yer aimin to travel along the Mississippi River, go east about two hundred fifty miles or so to the little burg of

Arkansas City. The last stragglin' streams of the White joins the Mighty Mississippi there."

"Thank ya, again, Mr. Carter," John waved to Jack, mounted the wagon, and gave the giddy-up signal to Biddy.

"Goodbye, John," Jack Carter yelled, waving to John. "God go with ya, boy."

John followed Jack Carter's directions and converged on the Mississippi then traveled another twenty miles, which took him south into Arkansas's foothills. The rocky paths challenged Biddy's footing, causing John to consider that a mule would have been a better choice for this terrain. However, he quickly dismissed that thought, for Biddy was his best friend, and he could never part with her.

The wagon creaked in a slow, easy pace, and Biddy nickered. "Ya had trainin' at home pullin' a wagon. So, what ya complainin' fer?" he admonished the mare.

She turned her head and blew hot air out of her nose in protest.

John ignored the insult and enjoyed the ride, watching God's world unfolding and engulfing him. He inhaled as if to devour its beauty. Balsam pines stretched their Christmas tree-scented limbs into the high azure sky. Those trees looked like hands lifted in praise, and his heart sang: "How great Thou art. How great Thou art." And he prayed. Most often, his prayers were of thanksgiving. Those were the easiest—and so abundant. "Lord, what a beautiful day Ya made. In Ya, all things are beautiful."

As he traveled, John felt insignificant compared to the wonders of God's world, until his heart and mind drew from its well of remembrance. He recalled the many times that Ma had read from the Bible, teaching John one of her favorite verses of the Psalm. Those words were etched into his mind. He recited Psalm 139:14, "I will praise thee; for I am fearfully and wonderfully made: marvelous are thy works; and that my soul knoweth right well."

Other times, he prayed for direction: *Which trail should I take? Is this water safe to drink?* Always, he prayed for protection.

He pulled up beside a stream, built a campfire, and hobbled Biddy to keep her from wandering off during the night. Then he bedded down by the inviting embers glowing warmth. He looked up into the starry night and wished he could see the invisible stars far beyond. He was awestruck and thanked God for His providence, "Thank Ya, Lord, for keeping me safe today. Now, as night comes, place Yer angels on my left, on my right, and over me. Thank Ya, Lord, for Ma and Pa, and fer their constant prayers."

"You are a good friend, John," replied God. *"It is My pleasure to care for you. Your Ma and Pa were also good friends, and I shall never forget them. I have already prepared a place for them with Me in Heaven."*

The fairies also gathered around God and gave him thanks for a safe journey and a new friend.

John slept. However, it was a fitful sleep. His dreams were as if he was fighting for his life. "What are Ya tryin' to tell me, Lord?" John prayed.

He awoke to see the sun just glowing white over the eastern horizon. He rubbed his eyes, remembering the leftover cornbread the blacksmith's wife had wrapped up for him. "Cornbread would be mighty tasty this mornin', Biddy," John said.

At that moment, the hair on the back of his neck prickled, and he heard Biddy stomping and pawing the ground. John suddenly jumped from his bedroll and grabbed his rifle lying close by. "What is it, Biddy? I never seen ya act like that afore."

Above his head, he heard the unmistakable scream of a cougar, and John froze. Biddy continued pawing the ground, now twisting in fright. In the early morning light, when shadows make things indistinguishable, John could not see the cougar. How could he get off a good shot when he could not see the threat? "Come on out, ya coward!" John yelled, trying to sound brave and calm, while he was neither brave nor calm. He cocked his rifle, Biddy squealed in a fight or flight posture, and the cougar sprang. It soon became evident that John was not the cougar's intended target. It was Biddy.

Courage and Hope danced around Biddy, trying to reassure the mare. Energy from emerald and topaz gemstones swirled around the horse, to no avail.

"No-o-o!" cried John in fear and anger. Blam! He did not have time to aim, hold his breath, and squeeze as Pa taught him. He just fired his rifle. The first shot hit the shoulder of the hundred and forty pounds of killing power. Blam! The second shot dropped the cougar, though not before lethal claws ripped open the mare's neck. Then the cougar hit the ground with a deep thud and angry screams. It took several long, frightful minutes of subdued protest before the cougar gave up and died.

John stood stiff, alert, watching, ready to get off another shot if needed, while Biddy was wide-eyed with pain and terror. John dropped his rifle, rushed over to Biddy, and fell on her blood-soaked neck. Never had he come so close to losing his best friend. The mare nickered her soft, warm horse breath into John's neck.

After calming Biddy, John removed her hobble then led her to the cool stream, where he bathed his friend's torn flesh and made a mud plaster for her wound. The friends tried to sleep again, but rest did not come. So, John hitched up Biddy to the wagon, being careful of her tender neck, and moved on following the river. Travel was slower with frequent rest stops, water, food, and John's care. Eventually, Biddy healed.

"Thank ya, Lord for keeping Biddy and me safe. Thank ya, for healing my friend's wound."

"*You are welcome, My son,*" replied a compassionate God.

Chapter 7

Cane Grinding In Louisiana

Late one afternoon, after a week of slow, healing travel and rest, The Mighty Mississippi River led John and Biddy to the small farming community of Alma, Louisiana.

The Louisiana Territory was in the shape of a boot. Alma was located at the top of the instep, not too far south of the Mississippi State and Louisiana Territory line.

As the wagon bumped over the uneven wagon trails, John noticed what looked like corn fields on both sides. "Ya reckon that's corn, Biddy? It kinda looks like corn. Hm? Then again, it might be sorghum. Look at them leaves, Biddy. They is long like corn and sorghum, but corn and sorghum leaves is yeller. This here crop is purple-green like." He reached out to touch one of the leaves. "Whoo, boy! Good thing I got leather gloves on, Biddy. Them leaves would cut skin for sure with them wiry edges. I never seen stalks like them with red rings about them."

As he and Biddy moseyed down the wagon trail, a warm July breeze blew through the rows. The long, thin leaves rustled and rippled in the warm air, reminding John of the whispering pines at home. After a mile or so, he spotted the end of the field, and the crop began to dwindle to a few straggling rows. Then John came to a large clearing where he saw a cluster of buildings in the shade of pecan and oak trees. "Someone takes real good care of this here land, Biddy. Them are good-sized barns."

The barns were big and tall, big enough to bring in a herd of cows for the winter. Atop each barn was a full-size loft, not as tall as the lower level, still tall enough for a man to stand up and toss stacks of feed corn or bales of hay. Alongside the barns stood smaller work sheds.

"That's a right smart idea," John said aloud. "One of these days, I'd like to have a shed for storing farmin' tools, burlap sacks, saws, axes, and the like." Then something caught his attention. "Looky yonder, Biddy!" John exclaimed. "I wonder if that there house is one of them plantations I heared about during the war."

John stopped Biddy to admire a neatly manicured lane, lined on each side with majestic oaks that led to the plantation, standing tall and gleaming white. Round columns guarded the inviting front double doors. White rocking chairs dotted the expansive porches that wrapped around three sides of the house.

"What a mighty fine house," he said to Biddy. John pulled the horse and wagon in front of one of the work sheds and wiped sweat from his brow with a dirty sleeve.

"Can I help ya?" a friendly voice rang out from the open wooden door of a work shed. The door, made from ancient cypress, hung with hinges made from cowhide.

“Howdy. The name’s Wilkins. John Wilkins from Missouri. What kind of field is that there?” John inquired, pointing his limp, soggy hat at the fields he had just traveled through.

“Howdy, John. I’m Abe Smith, and I own these sugarcane fields.”

“Sugarcane?” quizzed John. “What do ya use ‘em fer?”

“Syrup mostly, and fodder for the livestock. Some of the womenfolk make baskets or weave chair seats from the stalks and sometimes hats from the leaves,” replied Abe. “Ya lookin’ for work, John?”

“I sure could use some,” John confessed. “I’m a-runnin’ low on supplies, and my mare is recoverin’ from a fight with a cougar.”

“Well, ride on to the bunkhouse over yonder and stow yer gear. You can corral yer horse and feed up.”

“Thank ya, Abe.” John put his soggy hat back on and touched the brim in acknowledgment. He moseyed over to the corral where he gave Biddy a small lard can-full of oats. She nickered her thanks.

For the next six months, John stayed and worked with Abe Smith on his plantation. There was plenty of work to do since fence mending was a constant chore. Abe had a herd of new calves that needed branding, Mrs. Smith had chickencoops that needed repair and cleaning. Besides the cane fields, Abe had five acres of vegetable fields that needed tilling, cultivating, and harvesting.

At the end of each workday, John went back to the bunkhouse for the evening and took inventory of his sore muscles. When he pulled off his work gloves and saw the angry white blisters on his hands, he winced. "Look at them blisters," John exclaimed to Randy, his bunkhouse mate.

"If them blisters bust open, yer a-goin' ta have mighty bad sores. Not too good for a man who does hard work with his hands. They'll toughen up," said Randy. "Here, smear some of this here salve on yer hands."

"Thanks, Randy," replied John. "Them open sores will have competition," said John. "My back and legs is tryin' to see who can hurt most. My back most often wins."

Although the work was hard, it was pleasant, and the pace was fast. As he worked through the day, he thought of Ma and Pa, "Wonder what the family was a-doin' back home? It must be 'bout supper time. I'm hopin' that they and baby Beth is still well. I bet baby Beth is tryin' to sit up by now."

In October and November, harvesting vegetable crops was complete. The vegetables not eaten, Mrs. Smith canned or shared, and there was not one spare inch of space in her root cellar. John thought it was a colorful sight to behold. "Ms. Smith, ya surely keep a mighty nice root cellar. I don't think I ever saw so many jars of canned goods. I reckon it takes a lot of work to put up all them fruits and vegetables."

"Why, thank ya, John," responded a pleased Ms. Smith. "It's mighty nice to have someone notice the hard work it takes. But I enjoy doin' it. Most, though, I enjoy watchin' my boys eatin' it."

During early fall, work slowed a bit, and everyone enjoyed time on the big, shady porch, rocking, swatting flies, and gnats, and drinking sweet tea. However, that did not last long, for November was sugarcane harvest and butchering season, and on its heels, Thanksgiving. John and Abe, along with Abe's sons, Keith and Lloyd, and their teenaged sons, started hacking cane stalks to the ground with long machetes.

"Watch out for yer legs and knees," Abe warned John. "Them machetes are heavy and sharp."

It took the four men about an hour of hard cutting to finish off two rows of cane. They had no intention of cutting the entire twenty acres, just enough for next year's seed. Abe explained as he picked up a freshly cut stalk, "Ya see this section here?" Abe pointed to a little teardrop-shaped growth on the side of the sugarcane stalk he held between his big stubby thumb and fingers. His fingernails were torn ragged from the rough leaves and stained black from cane juice and dirt. "We'll need to cut the stalks so that each section has at least one of these nodes like that. We'll put them in burlap bags and hang them outside the smokehouse. In the spring, we'll plant the dry sections, and we'll have a new crop of sugarcane in the fall. So long as we remember to save seed stalks for the following year, we will always have sugarcane."

John picked up a knife and tested it on the hairs of his wrist. "Whoa, mister! That's sharp!"

"Yes, sir. Each year before harvest and butchering time, we gather the knives and sharpen them on the whetstone." Abe pointed his knife across his shoulder, indicating a huge, round stone.

The two new friends talked as they wandered over to give John a better look at the piece of equipment. "Never seen one of them afore. How do it work?"

"Ya sit on that seat and pump those foot pedals like a pump organ. That spins the stone. It will put an edge on a blade right quick."

"Reckon I could give 'er a try?"

"Don't see why not. That will be yer next job. There's a bunch of dull knives over yonder," Abe said, pointing to a bucket full of knives.

John sat on the saddle-shaped seat and started peddling.

"Keep the blade facin' down like this and slightly slanted in toward the wheel, about like that," Abe said, indicating a slight twenty-two-degree angle.

John quickly got the knack of the wheel and sharpened twenty butcher knives so that their blades gleamed in the sunlight. Three of the knives went to the kitchen for Mrs. Smith. Although his back ached from three hours of bending over the spinning stone, he was proud of his accomplishment.

When the knives were razor-sharp, Abe, John, and others sat on old tree stumps in the shade of a pecan tree and cut thick cane stalks while they talked.

"Man alive, Abe, them little hairs on the sugarcane stalks is wicked," John protested, scraping needles from between his fingers with his knife, being sure not to cut the skin.

"Yeah, they will remind ya all night of all the fun yer having today."

"How do ya stop the itch?" John asked.

"Ya just have to let it wear off," Abe chuckled.

The cane juice and pulp fibers stuck to the knife blade, slowing down the work, so John cleaned the knife blade on his overalls, and he was surprised when the cane juice left black stains on his pants.

Just like sharpening the knives, cutting cane was hard, still John enjoyed working outside with the good company of Abe and his family. They were a close-knit family like his own, and he felt right at home. He still felt sharp pangs of homesickness in his heart and missed Ma and Pa.

However, John did not have much time to be homesick. Fall in Louisiana was thrilling. The air was finally fresh and crisp. The November sky was high and blue, so high that the buzzards soaring on the wind currents hundreds of feet up looked like tiny specks. As the sun crawled across the short part of the sky, the colors gradually changed from shades of azure to purple and then faded to white. As the sun set in blazes of burnt orange and red, the western horizon looked as if it were on fire.

The next day was more work, a little rocking, and of course, sweet iced tea. Sounds of work and laughter filled the yard around the house. Happy, squealing children played in the fallen leaves of pecan trees where Mrs. Smith kept areas around the house raked clean to discourage any snakes and vermin from hiding there. Not that vermin would take up residence for long, for Max, the faithful shepherd-mix dog, made sure of that, and he took his job seriously.

The fairies who followed John since leaving home, fluttered around Max, enjoying his company. Curiosity considered Max to be an interesting conversationalist.

When he was not out chasing squirrels among the pecan trees or following Abe in the fields, Max lounged in the yard as a plethora of children hugged and rolled on top of him. For his noble efforts, Mrs. Smith gave the dog a big plate of table scraps. "Good boy, Max. Ya worked hard today. Eat up," Mrs. Smith praised Max. "Hey! Ye're s' pose' to chew it not swaller it whole!"

Curiosity also enjoyed romping with the dog and children. As she played, the amber gemstones in her gown filled the air with a pleasant orange glow. The squealing children and barking dog entertained the little fairy until she was exhausted. Serenity and Hope laughed and rolled with giggles at Curiosity's frolicking.

One morning, the second week of November, turned out to be frosty and bright. Abe, Keith, and Lloyd invited John out to an open area behind a work shed.

"What's that there hole fer?" asked John.

"That there is the butchering pit," replied Keith.

John estimated the pit to be four feet square by three feet deep. He watched as Lloyd attached a top crossbar on a wooden frame that stretched the length of the pit. Abe and Keith positioned a wagon close to the edge of the hole.

"Ya ever butchered beef, John?" Abe called to John when the wagon was in place.

"Not beef, but if it's anythin' like butchering a hog, I can do 'er," replied John.

John looked in the wagon bed and saw the biggest beef carcass he had ever seen.

"Big un, ain't he? And he's only a 3-year-old," Lloyd laughed. "I killed the bull before sunup."

"Man alive!" John exclaimed. "I never seen a bull that big. How ya gonna butcher it?"

"See how Keith tied the hind legs with leather straps? We's gonna hang the carcass up on that hook and pully on the cross bar," Lloyd explained.

Even with the pully system, it took all four big men several attempts to lift the carcass and secure it to the top of the cross pole. When they finally got the carcass up, they all took a breather.

"Good work, boys," Abe complimented his sons and John. "Keith, yer the beef expert. How much do ya reckon that beef will dress out at?"

"I 'magine after he's dressed, he will turn out about five-hundred pounds of beef," Keith said between several exhausted breaths.

"That'll keep us all in beef until next fall," Abe estimated.

After a brief rest to catch their breaths and clear their heads, the four men started back to work. Just as John remembered about butchering hogs, there was a method and skill to removing the head and guts and letting the carcass bleed out. Abe split the belly down the length of the carcass, and everyone cleaned out the gut, allowing the innards to fall into the pit.

"Them trash pieces will make mighty good soil for Ma's spring vegetable garden two years from now," Keith observed.

John had no qualms about removing the hide. He demonstrated his skill with one long, continuous slice without removing too much of the fatty layer underneath. With each man working on a side and making small downward cuts, the men removed the heavy hide then loaded it onto the wagon.

"John, you and Keith help Lloyd tote the hide and hang it on a shed," Abe instructed.

Once nailed to the outer wall of a work shed, the hide would dry and cure in the sun for six to ten months.

Mrs. Smith came out to the smokehouse to inspect the hide. "My. My. That hide should make new covers for my dining room chairs."

"I need a new apron in the farrier shed, Ma," said Lloyd.

"Looks like there will be plenty for a least one new apron," Ma assured him. "I got some sweet tea waiting fer ya boys at the pit."

When Mrs. Smith finished inspecting the hide, she and the boys returned to the pit where they found the sweet tea. Even though it was a crisp day, and the sun was hot, the refreshing drink was a blessed relief.

"Ya boys be sure to make generous cuts of meat," Mrs. Smith instructed.

Keith, Lloyd, and John made skillful cuts, dividing the carcass into perfect cuts of meat. Keith and Lloyd loaded the cuts of beef onto the wagon. Then drove the piled wagon to the smokehouse where Mrs. Smith waited.

"John," Mrs. Smith began, "here are clean pieces of burlap. Wrap each cut of beef in the burlap and tie them with those strips of leather." Mrs. Smith pointed to long leather straps hanging on a nail. "Lloyd, yer tall. Help John heft the beef onto them hooks."

"Them hooks is considerable bigger than the ones we use back home to hang pork," John noticed, pointing to the hooks hanging from the smokehouse rafters.

In the middle of the wooden smokehouse, a red brick fireplace, loaded with new wood, burned slow, low, and smoky, creating the perfect atmosphere for curing meat.

"John, the woodpile is out back of the smokehouse. Would ya bring in a load? Watch out for rattlesnakes."

From his experience back home in Missouri, John gave rattlesnakes and copperheads a wide berth. Next to the woodpile, John found an old, twisted fig tree that must have been twenty years old. He picked and savored their pink meat and tiny seeds. He pulled a few more and carried them to Keith and Lloyd. "There ain't nothin' like fresh figs," he said, handing figs to Keith. Then he caught himself. "Hope ya don't mind me pickin' some, Mrs. Smith."

"Land sakes, John, ya pick as many as ya want. These are the last for the season, anyways. I already put up thirty-two jars of preserves in the root cellar. Can't give my boys enough fig preserves on hot buttered biscuits."

After taking a break to gorge on figs, Keith stoked the fire with dry oak wood to fill the smokehouse with eye-burning smoke. "These cuts of beef will hang here for several months, slowly roasting in the dry heat and smoke," Keith told John.

With the smokehouse filled and the hide hung to dry, the men turned their attention to harvesting the remainder of the sugarcane. Even with the cooler temperature and low humidity, cutting sugarcane was hot, sticky work, just like cutting seed plugs.

The two brothers and John wielded machetes to cut the canes, leveling them to the ground. Two brothers-in-law and three cousins followed, picking up the long canes, trying to avoid the razor-sharp leaves that sliced quickly through work pants and flesh. The super-fine, almost invisible needles on the stalks also made work uncomfortable as John had found out earlier.

"Here comes Seth and Caleb," Keith shouted. "Hi, Seth! Howdy, Caleb. Mighty glad to have ya men come help."

Seth and Caleb were former slaves at the plantation. Now, however, through the generosity of Abe Smith, they owned farms nearby and walked across their fields to help the family with the harvests. Abe and his wife had always treated their slaves well, so Seth and Caleb were happy to come back to help with the harvest, for this had been the only home they knew. Now as free men, they were part of the community as well as part of the family, and they shared in Abe's harvest.

With seasoned skill, the men stripped leaves and tossed the canes up to a younger cousin balancing atop the growing mound of fresh sugarcane stalks.

"Woah," Billy yelled, trying to keep his balance. "I almost can't keep up with ya guys."

"Oh, quit whinin' and keep workin'," yelled Leroy, another cousin, with a devilish grin. "What do ya think we do down here, wait for ya?"

"Ya jest keep a-throwin'. I'll let ya know when to quit," teased Billy. Still, Billy knew he had to work fast to tie stalks into bundles of twenty or so and pack them tight on the wagon to stay ahead of the throwers.

It took two and a half days of hard, back-breaking work to harvest twenty acres of sugarcane. Each day, by the time the men returned to the barn, they were hot, tired, and hungry, and Mrs. Smith had dinner on the table.

"What's fer dinner, Ma?" called Lloyd.

"Fried chicken, black-eyed peas, collard greens, chicken with drop dumplin's, hot biscuits and cornbread," replied Mrs. Smith. "I got a smoked ham left in the smokehouse. Will that do?"

"As long as ya got some corn on the cob to go with it," Lloyd said, smacking his lips.

Mrs. Smith knew how to cook hearty food for her hungry family, and there was always lots of it.

Finally, Thanksgiving Day arrived, and the excitement in the air could be sliced like a piece of pumpkin pie. Squealing children, a barking dog, and fairies ran around the yard playing hide-and-seek or catch-me-if-you-can, while bustling women scurried to-and-fro, trying not to get in each other's way. A lot of work and visiting went into preparing a traditional turkey and dressing dinner with all the trimmings.

Out in the yard, the men hauled wagons loaded with the cane grinder equipment and set it up under a pecan tree in front of one of the barns. The framing for the grinder measured thirty inches square and five-feet high.

"Hey, Pa! Can ya help me lift this frame up?" asked Keith.

"Here comes Seth and Caleb with their families," shouted Abe. "I'll ask the men to help hoist the frame. Hi there, Seth. Howdy Caleb, will ya come on over here and help Keith lift this frame."

"Proud to," replied Seth.

Seth and Caleb kissed their wives, Sara, and Minnie, who then joined the other women in the kitchen, while their children joined in the fun playing in the yard.

"What ya got there, Minnie?" Lloyd shouted to Caleb's wife.

"Sweet tater pies," Minnie shouted back with a wink.

"Put one back for me," Lloyd joked.

Seth helped Keith lift the thirty-inch frame, and Caleb secured the metal grinder head to it.

"I got the bucket and brush to clean the grinder cylinders and the trough," shouted Abe.

A wooden trough attached to the grinder head directed the juice into waiting barrels.

"Where's the pole and the mule?" called Abe.

"Here comes the pole, Pa," answered Keith. "Lloyd and John is toten' the pole from the barn."

All three men lifted the twelve-foot, aged cypress pole to an upper metal shaft of the grinder head.

"John, will ya fetch the mule and fasten the end of the pole to the critter's harness?" Abe asked.

"The mule's a-comin' now," answered John. "Reckon that mule knows what to do?" John asked with a wink.

The mule, a family pet, knew his job well. He never stopped his monotonous walk around the grinder except when it was time to change riders. Giggling children, sometimes two at the time, if they were the smaller ones, rode on the mule's back and tried to urge the mule to go faster.

Once the mill was secure and operational, the mule started walking, and the men started feeding the cane stalks into the metal cylinders. Impatient children gathered around the mill and waited noisily for a mason jar of juice.

"Lloyd, load 'er up," called Abe. "Keith and Seth, ya keep the cane stalks comin'."

"You children keep them fingers away from them cylinder teeth, now," someone would occasionally warn. "Else we will have finger juice in our cane juice. You remember what happened to Big Jim's fingers when they got too close to the cylinder?"

"Yes, sir," the children chimed in, hiding their fingers under their little arms in a protective manner. A severe injury last year had made quite an impression on the little ones. Those powerful metal teeth of the cylinders could easily crush or sever tiny fingers.

As the drowsy mule walked his circular path, sweet, sticky juice flowed from the grinder's teeth, down the trough, and into a waiting barrel sitting on a wagon. After passing through the mill, the crushed cane stalks fell to the ground.

"Keith, run over to the barn and git the long-bed wagon," Abe called. "John, we're gonna load up the pulp and store it in that shallow hole behind the barn. Caleb, will ya show John where to go?"

From time to time, Abe filled a pint jar with the green cane juice and passed it around for tasting. The green, watery juice was thick and cloudy with pieces of cane pulp. However, once the juice settled, the pulp sank to the bottom, leaving a clear, sweet liquid. The harvest filled twenty barrels of juice ready for the eighty-gallon cooker.

The fairies, Curiosity, Hope and Serenity, flew through the cane juice as it flowed from the grinder. By the end of the morning, the fairies' gowns and wings were sticky with sweet juice.

While the men tended the cane grinding, the women readied the Thanksgiving tables.

Earlier in the day, Abe and Lloyd had set up four sawhorses under a hickory tree and laid long boards lengthwise. The women then covered the boards with yards of gingham fabric. Lillie May, Lloyd's wife, brushed away fallen leaves from the make-shift table covering, and Jamie, Keith's wife, planted a juicy, golden-brown turkey with cornbread stuffing on the table. Minnie and Sara brought out multiple side dishes of vegetables fresh from the garden. There was fried okra, crowder peas, black-eyed peas, sweet creamed corn, mashed potatoes, baked sweet potatoes, and sliced tomatoes and onions. For dessert, there was pumpkin pie, blackberry cobbler, Minnie's sweet tater pie, apple pie, and chocolate cake. When hot, delicious food filled every inch of the table, the boards groaned and threatened to crack.

From the back porch of the plantation house, Mrs. Smith rang the dinner bell and called, "Di-n-n-er." Then, she stepped back to watch with joy and amusement as children scrambled from the mule. Sand buckets spilled their contents where they fell, and swing sets slowed to a squeaking stop.

"Push through that last stalk of cane, Caleb, and let's go eat. Lloyd, unhitch that mule and give him an extra helping of oats. He's earned it with all them children hangin' all over him." The mule followed Lloyd without the usual mule hesitation and brayed his gratitude.

With everyone assembled, Abe, the patriarch of the family, removed his sweat-stained hat and said, "Let's pray. Lord, we thank Ya for this bounty Ya have provided. Thank Ya for another safe year with faithful friends and good neighbors. Now we ask Ya to again bless these hands that prepared the food. In Jesus' name."

Everyone said, "Amen," and the feast began.

God smiled upon the Smith family, John, Caleb and Seth and their families, and said, *"It is My pleasure to provide for families who acknowledge and appreciate My gifts."*

Even with all the laughter and chatter, the hungry crowd stripped the table clean of its bounty in less than thirty minutes. Still, someone always came back to scrape one last bite of creamed corn from a wrought iron pot. Children pushed and shoved for the last finger full of the chocolate icing from the cake plate, and Lloyd could not resist another slice of sweet tater pie. Surely, no one left the table hungry.

After Thanksgiving dinner, the men started a friendly game of horseshoes. Then the women and men battled in a game of tug of war, and laughter erupted when the men let the women win.

In the evening, Caleb and Seth gathered their wives and sleepy children and said their goodbyes. "Abe, call us any time ya needs extra hands," Caleb offered.

"I always do, Caleb. I appreciate yer work and friendship," said Abe shaking Caleb's hand. "Don't fergit, we got a smokehouse full of beef."

With a wave of his hand, Caleb acknowledged Abe's generosity.

In the weeks following, men took turns, two by two, adding raw juice to a large iron kettle mounted into the belly of an igloo-shaped brick furnace.

"John," Abe called. "Feed the fire with more wood. Use one of them lighter knots if ya have to."

"What's that there, Abe?" John pointed to a piece of dense wood with rings around the circumference from its pointed top to its rounded bottom.

"That there is a lighter knot. It's that dense, heart of an old pine tree that was cut and left in the woods. Ya find them around pine tree stumps and such. They're the best I've ever seen for lightin' a fire. "

"Why's that?"

"Reckon 'cause being the center of the tree, it's packed full of resin."

John loaded the wood under the boiler, and as blue tongues of fire danced under the round, cast iron pot, the juice came to a rolling boil. Lloyd raked out embers letting the fire burn down to a steady glow.

"We'll let that juice simmer for hours, so we'll need us all to tend it," Abe instructed.

"John and me'll take first hour," Keith volunteered. He turned to John and explained, "It's hot, sweaty work, and we have to pay close attention. Over there's a pail of water and a rag. Wrap the rag around a sturdy stick to clean off the sides of the boiler afore the foam turns to crystals. If ya don't keep the foam down, ya'll have more sugar crystals than syrup. Ya have to watch for a boil-over, too. Get hot, foamy juice a-runnin' down yer britches, and ya'll know it right quick. And don't let them kids bother ya none. They're just waitin' like buzzards for the sticky foam."

John followed Keith's instructions to keep the boiler clean. Then out of curiosity, he used a small stick to scrape a bit of foam from the kettle and tasted it. "No wonder them kids is wantin' that sticky foam. It tastes like taffy candy," John said, tossing the stick to the ground. "How long will it take to boil the juice down to syrup?"

"It'll take nigh on to five hours. That's why we switch off every hour. It's hot and dangerous work. And ya got to worry about them kids."

Of course, it was Curiosity who picked up the stick of sweet, gooey foam and tasted it. *"Serenity! Hope! Come taste the candy,"* Curiosity called. *"It's almost as good as wild honey from the garden."*

After five hours of simmering, the cooks ladled hot syrup, thick and brown, into clean bottles and sealed them with melted wax. Then they refilled the kettle to cook more cane juice. The cooking yielded enough syrup for all the families, including Seth and Caleb, to fill their larder with dozens of bottles of syrup.

"Ma, ya got enough syrup to make a pecan pie?" begged Frank.

"I reckon," answered Mrs. Smith. "But ya know well, I don't make one pie. I have to make at least four at one bakin. I got ya boys who like pecan pie."

"Grandma, I like to punch holes in yer biscuits and fill them with syrup," one grandson said hopefully.

"Yes, and ya make a mighty mess, too. Ya got syrup a-runnin' down yer chin, fingers and arms and a-drippin' off yer elbows."

"Ya have to admit, Ma, it's mighty good eatin' for a hungry little boy," Frank laughed, remembering when he had syrup dripping off his own elbows.

"Them boys, they is always hungry. Can't fill 'em up though I try," teased Mrs. Smith.

Chapter 8

Jake and Marsha

A shaft of light pierced the rising fog of the Florida wilderness, and silver fingers danced through leaves shimmering with dew. As Leo crept out from under the tarp, he stretched, releasing the remaining sleep from his muscles, and grabbed biscuits left from supper. With pioneer determination, he tromped through the wet grasses and palmettos to the place where Susan wanted her garden. A male cardinal flit from tree to tree chirping his morning song and keeping a keen eye on Leo, hoping for a handout. Not to disappoint the bright red bird, Leo sprinkled the last crumbs of a biscuit on the ground. "I wonder how long it will take ya to find this here biscuit?" Leo spoke to the quizzical bird.

By the time Leo cut and whittled oak limbs for stakes and paced off the dimensions of the garden, the cardinal, and his mate were devouring the crumbs. Leo enjoyed the birds' company and their cheerful songs, and as he worked, he talked to the Lord as old friends would do.

"Well, Lord, I'm a-startin' Susan's garden. I sure hope Ya will be kind and send rain, so's we can have plenty of veggies.

This here's a fine morning, Lord, and a mighty fine place You give us for a home. Oh. Here's a root. Help me, Lord." With his ax, Leo gave the root a mighty whack and was surprised at how easily it split. "Thank Ya, Lord. Did I tell Ya how excited I be to have a baby comin'? This here's just another one of Yer blessings. I am grateful. Thank Ya, Lord for always being near, for Yer wisdom and protection."

Leo's conversation with the Lord, continued in this manner as he worked turning soil in the garden. What a delightful way to start the morning.

Interrupting his work and meditation, a voice rang out, "Hello there."

Leo squinted into the sun and wiped his brow with his bandana and replied with caution, "Howdy!"

The young man sitting on the buckboard continued, "The name's Jake Kelly, and this here is my wife, Marsha."

Marsha nodded her greeting and smiled at Leo.

"Welcome, Jake, Marsha," Leo said nodding to the strangers. "Git on down and visit a while. Where ya from?" inquired Leo.

"We're a-homesteadin' about 160 acres just over west of here," replied Jake. "We built a cabin on the east boundary not far from here, but she burned down last week. That fire destroyed all we owned, which weren't much 'cept for our land," Jake explained. "We is startin' out to see if we might like another place better. Don't see as how we can find a better place though. Had the river close by and a little garden and fenced yard for a milk cow. Told Marsha we might as well clear away the rubble and build again. Ya been here long?"

"Nah. We just got here ourselves and marked off what we need to set up housekeeping in this here tent," Leo said, pointing to the tarp covering the myrtle bushes. "My name's Leo Bates. My wife Susan is over yonder fixing breakfast. Will ya join us?"

"Don't mind if we do, just to be neighborly," replied Jake helping Marsha down from the wagon.

"Are we on yer land, Jake?"

"Nah. This here's still public land. If ya aim to settle here, I'll ride over with ya to the land office in Newnansville, just north across the river," Jake offered. "There, ya can apply for a homestead."

"Well, seein' as how our wagon broke down," Leo said, pointing to the lame wagon, "we is interested in settlin' down here, and we'd be mighty glad to have good neighbors. How much do ya reckon I'll be a-paying for this here land?"

"If I 'member correctly, ya pay a five-dollar application fee for 160 acres and after five years, if ya build and improve the land, ya pay a filing fee for the certificate of ownership," Jake said. "If ya want to buy the land out right, I think the land office is asking a dollar and a quarter per acre."

"That sounds fine," Leo said, trying to contain his excitement. "What's the rest of yer land in?" Leo continued.

"Timber, mostly. Marsha had a vegetable garden, and we run a few scrawny beef cows in the woods," replied Jake. "Where ya from?"

"We come from up near Madison County way. After my ma and pa died, Susan and me left the homestead to my siblings and we set out for a new place. When the wagon broke a wheel, I says to Susan, 'Well, Susan, honey, I guess this is where the Lord wants us to be.'"

"Yer right about that, Leo. Where the Lord puts ya is where He wants ya," said Jake.

"So, yer a believer, too?"

"Mighty right. I don't see how a family gets along without the help of the Lord," Jake confessed.

"Let's wander over to the tent and see if Susan has breakfast ready," Leo invited.

When they neared the firepit, Susan was just taking biscuits and bacon from the fire.

"That bacon and biscuits smells mighty good, sugar," Leo praised Susan. "Hope ya got enough for company. Jake, Marsha, this is my wife Susan. Susan, these are our neighbors over west of here, Jake and Marsha Kelly."

"Welcome, Jake and Marsha. It is so nice to meet neighbors," Susan said wiping her hands on her apron and extending her hand in welcome. "Breakfast is ready. Shall we sit together?" asked Susan as she wiped her sweat-moistened hair from her eyes.

"Marsha, ya and Susan can sit on our fancy log seats here," Leo said pointing to sections of stumps he had cut from fallen trees. "Jake and I will get comfortable on the ground. Jake make yerself to home." Leo chuckled. When everyone found their position and the laughter died down, Leo said, "Jake, will ya give thanks for the day, for good neighbors and our first meal together?"

"I would be honored," replied Jake. "Let's pray. Lord, our God, we thank Ya for this fine day and new friends. Thank Ya for the safety and shelter Ya provide and this fine breakfast. In Jesus' name. Amen."

When Jake began his prayer, the fairies, Faith and Joy danced all around the camp, spraying their sparkling blue and yellow crystal lights over Jake's head. "*God will certainly be pleased to hear that these four people are believers*," said Serenity writing the events in her journal.

Susan could hardly contain herself when Jake finished the prayer. "I am so glad ya are believers. I already feel a common bond with ya. Now I know this is where the Lord wants us to be."

When breakfast was over, Jake and Marsha rose to thank their hosts and continued looking over their land. "We're mighty glad ya dropped by, Jake and Marsha," Leo said shaking Jake's hand. "Come back any time. We'll put on another pot of coffee."

"Goodbye, Susan. Thank ya for a lovely breakfast," Marsha said as she stood.

"Goodbye, Marsha, dear. I hope ta see ya again soon," said Susan as she embraced Marsha.

When the new friends were out of sight, Leo pulled Susan to his side and said, "Thank ya for breakfast, honey. How do ya like our new neighbors?"

"I think they is just fine. Maybe we can have Bible study some evenin'," said Susan.

"I'd like that, too," Leo agreed. "Right now, I have to git back to yer garden."

Chapter 9

John Wilkins In The Bayou

When Louisiana's cane grinding and syrup making season came to an end, John Wilkins said his goodbye to his new friends, the Smith families, and moved farther south to the Louisiana Bayou country. There, he found himself standing "knee-deep" in Bayou cypress swamps.

The local people living in the Bayou country, the Cajuns, were masters of the swamp. However, their mastery of this land took many difficult years to achieve. They originated in French Canada in the 18th century. Because these French Canadians refused to pay homage to the British monarchy, British soldiers forced them to leave their homeland. Some refugees found themselves in the unfamiliar wilderness of the Louisiana Territory.

John found these swamps interesting, although fearful. While he knew about pine trees, he was unfamiliar with the cypress trees. He quickly found that cypress trees sent up unique, rounded shoots from the tree roots, the purpose of which was unknown. Every growing boy in the Bayou knew to avoid cypress knees, submerged or not, that cracked toes and scraped skin from tender shin bones.

"Looky at them pine trees a-growin' in the swamp, Biddy. We got pine trees back home, but not like these, and not a-growin' in a swamp."

As John and Biddy moved closer, John spotted two boys off in the distance. Their excited voices carried back easily to John's ears.

"There's one! He's a big un, too," yelled Billy Bob. "Stick 'im good, Josh!"

"I sees 'im. Shush! Stay right there, Mr. Bullfrog," said Josh, a nine-year-old Cajun boy with his frog gigger at the ready. "Got 'im!"

"How many's that make, Josh?" asked Billy Bob.

"I gots four. How many ya got?" replied Josh.

"I only gots three. But I gots nine brim, but some are little uns. Them little fish'll be just as good as frog legs, all fried up crisp like," said Billy Bob licking his lips. "We best be gittin' home."

"Look out!" warned Josh. "Don't go up that-a-way! There's a big fat moccasin on the bank. See 'im?"

Pine trees grew among the swamp cypress where fishing for brim and gigging frogs were favorite pastimes for young boys. However, they knew they ran the risk of meeting up with a cotton-mouth water moccasin.

As John knew from experience, cutting pine trees for milling and harvesting pine resin was a dangerous yet highly profitable industry. John recalled the time he spent with Pa felling timber in the hills of Missouri.

Re-living that time brought back the memory of Miss Anne Marie. John whispered Anne Marie's name to himself as if calling an angel's name. Those memories continued to sting his heart. Still, he cherished remembering the beautiful times they shared watching the evening sky, so he forced himself to choke back the memories. The pain of losing her was still as fresh as it was before John had left Missouri. “I can’t think about Miss Anne Marie, Biddy,” he said to his mare. “We’s got a whole new world around us. It ain’t that I don’t love Anne Marie no more. It’s just that it hurts too bad to keep a-thinkin’ about her.”

John shook the cobwebs of pain from his mind, and he looked at the new world around him. It seemed to John that there was plenty of work available here in Bayou country. “With all this here timber, there must be a sawmill near ‘bouts,” he said to Biddy. “Let’s go find a sawmill, girl,” John said as he gave Biddy a gentle kick.

As it turned out, there was only one sawmill, owned and operated by a second-generation French Cajun. Henri Dubose was a kind, generous man, overweight, yet his thick girth was deceivingly firm and muscular from heavy work in the timber fields.

It was an immediate and profitable friendship between John and Henri. Henri was indeed impressed with John’s skill as a timberman and appreciated his work ethic. After lengthy discussions over many morning coffees, they found they shared the same strong faith in God. It was this faith that solidified the bond between the two timbermen.

“Why don’ you come to home wid me fer suppa,” Henri invited John. “I wan’a introduce you to my wife. She a fine woman.”

John accepted the invitation to supper, where he met Henri’s wife, Hina Hanta, a woman of Choctaw heritage.

“Hello, John,” Hina Hanta greeted. “I can see in yer eyes yer wan to know about my name.”

“Well, Yes, ma’am. Don’t want to be rude, but it’s not a French name,” replied John.

“Dat alright, John,” Hina Hanta assured him. “In my native tongue of Choctaw, my name mean’ ‘Way of Peace.’ Henri call me Mère, French for mother. Henri and I have had ten children together. Sadly, dough, only three of dem live.”

Although approaching middle age, Hina Hanta was a beauty, with thick dark hair, high cheekbones, generous lips, and sparkling eyes that, indeed, smiled greetings of peace. Her kind heart was as generous as her plump body.

As they visited, a young woman entered the sitting room, and Hina Hanta introduced her. “Here’ my youngest now. Mr. John, dis is my Babette.”

John was immediately mesmerized. Babette shared her Mère’s beauty, for she had the same characteristic long raven-black hair, high cheekbones, and dark eyes of her American Indian ancestors. Hina Hanta continued, “Henri name our daughter a favorite Creole name, meanin’ ‘baby.’”

Henri broke in and said, “Mère, John’s a Bible believin’ man. John, in Hebrew, Babette name mean ‘My God is plentiful.’”

Hina Hanta continued, “We chose da name Babette for da precious double meanin’.”

Silently, John agreed that Babette was precious. He enjoyed supper with Henri and Hina Hanta, all the while, his eyes were on Babette.

“Ms. Hina Hanta, I surely enjoyed my supper. Ya cook as good as my Ma.”

“Dat a big compliment, John. I certain yer ma’s a wonderful muder. After all, she raise a wonderful son.”

"Ya come anytime, John," Henri invited. "Ya don have to wait fer an invite."

"That's mighty kind of ya, Henri. I'd love to stay longer tonight, but I need to get some sleep. We have another full day tomorrow."

Babette walked John to the door and extended her slender hand. "Good night, John. I hope ta see you again soon."

John's heart sang as he walked back to his tent.

God turned to His Son and said, "*We have known Henri and Hina Hanta for a long time. They are good people and good friends. These will be the right friends for John.*"

For the next few months, John worked hard for Henri, cutting timber, and dragging up cypress trees long submerged in the river. Once reclaimed and milled, these century-old trees revealed rich tones of deep brown and blackish wood, often filled with deep cavities. These cavities, caused by a fungus growing inside the submerged tree, gave the timber its name, pecky cypress, and it came to be a highly prized variety of cypress wood.

Even though the terrain was foreign to John, he adapted to the Bayou country and appreciated the ancient swamp with its stands of slash pine and cypress trees. What he did not enjoy was having to maintain a constant vigil for alligators and cotton-mouth water moccasins, both deadly in the swamp. While Missouri had cougars and bears, they were nothing like the Bayou's highly fierce alligators and water moccasins.

"Henri, how do ya work fer fear of snakes and alligators?" asked John, swatting at the air.

"Ya gits use to it. Jes make lot of noise, an' da run away," laughed Henri.

There was another potentially deadly swamp creature, sinister and persistent. The warm, swampy waters of the Bayou were the perfect environment for mosquito nurseries and the dreaded mosquito-borne disease, malaria.

John found working difficult trying to swing an ax, look out for snakes and alligators, and swat mosquitoes at the same time. To make matters worse, an older Cajun worker told horror stories of men contracting malaria from mosquito bites. The malaria victims became so weak and jaundiced that yellow bile, the outward symptom of a diseased liver, rubbed off on their sleeves when they wiped their sweaty faces. That is just what happened to John. He contracted malaria and suffered for weeks, reeling from a high fever.

"John, ya do good work, an' I 'preciate it," assured Henri. "But, John, ya need ta stop an' go ta home. Ya need to git plenty of rest. That' da only ding dat will fight de malaria."

Because he was feeling too ill to work, John took Henri's advice and went home to bed. In his tent, John continued to run a fever and became delirious. "Ma," John called through his delirium. "Ma, I'm hot. Water, Ma. Anne Marie, where ya been? I been lookin' for ya. No! No! No! Come back, Anne Marie. Ma?"

After the burning fever, chills set in. John alternated between burning with fever and quaking with chills. Because the chills were internal and severe, nothing could warm him. How could a person burn with fever one minute and shake with chills the next? Finally, and mercifully, he lost consciousness.

After three days, when he opened his feverish eyes, he found Babette, kneeling beside his bedroll. "John, take dis soup. Dis is red bean soup, sof an' warm," she encouraged.

"Ya mus drink da wata, John. I boil it, so it pure." She nursed him through his fever and chills using tribal medicines.

"John, dis beava fur blanket will warm ya," Babette said quietly.

She covered him with a thick blanket of beaver fur and lay with him to keep him warm through the chills. When his fever returned, Babette threw off the blanket and bathed his face with cool water. She boiled swamp water and made mud plasters to draw out the poison and cool his fever. Babette spooned more Cajun red bean soup down his fevered throat. And she prayed and sang Choctaw songs of healing.

Through the fog of his delirium, John heard Babette praying and singing, and it touched his heart, reminding him of Ma praying for him. That memory of Ma's prayers and listening to Babette praying provided great healing and comfort to John. The greatest healing, however, was his deep faith in God.

Many times, in his spiritual life, John had witnessed God's healing, forgiveness, and provision. That is why Pa's scripture reading was so special to John. "Fear thou not; for I am with thee: be not dismayed; for I am thy God: I will strengthen thee; yea, I will help thee; yea, I will uphold thee with the right hand of my righteousness."

During his convalescing, John and Babette talked many hours about their mutual faith in God and their dependence upon Him. "Babette, I knowed yer ma and pa is a-belivin' in the Bible and in God. Are ya a-sharin' their faith?" John asked one day as they talked.

"I do believe, John. And you?" Babette asked.

"I learned my faith at my Ma's knee and from Bible readin's after supper. Pa always read the Bible to us kids."

Sitting nearby, Hope rested her chin in the palms of her hands, and Faith fluttered in the air over John and Babette. Faith asked, "*God do you see?*"

"*Yes, my dear,*" replied God, pleased with how His plan for John and Babette was unfolding.

John and Babette also shared their family values. He admired her compassionate heart, her work ethic, and her diligence. "Babette, how do ya feel about yer family?" John asked.

"Da family is important ta me, John. I would do nothin' to disappoint dem. My Mère, she is very good wife to my Père. She teach me to be a good wife and Mère, too."

Eventually, John began seeing Babette through different eyes. She was not just a nurse or a friend, she also exhibited qualities he wanted in a life mate, wife, and lover.

"Can I touch yer hair, Babette?" John begged. "Oh," he whispered. "It's so soft," he crooned as he ran his fingers through her raven-black Choctaw hair.

"Be still, John," Babette whispered. "We mus not give da impression dat we do wrong."

He obediently removed his hands from her hair. Oh, how he yearned to hide his face deep in her neck and breathe in her sweet musk scent. However, he knew Mère and Père would disapprove. So, he had to be content just to admire Babette's hair and look into her eyes. Her dark Choctaw eyes spoke of love one moment and flashed fire the next.

When John gathered his courage, he asked, "Are yer eyes speakin' love to me, Babette? I love yer dark Choctaw eyes, and I never want yer eyes to speak nothin' but love." John knew he must learn how to excite her eyes to speak love to him and how to avoid the fiery flashes.

As soon as he was able to stand on his own without feeling the room spin, John went to Henri to ask for Babette's hand in marriage.

The fairy, Courage, followed John down the path leading to Henri's cabin. Passion was all a flutter with anticipation. *"You must be demure,"* Courage instructed young Passion. *"You must not be too hasty."*

"I am much too nervous to be hasty, Courage," Passion assured.

"Howdy, John," Henri greeted him. "Have a seat on dis here hickory nut tree and take a load off. What on yer mind, John?"

With energy from her emerald gemstones flowing over the nervous young man, Courage hovered above John's head.

Henri sat quietly and listened, too quietly for John's comfort. Henri showed no emotion as John alternately wrung his hands and rubbed his sweaty palms on his buckskins. He ran his fingers through his brown wavy hair. Then John cleared his throat and rubbed his hands on his britches again. His tongue stuck to the roof of his dry mouth, and he choked on his words.

"Well, sir," John started, faltering. He cleared his throat. "Well, Henri. I come to," John paused, unable to say the words. "I jes come to visit," he stammered.

"Why John, ya jes seen me at da timberland," Henri teased.

"Henri," John wrung his sweaty hands then ran them on the back of his neck. He could not say the words he needed—no, the words he wanted to say. Again, John cleared his throat and tried to start over again.

Henri stood. Holding his hands behind his back, he paced to the front door. Henri turned. He paced back again to face

John. “John, are ya tryin’ to ask me somethin’?” Henri asked, knowing what the question was.

John was in agony, and he thought Henri was enjoying his agony a little too much.

Finally, the mighty Cajun relieved John of his pain. “Yer a-wan ta wed my daughter?”

“Yes, sir, that’s it. Henri, I would be much obliged if ya would give me the honor of marryin’ yer daughter, Babette.” John was much relieved that he could get out the words.

The mighty Cajun grabbed John by the shoulders and pulled the nervous young man into his big, burly timberman’s arms. “So, ya wan ta wed my daughter? Mère! Mère!” Henri shouted. “John done ask ta wed Babette.”

Hina Hanta came running in from the next room, for she had been listening to the whole conversation. “Oh, John, we are pleased to have ya as our son. Babette told us how ya shared yer faith in God. We’ve been hopin’ fer dis.” She embraced a shaken John.

This warm act of acceptance immediately melted the tension that gripped John’s heart.

In his broken English, Henri said, “John, I am glad ta have ya as my son-in-love.”

“Have ya ask Babette?” Hina Hanta asked.

“No, ma’am,” John replied. “I wanted to ask yer permission, first.”

“She know,” said a demure Babette from around the corner.

John stood as Babette entered the room.

“I have been wan’in dis ever since ya was sick, an’ we talk about da Lord in our lives,” whispered Babette.

Standing, holding Babette’s hand, John said without hesitation, “Babette, will ya do the honor of bein’ my wife?”

Babette beamed. “Yes, John.”

“When do ya want to get married, then?”

“Mère, may I wear yer weddin’ dress?” asked Babette.

“Of course, ya may, my child. I will git it tomorrow.”

“Père, will ya say da words?” asked Babette.

“I will,” said the big burly timberman with tears in his eyes.

“John, I would like ta be married day afta tomorrow,” Babette whispered as she fell into John’s arms.

On a warm summer day, with a gentle breeze stirring the leaves, John and Babette were married. John thought he had never seen anything so beautiful as his Choctaw bride, dressed in a white buckskin dress with ceremonial beads and long fringe. Her black hair cascaded over her shoulders and down her back. Oh, that hair, and her eyes. Her eyes spoke of love as she repeated her wedding vows to him.

The fairy, Joy, joined Serenity, Faith, and Hope, as the fairies surrounded the wedding couple with their gemstones of watermelon tourmaline, sapphire, and topaz lights. Young Passion hid behind Babette’s white buckskin dress. The red glow from Passion’s rhodonite gemstones bathed Babette in an enchanting glow.

“Babette, I love ya, an’ promise to care for ya an’ make ya a good husband.”

“John, may our Lord give me love for ya until we die.”

“Welcome to da fam’ly, my son,” Henri said in a soft voice.

Mère wiped tears of joy from her eyes and hugged both John and her daughter in her tender arms.

When, at long last, the wedding celebration ended, John led his bride to his tent then stopped her before she could step inside. "We need to do this right," he told a surprised Babette. So, he scooped up his bride into his strong arms and drank in her loving eyes. He kissed her. He kissed her deeper still and took his bride into his tent. She returned his deep kisses and wrapped her arms around his neck and her slender legs around his thick legs and whispered, "Mon amour."

Then, John kicked the door flap shut.

Mère had already made a warm and inviting fire for them, and they lay together under soft, beaver fur blankets. Even though a tent was not a perfect honeymoon accommodation, they did not seem to notice. At last, John took possession of that raven-black, Choctaw hair, filling his hands with thick strands. He buried his face into her neck and breathed in her warm, sweet musk, and quivered as she surrendered herself. With equal eagerness, she took possession of him, and John saw love in her dark eyes. He took her in his embrace and devoured her, letting passion overtake them.

Serenity gently took Passion's arm and led her friend out of the tent. "*We must not intrude,*" advised Serenity again.

John and Babette made love, whispered, and spoke of plans for their life together. Then they made love again and again. After they shared their passion, they prayed, asking for the Lord to bless their plans and their life together.

"I have many blessings in store for you, John," God said. "*You are a good and faithful friend, and I will always be with you.*"

In the fullness of time, God answered their prayers, and Babette gave birth to a healthy baby boy. John was so proud; he called him Gil, remembering his own pa. As John held his wife and firstborn in his arms, he cherished Babette more than he believed possible. He doted on his wife, the mother of his son, and still buried his face in her hair at every opportunity, sometimes at inopportune moments. Motherhood only enhanced her beauty.

Sitting before the fire, he tenderly cuddled Gil and spoke to his son of great love. He inhaled Gil's sweet baby scent and kissed the back of his neck. He inspected each little finger and fingernail, each little toe and toenail. He had Babette's long slender fingers and her dark Choctaw complexion and dark eyes. The stubby tiny toes were like John's. Gil's ears were on the small side and lay close to his head. They were beautiful ears, like John's pa. What a warm and beautiful combination of love and family.

The fairies stayed close by, adoring the newborn and playing with him. They were, again, glad to have a child who could see and hear them. Even though Gil was too young to comprehend, his eyes followed the fairies as they flitted around the room, turning summersaults and playing leapfrog.

While Babette nursed the baby, John caressed Babette's hand and touched her fingers to his cheek. He felt Gil's tiny fingers that grasped Babette's breast. John had an overwhelming desire to memorize this scene in detail, and he spoke to Gil of God's eternal love. John also promised his firstborn that he, his pa, would teach him about faith and trust in God.

Always near, Faith clasped her hands to her heart as she listened to John speak to baby Gil of God's love.

While John loved and doted on his little family, Mère doted on and loved the three of them.

Reluctantly, proudly, John went back to the swamp to work timber. When he returned home, Mère had supper on the stove, and Babette was nursing Gil. John's heart thrilled as he tossed his hat to one side, ran to Babette, and pressed her and baby Gil to his heart. His life was complete, and he breathed a prayer of thanksgiving.

God and His Son, Jesus, looked approvingly, sharing the joy of John's thanksgiving.

Once again, John took his wife and his nursing son in his arms and held them close with no desire to let go. "I love ya, Babette," John whispered. "And I love this beautiful son ya done give me."

"I love ya, too, John," Babette whispered. "I am glad ya like the son. I am proud ta be yer wife."

Six months later, in August, baby Gil became fussy. Gil would not nurse, although Babette nursed effortlessly and had plenty of milk. In desperation, John ran to fetch Babette's mother. When Mère came into the tent, Babette cried, "Mère, dere somethin' wrong wid my baby. He has fever. He will not nurse. Mère, my baby, he is sick."

When Mère saw the rash, she pushed John and Babette out of the tent and sent them to live with Henri. Mère recognized the rash from her own babies who had not survived, and her great sorrow returned. It was not good.

Baby Gil ran a fever, and the rash turned to pustules and spread. Pocks covered Gil's tiny body, and when the pocks burst, they oozed. Wherever the pus ran, more pocks formed, burst, and ran pus. The vicious cycle continued, more pus, more pocks, more agony.

Instinctively, Mère kept the tent dark and warm. She sat cross-legged on the dirt floor and rocked baby Gil in her arms. She made a poultice from slippery elm and swamp water to soothe the pocks and sang the old Choctaw songs she had sung so many times before. She rocked and sang and prayed until baby Gil no longer fussed. He no longer cried. He was much too sick.

Physically and emotionally spent, Hina Hanta coated her face and hair with white ashes from the fireplace, signifying her mourning. "My God, my Fader, I send back ta ya, our baby, Gil," Hina Hanta prayed as she wrapped baby Gil tightly in a beaver skin blanket and laid his beautiful, lifeless body on fresh hay. "Fader, let Yer fire cleanse dis house an' dis sweet baby," she continued to pray as she took a smoldering stick from the fireplace and stepped out of the tent.

Hina Hanta sang the Choctaw song of sorrow as she lighted the frayed edges of the tent. Over and over, she sang and blew smoke and prayers up to her gracious God.

The fairies sat on Hina Hanta's shoulders as if to comfort her. *"God! Are you there? Do you see what has happened?"* cried Compassion.

Faith, with Serenity by her side, tried to calm Compassion. *"Remember, dear, that God has all things in His hands, and He has a plan for John and Babette. We must not doubt. We must believe in Him and offer encouragement to His young friends."*

From outside his cabin, Henri saw the smoke and then the flames licking the sky. He remembered Hina Hanta's mournful song, and he knew. Père grasped John and Babette together in his arms, and they wept and prayed until there were no more tears to cry.

As the weeks passed, John and Babette tried to live their lives as best they could, yet their grief would not allow life to be normal. "Babette, I brung ya a new tent," John said as he unloaded the wagon. "I hope we can make this a lovin' home just like afore."

Babette cried and said, "I'm much obliged, John. If ya set da tent up, I will try ta make it happy." Babette went through the motions of making it a bright, happy home, and John went back to the swamp with Henri and tried to occupy himself with cutting timber. John pounded logs with fury as if pounding away his grief, while memories of baby Gil, still fresh in their hearts, consumed their joy altogether. At night, they went to bed and held each other, praying, and crying themselves to sleep.

Père saw that his children were both wasting away from sorrow, and though it broke his heart, he encouraged them to leave the Bayou and seek a new life. "My children, I can see dat ya hurtin'. I don wan ta send ya away from me, but dat is what ya need. Ya need ta put yer misery behind ya. So, go, wid my love."

John and Babette spent their evenings talking, crying, and praying, and asking for guidance. At last, with great reluctance, they took Père's advice. So, in November, after a sad Thanksgiving dinner, John hitched up Biddy to the buckboard, loaded their tent, and their few belongings.

Goodbyes were hard. Never had Babette said goodbye to her family. "Mère, I don wan ta go," Babette cried. "Jes because we lose a baby, don mean we need go away. We can still live here close to ya an' Père." She clung to Mère and poured out tears.

"I know, my child, but ya need ta leave ya heartache here and find a new life wid John," Mère encouraged her daughter.

John kissed Hina Hanta and clasped Henri tight in his arms and shook with the remaining fragments of his grief. He did not want to let go. Today was the second painful time he had to leave his family.

"God go wid ya, John," Henri said through his tears.

"Thank ya, Henri. I wish there was some other way," said John, reluctant to leave, still willing to take Henri's advice.

"No, dere is no uder way. Dis is best," Henri whispered into John's neck. Henri sadly gave John a gentle nudge and said, "God has a mighty job fer ya ta do, John."

How did Henri know to say those words? Those were Ma's words. John had meditated over those exact words so often.

John helped his wife up to her place in the wagon, close by his side. His stoic Native American wife, the Mère of his firstborn child, stared ahead with dead eyes as John gave Biddy the "giddy up" command. Before Mère and Père were out of sight, Babette turned and waved goodbye. Through her tears, she said in Choctaw, "Farewell until we meet in Heaven."

Their travels took them north up from Bayou country to Mississippi, down across the lower edge of Alabama and along the Gulf coast of Florida. They stopped when they needed provisions, and John found work. They also found a community church where they met friends and found much-needed strength. When John earned enough money for supplies, they moved on, searching for their new home.

When they reached the gulf coast of Florida, they began to feel small healing in their hearts. They saw and heard the waves from crystal blue water crashing on white sandy beaches and remembered the power of God in all things. They listened to gulls calling as if singing out praise for a new day.

They breathed in the warm salt air and let the bright sunlight bathe their faces, renewing them in the peace and joy of the Lord.

The fairies, too, enjoyed the white, sandy beaches and warm saltwater. Curiosity sat on the sand and dug her bare feet into the cool, hard, packed beach. When she stood, she brushed the sticky sand from her gown, and for the first time, noticed the lavender down peeping under the layers of orange and yellow organza. The layer of lavender down had changed into full, feminine feathers.

John and Babette camped on the coast, enjoying the lulling effect of the ocean. However, after the first tropical storm that nearly destroyed their wagon and its contents, they decided to move on. Although Babette was born in the swampy area of the Louisiana Bayou, she and John longed for dryer land. They no longer wanted to fight the swampy elements filled with malaria and fever. So, for two weeks, they traveled, following the rising sun. Along their way, they discovered small farming communities and homesteaders with one-hundred-sixty-acre tracts of land. Some land was swampland, while others were dry and barren. Although the communities welcomed John and Babette, the young couple felt this was not the right place for them. So, they traveled on.

Chapter 10

The Ties That Bind

Standing before the freshly staked garden area with his shovel and ax at hand, Leo studied the job ahead of him. Nothin' to do xceptin' to do it, he said to himself with self-discipline. With that, Leo stepped into the staked-out area and pushed his shovel into the Florida wilderness. Almost immediately, the shovel hit a root forcing the shovel's handle up into Leo's belly. After the jolt of pain subsided, Leo picked up the ax and retaliated, chopping the root with pent up frustration. He worked most of the day chopping roots and turning over soil. At last, when he thought his back could endure no more, he stretched out his screaming muscles and turned to view his progress. With surprise, he saw that most of the garden area was clear. He wiped his sweaty face and whispered a prayer, "Thank Ya, Lord. Sorry I was so bull-headed. Won't Susan be surprised?"

With renewed strength, Leo continued clearing the area. Just as he finished, Susan came with a jug of creek water. He drank deeply and kissed Susan with cool, wet lips. "Let's lie in the shade a bit. I'm pure tuckered out."

In silence, they lay together on a smooth carpet of pine needles and gazed through the tall long-leaf pines into the deep blue of the afternoon sky. Leo pulled Susan into his arms, and the warm breeze lulled the tired settlers into a gentle sleep.

Silk organza in shades of olive green and yellow swished in the air as Peace and Joy fluttered about the sleeping lovers. Hidden in the layers of fabric of the fairies' dresses, matching crystals flung vibrant colors like twinkling stars in the night sky.

"*Don't they look sweet resting together like this,*" whispered Peace. Joy was in complete agreement as she danced and twirled in the forest air.

A crow flying through the forest breeze, announcing all is well, awakened Leo. "Yes, Lord," Leo agreed, looking into the face of his sleeping wife. "All is well."

When Susan squirmed in his arms and opened her eyes, Leo kissed her gently on her head and playfully wacked her behind. "Time to get up, lazybones."

With reluctance, Leo stood and pulled his wife up and into his arms. "Let's set up our bed in our new myrtle tent," he whispered and breathed in her sweet musk scent. Then he turned his attention to unloading the corn shuck mattress and linen from the wagon. With the vintage mattress nestled in their myrtle bush tent, Susan unpacked the linen and shook the delicate pieces into the fresh air, fluffed the goose feather pillows she had brought from the old homestead, making an inviting nest for her and her husband.

Meanwhile, Leo wandered over to the freshly tilled garden and considered how he would plan the rows. The length of the garden ran north and south, allowing for plenty of morning and afternoon sun. He studied the natural tree borders that would give protection from wind and frost. Most of Florida's sugar-sand was flat and devoid of a slope, so at least he would not have to worry about planting in contour to the slope. While water was an issue, drainage was also important. Most crops don't like to sit in water. During the night before, he had noticed that the moon was almost full. This was the perfect time to plant above-ground crops. "Thank Ya, Lord, for the wonders of Your creation. Ya surely give us abundant signs and wisdom for planting and growing crops." He staked out even rows of bush beans, black-eyed peas, cabbage, and squash. By the time he finished the last row, the late afternoon sun was beginning to sink behind the trees, so he put away his tools and fetched another cord of wood from the wagon, and started a fire for supper. Soon, coffee boiled, filling the campsite with promises of soothing coffee and biscuits.

By the time supper was over, Susan had put away the dishes, and the daylight was dimming. A pair of cardinals, the last birds to return to their nest for the evening, sang their distinctive evening song. Leo scattered the smoldering firewood, saving the biggest pieces for the morning's breakfast, and then joined Susan under the myrtle tent.

"It's been such a nice day, Leo," crooned Susan.

"It sure has, honey," agreed Leo. "Got a new home and new neighbors; we're safe and, oh, yeah, a baby on the way."

As they sat on the corn husk mattress, Leo reached for Susan's hand and prayed, "Lord, we thank Ya for providin' us a new home and new neighbors. Thank Ya for Yer constant provision, mercy, and forgiveness. Bless our family and continue to keep us safe. In Jesus' name. Amen."

Leo kissed Susan and said, "Good night, honey. I'm glad yer my wife and the mother to our child."

“Good night, Leo, dear. I’m right proud to be yer wife,” replied Susan.

Down by the creek, frogs and crickets sang as the couple drifted off to sleep in each other’s arms. A hint of earthy musk, moss, honeysuckle, and roses filled the air, as did the sound of ruffling silk organza, as Serenity added these notes to her journal.

The following day, as the Florida wilderness was coming alive with the sounds of birds, Leo stepped out from the myrtle tent and stretched, breathing in the already hot Florida air.

Judy, his horse hobbled to the wagon, whinnied her greeting. “Mornin’, Judy. Are ya ready for breakfast?”

From the wagon, Leo fetched the feed bag filled with fresh oats and placed it over the horses’ nose and mouth, then unloaded his plow. “Eat up, Judy, we got work to do.” The gentle horse blew her warm horse breath into the feed bag in reply as Leo harnessed her up.

“Giddy up, there, Judy,” Leo said inhaling deeply for strength. He pushed the point of the plow into the dry soil and Judy plodded deliberately forward. Leo’s boots broke the clumps of sod, releasing a sweet fragrance, rich with years of decaying leaves. When Leo spread the precious seed, he prayed, “Thank Ya, Lord, for good soil. Bless this here garden and give us a good yield.”

Just as he finished plowing, he heard the familiar sound of heavy chains bouncing on the sides of a wagon bed. “Whoa there, Judy.” Leo welcomed the chance to rest and wiped his sweaty face with his bandana. “Howdy there, Jake. Welcome, Marsha,” Leo called as the wagon pulled up into the clearing.

When Jake had built his first house, he had used heavy chains to pull stumps from the ground or to secure milled lumber in his wagon for hauling. Today, though, the chains jingled a merry sound announcing their arrival.

"Howdy, Leo."

"Is Susan up, Leo?" Marsha grinned, knowing full well pioneer women do not sleep past sunup.

"Yes, she's been putterin' about doin' something. She's got a pot of coffee on the fire. Go on into the tent. She'll be right glad to see ya."

"Let's walk on over to the fire, Jake. I done found us some wood, so's we don't have to sit on the ground." During the afternoon before, Leo had found a fallen tree that was still in good condition. He had cut the trunk into five pieces and placed them around the firepit. There, he offered Jake a seat. "How's yer new house building comin'?" Leo asked.

"We decided to rebuild on the original site since there is water close by, so now I just got to start cuttin' timber," replied Jake.

"Need any help? I been cuttin' timber since I was eighteen, and I got all the equipment to set up a sawmill."

"Well, thank ya, Leo. That's mighty fine. I was wondering what I was gon'a do since my sawmill burned up. I can't tell ya what that means to me. The Lord surely provides, don't He?"

Susan and Marsha came out of the tent giggling at some small thing. The china teacups Marsha carried rattled in matching saucers, and Susan carried tin cups.

"Have ya boys had coffee?" Susan asked.

"We was waitin' on ya gigglin' girls," Leo said, winking at Jake.

"Oh, you," Susan said, pretending to be mad.

Susan poured coffee while Leo passed the plate of biscuits.

"Jake," Leo said between a mouthful of biscuit, "Susan and me was wondering if ya all would like to have Bible readin' together sometime?"

"Why sure," replied Jake with a big grin and looked at Marsha. "Why not right now?"

"I'll git the Bible," Leo replied and disappeared into the tent.

From their customary perches nearby, Joy, Serenity, and Peace flew down at the mention of the Bible. Gemstones of peridot and topaz sparkled through layers of silk organza. "*Did you hear, Joy*?" Peace whispered, "*They are going to read the Bible. God will definitely be pleased*."

"*I added that to my notes*," Serenity added.

"I'm so glad to have Christian neighbors," Susan said.

"We're mighty glad to have any neighbors," laughed Jake. "But Christian neighbors is the best kind."

Their first worship service was sitting around the breakfast fire. The logs Leo had cut were perfect seating while another log accommodated food and coffee cups. Leo and Jake took turns reading favorite scriptures from the Bible and adding stories of how his favorite reading had affected his family's life. Then Susan and Marsha sang hymns. Marsha sang, "To God be the glory, great things He has done." When she finished, they were quiet, basking in the same spirit of worship.

The fairies' tiny bodies shivered with peace and joy, and the gems in their dresses cast a shining array of colors over the campsite.

Not wanting to end the atmosphere of love and worship, Jake finally rose and said, "Let's pray. Our Father, we thank Ya for being a part of our friendship with Leo and Susan. Thank Ya for bringin' them here. Bless our homes and our work and keep us safe. In Jesus' name. Amen."

Jake stood with Leo, shook hands, and they patted each other on the back. Marsha and Susan hugged and wiped away their tears. So, the new friends made their homes as neighbors.

Jake and Susan's visits were frequent. Jake helped Leo in the garden while Marsha and Susan puttered about the tent. "I got some salt pork, here, Marsha. Do ya like salt pork?" Susan asked.

"If I'm from the south, then I like salt pork." Marsha laughed. "But I reckon I need to be careful what I am a-eatin' for a while."

"Why's that?" Susan inquired, still looking down at the biscuits she was making.

Marsha blushed and replied, "Cause Jake and me is goin' ta have a baby."

"Oh, Marsha, that's wonderful," Susan squealed. "We is too. We is expecting a baby in the spring. When you reckon yours will come?"

"In January, I'm a-thinkin'," replied Marsha. "Will ya be with me to help?"

"Of course, I will," replied Susan, hugging Marsha. "And you will be with me?"

"For certain, I will," beamed Marsha. "Now, where's the coffee pot?"

"Over there, and water's in the bucket," said Susan pointing toward the fire.

Outside, Leo smacked his lips. "Ya smell that, Jake? Salt pork and biscuits!"

"Ya thinkin' what I'm thinkin', Leo?"

"Yes, sir. Let's go," Leo said, moving the horse and plow to a shady area.

"O boy! That breakfast smells mighty good," exclaimed Jake.

"Jake, ya know good and well ya already had breakfast," laughed Marsha.

"That breakfast's done gone, sugar, and Leo and me's been workin' hard."

"Sit right down, Jake," Susan invited. "And will ya say grace?"

All kidding forgotten, the four friends bowed their heads, and Jake offered thanks. "Lord, thank Ya for a new day and for Yer help and protection. Thank Ya for these wonderful friends and tasty food. Amen."

Chapter 11

John and Babette Arrive

Although Babette was strong and resilient, the buckboard's wooden bench was beginning to take its toll on her whole body and mind.

"How long do ya want ta travel, John?" Babette asked, hoping to stop soon. "I tink my back, she won't go much more."

"I reckon we come another two-hundred miles now. I'm watching out for some sort of clearing soon, honey," John said trying to console his tired wife.

However, it was another thirty grueling miles bumping over sugar sand, switch-grass, and gopher holes before they stopped under a spreading oak tree.

"Do I hear water, John?" Babette asked in a tired though hopeful voice.

"Don't know," answered John as he urged Biddy to move forward. Biddy whinnied as she stepped carefully as the ground beneath her hooves had become moist and smelled earthy like decaying leaves.

"Ata girl, Biddy. I smell it, too. Move us on down," John urged his mare. "Babette, Biddy smells water," John announced with renewed energy.

Biddy moved the wagon over the soft, moist soil and through a sparse thicket of young oak trees and palmetto bushes, then stopped. Babette inhaled with delight at the scene before them. A small river. Clear, cool water skipped over fallen trees and teased long grasses growing in the river's white sandy bottom. Dancing in the water's current, the grass seemed to wave, inviting Babette into the refreshing water.

For a long moment, John and Babette sat still taking in the river's beauty and the surrounding terrain.

"Look, John," Babette sighed pointing across the river. "Pine trees. Hear da warm breeze whispering dere prayers into the blue sky. Oh, John. Dis is where I want to be."

"Come on down, honey, and we'll cool off in the water. I'm sure we could all use a drink," John said, holding out his arms to his wife.

The fairies, following close behind, flew with excitement over the river and plunged in. Even though their wings and organza gowns were wet and limp when they bubbled up, still they reveled in the sensation.

Biddy blew hot dust from her nose as John unhitched her from the wagon and led her into the water where she drank her fill. As John and Babette walked in the cool water and listened to God's beautiful world around them, John heard a familiar and happy sound in the distance. "Do ya hear that, Babette? It's a sawmill."

In his excitement, John lifted Babette by her waist and twirled her around. Babette threw her head back and laughed like a young girl before they both fell, sinking into the water. When they came out of the water and found their footing, John held Babette in his embrace and savored the cool water running from his hair, down his face, through his now thick beard before flowing over Babette's body. They stood in each other's embrace, and John breathed a prayer, "Thank Ya, Lord for a safe journey, and now this water and a new home."

"You are most welcome, My son," said God. *"We hope you enjoy the peace and prosperity of this home and find new friends."*

As if sensing it was time to go, Biddy waded through the water and nudged John. "Good girl, Biddy," John praised his mare. "We're ready to go, too?" With those words, John grasped Biddy's reigns and Babette's hand and led them back to the waiting wagon.

With Biddy hitched up to the wagon and Babette in her place beside her husband with renewed spirits, John gave Biddy the "giddy up" signal. With a nicker, his faithful mare navigated the gopher hole-pocked Indian trail. It was as if Biddy sensed John and Babette's excitement of finding their new home.

As they neared a clearing, John's heart thrilled at the sound he associated with so many precious memories. "Ya 'member me tellin' ya Pa worked a sawmill?" he said to Babette. "I 'member so well moseying up to the hills of Missouri to the loggin' camp. That was mighty hard, and sometimes dangerous work. But hearing the sound of the saw reminds me of how satisfying it was."

Babette squeezed John's arm with knowing love and her sense of excitement, and John kissed her forehead, and they moved on.

"Whoa, Biddy," John called to his mare when they arrived at the sawmill. "Howdy!" John sang out when the saw silenced.

Leo and Jake looked up. Sweat and sawdust covered their bodies.

"How do," yelled Leo wiping the sweat from his forehead. "Git on down and come on over."

John clicked to Biddy, asking her to move Babette into the shade of a turkey oak. He squeezed his wife's hand and climbed down from the wagon. "I'll go talk to 'em and ask 'em what's the name of this place." John breathed a prayer as he sauntered over to the sawmill.

Babette shaded her eyes from the intensity of the bright Florida sunlight. In the clear, azure sky, a pair of hawks flew screeching, urging their fledglings to take flight. Tall pines pointed to the sky as if to say, "This is home, Babette." Babette's heart thrilled as she breathed one word, "Home," and watched John shake hands with the two sawdust-encrusted men and hurry back to the wagon.

"They says this here is called the Gracetown sawmill, and they gave us a hearty welcome. One man's name is Leo Bates and t'other is Jake Kelly. Leo says his place is about a mile east, and his wife, Susan, is there. We'll go call on her if ya like."

"I'd like dat, John. It been long time since I've had a woman friend."

They traveled the wagon trail for a mile. Palmetto fronds and wild myrtle scraped the wagon's sides, making high-pitched scratching sounds on the wooden boards. As they continued up the wagon trail, their joy and anticipation grew. Coming into a clearing, they saw a small lean-to and a dirt firepit with tree logs around it.

Susan was in the clearing feeding her chickens and stopped when she saw the unfamiliar wagon pull up. Moving closer, she saw Babette, John's Choctaw Indian wife. "Well, my sakes. Git down and come on in out of the hot sun." As her guests entered the lean-to, Susan stopped at a cypress bench standing next to the entrance. There, she retrieved a gourd ladle from the bucket of water sitting on the bench and filled a tin cup.

"Would ya like a drink of water? Here, my dear. Ya look plumb tuckered out."

Although Babette drank her fill of water at the river, she graciously took the cup from Susan. As she did, her hands brushed Susan's, and her host returned the gesture by laying her hand on top of Babette's. Babette drank deeply then handed the cup to John.

"Thank ya, ma'am," John said to Susan. "It's mighty kind of ya." Then John recited Mark 9:41, "'For whoever gives ya a cup of water to drink in My name, because ya belong to Christ, assuredly, I say to ya, he will by no means lose his reward.'"

"That's from the Bible, ain't it?" Susan almost squealed.

"Yes, ma'am," replied John. "Are ya a believer?"

"Yes, indeed. My husband, Leo, and our friends, Jake and Marsha, is believers, and it's so nice to have more friends who is believers," replied Susan. "Where ya from?"

"I'm from Louisiana Bayou country," replied Babette. "Dis is John, my husband, he from Missouri."

"My, ya've come a long way. Ya must be tired. Do ya want to lie down?" Susan offered.

"Go on, *Mère*," John encouraged Babette.

"My name's Susan," she whispered her introduction to John.

"Nice to meet ya, Susan. Thank ya for being so kind to my wife."

"John, if ya want'a go back to the sawmill, I'll sit with Babette. Leo and Jake should be comin' back real soon."

"Thank ya, ma'am. If yer sure, it's no trouble."

"It's no trouble at all, John. I'm glad to have the company. Besides, I'm thinkin' she's goin' to sleep awhile."

When John left the little house and climbed on the wagon, Susan waved before going back inside. Just as she thought, Babette was asleep. So, Susan took down her Bible and turned to Psalm 121 and read silently:

"The Lord will keep you from all harm—
he will watch over yer life;
the Lord will watch over yer coming and going
both now and forevermore."

Susan busied herself making dinner while Babette slept. The night before, Susan had put on a pot of dry beans to soak. Now, she added salt pork, covered the beans with water, and put them over the fire to simmer. She knew Marsha would bring cornbread. "I hope Marsha brings a pile of cornbread since we have two guests."

The beans were ready by the time Leo, Jake, and John returned from the sawmill. Marsha arrived by horseback with plenty of hot cornbread. With the commotion from outside, Babette awoke refreshed and hungry. The men were excited to share what they learned about John and Babette during their working together.

"Susan, honey, John, and Babette are believers just like us," Leo nearly shouted.

"They want to join our Bible readings," added Jake.

And so, it was. Christian fellowship between the pioneers of Gracetown flourished. Over the next few years, the Lord blessed Gracetown with hardy babies. Born to Leo and Susan Bates were Maxie, Fred, Luther, and Leo, Junior. Born to Jake and Marsha Kelly were Maddie, Ben, and Joseph. Born to John and Babette Wilkins were George, Thomas, and Henry.

Just as generations before them, the new parents brought up their children in the love, and admonition of the Lord. "The ties that bind" continue through another generation.

The pioneers helped each other build and refine simple log houses, prepare gardens, and harvest timber and turpentine. During one of their frequent visits, John mentioned to Leo, "The Lord has been real good to us, hadn't He Leo?"

"Yep, He has."

For a moment, the two friends sat in silence as John smoked his pipe and Leo whittled. He kicked at the curly shavings covering his brogans. Finally, Leo asked, "What's on yer mind, John?"

"I'm a-thinkin' as Gracetown grows, we might be a-needin' a bigger place to store our timber and crops and such," said John drawing long on his pipe. "My shed is a-gittin' a mite small."

"That's a right good idea, John," agreed Leo. "We also be a-needin' a meeting place, too."

"Mighty fine," said John with another draw on his pipe. "Let's talk it over with Jake and see what he thinks."

"First, John," said Leo, "let's talk it over with the Lord."

Thus, planning for a new barn began.

The fairies danced with glee. "*This is exactly what God charged us to do*," exclaimed Serenity.

"*And it was the men's idea, this building a barn*," replied Courage, still dancing.

"*God, did you hear?*" asked a grateful Faith. "*The men are going to build a barn.*"

"*Yes, my dears,*" replied God. "*I knew they would. When you first came to Us in the garden, you thought We were lonely and had no friends.*"

"*Yes, sir. We were afraid You missed the first man in the garden,*" replied Faith.

"*As you see, my dears. We are not alone,*" replied God the Son, Jesus. "*As long as We have friends like these faithful men and women, we will always have devoted companions.*"

God the Father looked at the Son with approving love and replied, "*And these are the right men. They will continue to love and believe in Us, Son, and We will be with them always.*"

Chapter 12

"There she be. That's our warehouse."

John choked on a cloud of dust that rose from the caravan of buckboard wagons hauling the last of two-hundred loads of timber. George drove the lead wagon, and Thomas followed. The good-natured bantering between the brothers thrilled John's heart and livened up their labor.

John chuckled as he recalled the year Thomas was born. After helping a neighbor, Mr. Lester Crown, clear a piece of land and cut timber for a new house, Mr. Crown had paid John with a runt mule named Nester. As Thomas grew, that mule had stayed by Thomas's side protecting and playing with the toddler. Thomas could not say "Nester," so the runt's name became Nessy, and the two of them were inseparable. They had played together, Nessy had followed Thomas everywhere, and the two friends had eaten the same food, no matter what it was.

When Thomas was a strong, robust three-year-old toddler, he played chase with Nessy or rode the mule's back. John enjoyed watching his son and the runt mule play together. He considered Nessy to be the best in-kind payment he had ever received, for when Nessy was not protecting Thomas, he was a valuable work animal.

That year, without warning, Thomas came down with yellow fever. Through Babette's tireless care and prayers, Thomas survived. However, the entire time Thomas was ill, that runt mule pined for his little friend. He would not eat and would not play with any of the other children. Nessy was vigilant and stayed outside Thomas' bedroom window, pining for the tot. The mule would bray a mournful sound to let Thomas know he was there, and when Thomas began to recover, he called to Nessy. It was as if the tot and the mule had their own language.

All through his illness, Babette was a vigilant mother and stayed by Thomas's bedside. "Thomas, baby, yer muder is here," Babette reassured her son. After ten long days, the fever broke. "Baby, drink dis water," Babette encouraged Thomas. "Ya need to drink da water, Thomas, so ya kin get well. Baby, take dis bean soup. It make ya feel better."

Babette boiled water and forced her sick baby to drink. She made soft red bean soup and spooned the warm liquid into him, just as she had when John had malaria. It took him several more months before he was healthy again. Nevertheless, he was back chasing Nessy, and the mule became even more protective of his best friend.

In the evening, John and Babette sat on the front porch of their rustic home and watched George and Thomas play. John enjoyed his pipe, and Babette mended torn shirts and jeans. That faithful runt mule brayed with joy as he ran away from Thomas.

"Pa! Nessy run," Thomas squealed in his baby talk. "Run, Nessy. I catch ya."

Nessy instinctively knew not to kick when Thomas was chasing him. However, he would give the tot, what seemed to be, a mischievous backward glance. Then, abruptly, Nessy sat down, causing Thomas to bump into his back.

Thomas squealed, "Pa, Nessy go boom, Pa. Nessy go boom."

Thomas wrapped his arms around the mule's neck and squealed with delight before falling to the ground. The toddler quickly got up with a mouth full of dirt, turned, and ran, expecting Nessy to give chase. "Nessy, git me. Run, Nessy! Git me." The mule's sitting prank gave him the advantage of not missing a step.

John released a swirl of tobacco smoke and chuckled to himself, Smart mule. That was just what Nessy wanted.

The chase continued in the opposite direction this time. Nessy kicked up his heels and brayed as he chased his little friend, and John laughed until his sides ached. As his laughter subsided, he remembered God's goodness and offered a prayer of thanksgiving with another swirl of smoke.

"Thank Ya, Lord, for that runt mule and for healing my boy. Thank Ya for my Babette. She's a wonderful wife and mother."

"You are welcome, My son," God replied. *"You, John, are a good husband, father, and friend to My Son and Me. It makes Us happy to see you and your family happy."*

A wagon wheel hit a gopher hole and sent a jolt through John's body, interrupting his reminiscence. When he had been young, his body fought back at every pain of broken bones and crushed fingers. Now, however, it took longer for his aging body to fight back. As if in empathy, his bones and the faithful wagon creaked and groaned when they thudded over gopher holes as he traveled through Florida's sand and switchgrass.

Every assault from a gopher hole on one of the forty-four-inch, steel-rimmed wheels reminded him that years of farming timberland either strengthened or ravaged a young man's body.

"Easy, Biddy," he encouraged his golden mare.

That mare, now paired with Brownie, a young gelding, was a kind and patient mentor, showing Brownie how to work with, not against, the bit and bridle.

"When we git to the sawmill, Biddy, I'll put on yer feedbags, so's you and Brownie can eat," he promised his companion.

John drew on his pipe again and let his mind drift with the fragrant smoke as he remembered the years when building began.

George led the three-wagon caravan hauling timber and pulled up to Leo's sawmill. When all three wagons arrived, John, George, and Thomas began to unload logs.

Sitting in the shade of a live oak tree, Leo was sharpening the teeth of his fifty-inch blade, while Jake filled the boiler with river water and loaded the belly of the wood burner with scraps of pine. Leo and Jake set up a section of a long-leaf pine log to the freshly sharpened blade, and the engine screamed with pent-up steam. With one mighty spin from his work-calloused hands, the heavy cylinder roared, and the steam engine had no option other than to spring to life.

"Stand back, George, lest ya want a mouth full of sawdust," Leo warned. "Thomas, shove another log this way."

In minutes, the gleaming saw blade sliced through a thirty-foot section, spewing long tails of sawdust into the hot, now pine-scented air. By the time the hungry sawblade gnawed through the first cut, sweat and sticky sawdust coated Leo's and Jake's short muscular arms and hairy chests.

"This last load of timber will be fer the roof trusses," Leo yelled out his promise.

"I'm thinkin' it will take 10,500 board feet for them trusses. That'd be about twenty, one-hundred-foot trees."

With the last load of timber milled into lumber, the tired men re-loaded the wagons and headed two miles to the barn's building site. As they came into the community of Gracetown, John basked in the sound of laughter from children. His five-year-old grandson, Henry, Thomas's firstborn, was leading the pack of rowdy children waving stick-swords in the air.

"There's a pirate ship!" called Henry, waving his sword. "Surround it, mates."

"Whoa, there, Capt'n," John said, playing along. "Permission to sail on."

"Permission granted, Grandpa," Henry yelled, pointing forward with his stick-sword.

John's youngest grandson, Timmy, still in diapers and on wabbly toddler legs, tried to keep up with the older children. Although he was always a wobble-and-bump-in-the-dirt behind, he was determined to play. At least he was until his older brother, Henry, invited him not-so-nicely to leave.

"Go on, Timmy! You's too little to play with us." Henry gave Timmy a push, and the toddler fell on his butt into the dirt.

The fairies, Joy and Courage, hurried to the toddler and whispered encouraging words in his ear. Then, Timmy giggled and hoisted himself out of the dirt, diaper end first, and continued following the older children.

At the building site, John and his sons, George, and Thomas, joined Leo's four sons, Maxie, Luther, Adam, and Leo, Junior. Jake Kelly came later with his two sons, Ben, and Joseph, while Leo stayed at the sawmill.

"George, git Maxie and Luther to help ya roll off that there top log," shouted John. "Thomas, can ya hop on down, and when the log hits the dirt, hitch up that mule?"

"Here it comes, Thomas. Stand back and keep them children back," George shouted.

The log hit the ground with a mighty thud that shook the men to the bone.

"Let's git 'er done, boys," shouted John.

George and Maxie tied ropes on the log, two on both the top and bottom for guide ropes. Then, Thomas hitched up Nessy to a harness fitted with a rope and pully attached to a thirty-foot log. After the ropes were secure, Thomas coaxed the mule to pull. "Pull, Nessy! Pull! Pull, mule."

Nessy pulled and strained, digging his hooves into the dirt so that John could almost see the concentration in Nessy's squinting eyes. Thomas continued to coax the mule to pull the log, and Nessy, always eager to please Thomas, pulled harder.

Finally, as the log gave way and moved, its momentum made the task easier. Thomas instructed Nessy, "Bring it over here, Nessy. That-a-boy."

"Hold tight to them ropes, boys!" shouted John.

George, Joseph, Fred, and Adam guided the top ropes to keep the log from swinging. Maxie, Henry, Ben, and Luther guided the bottom ropes to keep it in position.

With no small timing and effort, men and beast groaned, straining their muscles, and finally lifted the first thirty-foot log to the edge of a four-foot foundation hole. The log teetered on the foundation's side while men and mule continued to maintain control with the ropes. With one more orchestrated pull, the log surrendered and fell into the foundation. Nessy let out a long bray, and the men cheered.

"That there's the first one," called John. "Only three more to go."

"Let's get 'er done, then," said George.

Hearing all the cheering and laughter, the toddler, again turned away by his older brother, came over to work with the big men.

"Git on out of the way, Timmy," John scolded his grandson while nailing long pieces of lumber to the corner posts.

"Go find yer Mama, Timmy," scolded Uncle Maxie.

Although Maxie was Leo's oldest son, Timmy loved the big burly man as much as he loved his real Uncle George.

"Git on now, Timmy," John prodded again. "It's dangerous here."

However, the three-year-old did not understand the danger. Timmy just wanted to help, and besides, it looked like such fun, and the dirt was delicious.

Jammed between a mammoth root on the side of the foundation hole and the edge, the last stubborn log stuck at a seventy-five-degree angle.

"Let's take a break," said Jake wiping his face. "This here log is going to take extra coaxing."

"Git on out of the way like I told ya, Timmy," his grandpa scolded and swung his sweaty hat in the vicinity of the toddler. "Now, git!" John turned to the others. "Ready, George? Maxie? Ben? Ready, Joseph?"

They all answered collectively, "Ready."

"Thomas, git that mule to pullin'."

As expected, it took extra effort and concentration from the neighbors and Nessy to pull that log to the final ninety degrees. Muscles strained, and nerves stretched to a near breaking point. While Thomas and Nessy pulled, the men holding the guide ropes attached to the log kept keen eyes and steady hands on the ropes. John and Jake stood at the hole to guide the belligerent pole into place. When the pole hit the eighty-five-degree angle, John yelled, "Thomas, unhitch Nessy and move him out of the way."

Eight strong men, nearly spent, strained every muscle to guide the log to its final resting place. They were determined not to let a log win that fight.

"Let 'er go!" called Jake.

The men holding on to the top guide ropes turned the ropes loose and stepped out of the way. The thirty-foot trimmed pine log slid through the earth and then dropped its one-ton weight into its place in the foundation. The ground shook when it hit its mark.

Even before they could get the pole stabilized, John and Thomas heard the wail of a child in pain.

"Timmy! Where's Timmy?" John turned to the left and scanned the area for the tot. Then he turned to the right, searching. His heart pounded in his chest.

In wild, distraught fear, Thomas ran searching, calling his son. They did not see Timmy anywhere. "Timmy?"

Leaving the pole in the capable hands of their neighbors, John and Thomas ran in panicked circles looking for the toddler, calling as they searched. "Timmy! Where's Timmy?"

Just before John collapsed from fear and exhaustion, he heard Babette's voice. "He over here, John, dear. He git in da ant bed and git his little leg chewed up, but he be okay."

John felt like adding a little red behind to Timmy's painful ant bites. Instead, he grabbed the toddler and devoured him with kisses and hugs, repeating over and over, "Thank Ya, Lord. Thank Ya, Lord."

In patient love, God said, *"You are surprised, John? Don't you know by now that I look out for even the littlest of My children? Now, be at peace."*

When John regained control of his nerves, he continued to yell instructions.

"Let's call it a day. We'll do better if we start the framin' tomorrow after a good rest."

"Rest?" laughed George trying to lighten everyone's spirits. "I still got to go home and do chores."

"Not me," quipped Thomas. "I don't got no chores," he said, pushing George in the shoulder. Both men knew that was not true, for pioneers always had chores that needed doing.

When building resumed the next day, the pioneers began constructing the frames for the barn walls. "It'll take all of us to build a wall frame and lift 'er up," said Jake. Thomas, hitch up Nessy to the wagon and bring them framin' pieces over here. Ya all know what to do. We want a bay of four windows, twenty-four inches below the roofin' on three sides, and a large double door on the west side. Thomas, you, and Luther make sure them corner posts is plumb. Maxie and Fred grab a beam and hammer it to the bottom of all the corner posts. George and Ben, ya git up on the ladder and nail a beam in the middle. The rest of us will attach studs and braces to the frame support."

Then, John called on Nessy again. It took all eight men and that mule to hoist the first wall in place. Over the next two weeks, the men fashioned three more walls and hoisted them up, taking frequent breaks for safety.

"It's beginnin' to look like a proper buildin'," said Jake.

"Yes, them walls is the second hardest part. Next comes them trusses," John added.

"The lumber ain't here yet, Pa. I'll ride back to the sawmill to see if'n they is ready," offered George.

"We can't start on them trusses until the lumber arrives," said Jake. "This would be a good time to break for the week. We'll begin again after Sunday."

On Sunday, the pioneers gathered at Jake Kelly's house for worship. As usual, John, Jake, and Leo took turns reading Scripture and explaining them to the little ones. The next generation—George, Thomas, Maxie, and Fred—were now old enough to add their favorite Scriptures to the readings. The worship was one of praise, faith, thanksgiving, and of course, asking for safety for the next day. After worship, the families returned to their homes full of hope and love.

Passion was always searching for love. However, since her maturity, she realized passion and love took many forms.

The evening was quiet as babies lay sleeping, and the couples shared their sweet whispers for the future.

"All is well, Son. Let's give them a peaceful night's rest," God said.

The truss lumber arrived from the sawmill on Monday afternoon, and the men worked in teams of two, constructing the trusses. In addition to the main trusses, the builders fashioned a small section atop the main roof. This small section, the capstone with its over-hanging eves, created an opening on all four sides of the roof, venting the building.

With the tall ceiling, large windows, and the vent, the building would stay cool and dry. Thanks to a pot-bellied stove in the center of the main room, the building would also stay surprisingly warm in the winter.

"Jake, where'd ya store them tin pieces that come up from 'Jacksonsville'?" asked John.

"They's stored at my livery stable," replied Jake. Earlier in the year, Jake had ordered sheets of interlocking tin, which had arrived from Jacksonville via riverboat.

"Thomas, when that tin gits here, git Nessy to haul them tin pieces up top," instructed John. "Fred, ya game to nail in tin with Ben?"

"Guess we can. I ain't never worked with tin afore," replied Fred.

"Ya'll git the hang of it. Just watch out for them sharp edges. They'll sneak up on ya and cut up yer hands and legs," George warned with a knowing chuckle.

Leaning against a truss for stability, Fred and Ben positioned a twelve-foot long section of tin perpendicular over the truss rafters. With his hammer, Fred secured a length of tin to a rafter. Each edge of the tin took six nails, and Fred hit each nail every time with three blows of the hammer.

"Looky there! Eighteen blows and didn't miss nary a time," boasted Fred. "Let's see ya best that there, Ben."

Ben accepted the challenge, "Yer on." Ben matched Fred blow for blow.

"Throw us up another piece," Fred hollered down to Thomas. "We got us a competition up here."

The good-natured competition between the friends and neighbors kept the work exciting and moving along at a quick pace. As the friends nailed the tin in place, four other men worked on the loading platform below.

"Did we git them cedar timbers from Leo at the sawmill?" Jake asked Joseph.

"Yes, sir, Pa," replied his son.

"Let's git them timbers on the loading platform and nail 'em together," instructed Jake.

They laid out fourteen, seven-foot by one-foot cedar timbers over the piling supports and nailed them together with cross timbers for added support. Two sections of cedar timbers made a seven-foot by seven-foot door.

"Where's them wheels?" called John.

"Over here, John," replied Jake. "Them tracks, too."

Four heavy iron wheels and matching tracks had also come by riverboat from Jacksonville.

"Is them doors done?" yelled Jake.

"Yes, sir, Pa."

"Did ya remember to nail in cross braces?"

"Yes, sir."

"Then, we's ready to put on the wheels."

Once the thick cedar doors' construction was complete and the wheels attached, it took these six men to heft the door up into the opening and coaxed the wheels into the matching iron tracks.

"Whoa, whoa!" yelled John. "I'm losin' my grip. Set 'er down! Set 'er down!"

John's corner of the door hit the loading platform so hard that it rattled the structure, and the sound reverberated through the inside timbers.

"Ya okay, John?" asked Jake. "Did it git yer foot?"

"Nah. But my blisters got blisters, and my back says it's done workin'."

"Let's call it a day," Jake announced. Again, there were no complaints about stopping.

Earlier in the day, Jake and Leo Junior had placed eight-foot timbers across three sawhorses to make a dinner table under the canopy of a giant live oak tree. Susan, Marsha, and Babette covered this make-shift table with yards of red and white checked fabric, then began loading the table with food. There were several platters of fried chicken, just as many bowls of sweet corn topped with mountains of melting butter, biscuits and chicken gravy, enough fresh pole beans, fried okra, cornbread, and milk for the army of tired, hungry men. For dessert, there was a blackberry cobbler. For obvious reasons, Leo would have preferred a chocolate cake, and he beamed when Susan placed her chocolate cake in his hands.

"This is for you, husband," Susan's eyes gazed at Leo with understanding love.

"Thank ya, honey. Yer priceless," whispered Leo.

Once everyone was seated, Jake asked for silence. He removed his sweaty hat and bowed his head. "Thank Ya, Lord, for a safe workday and for this bounty Ya set before us."

Everyone collectively said, "Amen." Then the reaching, eating, talking, and laughing began.

Faith, Hope, Courage, and Joy played with the little children and babies, feeding them spoons full of chocolate frosting and blackberry cobbler. It was not an easy task for Joy to contain herself, for she so delighted in the children.

Looking upon the families with pride, God said, "*We have done well, Son. However, I don't boast for what We did.*

Instead, I am proud for what the members of these families have done."

"Yes, Father. We have protected and provided for them. Though it was the hard work and perseverance of these brave pioneers that brought them here today, and they continue to be thankful."

After dinner, everyone found a comfortable spot for a short rest to let their dinner settle. Young married couples found quiet places to whisper their words of love to each other. The ladies visited and wiped little hands and lips full of chocolate icing. Some men enjoyed a relaxing pipe of tobacco while others had a third serving of blackberry cobbler or joined in a game of horseshoes. Fred and Ben compared cuts from the tin, counting to see who had the most. Their mothers were not amused. Soft conversation, the sound of clanging horseshoes, and the squeals and laughter of children filled the community. Then it was quiet, allowing for a much-needed nap.

The first to stir was Leo. As he passed, Leo kicked John's foot good-naturedly. After that, the other men roused from their resting places and followed, and the building resumed.

"Ya boys want to help work on the building?" Leo called to the ten and twelve-year-old boys still playing horseshoes.

"Yes, sir!"

"Yeah!"

"Sure do! What ya want us to be a-doin'?"

"Run over yonder to the shed and find a couple of gallons of white paint and brushes. You can start paintin' the sides as fer up as ya can reach."

The young boys, eager to be a part of the historic building, ran, pushing and shoving to see who could get a can of paint first. Those who did not get a can of paint turned their attention to paint brushes. It was a big game. The next game was to see who could avoid being the target for white splatters. It was difficult to say what most of the paint covered, the boys or the building.

In 1899, after years of arduous work, the last board nailed in place, and the last coat of paint slopped on the sides, the barn was complete, and the residents of Gracetown celebrated. When the noise subsided, Leo Bates quoted Malachi 3:10, "Bring ye all the tithes into the storehouse, that there may be meat in mine house, and prove me now herewith, saith the Lord of hosts, if I will not open ya the windows of heaven, and pour ya out a blessing, that there shall not be room enough to receive it."

"There she be," announced John Wilkins. "That's our storehouse."

One of the young boys covered in white paint from head to toe, shouted, "Hey, Mr. Wilkins, why don't we call it the warehouse?" And with that, the name stuck, and the barn was forever known as the warehouse.

While the pioneer builders had no idea what influence the warehouse would have in the years ahead, God knew. As years and even decades passed, the warehouse would change lives.

"To God be the glory, great things He has done," whispered Leo.

Someone quoted Psalm 116:15, "I will offer you the sacrifice of thanksgiving, and call upon the Name of the Lord."

Over the next two years, Gracetown doubled in area and population, and Leo Bates' sawmill buzzed, turning out timbers to build more houses. “The ties that bind” continued to anchor and unify the small town.

Chapter 13

Market Day In Gracetown

Years after the building of the warehouse, John, Leo, and their sons diversified their timber farms.

"How's yer garden, Leo?" asked John with a draw on his pipe.

"Got some new seed to put in. So, in addition to my black-eyed peas, potatoes, and okree, I will have pole beans and corn," replied Leo. "How's yorn?"

"Same as yesterday, sweet potatoes, black-eyed peas, and kale," reported John. "How ya goin' ta keep yer cattle out'a yer corn?"

"I put up a rail fence on my back twenty, so them cattle is grazing in another field," said Leo. "Ya goin' ta put in sugar cane, John?"

"'Course I am. Couldn't live without cane syrup," jested John.

After each harvest, the friends loaded their wagons to make the trip to the warehouse. On one particular trip, John was in the lead wagon. As a novelty, he attached long strips of braided leather to a wooden handle. He used this tool to keep his team's attention to the task at hand, for by now, Gracetown was a bustling place with horses and wagons.

Crack! "Let's go, Jack," John urged the gelding, cracking the whip above the animal's head. Biddy had long been retired, and John had bought two new horses for his farm, and, like Biddy, he treated them like pets. He took great care not to let the biting ends of the leather whip touch his horses. "Keep on up, Pete," John encouraged the younger of the two horses.

Hearing the crack from John's whip, several bare-foot children ran through the dusty street, jockeying for position to see the "cracker." Eugene, a chubby little eight-year-old, stumbled as he ran through clouds of dust, with a wayward overall-strap flying about his head, threatening to box his ears.

"Here comes that cracker," Eugene yelled.

"That's John Wilkins. He's a real Florida cracker!" Beau clarified, tripping over the frayed legs of his too-long overalls.

Crack! Crack! "There ya go, Jack, boy," John coaxed his gelding again. "Don't want to disappoint them kids."

"Hey, John, what did ya bring to market?" Isaac Gray called from a distance. Isaac, although one of the newer residents to Gracetown, considered John a good friend.

"The usual," John called back. "Kale and black-eyed peas."

"Yee-ha," Isaac sang out. "I'll trade ya for some of my sweet corn."

"Done," replied John, blowing a cloud of blue smoke from his pipe over his head.

So, market day burst upon Gracetown, filling the small town's tranquility with a myriad of sights, sounds, and smells to tantalize everyone's senses. Just as John and Isaac planned to trade their kale, black-eyed peas, and corn, other local farmers came to the warehouse with their goods ready to banter and barter.

"Ya sellin' that hog, Bill, or just showin' him off?" Jess teased Bill Watkins.

"I'm a-sellin' him, but not to the likes of you, Jess Thorpe. I doubt if ya'd even know what to do with a hog." Bill grinned.

"Gee," John called a command to Pete and Jack to turn right. "Too far, Jack. Haw."

An experienced and gentle Jack obeyed John's command and turned back left. Jack followed. "Good boy, Jack," John praised his faithful gelding again.

As more wagons arrived, moving into que at the warehouse, horses whinnied and snorted to each other in horse-speak and engaged in pawing and shoving matches.

"Whoa there, Pete. Settle 'im down, Jack."

Bare-foot boys ran among the wagons peeking under canvas and burlap coverings to discover what delicacies they hid. Between these scampering bare feet and horses pawing the dirt road, clouds of dust and an earthy musk from leather tack, sweat, and horse manure filled the hot Gracetown air. Ladies, eager to inspect fresh farm produce on market day, shared new recipes and bragged on their latest quilting creations.

"Mornin', Evelyn. My, that's a fine new shirtwaist," Mrs. Godwin said, admiring Evelyn's new gingham dress.

"Where'd ya get the cloth?" chatted her neighbor.

Everywhere one looked was a group of chattering women bedecked in bright-colored calico frocks and matching bonnets. Most of them carried hand-woven baskets, and their aprons, cut from flour sacks and trimmed with bits of lace, added to the colorful scene.

"My lands," exclaimed Mrs. Tawny, covering her nose and mouth with her hanky. "Pew. What an odor."

Her companion, Mrs. Murphy, who came to trade her fresh milk and butter, agreed then quipped, “My man done told me that was the smell o’ money.” Both women giggled, knowing it was the truth. “When he comes in from the barn after feedin’ up, I tells him to rake the money off’n his shoes,” added Mrs. Murphy with a giggle. The ladies muffled their laughter into their hankies and enjoyed market day just the same.

Gracetown continued to grow, adding residents and businesses. The warehouse remained the agricultural center for the growing community. While horse and wagon transported crops to the warehouse through 1918, the introduction of the motor car brought added motion and commotion to market day.

“Whoa, there! Slow down there, Dave,” shouted Dave’s neighbor. “What’a yer doin’ speedin’ through town like that?”

“I ain’t speedin’, Amos,” quipped David. “Yer horse is just slow.”

At the blinding speed of twenty miles per hour, a Model T truck put-putted on narrow inter-tube tires, trying to avoid potholes in the sandy roads. It was a wonder that a vehicle could travel even five miles a day on pothole-filled roads that had an insatiable appetite for rubber tires.

While many farmers took the slow and arduous drive to lucrative northern markets, others chose a less precarious route. Three miles east, steamboats waited to transport commodities a shorter distance upriver. Even though their smaller markets were not as lucrative as the northern markets, fresh produce still brought a competitive price.

As heavy-laden trucks and wagons pulled out from the warehouse, the town's people prayed for a safe journey and a good sale and savored the last whiff of fresh beans, bell pepper, and corn packed into tall wooden hampers. If perhaps a stray melon fell from a flatbed truck, as some farmers ensured would happen, little bare-foot boys gobbled up the sweet fruit. Teenage boys could not resist sneaking a protruding leaf of golden-brown tobacco from the course burlap covering. To be sure, a leaf or two of tobacco would enhance a lazy afternoon of fishing.

When the good residents of Gracetown were not farming or transporting their goods to market, they worked together as a community harvesting timber from acres of tall, slash, or long-leaf pine.

"Howdy, Leo."

Leo stepped away from the insatiable saw blade, wiped the sawdust encrusted sweat from his neck, and greeted his neighbor, James Moore. "Howdy, James."

"Ya got time to mill this here timber? I'm a-startin' a house fer my daughter and her new husband."

"Sure, James. Congratulations! Next week good fer ya?"

For the next thirty years, the sawmill hummed, and Gracetown grew, and John Wilkins' youngest son, Thomas, and his wife, Linda, blessed John with five more grandchildren. That year, the youngest was Edward, who, in the fullness of time, started his own home and family in downtown Gracetown.

In the Spring of 1950, Edward's first son, Kevin, was born. Upon Kevin's first presentation to family and friends, the near centenarian, John Wilkins, proudly introduced his great-grandson to his friend, Leo Bates. Baby Kevin made his presence known with a mighty howl and an angry red face.

Leo punched John in the arm, "Chip off the old block, eh, John?"

However, one year and two months later, the tables turned when Leo Bates' second grandson, Leo III, presented the family with a baby girl named Kathryn.

When Leo, the aging pioneer, proudly shared his beautiful sleeping great-granddaughter, John, his best friend over these many years, said, "She don't do much, do she? Kind'a like her great-grandpap."

The ribbing was good-natured and all in fun, for the two old pioneers were the closest of friends and proud of each other's families.

Not long after the presentation of the babies, John and Leo entered their eternal rest. They had a right to be proud of their families and their work building the warehouse.

Chapter 14

Progress Comes To Gracetown

After 1950, Gracetown and the warehouse experienced significant changes. No one knew the exact date that the small town's name changed; but changed it did. The residents' southern drawl may have had a hand in giving Gracetown its new name. However it happened, the name of Gracetown forever changed to Graceton.

The railroad came, first as a slow-moving freight train, then as a high-speed locomotive. This new mode of transportation usurped the wagon, Model T truck, and steamboat as the preferred means for moving crops to market and people to new destinations.

Through two wars, the families of Graceton gathered, wept, cheered, and embraced their anxious yet excited boys festooned in military uniforms. Year by year, some of these same families arrived at the warehouse in horse-drawn wagons to receive the flag-draped coffins of their fallen sons. With each arrival, the mayor hung a silver star on the front exterior wall of the warehouse. Each star, measuring six inches tip to tip, gleamed, as it were, with the sunlight of freedom. Long years later, these same families came to support each other, to weep, to cheer, and to embrace their returning men, no longer boys, but war-wearied men.

However, most of the time, the warehouse was a happy place where residents gathered to discuss new or pressing matters of agriculture, civic issues, or socialize.

"Heard the highway is comin' through town," Henry lamented. "That's goin'ta change things 'round here."

"Yep," agreed Leo Junior. "Don't mean we need to be a victim to progress, though."

"Remember back when we built that there warehouse, Thomas?" George asked his brother in a reflective voice.

"Yep," replied Thomas. "Them were the days. That were really blood, sweat, and tears, weren't it?" Leo paused to study the building and then remarked, "Looks like the ol' girl needs a new coat of paint. I can see them original timbers have grayed."

"Ya gonna climb that ladder, Thomas?" George asked, laughing.

"I reckon not. Let them young men take over," Thomas laughed. "Guess I become a victim of old age."

Once pristine with glowing white oil-based paint, exterior walls now revealed original sturdy pine timbers grayed by the sun. Sturdy gables still supported the once shiny tin roof, now rusted with age. Yet, there was something mysterious and drawing, even inviting about this old relic. Strangers gawked and saw only another old building screaming through opened mouths of chipped paint, "Paint me!" However, the citizens of Graceton gazed lovingly at their "beloved old lady." They did not see chipped paint and rusty tin. Instead, they saw decades of emotion, activity, and history.

The interior structure of the Warehouse allowed sounds to reverberate and echo through her enormous open rafters. A hard rain magnified into a deafening roar, while a gentle rain sounded like a whisper.

Sadly, as time dictates, the older Florida pioneers and builders of the warehouse died, as did small farms, the old sawmills, and turpentine. For a season, the warehouse sat empty and neglected.

Passion's brilliant rhodonite stones, hidden among the layers of her red silk organza gown, appeared blacker and pinker than their normal red as the fairy lamented, *"Graceton is not the same now that the old pioneers have gone. Everything is so fast now. I miss how horses and wagons once moseyed down dusty roads to the warehouse. I miss how farmers and their wives gathered at the warehouse to exchange stories and vegetables."*

"Passion, dear, your balance is off," consoled Serenity. *"Why don't you return to the garden for a while?"*

"I agree with Passion," added Faith. *"I also agree with you, Serenity, dear. I miss the pioneers, too. However, we must focus our energies more on this new generation of young people than on the past."*

"Very wise, Faith," added Hematite. *"We must not let God down. Just because the old pioneers are gone doesn't mean that God will stop caring for His friends."*

As God passed by, He overheard the fairies' conversation and said, *"Thank you, Hematite. You are always so reliable and positive. And you are correct. I have not forgotten My friends. Just because they are young does not mean they do not need Me. I also have a plan for the warehouse. As originally planned, I want to use the warehouse to store all the blessings and gifts that my friends do not claim. I will wait as long as it takes until they ask."*

"Why do they not claim Your gifts, Sir?" asked Curiosity. *"I would love to have as many gifts and blessings as I could have. Do Your friends not know how generous You are?"*

"No, my dear. They merely don't know how many gifts and blessings I have for them. That's why I need the warehouse. Now, my dears, you might enjoy getting to know the pioneer's great-great-grandchildren."

PART TWO

Chapter 1

Kevin and Kathryn

"The train's coming! The train's coming! I'll race you all to the knoll!" Kevin Wilkins yelled.

The fairies, continuing to keep close vigil over God's friends, watched in amazement as the excitement unfolded.

"*What is happening?*" asked Curiosity.

"I am not certain," replied Wisdom, "But, *I do think it is unwise to be here."*

At the railroad crossing, lights and bells rang and flashed in sync. The ear-splitting warning announced the approach of 200,000 pounds of hot iron and stainless steel. The Silver Streak's locomotive engine looked like a vicious stainless-steel bulldog with a flat nose and red, white, and blue stripes. Even when the Silver Streak stood motionless at the depot, this huffing, hissing, "ground-pawing bulldog" boasted a commanding presence of a sixteen-foot height and a ten-foot breadth. This machine was something parents feared, and children idolized.

At a new speed record of 79 miles per hour, this silver goliath gobbled up wooden railroad ties and iron rails made slick and shiny from constant wear. However compelling, this mass of roaring stainless-steel, this powerful diesel engine, was subservient to the engineer's hand on a small throttle.

In the 1950s, the Silver Streak made its regular 1,300-mile route from New York to Miami in a twenty-five-hour blur.

Throughout the country, at any one time, four-thousand passengers, some sleeping in Pullman cars, some sitting in luxury coaches of the lounge cars visiting or reading, all traveled in serene peace and comfort. Only on rare occasions did travelers from up north come to the tiny burg of Graceton, Florida, to visit families and friends. At those exciting times, the engineer pushed another small lever to engage the airbrakes and bring the roaring locomotive and its twenty-one cars to a labored stop. Twelve, forty-two-inch iron wheels on three axles squealed, iron against iron, as the demanding airbrake hissed a command.

Hot air from this laboring goliath was pungent with the strong odors of diesel fuel and brake fluid. However, today, the train would not stop.

Rex Cross, a thirty-year railroad man and now engineer of the Silver-Streak started his eight-hour shift at six o'clock in the morning in Savannah, Georgia. By mid-morning, he guided his submissive beast through Graceton, where he knew every inch of the tracks. When he was young, he had committed to memory the timetable for his regular stops on the route and was always on time. When the Silver Streak flew through Graceton, towns' people looked at their vest pocket watches and kitchen clocks and commented, "Here comes the train. Right on time, Cross."

Rex Cross knew every whistle stop on his route and recognized passengers who traveled with regularity. Almost like Santa Claus, he learned to anticipate a band of happy children who raced every day, except Sunday to the grassy knoll at the main intersection of Graceton. He enjoyed watching their smiling faces and looked forward to their exuberant waves and cheers. And of course, he always waved back and blew his high-pitched air horn for their added excitement.

After the Silver Streak made its daily pass through Graceton, other trains ran every thirty minutes. These were the very slow-moving freight trains that children loved counting the cars and guessing at their contents as the rattling freight cars thumped over the tracks. Adults, however, were not as excited as the children. It was not uncommon for a freight engine to pull one hundred cars and creep at twenty miles an hour through town. Anyone in a hurry usually turned around and traveled the back route instead of waiting.

Sometimes, the freight cars hauled logs on their way to northern mills. Others carried building materials or machine parts, and still, others hauled farm equipment, seed, and fertilizers. With the invention of refrigerated cars, the freight trains transported vegetables, citrus, and even flowers across the country without spoilage. The contents of some cars were obvious, for nothing else smelled like cattle or hogs. During WWII, freight trains carried tanks, machine guns, and other machines needed to win the war. Today, however, as every day, in Graceton, the children thrilled as the mighty Silver Streak flashed through town.

"The train's coming! The train's coming! I'll race you to the knoll!"

Why was the goliath Silver Streak such a daily thrill for the children of the small town of Graceton? Was it the racing, tumbling, and giggling to reach the knoll first? Was it the power of the giant hulk of shiny stainless-steel? Was it the heat and force of wind from the mighty locomotive? Was it the sense of danger from being so close to such a powerful raging bull? Or was it merely the joy of being young and carefree?

Seven giggling, awkward children, ages six to twelve, ran pushing and tripping over each other, rolling in the grass, and looking more like long-eared puppies than children.

"Last one to the grassy knoll is the cow's tail," Kevin hollered, laughing and looking back, especially to find Kathryn. "Come on, Bobby, you can do better than that," Kevin teased. "Oh no, you don't, Al. You can't trip me up that easy," Kevin yelled, eluding Al's long eleven-year-old feet. "Ow," wailed Kevin. "Ya little runt." Kevin stumbled and rolled to catch his balance. "Just wait! I'll catch you and give your carrot head a good knuckle scrub."

"If you catch me!" Jim Bob shouted as he turned and ran backward several paces. No sooner were the words out of his mouth than Jim Bob fell over Al, who was kneeling and waiting for the unsuspecting friend.

"Come on, Kathryn," coaxed her best friend, Helen. "You don't want to be last again and let Kevin call you the cow's tail."

Kathryn willed her long slender limbs to keep running, knowing her legs would prefer to curl up under a fuzzy blanket with a good Nancy Drew mystery. In an excited frenzy of anticipation, the children raced to see who would be the first to reach the knoll's soft green grass located just west of Mr. Martin's Sunshine-Swifty Grocery store. The Seaboard Railroad had constructed a mound of grass and rock to be a protective buffer for pedestrian traffic. It was this prime real estate, a mere fifty yards from the Seaboard depot and train tracks, that provided a safe vantage point for the children to watch and wave as the Silver Streak diesel locomotive roared through the small town.

Dashing Al's and Jim Bob's hopes of beating him to the grassy knoll one day, Kevin arrived three strides ahead of all the other children. Upon his arrival at his coveted goal, he raised both arms above his head and pranced a victory dance, taunting the other boys. "Still, the winner!" Kevin cheered.

Kevin Wilkins, the oldest of the children, was a stocky fifth-grader with broad shoulders, husky legs, and thick hips that showed promising signs of becoming narrow and muscular. He had a hint of Native American rugged allure in his complexion and high cheekbones.

"John and Babette would certainly be proud of their great-grandson," commented Grace, the fairy in the feminine, lavender gown.

"I am certain the pioneers are proud of all their grand and great-grandchildren," Compassion agreed.

Just like other boys of the 1950s, Kevin's thick auburn, almost black, hair was long on the top and sides and longer in back. With the aid of a popular, greasy hair cream product, Kevin brushed the sides of his dark locks back to a point at his neck. The name of this hairstyle was called "ducktails."

When Kevin ran, even the greasy hairdressing could not contain his dark auburn hair. Sweat, oil, and hair flew in all directions and looked as if his locks were wings that might take flight. Despite the dirt and sweat of an active fifth-grade boy, Kevin's natural body chemistry yielded a pleasant, spicy musk, unlike other boys going through the rigors of puberty.

After his teasing victory dance, Kevin fell to the ground rolling in the grass, giggling and gasping for breath. One by one, the other children arrived and joined Kevin in a free for all, running and laughing to celebrate the end of another race.

"The winner," Kevin declared between gulps of air. "I did it! Still the champion!" Then Kevin paused. "Where's Kathryn?" he shouted, scanning the street and knoll for Kathryn.

"She's coming, Kevin," shouted Helen. "Don't tease her so."

"Come on, Kathryn! You can do it. Run! Run!" Kevin encouraged Kathryn with a bit of a tease.

As usual, demure Kathryn was the last to arrive. Yet, her typical late arrival was not lost on Kevin. With one eye on his fellow rowdies, Kevin watched as a winded Kathryn fell to the ground.

Just as Kathryn arrived, the Silver Streak reached the knoll. As his giant silver train flashed through town, Rex Cross, the engineer, stuck his head out of the window and waved to the children, and of course, he did not forget to blow his loud airhorn. He rewarded the children with not one but two extra-long blasts of his horn.

The children cheered, even as the locomotive passed them, "Hey, Mr. Cross!" They continued to wave their gratitude to the engineer and still cried, "Blow your horn again! Blow your horn again!"

The rolling, tumbling, giggling children continued their frolicking until the red caboose's approach, signaling the end of the train.

"Hey, Mr. Blythe! Hey, Mr. Blythe! Throw me your cap, Mr. Blythe," begged Kevin.

"*Hey, Mr. Blythe!*" called Joy, then caught herself and blushed at her exhibition.

In the caboose, the conductor, Harmon Blythe, leaned out of the window when he saw the rollicking children and waved his blue-and-white-striped railroad cap to their delight. It only took a few quick seconds for the mighty passenger train to disappear down the tracks and out of sight. Still, the children waved until the red taillight was no more than a speck in the distance. After the speeding train passed out of sight, Harmon Blythe returned to his conductor's duties, verifying passenger lists, recording tickets, and checking arrival times for the next stop. Thus, the last joyous wave marked the end of another exciting day for the children of Graceton.

While Curiosity and Joy reveled in the excitement of watching the frolicking children and the speeding train, Hematite and Wisdom exhibited more self-control yet still enjoyed the new thrill.

As the children continued to engage in rolling and play-fighting on the grassy knoll, Kathryn bumped into Kevin and rolled over him.

"Woo hoo," Kevin exclaimed as he held Kathryn on top of him in playful wrestling. Kevin had a funny feeling quivering in his body that gave him a start.

Although more mature now, Passion enjoyed the emotion this game generated between Kevin and Kathryn, for Passion had seen this play before.

Kathryn Bates, thoughtful and reflective, was a year and two months younger than Kevin. She was tall, although not as tall as him. She was graceful with long slender legs that moved with natural, graceful motion. Straight, black hair, glowing in the sun, framed her tan complexion. Despite the gleaming of her hair, throwing flashes of rainbow colors back at the sun, they could not compete with her sapphire blue eyes and long, thick, black lashes.

"*Isn't she beautiful?*" Serenity asked Hope. "*She does favor her great-great-grandmother E-no-la in more ways than just her Seminole beauty. Kathryn has that Seminole poise.*"

Kathryn had the natural beauty of her Native American heritage. Still, she paid no attention to all that glittering, all that flashing of rainbow color. She hated her straight hair. Nevertheless, Kevin noticed the long tresses, and he thought her black hair was the prettiest, most tempting hair he had ever seen.

However, at night when Kathryn stood in front of her vanity mirror, she often made faces and hissed, trying to put her hair up in pin curls. She curled the straight hair around her finger, just to have it fall without restraint. "Oh, I hate this hair," Kathryn fumed. She did so want wavy hair with bangs teasing her long lashes. "I will never have a wavy ponytail like Helen's." Instead, she had daily fights with hair that resisted curls.

"Kathryn, dear, don't worry so about your beautiful hair," Serenity encouraged the young girl. "*Your great-great-grandmother, E-no-la, had beautiful Seminole hair. She was a beautiful woman, inside and out. You should be proud that you are just like her."*

Kathryn and Kevin had been sweethearts starting in Kindergarten and had an on-again-off-again relationship for the past six years. Their love affair began in earnest at lunch one day when Kevin, then a third-grader, secretly passed a note to Kathryn, the second-grade beauty that had caught his eye and his heart. With no embarrassment or apology, he wrote:

I love you. Do you love me?
Yes *No*

Kathryn read and re-read the note for what seemed a long time. Then, with her pink tongue directing her slender fingers and a stubby pencil, she made a mark and folded the paper along the original creases. However, she did not return the note to Kevin.

"What did she write?" Kevin asked his best friend, Al Kelly. "What did she write? What do you think she wrote?"

"I don't know," replied Al. "You will have to wait."

Kevin was in agony. "I got to find out before recess."

At long last, Kathryn passed the note, asking Linda to hand it back to Kevin. It seemed like all the kids in the third grade had handled it. The girls giggled, and the boys snickered. "Kevin's got a girlfriend; Kevin's got a girlfriend." When the third graders were all seated, waiting for their history lesson, Linda passed the note to Kevin and covered her giggles with her hand.

Kevin was sure everyone around him could hear and see his heart beating. His love-sick heart pounded with joy when he saw what Kathryn had written:

I love you. Do you love me?

Yes *No*

"She circled 'yes.' She crossed out 'no' and circled 'yes!' She loves me!"

Passion and Joy leaped and danced together with Kevin, celebrating the revelation.

Miss Williams, the third-grade teacher, cleared her throat and choked back her laughter. "Please turn to page 142 in your history book."

From that day on, Kevin teased Kathryn, telling her, "We're going to get married and live happily ever after in Graceton for the rest of our lives."

As much as Kathryn wanted to marry Kevin, she was not so sure of the destiny Kevin had proclaimed for her. She replied in a voice as self-assured as a second grader could, "Oh, no, Kevin. We're going to get married and move to a big city, and I'm going to own a fancy-dress shop." Although there was determination in her heart, she was happy just to be running, trying to keep up with Kevin with her belligerent straight hair flying, yet she wanted more.

Together, Kevin and Kathryn spent many such happy hours growing up in Graceton. As they grew, high school football games, ten-cent western movies at the town's small twenty-five seat theater, town picnics at the river park, and Sunday worship together filled the days of their childhood. These carefree days quickly fade into the responsibilities of young adulthood. Their childhood of running after trains gave way to taking long, private walks in the park and dreaming about their plans after high school graduation. Growing up in a small town held such peace and hope for them, and they cherished each blissful moment together.

At long last, black gowns and graduation caps with bright green tassels brought a new chapter in Kevin and Kathryn's lives, and with it, new challenges and emotions.

Beginning with his third-grade proclamation of love and marriage to Kathryn, Kevin dreamed of building houses, especially Kathryn’s house. So, it was no surprise that he chose architecture and building construction as his major in college, and he was joyous when he received a letter of acceptance from State College for the summer term.

Kathryn, however, was not so happy. She still had her senior year of high school, and she hated the thought of Kevin being so far away.

On the day he was to leave for college, Kevin’s parents, who were to drive him, waited for him to say goodbye to Kathryn. Feeling the same sense of loss, Kevin held Kathryn as she cried.

During his first days at State College, Kevin spent most of the time settling into his dorm, buying books, finding his classrooms, and meeting new friends. Then he had to find a job. Still, all he could think of was Kathryn.

Classes at State were not difficult. However, being away from home, his parents, and Kathryn, the girl he loved, made life seem much harder, and the days, oh, so long. His parents reminded him, “If it’s worth having, it’s worth waiting for.” So, he waited. And he waited.

Kevin wrote to Kathryn late at night after a full day of school and work:

My Dearest Kathryn,

The days away from you are almost to painful to bear. I am glad I am busy with classes and work, so time goes by quick.

I'm taking English this turm and hate it. It seems we have to right a essay every week. I don't git it. How will I ever need English in building construction? I am also taking a history class, and it ain't any better.

I made a "A" on my last algebra exam and that's great. I know I can apply algebra equations to building construction.

Oh, yes. I have a part-time job at the bookstore unpacking and shelving textbooks. It pays only fifty cent an hour but I figured if I can keep this job til I graduate, I can save $300 for us.

I love you Kathryn and can hardly wait until we see each other at Thanksgiving and Christmas,

All my love,

Kevin

In turn, Kathryn wrote to Kevin every day, telling him about her job at the dime store and the typical small-town news buzzing about Graceton:

My Darling Kevin,

Summer is horrible without you. All the other kids are going to the river or walking in the park while I am alone, missing you.

I have a summer job working at the dime store.

Remember the dime store? It's okay, I guess. The marble floors make the building comfortable, but the dark counters and wall paneling make it feel like a dungeon. Some say the big ceiling fans will keep us cool, but it seems they only push around the hot air.

My supervisor in the cosmetics and notions department is Mrs. Douglas. She's a cool teacher, and I am learning a lot about the makeup and dressmaking industries. Do you know what "notions" are, Kevin? I didn't either until Mrs. Douglas told me they are things like thread, zippers, buttons, and shoulder pads. I never knew there were so many things needed for sewing. There are beautiful buttons, different lengths of zippers, all colors of thread and pins, and other notions.

Guess what the biggest seller is? Curlers!

Since all the women and teenage girls in Graceton put their hair up in curlers every Saturday night, I sell a lot of curlers. The next best seller is hankies. No lady leaves home without a hanky in her purse. That's what I want for Christmas. I want a box of hankies embroidered in pink silk thread.

Oh, yes, remember, Robert, that six-foot boy in our class? He's the soda jerk. Well, when he goes on break, I get to fill in for him at the soda fountain. Mr. Johnson just put in a new counter, and of course, it's that dense mahogany and really big. It's so big I have to stand on a box to reach the countertop.

The counter has tall, glass columns all the way to the ceiling, and they look like white marble, but when Mr. Johnson turns on the lights inside the columns, they make a romantic yellow glow. All the kids sharing a soda at the little tables love it.

Oh, and Mr. Johnson added two more round tables, so now there are five. Of course, they are not JUST soda tables. They resemble shadowboxes with glass tops, and they are filled with jewelry. So, the girls ogle the jewelry, and the boys ogle the girls.

Mr. Johnson also added a new flavor of ice cream. Well, it's not really ice cream. It's lime sherbet, and it's really cool. But the kids' favorite is still the banana split.

The jukebox has all the latest hits, like "You Send Me," and "Earth Angel." The kids love to dance to "The Stroll," and I wish you were dancing with me. I miss you so, Kevin. I can hardly wait until Thanksgiving.

I love you,
Kathryn

In addition to the soda fountain, the dime store had a small, simple inventory that ranged from hardware to stationery to penny candy. At the front of the store, just inside the two heavy mahogany doors with brass kickplates and oversized brass doorknobs, stood a huge, inviting candy counter. The counter, made of mahogany, had beveled glass on three sides and the top. The beveled, diagonal cuts on the edges seemed to make the glass radiate the colors of the rainbow, sure to catch any child's eye.

From her vantage point of the nearby cosmetic counter, Kathryn enjoyed hearing the "oohs" and "awhs" from wide-eyed children when they walked through the store's massive double doors. Young children who had never seen so many kinds of candy, and each costing only a penny, tried to drag their mothers to a stop at the candy counter. Pushing and shoving was a daily occurrence as an assortment of children jostled for position, eyeing their favorite sweet treats. While a kind and patient clerk knew each child and their favorite, it was still a challenge keeping up with so many requests.

"I would like five Mary Janes, please," one timid girl said. "I gots a nickel."

The clerk took the nickel in exchange for a brown paper bag containing five peanut-buttery taffy pieces known as Mary Janes.

"I want Kits!" Yelled one little tike standing on tippy-toe and tapping his finger on the glass. "I want Kits!"

"What flavor do you want?," asked the clerk. "Vanilla, chocolate, strawberry, or banana?"

"The *lallo* one!" replied the four-year-old.

"Banana, it is!" said the clerk. "How many do you want?"

Little fingers fumbled with two pennies. "I gots two pennies," said the child dancing from toe to toe.

"Then you can have two packets," the clerk said, bagging two small packets of banana taffy candies wrapped in yellow paper. It was a bargain. Each packet contained three squares of candy. Little eyes gleamed as dirty hands reached for the brown paper bag.

"I want a B-B Bat!" said a little snaggle-tooth boy, pushing and shoving up to the mammoth candy counter. One can only wonder if the boy lost his front teeth pulling on the hard taffy candy on a stick.

"Fireballs, please," yelled a little red-haired boy with an already red-stained tongue.

"I want three root beer barrels!" said his friend old enough to hold on to the top edge of the counter with his dirty little fingers.

The rush on the candy counter ebbed and flowed all morning until exhausted mothers ushered their sugar-laden children home for a nap.

Kathryn filled her letters with all these activities, trying to make Kevin feel like he was home.

When he wrote to Kathryn, he told her about new things he was learning:

I learned something interesting in my finance class, and it could prove valuable to us when we are married. In the chapter on financial insurance, Professor McKeen taught that young men starting on their own needed to consider investing in insurance for both their businesses and their families. He said it is okay to invest small. He showed us how the investment could grow, but he stressed it is prudent to invest.

Kathryn, I am considering investing $2 a month for $100,000 worth of life insurance. Once I graduate and have a job, I know money could be a little tight, but I think it is important to invest for us.

I love you, Kathryn, and I want to provide well for you. I hope you will agree. We can discuss it at Thanksgiving. I can hardly wait to hold you in my arms.

Love,

Kevin

"You are very wise, Kevin," God said. *"Being a good steward of all you have is a great gift. I am proud of you, My boy."*

Sharing their lives long-distance through letters was a poor excuse for romantic dates, but it did keep them close to each other's hearts. Still, time dragged on. My, how time dragged on. At long last, graduation came, and Kevin was pleased to earn his four-year degree in architecture. However, he was reluctant to spend one more day and one more dollar away from Kathryn. So, Kevin chose not to attend graduation ceremonies to receive his diploma. All he wanted was to get home, marry Kathryn, build her a house, and spend many, many happy years as husband and wife and make babies.

When Kevin got back home to Graceton, his mom and dad welcomed him back to his old bedroom. His parents considered that still his home. He could look for a job and would not have to spend from his savings.

It took him two long weeks to find a job. Finally, he considered himself lucky when Mr. Cox, the owner of a building construction company in the neighboring town, hired him as an apprentice. The meager job paid minimum wage, one dollar forty cents per hour, which meant that Kevin brought home only two hundred dollars a month after taxes. While the job was not exactly what he wanted, at least he could add the experience to his résumé, and it would provide an income to support his bride. He knew the three hundred dollars in savings would not stretch far enough to build Kathryn a house.

More than anything, Kevin wanted to build a house for Kathryn and give her exactly what she wanted. Instead, each evening after work, he and Kathryn searched the newspaper ads for a home for sale and went looking at houses that would fit their budget. Kathryn found it to be very frustrating. It seemed that everything she liked, Kevin said they could not afford, and everything Kevin said they could afford, Kathryn did not like.

After many long hours of searching, they found a perfect little house that Kathryn loved, and Kevin said was within their budget. It was modest though charming and comfortable and had everything newly-weds would need. The house, painted white with yellow faux shutters, was in town, not far from the grassy knoll where they had once played as children. An old camphor berry tree grew just outside the front door, and a white picket fence separated the little house and other trees from the front sidewalk. Kathryn thought this little white house with yellow shutters and a white picket fence was the perfect little love nest.

In keeping with Kathryn's simple charm, she chose fine linen paper for her wedding invitations. The flowing script added to the elegance. The invitation read:

Mr. and Mrs. Leo Bates III, Request the honor of your presence at the marriage of their daughter, Kathryn Elaine Bates to Kevin John Wilkins, on Friday, June 15, 1962, at 7:00 p.m. at Graceton First Baptist Church.

"*Oh. I can hardly wait,*" gushed Passion. "*I am going to start collecting flower petals now to throw at the young couple when the preacher introduces them as Mr. and Mrs. Kevin Wilkins.*"

So, just as Kevin planned, they were married the third Friday in June 1962.

It was a beautiful, although modest wedding—ladies of the church decorated with candles and a few flowers of white snapdragons and mums. Kathryn's mother made the wedding dress, and Kathryn thought it was the most beautiful dress she had ever seen. The wedding announcement in the local newspaper read:

Her wedding gown was a tea-length gown of Chantilly lace atop sheer organza. The bodice had a "Sweetheart-neckline," which dipped gracefully in front and low in the back. Her fingertip veil was white tulle with tiny silk roses nestled in her black hair.

"I do so love organza," crooned Grace. "With the Chantilly lace, her gown will be so simple and elegant."

"The white tulle and silk roses will be beautiful in her hair," replied Hematite.

Kevin loved how Kathryn pinned up her straight black hair so that the strands played peek-a-boo through the tulle before cascading to her shoulders. He loved that black hair as much as she hated it, and he craved her delicate neck hidden in the tempting strands.

Their honeymoon, also modest by necessity, was a glorious, romantic weekend at the beach with no one intruding on their privacy.

"Can we go on the honeymoon?" begged Curiosity.

"Of course not," replied Serenity. *"You know we cannot intrude."*

"I wouldn't intrude," protested Curiosity. *"I just want to dig my toes in the sandy beach again, like I did when John and Babette crossed into Florida."*

At the end of a beautiful, albeit too brief, honeymoon, Kevin and Kathryn bid farewell to the rolling ocean and blue skies to return to work on Monday morning. Although it was difficult to return to work, still Kevin and Kathryn had no regrets. They had each other and memories of a beautiful wedding surrounded by all their friends and family.

In the following months, they had fun shopping together for furniture for their new home. Kathryn knew they had to be thrifty, and she tried hard to be a wise shopper and respect Kevin's budget.

Together, they looked through the Western Auto catalog for the big items.

"Look at this one, honey," Kevin said, pointing to the ad for a washing machine. "It's one hundred eighty-four dollars."

"Oh, I did want a washer and dryer combo." She pointed to the picture.

"But the combo is twice as much. I don't think we can afford three hundred fifteen dollars," Kevin told a disappointed Kathryn. "I'll build you a clothesline in the back yard."

After considering a clothesline, Kathryn agreed that the backyard's full sun would be a perfect place to dry clothes, and later, just maybe, to dry diapers.

"We still have to buy a refrigerator, and that's going to be another three hundred dollars," Kevin said, turning to the page in the catalog showing refrigerators.

"What about a telephone?" Kathryn desperately wanted a telephone to keep in touch with her family, even though they lived only two blocks away.

"I'm sorry, sweetheart. A one-dollar twenty-five cents a month phone bill just is not in our budget."

"But, Kevin, when you start your own construction business, you will need a phone," argued Kathryn.

"First, we need to buy insurance," replied a sensible Kevin. By this time, the monthly insurance premiums increased from two dollars to two dollars fifteen cents a month, so he had to make careful plans.

There were smaller items they disagreed on, too. Kathryn wanted bright, sunny yellow bath towels. She thought how beautiful and cheery yellow towels would look in the clean, white bathroom with black and white octagonal tile floors. Kathryn imagined opening the little window over the bathtub and letting in warm golden sunlight. She could just see the towels sparkling in the sunshine. On the other hand, Kevin preferred practical white towels, yet, with deep love, he gave in to Kathryn's wish for yellow towels.

When they went shopping at Woolworth's, they picked out two bath towels and two washcloths. Kathryn blinked in surprise when she heard the clerk say, "That will be three dollars fifty-nine cents, please."

"Oh, no!" Kathryn heard herself shriek. "I think we want white towels instead." She turned to Kevin. "I'm sorry, Kevin. I did not know yellow towels would be so expensive. The white ones are just fine, and they will be easier to keep white."

With their shopping bag filled with practical, white towels and a receipt for two dollars and fifty cents, Kathryn felt a little embarrassed for arguing in favor of yellow bath towels instead of the cheaper white. However, she did give a backward glance at the stacks of fluffy, yellow bath linen as they left the store.

Kathryn vowed to be a practical wife and follow the budget Kevin had made for them. She wanted Kevin to be proud of her. And he was. They were so happy together in their new home. Kevin was working for a builder in the next town and saving money. Life was wonderful. He loved to come home to the delicious smell of dinner and fresh laundry and a beautiful young wife. What could make him happier?

Two days after their second wedding anniversary, Kevin came home to find Kathryn standing in the middle of the living room with a silly grin on her face. "Hi, Sweetheart," Kevin said as he kissed Kathryn. "What's behind your back?"

"These," said Kathryn, revealing a little bonnet, booties, and a blanket. "Do you like them?"

"Baby booties," sighed Passion.

Hope clasped her hands together and held them at her heart. "*Kevin and Kathryn will have a beautiful baby,*" she said.

For a few moments, Kevin could not speak. Kevin was thrilled. Then he was scared, then petrified. Finally, he was thrilled. Suddenly, it was Kevin who had a silly grin on his face. "We're having a baby. We have to make plans," Kevin told her. "What color do you want the nursery?" Kevin asked as he turned around and around in the small living room. "A baby bed? Where will we put the baby bed?" Kevin hurried to the extra room and mentally measured space. "A stroller. We must have a stroller," Kevin babbled.

Kathryn kissed Kevin and said, "There's plenty of time, my darling."

In the weeks that passed, they talked about names for the baby with stars in their eyes. Kevin told Kathryn, "I don't care if it is a boy or a girl, as long as it is healthy and looks like you, Kathryn." Still, in his heart, Kevin wanted a baby girl.

"But I want <u>him</u> to look like you, Kevin," Kathryn added. "I want him to have lots of girlfriends, dress up and go to dances, play football and go to college."

Kevin countered, "I want <u>her</u> to have long black hair, like yours, tied in pink ribbons, dress in pink organza for Easter, and wear black patent shoes with white nylon socks trimmed with lace."

"*Why not one of each?*" Passion squealed.

"*Shh,*" admonished Hematite.

What a joy it was planning for a baby, and Kevin wanted the best. However, despite all of his financial knowledge, he was not ready for just how expensive baby furniture could be, so they looked in the newspaper for used cribs.

There were so many other things a baby needed: blankets, baby clothes, baby bottles, large-milk-size and small-juice-size, nipples, and a sterilizer, and lots and lots of cloth diapers. Of course, they would need a high chair and changing table. Kathryn wanted a rocker. To Kevin's surprise, the list went on and on.

At church, the announcement of a new baby on the way caused a frenzy of activity. The older ladies, who lovingly remembered when Kevin and Kathryn were babies themselves, gave Kathryn a baby shower. After the party, Kathryn, glassy-eyed with joy, surprised Kevin with a "show and tell" of all the gifts she received at the shower.

In the next few weeks, they found a baby crib for sale in the newspaper for only twelve dollars. It was natural wood, not at all the best color for a little girl, and it was a bit pricey, but Kevin wanted it for his daughter. When they got it home, Kevin went to work painting the natural pine wooden crib, making it clean and shiny white.

Curiosity wanted so much to help paint. However, the fairy ended up getting paint all over her wings and gown. *"What a mess,"* scolded Hematite. *"This will never do."*

Kathryn was so excited. She could not keep from dancing and twirling like a little girl. Kevin laughed so hard he nearly fell into the can of paint.

To say they were happy would not begin to describe their joy. They cuddled up together on the soft sofa, planning for the nursery, preparing Kathryn's overnight bag for the hospital, and still thinking of names.

"Kevin, darling, I would like to call our son Seth," Kathryn proposed. There was no need for further discussion. "Darling, will you paint the nursery blue? Blue, like a little bird's eggs, will be perfect for a little boy."

Of course, Kevin complied. Yet wherever he could, he added a little touch of pink like angels' wings. Pink angel wings would be perfect for a baby girl.

Afterward, he moved the baby bed into the freshly painted room. In his eyes, it was perfect. The once wooden spindle baby bed had a new coat of white paint and a sleepy Teddy Bear sticker displayed on the outside panel. It was perfect for his baby girl. Kathryn had folded the new layette from the baby shower and stored it in the used chest of drawers, now shiny and looking fresh with a coat of white paint and Teddy bear stickers.

When the big day came, and Kathryn went into labor, Kevin did the customary "new father" pacing. Up and down. Up and down—looking at the clock—more pacing. Both sets of grandparents, Kevin's parents, Edward and Joann Wilkins, were there. Kathryn's parents, Leo III and Mildred Bates were there. Then, after what seemed like an eternity, a nurse came out of the maternity ward to announce that Kevin had a daughter.

"*A daughter!*" sighed Passion.

"A daughter?" Kevin asked in disbelief and nearly danced around the waiting room. "I have a daughter?" He turned first to his dad and grabbed him in a bear hug. "I have a daughter!" Then he turned to Kathryn's mother and then her dad. "I have a daughter!" He beamed. Then he stopped. "Kathryn? Kathryn will be so disappointed. We have not chosen a girl's name. And the nursery is blue." He glanced at the nurse. "How is my wife, Kathryn?" he remembered to ask.

"She is just fine," the kind nurse answered. "She is a little weary right now and needs a nap. I'll take you to her, and you can visit for five minutes."

As soon as Kevin saw Kathryn, he went limp. She was so beautiful. No, Kathryn was radiant. Although she looked a little pale and tired, she was beautiful, just the same. "Kathryn," Kevin whispered.

Kathryn opened her weary eyes and smiled.

"We have a baby daughter, and she's beautiful, just like her mother," Kevin announced.

"A girl?" whispered a weary Kathryn. "Oh, I did so want a boy just like his daddy."

Kevin kissed Kathryn's fevered brow, then Kathryn sighed and closed her eyes. "You rest, sweetheart," Kevin whispered. "I'll be in the waiting room."

Returning to the waiting room to share in the celebration, Kevin was all smiles while his dad passed out cigars. Kathryn's dad laughed and patted his friends on the back.

However, all at once, when the doctor came through the swinging double doors, the celebrating stopped. The doctor took Kevin aside and spoke to the new father in a low voice, and Kevin went white. "Kevin, I am deeply sorry. Kathryn had complications and slipped into a coma. There was nothing we could do for her."

Hope and Serenity both shuddered at the news. Passion fell to the floor in tears. "*Kevin? What can we do for Kevin?*" she asked in shock.

"*There's nothing we can do,*" replied Hematite. "*You remember what God said. How could you forget through all these years? Only He controls life and death.*"

Sadly, with Kevin by her bedside, Kathryn died that night, leaving Kevin to wonder, “How could this be? What happened? We were so happy together. Our lives were just beginning. Now, Kathryn is gone!” Kathryn. Gone? How? How can this be? Kevin was beside himself with grief.

No one could explain it to him; although they all tried, they could not comfort or console him. It was shocking to everyone when Kathryn, once healthy, beautiful, and excited to be alive, succumbed to an obscure, deadly disease minutes after giving birth to her baby. Kathryn did not even have a chance to name her daughter, and Kevin was too distraught to think of anything except losing Kathryn.

“Kevin,” asked Kathryn’s mother, “would you like to call your daughter Katie, short for Kathryn?”

Through his pain-induced numbness, Kevin heard only, “blah, blah, blah, daughter, blah, blah, blah,” and mumbled in agreement.

The painful void created in Kevin’s heart engulfed him to the point of despair. He was so distraught about losing the love of his life, his soulmate, and his best friend that he felt he no longer wanted to go on living. Nevertheless, he pushed himself to keep living, for he had a baby daughter to consider. Still, in his despair, he felt he could not care for a baby alone. So he asked Kathryn’s mother and father if he and his daughter could live with them.

“Of course, you may, Kevin,” she said.

“What do you want the baby to call you?” Kevin whispered through trembling lips.

“I would like Katie to call me Nana, and please call Leo Papa,” she replied.

"Thank you, Nana. Thank you, Papa," said Kevin. "I will bring you Katie's things."

Somehow, Kevin found the strength to return to the little white house with yellow faux shutters that he and Kathryn loved. With what felt like a knife sticking in his heart and stomach, Kevin went into the nursery. The freshly painted blue and pink room no longer excited him. He packed up tiny baby clothes and diapers and loaded them into a borrowed trailer. Then he went back inside to get the shiny white baby bed with the sleepy teddy bear sticker on the outside panel and the matching chest of drawers. When he returned for a last look, his heart dropped. His home with Kathryn was empty, and his heart was numb.

Together, Kevin, Nana, and Papa discussed the baby's welfare and planned for her future. "Papa," Kevin began, "I think I need to return to college to earn a master's degree in architecture. Of course, I will look for a job and send money back to you and Nana."

Toward that end, Kevin left his precious baby in Nana and Papa's care, asking them not to tell their friends. Understanding how his heart ached and knowing that their friends would be most supportive of his brave decision, Papa and Nana respected Kevin's wishes. Nevertheless, he felt like a failure, a quitter. He had to believe he made the right decision, and that thought carried Kevin through another stage of his mourning and depression. Step by precious step, his heart began to heal.

Leaving Papa home to tend the baby, Nana dropped Kevin off at the railroad station with his few belongings and enough cash to find a room to rent. Like a zombie, Kevin boarded the Amtrak passenger train with a one-way ticket to Tallahassee.

Over the next several years, the fairies followed Kevin. Remembering God's instructions, they were obedient and did not try to change the course God set for them.

When Kevin got off the train in Tallahassee, he stood in the middle of the platform, as if helpless. When he finally shook the cobwebs from his mind, Kevin walked to the campus and found the same rooming house he lived in as an undergraduate. It was just as Kevin had left it. It was cheap, clean, and comfortable. There he dropped off his luggage and set out to look for food and transportation.

Kevin walked up to the Piggly Wiggly grocery store near the college to check the bulletin board. One ad stood out from the others: *For Sale. Cheap. Second-hand bikes. Refurbished. Call Larry 332-4456.*

"May I use your telephone, sir?" Kevin asked the man at customer service. "It's a local call."

"Why, sure," replied the kind man. "Do you have a dime?"

Kevin dug into his jeans and pulled out two nickels. "Yes, sir, I do," replied Kevin.

"There's the phone over there on the wall."

Kevin dialed the number in the ad. "Lord, help me find a bike that's not too expensive," Kevin prayed. "Hello? Yes, my name is Kevin Wilkins. I'm calling about your bikes. That sounds fine. Where are you located? I'm walking, so I will be there in about fifteen minutes."

"Did you find one?" asked the man behind the customer service desk.

"I think so. It's nothing fancy, but it will get me from here to there," said Kevin.

"By the way," said the grocer, "I couldn't help overhearing your conversation. Are you a new student in town?"

"Not exactly," replied Kevin. "I earned my undergraduate degree here several years ago. This is my first year of graduate school."

"My name's Ken Brothers, and I'm the manager here. We have a job opening for a stocker that pays minimum wage. Would you be interested? You realize as a student, you can only work ten hours a week? It's the college rule, and we employers know that student's first job is to study and attend classes."

"Yes, sir! That would be wonderful," Kevin replied, trying to contain his excitement.

"Well," continued Mr. Brothers, "go get your bicycle and then come back, and we can discuss the job."

Kevin purchased a second-hand bicycle for ten dollars and had money left for food. When he returned to the grocery, he and Mr. Brothers discussed the job.

"I can pay a dollar sixty an hour. The job requires heavy lifting, but seeing your build, I think you can manage it," said Mr. Brothers.

"Yes, sir, I can. When do you want me to start?"

"How about tonight, say, 9 p.m.? That's when the truck comes in, and you can work stocking shelves and distributing goods," said Mr. Brothers. "There will be plenty to do."

"That will be fine," replied Kevin. "However, I can work only Monday, Wednesday, and Friday nights. I have graduate seminars in the mornings."

"We can certainly work around that," assured Mr. Brothers.

Kevin filled out the necessary paperwork and shook Mr. Brother's hand.

"Kevin, I attend the First Baptist Church here in town. Will you be my guest at church this Sunday?" invited Mr. Brothers.

"I would be pleased to," replied Kevin. "I miss worship services with my folks back home. I know where the church is. I will meet you there at 10 a.m."

"Perfect," agreed Mr. Brothers.

Before leaving the grocery store, Kevin bought a supply of peanut butter and white bread.

"That will be seventy cents," Mr. Brothers said.

"I think there's some mistake," interrupted Kevin. "The bread is twenty-five cents, and the peanut butter is fifty-nine cents. That's eighty-four cents."

"Yes. But you forgot your employee discount," said Mr. Brothers with a smile. "Thank you for your honesty, Kevin. I knew you were a fine man."

The Lord blessed Kevin with a friend, food, transportation, a job, and a church.

"Thank You, Lord," Kevin breathed a prayer of thanksgiving.

God smiled and said, *"You are most welcome, My boy. It gives me pleasure to take care of you, just as I took care of your parents."*

That night, when Kevin got to the grocery store at 9:30 p.m., he found the delivery truck had already arrived. He had to sort inventory and have it ready for the managers before leaving work at 1:00 a.m.

Because Piggly Wiggly was one of the bigger grocery chains in the area, it was not unusual for him to sort through up to fifteen or twenty heavy crates filled with corn, green beans, tomatoes, green peas, black-eyed peas, and paper goods. Next, he unloaded rice, flour, sugar, and spices. If he had time, he would start on the laundry items. Tide was the big seller. However, a new product was catching the attention of customers. DUZ laundry powder was the big, new product whose marketing incentive was that each box contained either a washcloth, a hand towel, a dish towel, or a bath towel, depending on the size of the product that customers purchased.

When Kevin left the grocery store, he biked home to try to get to sleep. The next morning, Tuesday, his first-class was at 10:00 a.m. This was the once-dreaded English class, now an elective. English still plagued Kevin even after four years as an undergraduate. However, now that he was a little older and wiser, he appreciated English's value and how he might use it as an architect or building contractor. He wasn't taking this course because he had to, like in his undergraduate years. Instead, now, he took it because he wanted to learn.

His grocery store job did not give him the luxury of sleeping in, so halfway through the English class, he had to talk himself into an attitude adjustment to get through the hour.

"Mr. Wilkins," the instructor called on Kevin. "What is your major?"

"Architecture, ma'am," answered a drowsy Kevin.

The English instructor held up a photograph of a fieldstone fence surrounding an expensive two-story house. "Mr. Wilkins, will you please, tell the class how you would describe this product to your subcontractor and communicate to him how to integrate this product into the existing house and yard?"

"Yes, ma'am," replied Kevin. In reply, he gave a clear, oral description of the products he might use for building a fence.

"Very good, Mr. Wilkins," The instructor commented and continued. "Mr. Wilkins, do you believe you can use your English skills to write a winning proposal for a client?"

"Yes, ma'am," replied Kevin with confidence. He caught the vision of how English would be essential when writing a proposal with preliminary job specs. Kevin wanted his clients to visualize a magnificent two-story red brick house with its grand front columns and stunning river rock fireplace. He could paint a word picture to convince the client that a breezy porch with a gray slate flooring and a red door with brass hardware would make a great first impression for visitors and guests. Kevin even surprised himself when he could paint a delightful word picture of a white wicker porch swing bedecked with blue floral cushions, matching side chairs, all graced by full pots of lush green Boston fern hanging just above the porch railing on either side. He frequently referred to the endless essays he had written in college for proper tense and grammar.

His next class, at 11:00 a.m., was physical sciences, also an elective course. He smiled as he remembered his conversation with Dr. Sirmans, his program director. "Why are you taking physical sciences, Kevin? That seems a great waste of time and money for a graduate student."

Kevin explained to his director, "As an undergraduate, I took the course only because a science was required. Now, I want to take the course for the knowledge. Besides, it is an advanced course and will likely help me with my master's project and a job later. After all," Kevin continued, "I will need to know the properties of different natural resources."

He enjoyed the natural sciences most and took great care to learn the different types of rock and stone, their weights, and their densities. He was sure to need to know things like the strength and assets of slate versus granite, for example, in his building career, and now with a better grasp of English, he was confident he could write a convincing proposal.

After physical sciences, he grabbed a quick modest lunch of peanut butter crackers.

The day before, the Lord had blessed Kevin with a second job at a downtown bakery, and Kevin did not want to be late.

Mr. Simms, the baker, started his busy day of measuring, mixing, and baking at 2 a.m., so that by 9 a.m., all shelves would be full of tempting baked goods when he opened his store for business. From experience, Mr. Simms knew he must open the bakery on time, since early morning customers, eager to be first in line, would have noses pressed against the glass door. By 3 p.m., he had sold all the baked goods, including two dozen loaves of bread, peach pies, lemon meringue pies, pecan pies, six different kinds of cookies, endless donuts, vanilla pound cakes, and special-order cakes.

When Kevin arrived in the afternoon and took stock of the work to do, he winced, thinking that Mr. Simms used every pot, pan, and baking sheet he owned each time he baked or cooked filling and frosting. There was never a lack of pots and pans to wash, dry, and hang back on the racks, and so much activity made the time go quickly. Then there were piles of flour and sugar to sweep up. The hardest of all was dissolving and wiping away the greasy shortening.

After all this washing, drying, and sweeping, Kevin carried in fifty-pound bags of flour, sugar, and shortening for the next day's baking. Then, he was off on his bike to make his last class for the day. His building construction class was

Tuesday and Thursday, beginning at 7 p.m. and lasted two hours.

His long day was beginning to catch up with him, so he was glad this class was construction theory. Each building project piqued his attention and held him spellbound. He studied the textbook and lecture notes and often consulted with his professor. “Dr. Fry, what would make this design better, more durable, more resilient, or more cost-effective? What products would be best for this project? Can we make this design safer?” Even before the phrase “think outside the box” was popular, Kevin was doing just that. He wanted to be innovative and, at the same time, build safe houses and office buildings.

When his construction theory class was over, he peddled his bike, much slower now, back to his room at the boarding house. There was only time for a quick shower before falling into bed for a nap before starting on homework and study. If he were lucky, he would sleep well until time to start all over again at 8 a.m.

This rigorous schedule of work and classes dragged out Kevin’s two-year degree to four years. During the summer months and after graduation, he worked full-time at the grocery store to send money home to Nana and pay off his college debt.

From Kevin’s short notes home, Nana could tell that he was a conscientious, thoughtful provider for his little family. He sent Nana money every month, and Nana knew that even though distance separated them so that he never saw his daughter, Kevin loved his child. Nana sympathized, knowing that Kevin could not be there as his child grew up. Still, his tireless work and study kept his mind keen on school and providing for Nana and his daughter. However, all his relentless activity did not lessen the pain of losing Kathryn, his beloved wife.

As Katie's guardians, Nana and Papa made every effort to raise their precious granddaughter just as Kathryn would have wanted. Sadly, though, Leo "Papa" Bates died before Kevin finished his degree. So, alone, Nana raised Katie just as they had raised Kathryn without her beloved husband beside her.

Chapter 2

Katie

> But Jesus said, "Suffer little children, and forbid them not, to come unto me: for of such is the kingdom of heaven."
>
> – Matthew 19:14

From the garden, God the Father and God the Son watched over a new little friend, Katie, and her grandmother, Nana.

"She's an active little thing, isn't she?" chuckled God. "*She's going to need someone special to guide her endless energy and curiosity,"* God the Father said to His Son.

"I would like to be that special person, Father," said God, The Son. *"I know exactly the plan I have in mind."*

"Very well," replied God, the Father. "*This might satisfy two needs at once. Give it a try."*

"We want to go, too!" begged Curiosity, Faith, and Joy.

"We think that would be a wonderful idea, My dears," said God the Son. "*Katie is still young enough to see you and talk to you. We think it will be good for both Katie and you."*

Mildred Bates, Nana, struggled with sorrow from losing her precious daughter, Kathryn, and then her husband, Leo. Nana found it challenging to mourn while, at the same time, showering love and happiness on her active granddaughter, Katie. In her sixties now, Nana found that raising an active, intelligent granddaughter was not for the faint of heart. Katie, unlike her demure mother, was independent and fearless. She would rather climb a tree than read a novel. She had no time to sit quietly and paint or sew or embroider. Instead, Katie spent her time under the front porch of Nana's house on Main Street, searching for doodlebugs and roly-polies. When Katie tired of these harmless insects, she quickly turned her attention to talking with worms. If, while forcing an uncooperative worm from his twig, the worm puked greenish brown juice on Katie's fingers, the little raggamuffin simply wiped the worm juice on her shorts. She equally enjoyed dirt and mud, and one must have mud to make mud pies.

Through trial and error, Nana learned that any challenge Katie created, the active little girl's love matched the frustration with precious rewards ten times over. Because Katie had her mother's beauty, arrows of bittersweetness pricked Nana's heart as she watched Katie grow.

Towering magnolia trees, with their thick bark in shades of brown and gray, and pungent camphor trees with their obnoxious black berries, lined Graceton's main street where Mildred Bates lived. The Magnolia's flowers gleaming alabaster white, screamed, "See me! Touch me! Feel me!" However, the slightest touch from an admirer's hand destroyed the delicate flowers turning them brown.

Fairies danced around the magnolia tree, watching an active little girl with a giant imagination play. Unfortunately, the fairies were not ready for the non-stop activity.

"I love magnolia trees and their pretty white flowers," crooned Peace. "*Their flowers smell so fresh, and the carpels and stamens in the center make a wonderful place to curl up and take a nap."*

"It looks as if there will be no time for a nap," giggled Passion. "*Keeping up with this one is going to take all our energy."*

The shade of the magnolia tree where Katie played was a happy place, full of flowers, birds, insects, and now fairies. It did not take Katie long to notice the fairies as they danced and fluttered around the tree. Curiosity watched intently when Katie pointed out a strange cluster of orange-and-black-striped insect eggs farmed by carpenter ants. Katie watched in amazement as the docile ants crawled over the stiff eggs attached to the tree's enormous roots. Using a stick, Katie poked the strange orange eggs to see what might ooze out.

"Hello, Mr. Ant," Katie said. "You have beautiful eggs. I want to see what's inside. Can I open your eggs? My, they have hard tops, and I can't poke one open. Oh, well. I didn't want to see inside anyway."

The magnolia tree trunk, covered with thick, brown bark, might not be of great interest to most people, but to Katie, the magnolia tree's bark looked like big chunks of chocolate. It was a kid's greatest fantasy. Jaws tightened, goosebumps popped, and shivers ran up and down her entire body as thick, sweet chocolate bark hit Katie's tongue. "Pewy!" It tasted nothing like chocolate. So, Katie turned her attention to her swing set.

"Let's go swing," encouraged Katie.

Reluctantly, the fairies left their game of chase around the shady magnolia tree and followed Katie as she ran toward the swing set.

Joy echoed Katie, "*Let's go swing!*"

"*Okay,*" agreed Passion. "*I want to go high and fly through the air.*"

"*You fly through the air all the time,*" scoffed Curiosity.

"*Yes, but on the swing, I won't have to use my wings,*" giggled Passion.

"*Do you know how to fly on a swing?*" inquired Joy.

Passion thought a moment then lied, "*Of course, I do. Do you remember the rope Charles hung from the tree for Cassie and Cody? That was fun.*"

"*Yes, but this looks different from a tree swing,*" said Grace with trepidation.

God the Father chuckled, watching the little girl and the fairies playing together. He turned to God the Son and said, "*It is good to see the fairies at play.*"

"*Yes, Father, it is,*" replied the Son. "*But they will soon need to return to the garden for a nap.*"

One of the two seats of Katie's swing was forever lopsided from the effects of being forced around and around in circles and then allowed to unwind in squeaking protest. A rusty, teeter-totter, unsteady from wear, yet still functional, completed the "venue of adventure" that was Katie's swing set.

Focusing on Katie's movements, the fairies watched as their playmate took her place on the best swing seat, pushed back, and started pumping her legs. First, she went slow, back and forth. Then she went higher and faster, swinging through the air enjoying the exhilaration of unrestraint.

"That looks easy," commented Joy.

Curiosity was the first to flutter down to investigate the swing set. With heightened anticipation, the fairy sat on Katie's shoulder, and with each hand, grabbed a handful of the little girl's hair.

Squeak, thump, squeak, thump. The squeaking sound was the sound of the chains scraping on the hardware. The thump, thumping noise was the back-left leg of the swing lifting off the ground and pounding back down again with a tantalizing thud. The continued thump, thumping of the leg gouged a hole in the dirt as Katie hurled forward into the warm summer sky.

Ignoring the fact that she didn't know how to swing, Passion flew up and sat on Katie's head. As Katie swung forward, Passion gasped, and her eyes popped. The surprised fairy grabbed two hands-full of Katie's hair and steadied herself with her wings. "*We-e-e!*" Passion sang. "*This is fun! Come on, Joy! Come on, Grace!*"

However, that fun didn't last long, for Katie quickly tired of swinging, and on her last forward motion, she let go of the swing's chains. Her forward momentum pushed her off the seat, hurling Katie through the air with long strands of black hair flying about her head. In a delicious surprise, the fairies grip on Katie's hair let go, and the little fairies tumbled through the air. Their silk organza gowns and gemstones sparkled in a blur of color.

With gay abandonment, Katie landed in the soft sand, scraping her knees. But no bother, she just jumped up, wiped the sand and blood from her knees and onto her mud and worm-juice encrusted Osh Gosh shorts.

Next, the magical swing set became a sturdy sea-going vessel with Katie as its fearless first mate.

"Ahoy! First Mate!" the old sea captain called. "Climb to the top of the mast. When you get to the crow's nest, search for land or enemy ships."

"Aye aye, Captain," answered First Mate Katie, and without missing a beat, Katie scrambled to the side of the swing set closest to the teeter-totter. After a bit of a stretch, Katie grasped the bracing bar with both grubby little hands and threw one leg across the bar, then the other leg. When she released her grasp on the horizontal bar, Katie squealed at the exhilarating sensation of being upside down swinging by her knees. The active little girl did not notice that her Strawberry Shortcake t-shirt no longer covered her bellybutton.

Curiosity followed Katie, and the fairy went all the way to the top of the swing frame and walked the bar like a balance beam. "*Look at me, Joy!*" giggled Curiosity. "*Come on up. It's fun.*"

At Curiosity's invitation, Joy, Passion, and Grace fluttered up the teeter-totter bar and joined their sister fairy. Together, the fairies walked across the top horizontal piece of the frame and pretended to jostle each other for position.

After hanging upside down until the blood rushed to her head, Katie pulled herself up and stood on the brace, pretending to climb high, high up to the ship's crow's nest. Once upon the bracing bar, Katie tiptoed as far as she could reach up to the opening of the large crossbar. The plastic cap of the crossbar had long since been missing. However, this offered opportunities for a little girl's vivid imagination and adventures.

"First Mate, Katie, when you see something, blow a signal to your shipmates," shouted the old sea captain.

Katie peered through the crossbar. Usually, she could see a bit of light at the other end. Today, however, something obstructed her view. “Captain, I spotted something,” shouted First Mate, Katie.

The fairies fluttered from their “balance beam” and hovered around Katie’s head, trying to get a look at what their little friend saw.

Katie took a deep breath, placed her mouth on the opening of the metal crossbar, and blew a mighty signal to her fellow shipmates below. Katie imagined the sound was like that of a deep bellowing foghorn, while it was more like a muffled whisper through a rusty metal tube.

Katie scampered down from her perch, followed by the fairies.

Curiosity and Joy had never experienced such energy before. It was tiring, yet they did not want to miss a moment of Katie’s adventures, so the fairies kept up the best they could.

Scanning the ground, Katie found a stick that would work well as a probe. Again, she scaled the pretend mast. First Mate Katie poked into the open crossbar using the probe to release the obstruction; her tongue stuck out and wiggled on her lips as if guiding the probe. With Katie's second jab, the obstruction dislodged and flew out, right into First Mate Katie’s face. Startled, Katie nearly lost her hold and wobbled on the brace where she was standing, sending a delicious electric sensation of fear through her body. Then the obstruction vanished into the tree. “Ha, Ha. Gotcha!” Katie shouted, startled, yet proud of her accomplishment.

“It’s a baby bat,” Curiosity squealed.

"Poor little bat," said Joy, empathizing with the small creature. "*Let's go find him and tell him Katie is fun to play with.*"

Katie jumped down from her position on the swing set and ran to the house, closely followed by the fairies, Curiosity and Joy.

"Nana! Nana!" Katie squealed as she ran to the house. "I have a baby bat in my swing set." Katie gasped for breath and held her chest in dramatic fashion, "Can you believe it? I have a baby bat!"

Fortunately, Nana no longer reacted in fear to Katie's squeals. "That must be a great adventure," Nana said. "The starbursts in your eyes are twinkling."

Because of those golden pulsating starbursts in her blue sapphire eyes, Nana called Katie, "My little sunbeam," and sang to Katie:

"Jesus wants me for a sunbeam
to shine for Him each day.
In every way, try to please Him
at home, at school, at play.
A sunbeam, A sunbeam,
Jesus wants me for a sunbeam.
I'll be a sunbeam for Him."

The fairies, returning from assuring the baby bat that Katie was a good playmate, heard Nana sing. "*What a sweet song,*" sighed Grace. "*I'd like to learn that song.*"

"To be sure," giggled Passion, "*Katie will sing it to us a time or two.*"

Long black hair cascaded in thick layers from the top of Katie's head and past her shoulders, complimented Katie's sapphire eyes. When the sun glinted off her black hair, streaks of auburn flashed, shining from between the black waves, and playing peek-a-boo with the sunrays. When Katie ran, her hair was ablaze with auburn highlights and billowed in happy unrestraint, and she pretended that her feet left the ground. She jumped over anything that got in her way, with the fairies following close behind. If it happened to rain in the afternoon, it was a joy to have a fresh mud puddle in her path. Yes, what joy! What fun, indeed? However, Nana did not think it fun to comb out globs of mud from the endless tangles.

Grace buzzed over Katie, brushing the dirty little girl with lavender organza, and sprinkling Katie with feminine light and energy from the amethyst and tanzanite gemstones hiding among the layers of silk.

"Hold still, Katie," Nana scolded. "The more you wiggle, the longer this will take to get you clean and sweet-smelling."

"I don't want to be clean and sweet-smelling," protested Katie.

"Don't you want to smell like tea roses like your Nana?" her grandmother asked.

"No!" Katie huffed, crossing her arms at her chest. "I don't want to smell like roses. I want to smell like mud!" Katie said, pouting.

Passion and Joy giggled, but still, they helped Grace shower the little nymph with energy from their yellow topaz and red rhodonite gemstones to change the little girl's cranky mood.

"Oh, you silly girl." Nana smiled as she continued working on the tangled hair. "What a mess," Nana fumed.

"Ouch! Ouch, Nana!" cried Katie.

"I'm trying to be gentle, Katie. There are so many tangles."

"Hurry," Katie begged through crocodile tears.

"Where is the ribbon? Do you have the ribbon, Katie?" asked Nana.

Interrupting her pretend crying, Katie looked all around. "I just had it a minute ago. I was running my fingernail over the bumps. I like to feel the bumps on the ribbon."

Passion cupped her hand to her tiny mouth and whispered to Katie, "*Look on your chair.*"

"Here it is," squealed Katie. "I was sitting on it."

"Okay, first a rubber band," Nana mumbled with the ribbon between her teeth. Nana removed the thick rubber band off her wrist and wrapped it around the black tresses. "Okay. Now the pretty, pink grosgrain ribbon. There. Don't you look pretty?" Nana said, approving of the sweet, clean granddaughter.

"My ears stick out, Nana. Can you make my ears stop sticking out?" cried Katie.

"You have beautiful ears, my Katie," Nana said, trying to comfort her granddaughter. "They are just what God wanted you to have." Nana sang a song to Katie about her little ears:

"O be careful little ears what you hear.
O be careful little ears what you hear.
There's a Father up above, And He's looking down in love.
So, be careful little ears what you hear."

"*Aw,*" whispered Joy, "*Nana knows so many cute songs.*"

"*We need to learn that one, too,*" added Grace.

"*Not to worry,*" giggled Passion again, expecting to hear the song many times each day.

"Don't you look sweet," Nana said, patting Katie's hair. "Because you were so good and brave, I have a surprise for you." Nana reached in her apron pocket and took out a bottle of nail polish. "Here, what do you think of this, Katie?" asked Nana.

"Oh, it's pink! I love pink! Is it really for me?" Katie chattered.

"Yes, it is. It's just for you. The label says it is cotton candy pink."

"Cotton candy?" shouted Katie with glee. "I love cotton candy!"

While Nana painted the dainty little fingernails, she took advantage of a teaching moment and told Katie stories of brave women who were also beautiful ladies. Although Katie was confused about being a strong woman and a gentle lady, she loved to listen to Nana tell her stories.

"Tell me the story about 'Ms. tin Boone'," Katie asked Nana.

"You like that story, don't you, Katie?" asked Nana. "You should know that story well enough to tell it to me."

"Okay!" Katie agreed and told Nana the story. "Ms. tin Boone lived in Holland and was in prison."

"Her name is Corey ten Boom," Nana interrupted.

"Oh. Ms. Corey ten Boom," said Katie. "Well, anyway, a mean army came to her country and made her and her friends live in prison. Her little sister died. The mean army was cruel to her friends, and they died, too. But Ms. ten Boom was not mad at them. She asked God to help her love her enemies."

"Very good, Katie. Do you know why the army was cruel to Ms. ten Boom and her friends?" asked Nana.

"'Cause they were Jewbish?" asked Katie.

"That's right. Ms. ten Boom and her friends were Jewish and loved God," answered Nana. "Ms. ten Boom was strong because she suffered cruelty from her enemies and still encouraged her people to be brave and love God. That is a strong woman."

"Did she cry?" asked Katie.

"I would imagine she did. Nevertheless, she also asked God to teach her to love her enemies. That is a beautiful lady. There. Now let's do the other hand."

"Tell me the story of the beautiful queen next, Nana."

"You tell me the story," teased Nana.

"Okay. Once upon a time, there was a beautiful queen," started Katie.

"That was Queen Ester," interrupted Nana.

Katie continued, "She found out that some mean man was going to hurt her people bad. So, she went to visit the king, but she didn't have a party invitation. She told the king her story, and he said he would protect her people."

"Do you know where that story is from, Katie?" asked Nana.

"The B-i-b-l-e!" shouted Katie with pride.

"That's right. How was Queen Ester brave?" asked Nana.

"'Cause she didn't have a party invitation from the king, and she went anyway," said Katie.

"In those days," added Nana, "no one could speak to the king without an invitation. A displeased king would mean death to an intruder. Queen Ester was very brave," added Nana.

"And she was beautiful, and the king loved her," chimed in Katie.

"Very good, Katie. Queen Ester was a brave woman and a lovely lady who risked her life for her people. Can you be a strong woman and a kind and beautiful lady, Katie?" asked Nana.

"Um, I will try, Nana," said a sincere Katie.

"Done. Ten perfect cotton candy pink fingernails," said Nana.

Grace, Passion, Joy, and Curiosity fluttered around Katie, looking at the cotton candy pink fingernails.

"Oh, how lovely," crooned Grace. *"Can I have pink fingernails?"*

"I've never heard of fairies having pink or any other color fingernails," quipped Curiosity. *"But you can ask Sir. Maybe He will agree since you have worked so hard."*

"All of us fairies have worked hard," added Joy. *"I don't think we should ask for a reward. Remember, this whole thing was our idea to help God."*

Katie loved her beautiful pink fingernails and tried to be a brave woman and a beautiful lady. However, in keeping with Katie's wild pursuit of happiness, after a few short days, only tiny specks of cotton candy pink nail polish were all that remained of Nana's labor of love.

"How can I be brave and beautiful?" Katie asked as she sat on a rock to think.

"Athletes are brave and beautiful," whispered Passion. *"The most beautiful athletes are gymnasts."*

"That's it!" cried Katie in a ball of enthusiasm, "I can be a brave and beautiful gymnast." Then, just as in everything Katie did, her imagination took over.

"Fairies?" Katie called in a melodic invitation. "I'm going to be a gymnast. Come play with me."

In her mind's eye, Katie watched as an excited crowd waited in eager anticipation. Chatter filled the arena about the world-class gymnast from Graceton. She would be performing that very day.

The fairies hovered in the air, waiting to see what Katie would do.

"I can't look," said Grace, "*What is she doing?"*

"Shh," whispered Joy. "*I don't know. I've never seen a gymnast before."*

"Oh, I have," lied Passion.

"When have you seen a gymnast?" asked an unbelieving Curiosity.

"Oh, many times," lied Passion.

The announcer stepped to the microphone. "Ladies and gentlemen, we are just minutes away from a spectacular event. It is my immense pleasure to provide a step-by-step account of this performance for you here in this arena and fans listening by radio. You are sure to be delighted. And here she comes now! Without further delay, it is my pleasure to introduce -- KATIE!"

The crowd cheered as Katie removed her long, beautiful cape revealing her white, sequined leotard.

The announcer continued, "Magnificent! Her well-trained body is ablaze with millions of sequins on her white leotard. She is ready to mount the balance beam."

From a standing position, Katie leaped up to mount the beam, and the crowd gasped as Katie teetered. Then, with outstretched arms, reflecting trained poise, Katie regained a perfect balance.

"She's going to fall!" gasped Passion.

"Don't worry," replied Joy. "*She doesn't have far to fall."*

"What grace, what poise," continued the enthusiastic announcer. "Quiet, please. Please. Katie is ready to begin her routine, and I must say, from the information I have in front of me, the routine is spectacular."

Katie stood on her tiptoes with her arms reaching up high, and her back arched in a salute to her trainer and her audience.

The fairies held their breaths, and Passion peeped from between her fingers.

"That was a beautiful salute to you, ladies and gentlemen. Now, she shifts her weight to her left foot and lifts her right leg ever so slightly so that her toe almost touches the balance beam. She pauses, arms gracefully outstretched. She is still pointing her toe, ladies and gentlemen. She glides her right toe from its pointed position in front of her and sets it securely on the beam. Perfect execution! She shifts her weight forward, maintaining expert form and balance. Now she glides the left leg from its backward hold, moving it forward to line up, again perfectly, with her right ankle. She takes four steps. As we would expect, the world-class gymnast finds secure footing on the beam. It's a flawless exercise," shouted the announcer, and the crowd cheers.

As Katie moved in fluid elegance, members of her adoring audience waited with bated breaths. The audience thrilled as Katie pointed her toe with charm and grace with each step.

"Katie is ready for her dismount," the announcer whispered. "Notice how her backfoot arches handsomely so that just the tip of her toe touches the beam behind her. She holds the pose, extending her two lovely arms above her head. She takes three wide steps on the beam. She leaps. She tucks her head into her torso for a perfect double summersault dismount. She plants her feet solidly on the ground and arches her back in her final salute to you, ladies and gentlemen."

The crowd went wild.

The announcer continued, "Such a picture of elegance and talent."

Well. In any case, that's how Katie saw herself.

"I told you she was going to fall," whispered Passion.

Feeling embarrassed, Katie was glad that only the fairies had seen her fall from the weathered wooden fence. Katie quickly picked herself up, dusted off the back of her cute cutoff jeans with the embroidered butterfly on the seat, and ran to the next venue.

As always, her adoring audience, two awkward puppies, a skinny orange tabby cat, and the fairies followed in close order. As Katie searched for her next feat, she rubbed her soon-to-be bruised bottom, then ran off to find a worm.

One warm day, Katie lay on her back, cradling her head on her arms, watching the clouds. The fairies fluttered about, flinging gemstone lights in the air while Nana weeded her rose garden. "Look, Nana. That cloud looks like a lady." Katie said. "She must be sleeping. It looks like she's wearing a white nightgown. Look it there. Those clouds look like angels with their wings over the pretty lady." She paused. "Nana, tell me about my mommy again," Katie begged.

The fairies, Joy, Grace, Passion, and Curiosity stopped fluttering about and sat close to Katie.

"Do you remember about Katie's mommy?" asked Curiosity.

"Yes," replied Grace. *"It was incredibly sad. Shortly after Katie was born, her mother, Kathryn, died."*

"Where was Sir?" whispered Curiosity.

"Oh, He was close by as always," replied Grace. "*We just cannot understand why God allows sorrow to break people's hearts. Only He knows His plan, and He cares."*

Although remembering the passing of her daughter broke her heart, Nana wanted Katie to know her mother. "Well, Katie," began Nana forgetting about the weeds in the rose garden. "You look very much like your mother. She had long black hair and beautiful blue eyes just like yours. The day you were born, God called your mother home to Heaven. God never told us why He wanted your mother to go to Heaven. Never forget, though, my Katie," Nana whispered, hugging her granddaughter, "God loves you. Your mother loved you very much, and so do I. Now, your mother is safe and happy in Heaven."

"Safe in Heaven," Katie mused. "That must be a wonderful place. But, Nana, I feel like that all the time."

"I'm glad, my Katie. You never have to be afraid, Katie," Nana told her. "We have so many friends who love you and will take care of you."

"And I have the fairies," giggled Katie.

Nana pondered Katie's reply about the fairies. Still, she considered it part of her active granddaughter's imagination.

> "Love is patient and kind; love does not envy or boast; it is not arrogant or rude. It does not insist on its own way; it is not irritable or resentful; it does not rejoice at wrongdoing but rejoices with the truth. Love bears all things, believes all things, hopes all things, endures all things." 1 Corinthians 13:4-7

Chapter 3

Daddy G

As God the Father and God the Son walked in the garden, they shared laughs about how they watched the fairies and Katie play together.

"Father, I remember that You have a plan for the warehouse," said God the Son.

"Yes, My Son," replied God the Father. "*I also remember how You said You wanted to be someone special for Katie."*

"Yes," continued God the Son, "*I would very much like to be the One to watch over Katie. I thought We could also restore the Warehouse to Your original plan."*

"I like that," replied God the Father. "*We are of one Heart, My Son. When do You want to begin?"*

"Right away, if it pleases You," said God the Son.

"Very well, Son. It will be a challenge."

"Sir?" whispered Curiosity.

"Yes, My dear?" replied God.

"We fairies are very tired. Would it be okay if we went back to the garden to rest?"

All the other fairies shook their heads in agreement.

"I think that would be a clever idea," said God. "*You fairies have done a splendid job helping Me to find friends who built*

the warehouse. You have also done an excellent job of attending to Katie. You certainly deserve a rest. So, off you go. Rest well, My dears," said a benevolent and knowing God.

The expansive interior of the Warehouse radiated a sweet omnipresence from every fiber of its ancient wood. When visitors entered the vintage building, the same questions followed: "What is that fragrance?" a visitor asked. "It smells..." She paused and breathed in the fragrance again. "It smells almost magical."

"That fragrance is indescribable," said another. "I can't get enough. I come here often just to inhale its essence."

"It smells like what peace and tranquility might smell like," added another.

"I think it smells like kindness. It reminds me of Grandma's pies. Or was it just Grandma?" a young girl said.

"I could stay here all day and bask in the aroma," said still another visitor.

"When I come, I don't know if I possess the aura or if it possesses me," someone commented. "I only know that I feel renewed and revitalized."

"Whatever it is, I simply want to be here in its presence." A woman breathed a deep sigh of satisfaction as she inhaled.

"I know what it is," Katie announced. "If I stand still, the Warehouse hugs me with peace and joy, and love." To Katie, it was that simple. For she knew it was because Daddy G was there.

"Daddy G," whispered Katie. "I heard it again."

The Warehouse's open rafters echoed the sweet sounds that lived in the massive building constructed by pioneers so long ago. The sounds were not only of the little Carolina Wrens that nested there year after year but also of happy, contented people. The Warehouse even echoed its sounds of silence into a reverence that penetrated the soul.

"What did you hear, Katie?" prodded Daddy G.

"It was like someone called my name," Katie continued. "Who's calling my name, Daddy G?"

Daddy G winked and replied, "*Maybe it is your special gift.*"

A special gift. Oh, how Katie yearned for a special gift. There were so many beautiful boxes in the Warehouse. On one of those many enchanting occasions when she was with Daddy G, Katie skipped ahead of Him as He took inventory or stored yet another spectacular gift.

"What's in that box?" Katie asked. "Can I see it?" she begged. "That's a big box! That must cost a lot of money," she said, prodding Daddy G for an answer. "That one is too small. I don't want that one."

Daddy G listened patiently to Katie's many questions and constant chatter. In His loving and always understanding voice, He replied, "*In the fullness of time, My Katie.*"

"In the fullness of time?" sighed a disappointed Katie. What did that mean? That sounded like a very, very long time to wait. Why would Daddy G not give her gifts now?

"My Katie," Daddy G instructed, "*some gifts you would not appreciate now. However, in years to come, you will cherish them.*"

"When will I get a gift?" Katie whined.

"*You already have gifts, Katie. You just don't recognize them,*" Daddy G said in His wise and kind manner. "*Don't you have everything you need?*" He asked. "*You have a brain, and it works well. You have a wonderful body.*"

"Yes, but—" Katie started.

"I know, Katie. You want something special." Daddy G understood Katie.

Occasionally, He surprised her with a frivolous toy. She remembered once He gave her "her heart's desire," a yellow dress with tiny fuzzy white dots, ruffles, and lace. He also gave her shiny black patent shoes and little white nylon socks with ruffled lace at the top. The men who worked at the Warehouse wore white shirts, and the women wore blue blouses. They did not wear anything as spectacular as Katie's yellow dotted swiss dress with ruffles and lace.

"Daddy G, look how far my skirt goes out," Katie laughed with glee as she twirled.

"My, that is fine," Daddy G replied. *"You look like a beautiful buttercup."*

"It's the most beautiful dress I ever had," Katie purred as she skipped and twirled around in her yellow ruffles.

Several times, she abruptly stopped her twirling and ran to Daddy G, grabbing him around a leg.

"Oh, thank You, Daddy G." Katie's spontaneous gratitude was deep and sincere, and she wore that yellow dotted dress as often as possible.

One particularly sunny day, as she was twirling, giggling, and admiring her yellow dress, she heard that sound from several days before. It was that same mysterious sound. She was not frightened. No, she was never frightened when she was in the Warehouse.

As she followed Daddy G on His rounds, Katie chattered. "Daddy G, I heard it again."

"What did you hear?" Daddy G asked in an omniscient voice.

"I don't know, 'xactly," Katie explained.

"Were you afraid?" asked Daddy G.

"No. It sounded soft and sweet."

"Then just keep listening, Katie. Someday you will understand," Daddy G encouraged Katie.

Daddy G was always busy at the Warehouse. When He was not managing the gifts or answering Katie's unceasing questions, He was helping others. Katie remembered how she once hid behind boxes and silently listened and watched as Daddy G talked with a disabled man. From her hiding place, Katie learned that the man's name was Lawrence. His story was so sad, and Katie's eyes filled with tears.

"Daddy G," Lawrence began, "when I was a boy, we didn't have enough food to eat. My dad was hard on us kids, but I was the only one he beat. I got a beating for not working fast enough or the way Dad wanted. He treated us more like indentured field servants than like his sons. I often went to bed hungry and with bloody stripes on my back.

"I couldn't wait to get away from home, so I enlisted in the army. After working in the fields under Dad's wrathful hand, the strict training I received in the military was a welcome relief. I was trained as a medic and sent to the European front during World War II.

"I recall during one battle calling out, 'Lord, if You get me out of this hell, I will serve You for the rest of my life.' Shrapnel from 150mm artillery rained down on my company. The burning shrapnel hit me as I ran to help a wounded soldier, and the burning lead severed an artery in my leg. I knew my injury was bad. So, I gave myself an injection of morphine. Then I had to struggle to stay awake. Amazingly, from out of nowhere, a young G.I. appeared and knelt beside me. He whispered comforting words and wrapped a tourniquet around my mangled leg, then left. I never saw him again. I still struggled to stay awake, or the burial patrol would leave me for dead. When help arrived, I passed out.

"Finally, I woke after five days, and an Army nurse told me I was in the hospital and that I had lost my right leg." Lawrence tearfully cried to Daddy G, "Why did I have to suffer abuse as a boy and then suffer this pain and physical handicap as a man? Why did I have to suffer so?"

Looking gently into Lawrence's sad and tearful eyes, Daddy G replied, "*Perhaps because there is a greater job God has for you to do.*"

"That's a lot to think about," Lawrence said.

Throughout the rest of his life, Lawrence pondered those events and Daddy G's answer. This physically disabled man became a valued worker at the Warehouse and kept his promise to God. He was no longer spiritually disabled.

"Lawrence," Daddy G said, touching Lawrence's shoulder, "*I have noticed your dedication here as a volunteer. Now, I need someone dependable to work full-time at the Warehouse. Would you like the job? You will not be wealthy on the small salary, but the fringe benefits are good.*"

"Yes, sir," Lawrence sang. "My wife will be pleased. She stays home with the kids, You know, and we sure could use the money."

"In this job, you can sit down whenever you need, and you won't need to do any heavy lifting. You simply need to be here to supervise the volunteers," Daddy G explained.

"Yes, sir. I will be happy to do that," beamed Lawrence.

Daddy G continued, "*I might also ask you to travel to the hospital and visit and encourage other disabled people. There are so many people in need.*"

"It's the least I can do, Daddy G," Lawrence answered. "And it will be my pleasure."

Happily, there was little sadness or sorrow in residence at the Warehouse. Many visitors returned to report their joy, deliverance, and restored families. Daddy G never tired but delighted in those reports, and He was never too busy to listen to them all. And there was another mystery: He always had the right advice for those in need.

A frequent visitor told Lawrence, "Every time I visit the Warehouse, Daddy G is so generous and always gives the perfect gift."

"I understand," Lawrence replied. "Even though I am here every day, I still receive the same generosity."

"Have you ever been turned down by Him?" the visitor asked Lawrence.

"No, not exactly turned down. But the advice or gift was not always what I expected or asked for."

During her frequent visits to the Warehouse, Katie watched and listened. Each time she heard someone's story, she marveled through her childish understanding of how, besides the gifts of comfort and support, Daddy G also had a perfect gift to meet every need. Katie also enjoyed the safety and tenderness of being with Daddy G and always felt welcome, and at any moment of the day, she could run into Daddy G's open arms where she knew no harm could come to her.

Katie wished that everyone could feel the peace, love, and safety of Daddy G's embrace. Katie knew that so many needed

Daddy G and wondered how He ever had time enough to attend to everyone's needs.

As Katie remembered stories told in the Warehouse, she heard that sound again. This time, it was a bit louder. Still, she could not understand. So, she continued to play.

In His wisdom, Daddy G chose and mentored volunteers who loved the work of the Warehouse, volunteers who loved talking to visitors, and who loved Daddy G. As He trained volunteers in tasks, Daddy G was patient and kind. Some volunteers, like Lonny, were simply happy to be there to open the door and welcome visitors. Janie was happy to sweep the floors or wash windows. Still, others understood that listening without interfering or being judgmental was their most essential duty. Volunteers, like James, learned that the act of sharing encouraged those in need and strengthened those who shared. Daddy G frequently asked this volunteer, "*James, will you deliver some gifts for Me? It's okay if you stay to visit. Sometimes recipients need instruction to help them understand their gifts.*"

"I'd be glad to," the young man answered. "When You gave me my gift, I appreciated Your help in understanding and teaching me to use it to its fullest potential."

Katie thought it strange that Daddy G trained people to give away the gifts. "Daddy G?" Katie asked.

"*Yes, My dear.*"

"Daddy G, why do You give away gifts? You could make lots of money if You sold them."

"Katie, it is more important to give to someone. Giving will motivate others to share in return. It's like dropping a pebble into a lake. The circles eventually spread over a greater

distance. Receiving a gift inspires and encourages people to share."

"I want to be a volunteer at the Warehouse," Katie chirped "and give away expensive gifts."

"Katie, dear, no gift is more precious than another," explained Daddy G. "*The only difference is how a person uses their gift."*

Then, she heard that sound again.

Chapter 4

The Warehouse

As God the Father walked through His garden, His radiance lighted everything in His path, casting a Heavenly glow upon His Creation. Yet, this day, God noticed something was amiss.

"Where are My fairies?" God called with laughter in His voice. "*Hope? Where are you? Serenity? Are you hiding? Joy? Surely, you are not sad. Hematite, always the balanced one, are you so unhappy?"*

Knowing where the fairies were hiding, God the Father became concerned, hearing no reply from them. "*Wisdom? You are the leader. The other fairies need you. Compassion? Have you become apathetic? Curiosity? Have you lost your spark?"* As God searched, He found that the gemstones' energy adorning the fairies' gowns appeared dim, almost unhappy. "*What's this?"* asked God with a smile, trying to encourage the fairies. "*Sadness is not permitted in My garden."*

"We're sorry, Sir," Curiosity said, emerging from her hiding place. The emeralds in the little fairy's gown no longer flashed their dynamic energy. "*We want to go back to the warehouse,"* sighed the little fairy.

"Katie needs us," added Compassion. Fire opals in Compassion's gown no longer radiated their red, pink, and yellow fire.

"Yes, and we miss her," agreed Hope. How sad to see the topaz in Hope's gown cloudy, no longer brilliant with energy.

Even Passion's red rhodonite did not shine as bright.

"I dare say she does need you," agreed God the Father. "*However, there are many others, besides Katie, who may need you as well. So, if you fairies have rested sufficiently, then you must go back to the Warehouse. Off you go."*

Immediately, gemstones glowed as the fairies squealed with delight and danced.

As the fairies began their flight back to the Warehouse, Curiosity turned and said, "*Thank You, Sir."*

"You are most welcome, My dear," replied a radiant God the Father.

With the Father's sweet words, Curiosity flew off to join her sister fairies.

Katie was ignorant of the fact that her great-great-grandfather, John Wilkins, had suffered perils leaving his home in Missouri and arriving in Florida with a new wife. Neither did she care that this same John Wilkins had helped harvest the ancient timbers of the Warehouse from the wilderness territory of Florida. Katie was equally indifferent that her great-great-grandfather, Leo Bates, had milled the timbers so many years ago. She knew nothing of the history of how the Bates and Wilkins pioneer families had settled Graceton and at what expense.

However, the fairies knew all these things. They remembered the joy, excitement, heartache, and often terror the pioneers had endured to build the Warehouse. Moreover, the fairies reveled in the joy as the pioneers celebrated the completion of the Warehouse.

Katie only knew that the Warehouse was the happiest place in the world. It was better than a circus because there were always activities to capture her attention and imagination. It was much better than going to school for obvious reasons. It was even better than attending a birthday party, unless, of course, it was her own birthday party. She was unconcerned that in the 1800s, a riverboat had steamed from Jacksonville to deliver gleaming tin for the roof. However, she was impressed that even the smallest sounds on that tin roof echoed in the enormous, open rafters.

Katie loved to stand in the middle of the Warehouse, surrounded by fairies, and shout, "Hello! Katie! Katie! Hello, Daddy G! Daddy G? Daddy G, I love you."

Once again, back at the Warehouse, the fairies giggled and danced through the rafters, over boxes, and around Katie.

Joy, no longer a sad, lonely fairy, shouted, "*Katie, Katie, Katie. Hello, Katie.*"

Curiosity joined in the excitement of hearing her echo, "*Hello, Sir. Sir, we love You.*"

Hearing their voices bouncing off the tin roof and echoing through the open expanse of the giant timbers excited Katie.

Katie had many friends and family who worked in the Warehouse. They were good friends and added to her happiness of being there, and now the fairies were back and continued to play games with Katie.

"Daddy G, everybody here is always so happy. Why are they so happy? Most of the time, I'm happy. But sometimes I'm not happy, but then one of my friends listens to me, and then I feel happy again." It was true. Katie had discovered that when she had a difficult day, and someone listened, just that little encouragement helped her get through her problem and make a good decision. Listening was the most excellent comfort a friend could offer. The fairies, especially Joy and Wisdom, were good listeners, but having fairies listen was not the same as having human friends listen and care.

"Daddy G, do You remember when Mr. Ted came to the Warehouse? He was not very happy, was he? But then he got happy, and he kept coming back. What makes people happy, Daddy G?" asked Katie, always full of questions.

Faith and Wisdom hovered about Katie's head, waiting to hear God the Son's answer.

"*Well, Katie,*" Daddy G tried to explain, "*here at the Warehouse, there is a kindred spirit.*"

"Huh? What is a kiddy spirit, Daddy G?" asked Katie.

At Katie's response, the fairies giggled, for they knew that this kindred spirit existed wherever God the Father and God the Son lived.

"A kindred spirit comes when people believe the same thing. Here at the Warehouse, everyone feels like they belong. It is important for people to feel like they belong. Wouldn't you agree?"

"Yes, Daddy G. I love belonging here at the Warehouse and belonging to You," Katie replied with giggles.

"I am glad you like being here. I like having you here, too," said Daddy G in a soft, understanding voice.

"We like being here with You, too," crooned Serenity, looking at God the Son with loving eyes.

God the Son returned Serenity's love with a wink.

With so many employees, volunteers and visitors working, talking, laughing, singing, and sometimes whistling, the Warehouse was a busy place. Despite all this activity, it was not noisy. Instead, it was an oasis of happy chatter, joy, and peace. Everyone worked well together and seemed to enjoy their tasks. Katie was quiet a moment as she evaluated this. Was everyone happy because they had a job? Or did everyone have a job because they were happy? Either way, Katie knew she, too, wanted a job.

"Daddy G, I want a job at the Warehouse," begged Katie. "And I want a gift of my very own."

"What kind of job were you thinking about, Katie?"

"I don't know." After thinking a moment and remembering the tantalizing secrets hidden from her view, she squealed, "I know! I can make sure all the boxes are in the right places, then open them to make sure nothing is broken."

"Hum," said Daddy G, feigning thought. *"I don't need a box checker, Katie."*

"Well, then, can I count the boxes?" asked Katie. "I'm a good counter, and I will be very careful, I promise. Oh, please, Daddy G, let me count the boxes."

"I'm not sure you are ready for a job like that yet, Katie," Daddy G. said in a sympathetic voice. *"I just like having you here and watching you play. I will know when you are ready for a job."*

"When will I be ready?" begged Katie. "I want to feel the kiddy spirit and have a job and be happy."

The fairies fluttered around Katie in a feeling of unity, for they knew her longing.

"Don't fret about it, My Katie," comforted Daddy G. *"Be happy and enjoy the friendly, safe feeling."*

Indeed, the Warehouse was a safe place. Katie noticed that people were not afraid when they were there. They all seemed to enjoy and even appreciate the safety of the Warehouse. Even though blocks and blocks of a heavy traffic highway fronted the Warehouse, Katie felt safe. It was an unusual feeling. Not that feeling safe was unusual, but in the Warehouse, that feeling was curious and mystical, almost reverent.

"I do feel safe, Daddy G," Katie said. "The Warehouse is a perfect place."

From the busy highway, the Warehouse looked like any other old wooden building whose rusty roof needed cleaning, and the wood needed a new coat of paint. However, this building was different. To Katie, it was mystical, even magical. It was unexplainable.

Just as quickly as her questions flowed, Katie's attention shifted. "Daddy G?"

"Yes, ma'am?"

"Do you think one of these boards came from one tree?" Katie asked, pointing to one of the longest floor planks.

Compassion, Curiosity, and Joy followed to where Katie's finger pointed as the chatty little girl spoke. The fairies hovered over the planks of wood, remembering the history held within the fibers of the timber.

"I imagine it could."

"The tree would have to be very tall, right?" asked Katie.

"Yes, ma'am. It would be very tall and incredibly old," agreed Daddy G.

Thick wooden timbers, expansive joists, and sturdy buttresses that formed the skeleton of the Warehouse still revealed skillful cuts from pioneer axes.

"Daddy G?" continued Katie.

"Yes, Katie," replied a patient, Daddy G.

"How old is the top of the Warehouse? It looks old and rusty."

"Well, since the building of the Warehouse was completed in 1899, the tin on the roof would be over seventy years old."

"Wow," breathed Katie.

As if enhancing the aura of their deep secrets, the wood released ancient fragrances. Among those timbers were red cedar: perhaps used for a trousseau chest, smoky, white oak that loving hands had carved into a cradle one year and a tiny coffin the next, southern cypress used to fashion a sturdy ladder for little ones to scamper up to bed or the front door of a cozy cabin.

The fairies recalled the joyful fragrances of remembered celebrations with European balsam, Norwegian spruce, or Douglas fir hiding the scents of Christmases past. It was as if the scents held happy squeals of excited children, waking up on Christmas morning to find a decorated tree reflecting the flickering light of a cozy fireplace.

Katie wondered if lots of toys covered the floor under the tree, or was there just one unique, handmade toy displayed for little eyes and hands to find, to caress, and to treasure. Katie imagined that she heard the tinkle of crystal as little hands lifted the cover from a forbidden candy bowl. She felt her taste buds explode as she remembered the taste of sweet delights of strawberry flavored disks filled with delicious jellies, or thick yellow ribbons of lemon-flavored hard candy, or classic peppermint candy canes.

Katie heard stories of children in a one-room schoolhouse, sitting on benches hewn from ancient pine, trying not to squirm lest splinters pierced their britches or pantaloons. The fairies remembered watching children write on black slates with chunky pieces of chalk, and they laughed when Katie had tried tasting chalk and found out quickly that it was not one of her favorite things.

When Katie imagined an aged grandmother napping in her rocking chair close to a low-burning fire, sweet thrills of joy filled her heart. Katie could see in her imagination the grandmother waiting to snatch up her school-weary grandchildren into her arthritic arms and smother them in thousands of hugs and kisses. Katie giggled to herself when she imagined the children, once released from arms of love, melted to the floor in a puddle of giggles. The children knew that chocolate chip cookies and milk always waited for them on the old worktable.

In addition to imagining hidden stories, Katie also played inside the cavernous space of the Warehouse, climbing ladders and walking beams when she thought no one was watching. She ran chasing fairies, dodging in and out between the boxes that filled every nook and cranny of the building.

"Chase me! Chase me!" squealed Joy.

"Can't catch me!" taunted Curiosity.

Just as Katie gave chase, Grace and Courage jumped out from behind another stack of boxes. "*Gotcha!*" *s*houted Grace, shaking with giggles.

Katie stopped in her tracks, and her body tensed. Squealing, she turned and ran in the other direction with the fairies in hot pursuit. That game continued until Katie or the fairies fell in a heap from exhaustion or became bored with the game. Then Katie turned her attention to climbing to the highest rafter.

"Look at me, Daddy G," Katie squealed as she climbed a ladder high up to the loft.

"What are you doing up there, Katie?" Daddy G inquired with amusement.

"I saw a little bird fly up here, and I wanted to see where he sleeps."

"Be careful, My dear. You're not a little bird, and if you fall, you won't fly," warned Daddy G.

"You would catch me, Daddy G," Katie replied in her child-like faith. Just as quickly, Katie's attention turned to a new interest. "Daddy G!" squealed Katie. "There are bats hanging upside down! I had a baby bat once, but Nana wouldn't let me keep him. He had to go back to his house in the swing set. Will you catch me a bat, Daddy G?" begged Katie.

"No, Katie, we can't disturb the bats. They have a job to do at night, so we better let them sleep," answered Daddy G, understanding Katie's fascination with the little creatures. *"Come down, please."*

Obediently, Katie climbed down a ladder onto a platform below, then squealed and giggled as she jumped into Daddy G's waiting arms. "Now, what can I do?" Katie whined.

"Here, Katie," said Daddy G handing her a broom. *"Would you like to sweep around the boxes?"*

"Oh, yes! You're giving me a job?" asked Katie with delight.

The fairies were also delighted for Katie. They fluttered around her head, whispering in her ear stories about the garden, all the while dusting their little friend with their gemstone energies. Katie giggled and sang as she worked, "Little feet, be careful where you take me to. Anything for Jesus, only let me do."

Daddy G beamed as He listened to the sweet words of the song.

As Katie swept, she was careful not to disturb the stacks of boxes and cartons, for intuitively, she knew that these were not just ordinary, but extraordinary boxes containing extraordinary treasures. Though some were simple cardboard, many others boasted lavish gold gilding or metallic paper reflecting colors of the rainbow. No matter the decorations, they all held unique gifts of all sizes and values. Even though Katie did not know what each box contained, the boxes fascinated her, firing her desire for a special gift of her own.

As she swept, the fairies hovered and fluttered about Katie as the chatty little girl asked more questions.

"What's inside the shiny boxes? I like the yellow one. Are those blue ones for a boy? Oh, this box wrapped in brown paper is not pretty at all. I wouldn't want that box. It must have something awful in it, like underwear or socks. Aw. Look at this box. It's all covered with dust. How long has it been here? Did someone forget it was here?"

As Katie played among the boxes, she could almost smell and taste the essence of each gift she imagined. To Katie, most were sweet happiness, intense joy, or exhilarating power, and she spent a great deal of time guessing the contents of each box. The ones that fascinated her most were the tiny gifts. Were they precious jewels of immense value? The large gifts tantalized her, too. Were they wrapped large to be a joke, or were they indeed priceless? Katie gave little thought to the gifts for boys. She had to admit, though, that the lovely wrapping paper in blues, purples, and greens was fascinating in a masculine sort of way. The gifts wrapped in pink flowered paper or yellow polka dots—perfect for girls—gave her the biggest thrill. Then there were tens of thousands of beautifully wrapped gifts just waiting in joyful anticipation of longing hands. Also, within the giant Warehouse were crowds of gifts wrapped in more subdued-colored paper and brown string. These gifts seemed to have a quiet yet commanding presence. The auras surrounding the gifts varied from dense with an unhappy feeling to others that almost seemed to glow. Even the sad and lonely gifts waiting in the shadows covered with dust peaked Katie's imagination. To her, these long, faded, and forgotten gifts tasted stale and bittersweet. Her heart broke thinking about who had forgotten them, and how long ago, and why. These lingering questions haunted Katie and left her sad and melancholy.

However, Katie had little time to be pensive, for there were just too many other gifts. There were so many happy, joyful gifts that intrigued her. Gifts stacked so high that they seemed to disappear into the open rafters. Feelings of joy and happiness in this special place that was the Warehouse far outweighed sadness and loneliness. The combined sense of love, safety, and magnificence encompassed Katie, and she was in awe at the strange sweetness that permeated the Warehouse.

However, a more magnificent, more engulfing, and more comforting sensation swaddled Katie. The most significant presence, the sweetest, the softest, and yet the most overpowering feeling at the Warehouse was Daddy G, and He was the most important part of Katie's life.

Chapter 5

Kevin

> I have loved thee with an everlasting love: therefore with lovingkindness have I drawn thee.
>
> – Jeremiah 3:31

The wooden chair squeaked as God, the Son, leaned back, hands folded. The fairies, Wisdom, Hope, and Compassion sat on the back of the chair, while the other fairies hovered and fluttered about the room.

"Tell me a little about yourself, Kevin," prodded Daddy G, sitting back in his modest oak chair.

"I don't know where to begin," said Kevin pensively.

"The beginning is always a good place to start," Daddy G said with a comforting smile, trying to relive the stress showing on Kevin's face.

For the next several minutes, Kevin told Daddy G about his family, the Wilkins. Kevin proudly told how his mom and dad taught him and his siblings to love God and depend upon Him. Kevin's demeanor changed when he related that his parents were no longer with him and how he missed them so. His sadness continued as he told Daddy G about marrying his high school sweetheart then how she had died in childbirth.

Compassion fluttered down to Kevin and sat on his shoulder, releasing the healing energy in her fire opals that adorned her gown.

"What became of the child, Kevin?" Daddy G asked.

"I was so distraught when Kathryn died that I could not think straight. I asked Kathryn's mother if she would take the baby and raise it for me. She's a wonderful lady. You probably know her, too—Mrs. Bates? When she agreed, I told Mrs. Bates that I would send her money each month to support her and my daughter. So, I left my daughter with her grandmother, and I went to college. Don't get me wrong. I did not abandon my daughter," Kevin said as he broke into heavy sobbing. "I am so ashamed."

As Kevin sobbed, Hematite joined Compassion, who was trying to add balance to Kevin's mind and body.

"Why are you ashamed, Kevin?" asked Daddy G. *"Leaving your heartbreak does not mean you are a bad person or a bad father. You did a very responsible thing in asking Mrs. Bates to take your daughter. You should be proud that you went the extra mile to support them,"* praised Daddy G. *"What's your daughter's name, Kevin?"*

"Her name is Katie — after her mother, Kathryn," answered Kevin in a low, sad voice.

"Oh! Katie? Our Katie," exclaimed Hope as her topaz gemstones radiated.

"This is Katie's daddy," added Wisdom. Her peridot gemstones competed with the topaz for brilliance.

"I think he is very brave," sighed Courage with admiration. Her emeralds under the layers of burgundy silk organza glowed.

The light show of the gemstones was indeed spectacular. Even more radiant, though, were the smiles the fairies wore.

"I see. I am sorry for your loss, Kevin," consoled Daddy G.

"Thank You. Well, one of the reasons I am here is that I will be graduating from college this term with a master's in architecture and a minor in business, and I was hoping You might have a job opening here," Kevin said, testing the waters.

"Hmm," said Daddy G thoughtfully. *"As a matter of fact, I do have an opening for a financial manager. However, this manager will be responsible for other duties as I assign them. Does that sound good to you?"* Daddy G asked.

Hope, Wisdom, and Courage danced together, showering God the Son with their gratitude.

Kevin beamed, "That sounds just fine."

"When do you graduate?"

"At the end of the month," Kevin replied.

"Very well," replied Daddy G. "*That would be on a Friday night. How does starting the following Monday morning sound to you?"*

"That sounds just right, Sir," Kevin chirped.

"By the way, Kevin," interjected Daddy G, *"in addition to your salary, which we haven't discussed, you will receive a stipend for incidentals and a small apartment as well."*

With that understanding, Daddy G stood to embrace Kevin with a pat on the back.

Kevin marveled. That's a strange way to end a job interview.

The following Monday, after graduation, Kevin reported to the Warehouse.

"Good morning, Kevin," greeted Daddy G.

"Good morning, Sir," replied Kevin.

"Oh, please," Daddy G waved off Kevin's formality. *"Everyone in Graceton calls Me Daddy G. I would be pleased if you would do the same."*

"Thank You, Sir," then Kevin stumbled over his words. "I mean, thank You, Daddy G."

The fairies gazed at God the Son through eyes of love, and He returned their affection with a smile.

On Tuesday, Kevin's second day on the job, a puzzled Kevin emerged from the financial manager's office. "Sir, I mean, Daddy G, looking over the books, I don't see much money coming in. How do I balance the books?" asked a bewildered Kevin.

"Oh, don't worry about that part, Kevin. I always take care of the income and balancing," replied Daddy G. *"You only need to keep a list of, let's say, expenses."*

"Is it legal?" Kevin asked, then blushed, not wanting to offend Daddy G.

"Oh yes," replied Daddy G with a little chuckle. *"You see, I have, what you might call, a trust fund."*

Knowing the true Source of the Warehouse income, Wisdom covered her giggle with her hand, looked at God the Son, and gleamed. God the Son winked at Wisdom and shook His head.

"I see," Kevin replied, though he did not see. Instead, he walked back to his office, scratching his head, and gave a backward skeptical glance at Daddy G.

On Wednesday, when Kevin reported to work, Daddy G called Kevin into his office. *"Kevin, I've been thinking about your job here."*

Oh, no, I'm going to be fired, Kevin thought to himself. "Yes, Sir," Kevin replied, with nervous sweat and fear consuming his quaking body.

"Yes," began Daddy G, *"it has come to my attention that there may very well be more additional duties than I first imagined."*

Kevin breathed a sigh of relief.

"Let's say your financial duties will be secondary. Instead, I am putting you in charge of a special section."

"I'll be happy to do anything, Daddy G," Kevin said when he caught his breath.

"I think you will like this assignment," Daddy G encouraged Kevin. *"However, it is not necessarily an easy assignment. You will face challenges, and you may even suffer minor setbacks. But don't be afraid. Remember, I am always here for you. Let's go out and evaluate the situation."*

How could Kevin say no? So, with a lighter heart, Kevin followed Daddy G as they toured the assignment area. At first, Kevin was a bit intimidated, for he had no idea his territory was so vast. When they got to the elementary school playground, they stopped to survey the area.

"Your territory starts here, and the playground will be a frequent stop. That's not so bad, is it?" Daddy G quipped.

"From here, you can scan a wide area and take any action necessary."

By now, Kevin was more than a little curious. However, the sight of a dirty little girl running and playing on the playground interrupted his curiosity. The little urchin with long, unkempt hair flying around her head skipped from the school playground's east side as two clumsy puppies and a skinny tabby cat followed. Although Kevin could not see them, a gaggle of fairies also fluttered about. The dirty little bundle of energy chatted and laughed as though talking to her best friends as she tumbled and skipped and fell in the dirt. With no notice, the little munchkin simply jumped up, dusted off the bottom of her shorts, and continued leaping and twirling and giggling to the other side of the playground. Then she stopped. She looked. She squealed, "Daddy G! Daddy G!" The dirty little urchin came running and flung herself at Daddy G, who was more than happy to embrace the little girl, dirt, worms, doodlebugs, and all.

Hope and Faith, knowing what was to come, watched for Kevin's reaction.

Kevin thought, What a greeting! I wish a child would come running to me and greet me like that.

"Hello, My dear," Daddy G said with obvious deep affection. *"I would like to introduce you to someone special. Katie, this is Kevin. Kevin, this is Katie."*

For an extended moment, Kevin froze. A blank stare covered his face, and he was unable to speak.

"Hello, Kevin," Katie sang in her happy little girl voice, still holding Daddy G's hand and twisting her dirty little body in vixen fashion.

Kevin still was unable to move. He was unable to find his voice.

"Daddy G," Katie whispered, motioning for her Confidant to bend down to listen to her secret, "I don't think Kevin likes me."

"Don't worry, My dear. He likes you," Daddy G assured Katie.

Faith and Hope giggled.

"Okay," Katie chimed. And off she ran to resume her running, tumbling, and giggling with her entourage following along. Silk organza rustled, and gemstones gleamed as the fairies looked back at Kevin and giggled.

"Kevin, are you okay?" asked Daddy G.

"I'm not quite sure yet," replied Kevin with a hard gulp. "Is that my…"

"Yes, Kevin, that is your little responsibility you have been caring for all this time," Daddy G replied in a quiet, understanding voice. *"This is your assignment. You are to watch over her, protect her, and help her in any way she might need you."*

"I don't know what to say. I don't know how to…" Kevin mumbled.

"Let's go together and visit Nana. I know she is waiting for you and will be pleased," assured Daddy G.

"What if she doesn't want me in Katie's life?" asked Kevin with fear.

"I don't think you need to worry about that," Daddy G assured Kevin.

The fairies, Joy and Serenity, followed Daddy G and Kevin to Nana's house. They didn't want to miss this homecoming.

When Daddy G and Kevin arrived at her house, Nana was in the yard hanging clothes. Just like Katie, Nana stopped. She looked. Then she ran with her arms held open wide the entire distance. "Kevin! Kevin!" Nana cried. They fell into each other's arms and wept.

After a time of sobbing, they stopped and looked at each other in disbelief. Kevin was not disappointed with Nana's greeting. Neither were the fairies.

Kevin performed his duties as a financial manager at the Warehouse with superb attention to detail. He also gave his "special assignment" his most excellent care. Kevin watched over Katie; he listened to her constant chatter and protected her. When she needed him, Kevin was always there for her. And to his surprise, when Kevin needed her, Katie was there. When either of them needed Nana, she was there for them. And of course, whenever any of them needed Daddy G, He was always there.

Kevin was living in a small apartment not far from the Warehouse. After Daddy G gave him the new assignment, Kevin wondered how he would make room for Katie. Would Nana want to come live with him?

With Daddy G close beside him for advice, Kevin began looking for a bigger house for his family. His family! How sweet were those words? Every time he spoke those words or even thought them, he got goosebumps, and his heart soared so that his happiness was immeasurable.

"Kevin," called Daddy G.

Kevin put down the newspaper and gave Daddy G his complete attention. "Yes, Sir," Kevin replied.

"Will you come with Me. I'd like you to look at a sweet, two-story ranch-style house in a neighborhood not far from your apartment."

So, Kevin and Daddy G went together to investigate the house. It was perfect. It was affordable. To say that it was a magnificent house would be stretching it a bit, but that's just what Katie thought, and Nana agreed. It *was* a magnificent house.

The day Kevin took his family to see the house, Katie flung open the front door and squealed, "Nana! Come look!"

"My my," said Nana. "It's so bright and cheery."

"Oh, it is a beautiful house," crooned Grace.

"And it will soon be full of love," added Joy.

"Nana, look! The curtains look like a bride's veil!" Katie said as she wrapped herself in the sheer white curtains, enhancing the blue living room.

Grace and Joy giggled as they became wrapped in the sheer curtains with Katie, and the fairies' amethyst and topaz gemstone created a soft glow through the fabric of the curtains.

Nana had already turned her attention to the french doors on the opposite side of the hall. As she opened the elegant, white, glass-paned doors, Nana gasped. "There's a dining room! A real dining room with lots of windows to open and let in the warm sunshine," she said, dreaming of the sunny room.

“Nana, there’s a dining room in the kitchen, too!”

Indeed, there was a little table in the kitchen, just right for breakfast or milk and cookies in the afternoon.

Nana worked with Kevin to agree on how best to decorate the dining room. First, of course, they would need a dining table and chairs. Nana was also hoping for a china cabinet. Though she did not have antique china or expensive porcelain, a china cabinet would be a place to display family treasures, Christmas cards, or Katie’s school papers.

Upstairs, Katie ran squealing joyfully with her puppies and kitten, and the fairies fluttered, twinkling with excitement. Katie had her own bedroom! “Nana. I have a bed with curtains!”

A full-size canopy bed was the first piece of furniture Kevin had moved into the house. He knew a twin bed would do, but Kevin just wanted his daughter to have a full-size bed with a canopy, dust ruffle, pink satin comforter, and pillows. Kevin was not disappointed when he heard her squeals.

“Nana! Oh, Nana! My windows have bride’s veil curtains, too!” squealed Katie with glee.

White ruffled Priscilla curtains with matching valance and tiebacks decorated the double windows in Katie’s bedroom. Kevin wanted Katie’s bedroom to be sunny and bright, and the white Pricillas were perfect for that purpose.

For a short second, Katie was quiet. “Kevin, does Nana have a bedroom, too?” Katie asked in a contemplative manner.

“Yes, ma’am. Let’s go see.” Kevin beamed as he took his daughter’s hand and led her two doors down the hall.

When Kevin opened the door, Katie gasped with joy and shouted, "Nana! Come quick."

Just before Nana entered the bedroom, Kevin instructed, "Nana, cover your eyes."

Katie's face could hardly hold the fullness of her excited grin, and happy fairies fluttered about her head throwing rays of light from their gemstones. As Nana touched the bedroom door, Katie squealed, "Open your eyes, Nana!"

Nana stood dumfounded. Her eyes widened, and she covered her open mouth with her hankie. Serenity and Compassion fluttered around Nana and showered the grandmother with watermelon tourmaline and topaz gemstone energies. These gemstones helped calm Nana's mind and emotions and brought her deep joy and peace into alignment. It was the most beautiful room. Kevin had picked out a queen-size bed in cherry wood with a matching dresser and chest of drawers. With crisp white sheets and plump pillows, the bed was fit for a queen.

"My wedding quilt," Nana said in a whispered gasp through her hanky. "You put my wedding quilt on the bed. Thank you, Kevin." Nana began to cry, and Kevin held her close. "It's a beautiful bed, Kevin," Nana said between her tears. After a moment of pensive reflection, Nana whispered, "I do miss Leo." Although Nana knew her husband was in Heaven and no longer in pain, she still felt like only half a person. Before Kevin's return, she had Katie to help fill the void of the empty side of the bed. Somehow thinking of being in bed alone tore her heart again.

“Maybe I can sneak in and sleep with you, Nana,” whispered Katie in a conspiring voice.

Nana kissed her granddaughter and wiped a tear away.

“Oh, Kevin, it’s beautiful,” Nana said again. “And doesn’t the whole house seem full and happy?”

Indeed the house was full. It was full of Katie’s squeals, slamming doors, and little feet running up and down the stairs. Even the fairies added to the joyful activities that were now Kevin’s home.

“It is a full HOME,” Kevin corrected as he grimaced at the door slamming. “How long do you think it will be before she finds the banister?”

“Weee!”

“Not long,” giggled Nana through the last trace of her tears.

To Kevin, Daddy G gave the joy of a happy home with his daughter and Nana and a full heart without regret.

Chapter 6

Mr. Bob

> Bring ye all the tithes into the storehouse, that there may be meat in mine house, and prove me now herewith, saith the LORD of hosts, if I will not open you the windows of heaven, and pour you out a blessing, that there shall not be room enough to receive it.
>
> – Malachi 3:10

Daddy G continued distributing gifts and blessings from the abundance of His Warehouse. Even though He gave many gifts and the right gift to each recipient, His supply never ended. Often, Graceton residents and visitors who came requested specific gifts, though others were unaware of their need. Those interested Katie the most and gave Daddy G the greatest satisfaction.

Just as in any small town, adult residents and some teenagers of Graceton knew their neighbors and their neighbors' business. Even Katie knew many of the townspeople who visited the Warehouse and liked most of them. However, there was one person she felt uncomfortable around, almost afraid to be around. That was Mr. Bob, and she was glad that Mr. Bob came around infrequently because he was always unpleasant, and he smelled terrible. Katie was too young to know that this horrible body odor was due to Mr. Bob's alcohol consumption.

Once, Mr. Bob was handsome, happy, well-groomed, and smelled clean and of aftershave. However, when his wife died, he changed. He secluded himself in his house and refused contact with friends. His pain was too overwhelming for him to bear, yet he did not want to give up his independence and receive love and help from his friends. He began to drink more heavily, he lost his job, and his children refused to visit.

Remembering Mr. Bob's last visit to the Warehouse, Katie cringed. Chaos filled the air with the sound of a racing engine, grinding gears, squealing tires, a galvanized trash can crunching, shouting, and cursing. The sounds of the Warehouse never sounded so vain.

When Mr. Bob brought his car to a skidded stop at the Warehouse, rocks and limestone billowed, sending the choking dust into the air. Mr. Bob flung open the car door in a fit of rage and appeared to be pulling on a man's leather belt. To Katie's alarm, she discovered that Mr. Bob pulled the cruel restraint too tightly around the neck of a very reluctant and frightened dog. All the while Mr. Bob pulled on the belt, tightening it on the dog's throat, the poor defenseless animal gasped for breath and whined in pain and fear. Finally, with Mr. Bob's last violent pulling, tugging, and cursing, the poor dog, fell from the car's interior and lay on the dirt and gravel. Too physically and emotionally spent, the frightened animal could not move.

"Get up, you blasted, good-for-nothing mutt," Mr. Bob snarled as he drugged the defenseless dog on his side through the rough gravel. At once, Mr. Bob stopped, picked up a large, jagged rock, and drew his arm back, threatening to hit the dog. "Do you want me to bash your brains in? Then get up!"

Hearing vicious words and frightened whines, Daddy G walked outside onto the loading platform.

"Hello, Bob," Daddy G greeted, taking control of a volatile atmosphere in a firm yet loving way.

"'lo," snarled Bob. "Know anyone who wants a worthless dog?"

"Why, I thought Dog was your best friend, Bob?" asked Daddy G.

"His only friend," Katie whispered to the fairies, Serenity and Hope.

"He's more blasted trouble and money than he's worth. Now the vet tells me he has heartworms and needs an expensive treatment. I can't afford no expensive treatment, and I wouldn't pay it anyway," growled Bob. "Just let the blasted dog die."

Compassion and Courage fluttered down, trying to give comfort to the frightened animal.

"I'm sorry to hear that, Bob," said a sympathetic Daddy G, *"I might know someone who needs a good companion and will be happy to give Dog a good home. Wait just a minute. I'll get the information for you."*

Daddy G disappeared inside the Warehouse, leaving a furious Mr. Bob, a cowering Dog, and a shocked Katie to suffer in agonizing silence.

Finally, with Katie, Compassion, and Courage close by, Dog lay down at Mr. Bob's feet and looked at his angry owner with begging eyes. Tan eyebrows that crowned Dog's sad, dark-brown eyes moved alternately up and down as Dog looked up at Mr. Bob. First, his right eyebrow went up, and his left eyebrow went down. Then it changed, his left eyebrow going up and his right eyebrow going down. This up and down movement just intensified the sad longing in Dog's eyes. He was a lovable, obedient dog and only wanted love in return. It was painfully evident, though, that he was not to receive love from Mr. Bob.

Katie looked at Dog's compassionate, trusting eyes and said to the fairy, Hematite, "Mr. Bob does not deserve anyone or any other animal as loving and kind as Dog." With those words, Katie reached down to pet Dog.

"Leave him be," Mr. Bob growled.

Immediately, Hematite and Courage flew to Katie's side, ready to defend their friend.

Katie withdrew her hand, then, with great resolve, decided to ignore Mr. Bob, and she continued to pet Dog. For her act of kindness, Dog rewarded Katie with a soft doggy tongue kiss on her hand.

"Are you 'deef'? I said leave him be," snapped Mr. Bob as he jerked the belt around Dog's now bruised throat. Dog coughed and whimpered in pain and surprise.

Serenity and Compassion hovered above Dog, showering him with their energy from watermelon tourmaline and fire opal gemstones.

Fortunately, Daddy G came out at that moment carrying a white box and a piece of paper torn hurriedly from a yellow legal pad. "*Bob, this is the address of Mrs. Carrie Rheinheart. She is a dear lady who just last year lost her husband of 65 years and needs a companion.*"

Mr. Bob reached out, huffing at the prospect of being anyone's companion. "I don't need no companion, and I don't want to be nobody's companion," snorted Mr. Bob with angry black eyes.

Daddy G laughed, "*Oh, no, Bob. Mrs. Rhineheart needs Dog for a companion.*"

Katie and the fairies, now hiding safely behind Daddy G, giggled.

At that, Mr. Bob almost looked startled and offended.

"I'd appreciate it if you would pay her a visit and let her meet Dog," continued Daddy G in a kind yet compelling voice.

Mr. Bob snatched the paper out of Daddy G's hand and turned to leave, again pulling the poor animal by the cruel belt wrapped tighter around Dog's neck.

"By the way, Bob, I just got in a new 'toy.' Perhaps you would like to see it."

Daddy G opened the rectangular box He carried and took out the shiny, reflective object.

"A mirror?" Mr. Bob snorted indignantly. "What do I want with a mirror?"

"Just try it," encouraged Daddy G. "*Who knows, you might need a good mirror when you shave, and it might be entertaining.*"

Daddy G made a joke, thought Katie. It was apparent to her that Mr. Bob had not shaved or brushed his hair or put on deodorant for several days.

Reluctantly, Mr. Bob took the mirror and checked it out, turning it over in his hand. "Just a regular ole mirror," he grunted. "Regular on one side and magnified on the other. What's so special about that?"

"Try both sides," prodded Daddy G.

Mr. Bob looked at his reflection on the regular side of the mirror. As he expected, he saw a self-assured, no-nonsense professional who considered himself an excellent manager. Didn't his employees love him? Didn't his colleagues admire his talents? "Sure, that's me," he affirmed. "I had plenty of years of experience as a successful business manager," retorted a self-satisfied Mr. Bob. "I had to be smart and firm; else, some employees would steal me blind. I was a good worker, then the company up and fired me." Mr. Bob snarled again. With that, he intuitively flipped the mirror over to the magnifying side. The expression on his face immediately changed from self-assured and firm to grossly old and with a look of shock.

Curiosity, Hematite, and Wisdom fluttered around Mr. Bob's head to see his image, then abruptly withdrew in surprise.

"What is this? A joke? Here," Mr. Bob said tersely as he thrust the mirror back to Daddy G., "I don't want your lying mirror."

With a slightly changed attitude, Mr. Bob turned, and with drooping shoulders, gave the belt around Dog's neck a gentler tug.

"Come on, Dog; we have a job to do."

Katie stood staring a moment and then asked Daddy G, "What did he see, Daddy G?"

"*Well, Katie, on one side of the mirror, he saw what he thinks of himself. On the magnified side, he saw himself as others see him.*"

"He didn't look so happy when he looked on the other side," quipped Katie.

Katie was in awe at the effect Daddy G had on Mr. Bob. Daddy G was not angry or stern. Instead, He was gentle and loving, yet firm. Katie noticed that Mr. Bob could not resist Daddy G's request.

In the two weeks that passed, Katie never saw Mr. Bob at the Warehouse, though she did see him driving his Malibu up and down the highway. What was most interesting was that, frequently, Katie and Daddy G saw Mr. Bob hauling lumber, carpet, or other building materials. Since he did not have a truck, the lumber or carpet stuck out the back window of his car, and each time, he was driving in the direction of Mrs. Rheinheart's house.

One afternoon, Katie and the fairies could not contain their giggles, and she ran to tell Daddy G the latest news. "Daddy G," Katie giggled, "now Mr. Bob has a trailer attached to his Malibu, and he has a refrigerator and a dishwasher in it."

"Well, Mr. Bob is getting to know Mrs. Rhineheart quite well," beamed Daddy G.

A week later, Katie stood with Daddy G, speechless, when they saw Mr. Bob walking down the sidewalk to the grocery store. Mrs. Rheinheart held his arm as they walked. She looked lovely, yet delicate, in her favorite blue jersey dress with white polka dots and lace collar. As she walked with Mr. Bob, she twirled her white ruffled parasol, and Mr. Bob grinned a funny grin like a little boy caught with his hand in the cookie jar. He tipped his hat as he and Mrs. Rhineheart greeted other people shopping on Main Street. An even bigger surprise was Dog! Dog appeared to be smiling! He seemed to prance with his head held high, showing off his new blue and red leash held gently in Mr. Bob's free hand.

"What made him change, Daddy G?" Katie asked.

"Mr. Bob found a purpose in life," answered a very satisfied Daddy G.

That strange yet funny behavior Mr. Bob exhibited lasted for the rest of his life. He finally found something, or someone, that could make him happy, and he took good care of Mrs. Rhineheart.

Watching from a distance, two of Mrs. Rhineheart's friends commented as that dear lady walked arm-in-arm with Mr. Bob, "Don't Carrie's house look right nice?" Ms. Carson said.

"My. Yes," said Ms. Daniels. "That Mr. Bob is taking such good care of her. And did you ever before see such beautiful roses as those in her garden?"

"Mr. Bob made her that garden," added Mrs. Carson. "It's like God sent him, especially to her."

Mr. Bob repaired and painted Mrs. Rhineheart's house and replaced all her old and failing appliances. Although he had never in his life done it before, he prepared the soil and planted a lovely rose garden outside her bedroom window. The garden bloomed with yellow roses, double whites, and tiny pink tea roses.

Each morning, Mr. Bob cut roses for Mrs. Rhineheart's afternoon tea. Later, the new friends, and Dog, enjoyed each other's company, sitting in matching rocking chairs on the front porch. They sat and talked and rocked. Many times, Mrs. Rhineheart reached out to give Mr. Bob's arm a tender pat and told him how much she appreciated his help and friendship, and then she reached down and scratched Dog's ears.

When it was time for Mrs. Rhineheart's nap, Mr. Bob washed clothes, dusted furniture, and mopped floors until her little house shined and a sweet fragrance of potpourri wafted through the open windows.

With Mrs. Rhineheart's passing three years later, the town's people watched with suspicion, afraid that Mr. Bob would revert to his old ways. Yet, to everyone's surprise, that never happened. At her funeral, Mr. Bob graciously and lovingly received everyone's condolences, and he was pleased to accept the many dinner invitations.

When it came to closing Mrs. Rhineheart's estate, Mr. Bob took considerable thought and care into whom he would gift her cherished knick-knacks. "Ms. Polly," Mr. Bob said, holding out a neatly wrapped gift. "I know Mrs. Rhineheart would want you to have this."

"Why, thank you, Mr. Bob," said Ms. Polly unwrapping the gift. "Oh. My!" Ms. Polly exclaimed. "It is one of her Hummels. The very one I admired so often. Thank you, Mr. Bob."

With tender care, Mr. Bob wrapped each cherished treasure with tissue paper or cotton before placing them into shoe boxes or sometimes an empty oatmeal box. Unsuspecting friends and acquaintances were much surprised and honored to receive vintage Hummels, Precious Moments, or Lenox figurines. Watching Mr. Bob gift Mrs. Rhineheart's treasures touched the whole community.

He and Dog remained in Mrs. Rhineheart's house and took their usual walks she once enjoyed with them. The neighbors looked forward to seeing the two friends, Mr. Bob and Dog, taking their routine stroll. Six months later, however, Ms. Kendrick greeted Mr. Bob.

"Good morning, Mr. Bob," greeted Ms. Kendrick. "My, you look nice this morning. Why, where's Dog? He's usually with you on your walks."

Mr. Bob choked back his tears. "Dog died last night. He was a good friend. He came to lie down with me and licked my hand, and then he was gone."

"I am so sorry, Mr. Bob. Is there anything we can do for you?"

"No, thank you, Ms. Kendrick. You are so kind," replied Mr. Bob.

"Well then, please come to dinner tonight," Ms. Kendrick invited.

Three weeks later, Ms. Kendrick again saw Mr. Bob on his daily walk to the grocery store. "Good morning, Mr. Bob."

Mr. Bob removed his hat and returned the greeting, "Good morning, Ms. Kendrick."

"Well," Ms. Kendrick said with a twinkle in her eyes, "who is this?"

With a broad grin, Mr. Bob squatted down and petted his golden retriever puppy, "This is Sweetums."

"My she is a beauty. How old is Sweetums?"

"She's still just a puppy, and she's chewing up everything. We're on our way to the grocery store to get a big chewy bone. Good day, Ms. Kendrick," Mr. Bob said, tipping his hat again. "Oh, by the way, you served a delicious dinner, and I certainly enjoyed your company," Mr. Bob complimented Ms. Kendrick.

"Do come again. How about Saturday night?" said Ms. Kendrick.

"I would like that, Ms. Kendrick. Thank you," said a gracious Mr. Bob. "Ms. Kendrick?" Mr. Bob started then cleared his throat. "Ms. Kendrick, may I walk you to church Sunday morning?"

Ms. Kendrick blushed and said, "Well, Mr. Bob, that would be lovely. Thank you."

Mr. Bob also became a faithful volunteer at the Warehouse, ready to help anyone in need.

"Hi, there, Daddy G," Mr. Bob greeted Daddy G in somewhat of a hurry. Sweetum's little legs could not make it up the loading dock steps quickly, so Mr. Bob picked her up in his arms, fluffed her ears, and kissed her on the head. "Do you have any plumbing equipment?"

"Well, hello there, Bob. I believe I do. Come on in and take a look."

There were more boxes to open than Mr. Bob imagined; however, the two friends finally found just what Mr. Bob needed. "Here it is! Ms. Jamison has a leak in her kitchen sink, and this will do the trick," reported Mr. Bob.

"Then, it's yours. You're doing a fine job, Bob. Hello, Sweetums."

The puppy barked a hello.

Mr. Bob carried Sweetums down the steps and put her in the puppy car seat next to him. Hurrying out of the parking lot to Ms. Jamison's rescue, the wheels of Mr. Bob's car kicked up a cloud of dust and limestone rocks.

For years to come, Mr. Bob used his gift of giving to help others.

Chapter 7

Ms. Mamie

> May the words of my mouth and the meditation of my heart be pleasing in your sight, O LORD, my Rock, and my Redeemer.
>
> – Psalm 19:14

Mamie Harden, Ms. Mamie, as everyone in Graceton knew her, lived a full life during her 73 years. However, one would be hard-pressed to call hers a full and happy life. It was just full, full of stuff.

Ms. Mamie was married for 52 years to Harold S. Harden, the town banker, and together they had two children, Sam and Caroline. Their children were the best dressed, best-mannered children in town. They also had the best toys, best books, best roller skates, and the best bikes.

Ms. Mamie was a member of the Graceton Garden Club and the PTA, although she never attended. She was past president of the Graceton Women's Club and was eager to relinquish the position yet continued to boast of the prestige. She still attended the Women's Club meetings, for it was a great way to catch up on town news.

When her children, Sam and Caroline, were in middle school, she was a chaperone for Sam's varsity basketball team and Caroline's school drama club. She would have chaperoned more often, but by the time she got around to signing up, there was no room for one more chaperone.

"I'm sorry, Ms. Harden," the teacher said. "Maybe next year."

Ms. Mamie, though embarrassed at the rejection, made excuses for herself, saying she was much too busy, and boasted of her other passions. She was an accomplished pianist and proud of it. She performed at the Graceton civic center every spring over the last five years and at various school functions. She often boasted of performing at Carnegie Hall, a boast never confirmed.

When she played at the Graceton civic center, she remembered walking onto the stage in long graceful strides. Her designer was right. "My dear," gushed her designer, "you simply must have the periwinkle chiffon gown. The fabric is simply delicious. Look how it flows about your ankles. And the matching sequined pumps are just divine. Periwinkle is certainly your perfect color. However, my dear, the emerald green taffeta suits you equally as well."

In addition, Ms. Mamie considered herself an accomplished homemaker. Well, a home organizer, anyway. "Mr. Harden," began Ms. Mamie as she sat on the footstool in front of her husband, "You know, dear, I am a very busy woman with my piano concerts and civic organizations. I simply do not have time to do housework. I want to hire a housekeeper."

"Very well," said Mr. Harden, always eager to dodge an argument.

"And I need a cook, and, oh, yes, a gardener. How can I possibly play the Steinway at Carnegie Hall with dirty fingernails?"

"Yes, dear," Mr. Harden agreed.

Indeed, she was a busy woman and a busybody, and she made sure everyone knew it.

Unfortunately, her children knew it all too well, and they eventually became resigned to the fact that Mother was just too busy for them. Ms. Mamie missed more school plays and ballgames than she ever attended. What could people expect? She was a great concert pianist and a busy hostess.

Today, however, Ms. Mamie was alone and lonely. Mr. Harden had died two years ago, and the Graceton civic center had not booked her in seven seasons now. Her children had grown up and moved away, living their own busy lives with spouses and children. They never called. Ms. Mamie consoled herself by saying she still had her garden club, and although she knew nothing about gardening, she just enjoyed visiting and gossiping. She attended the women's club from time to time, especially when there might be fresh gossip to hear and share. She used to attend the biggest church in Graceton. However, they stopped asking her to play the piano. So why go? She switched to a smaller church, hoping they would appreciate her talent. Soon, they, too, stopped asking her to play.

On this day, August third, she was very distraught. It was her birthday, and no one had called. No one had sent a card. Her children had forgotten, and her grandchildren had not phoned since they learned to drive. There was only one thing to do. Ms. Mamie dressed in her most becoming summer dress, white heels, pearl necklace, and earrings, and walked over to the Warehouse to unload on Daddy G.

Looking through the windows from their perches in the rafters, Katie and the fairies saw Ms. Mamie coming. "There's Ms. Mamie," Katie sighed to the fairies. "I don't like her much. She is a gossip and not very pleasant."

As soon as Ms. Mamie entered the big wooden door, she began. "Did you see that old Mrs. Rheinheart walking down the street this morning arm in arm with Mr. Bob? How shameful. Why Mr. Bob must be 30 years her junior," Ms. Mamie said with a feigned gasp. "And what a spectacle he made, tipping his hat like a proud peacock."

Daddy G replied, trying to defuse the conversation, "*Yes, Mr. Bob is certainly happier now that he helps Mrs. Rheinheart fix up her house. It's like he now has a purpose. And Mrs. Rheinheart needed a companion after her husband died. Dog is the perfect companion for her.*"

The fairy, Wisdom, hid her giggles behind dainty hands. Grace snickered, then caught herself and blushed.

Although shaken, Ms. Mamie continued, "Well, have you heard about that young woman, that single mother, with all those children? I would guess that her husband up and left her for another woman."

Again, Daddy G explained the actual situation to Ms. Mamie with kind yet convicting words.

"Well, yes, her husband up and left her, as you say. He was working at the local feed store when a grain elevator malfunctioned. Sadly, the entire contents of feed corn buried him. It was tragic. They were so devoted to each other, and he was proud of his children."

"Well, that may be, but…" began Ms. Mamie.

Katie's eyes popped, and she giggled when Daddy G cut off Ms. Mamie in the middle of her next sentence.

"*By the way, Ms. Mamie. Happy birthday. It is today, isn't it?*"

"Why, yes, it is. And you know, no one call…"

Before Ms. Mamie could finish that sentence, Daddy G broke in again. "*I have a birthday gift for you, Ms. Mamie.*" He reached behind one of the many boxes and pulled out a tiny box with a periwinkle-colored bow on it. "*This is just what you need,*" soothed Daddy G.

"Just what I need?" With shining eyes, Ms. Mamie eagerly opened the tiny box imagining diamonds, emeralds, or pearls inside, then she stopped. "What is this? A necklace?"

"*It is a special pendant for a special lady,*" explained Daddy G.

Curiosity nearly fell from the rafter on which she sat. Serenity and reliable Agate did fall and tumbled through the air giggling.

Incredulous, Ms. Mamie looked at the pendant. She secretly thought it was the ugliest necklace she had ever seen. The chain looked expensive enough, but the pendant…well, it reminded her of a plastic, valentine-shaped toy, filled with heart-shaped candy. She shook the heart, and it sounded like it had candy hearts in it. Thankfully, it was not overly big, though it was big enough. She held up the ugly red heart on the lovely chain and inspected the clasp. Ugh! It looked like a skinny black spider with long, thin black legs!

"*Why would Daddy G think I would like this*?" she asked herself.

"*I hope you will wear it, Ms. Mamie. It suits you, and I think you will learn to like it,*" said a sincere Daddy G.

"Why, th-th-thank you, Daddy G," Ms. Mamie stammered. "Of course I will wear it. Just for you," she lied. "Will you help me put it on?" Ms. Mamie turned to let Daddy G fasten the heart pendant around her neck with the ugly black spider clasp. Then Daddy G held a mirror for her to see how the necklace lay on her neck.

Ms. Mamie frowned at her reflection in the mirror, then tried to cover up her disappointment. "My. It's very red, isn't it?"

An offended Passion shrieked, "*What's wrong with red? I like red.*"

"*Yes, and it looks stunning on you, dear,*" Compassion said, trying to soothe Passion's hurt feelings. "*I think Ms. Mamie means that her necklace is not real. Your beautiful red rhodolite gemstones are real.*"

"Oh. Then why did God give them to her?" inquired Passion.

Ms. Mamie left The Warehouse, not feeling much better than when she arrived. However, Ms. Mamie was glad Daddy G had remembered her birthday, even if this were not what she would have hoped for in the way of a gift. She much would have preferred diamonds, emeralds, or pearls instead of this ugly plastic necklace.

On her way home, Ms. Mamie passed Mrs. Rheinheart and Mr. Bob going into the hardware store. Ms. Rheinheart looked frail yet radiant, and Mr. Bob seemed happy to be attentive to her needs and wishes. He was even pleased to have Dog. *How ridiculous Mrs. Rheinheart looks holding on to Mr. Bob's arm as if he was her beau, Ms.* Mamie thought to herself with disdain in her eyes.

No sooner had that thought entered her mind than something pricked her neck. “Ouch!”

“Oh, I see,” giggled Passion. “*God is so wise.”*

Ms. Mamie swatted at whatever it was that was pricking her neck. “Ouch!” This time, her hand struck the pendant clasp. The legs of the spider-shaped fastener dug into her neck, causing her to wince at the shock. “Stupid necklace,” she fumed.

Two weeks later, at the garden club meeting, Ms. Mamie was all set to enjoy a great exchange of gossip. However, each time Ms. Mamie shared a tidbit of second-hand news or whenever she inclined her ear to hear someone else share half-truths, the spider legs pricked her neck.

“Ouch!” Ms. Mamie yelped, disgusted.

“What’s wrong, Mamie?” asked one of the ladies.

“Oh, nothing to worry about,” replied Ms. Mamie. “Just a touch of…of arthritis or something.”

“Ms. Mamie, you should watch your words,” Wisdom whispered as an aside to Passion.

The spider clasp pricked Ms. Mamie’s neck many times during the next month. Tempted, she wanted to jerk the necklace from her neck to eliminate the pain. However, she had promised Daddy G that she would wear it, and there was just something compelling about that ugly heart-shaped necklace.

The next month’s garden club meeting proved to be a prickly one. Relieved to have the meeting over, Ms. Mamie walked her usual route home past the grocery, around the corner, and up to the elementary school. Just in front of the elementary school, little ones making their way to family cars or school buses forced Ms. Mamie to slow her pace. As Ms.

Mamie stood and watched pensively at the joyful youngsters, a young woman, a stranger, approached Ms. Mamie. She thought she knew all the teachers at the school, yet she failed to recognize this young woman. *Where have I seen her before?* Ms. Mamie thought to herself with squinting eyes.

"Good afternoon, Ms. Mamie."

"Good afternoon. Do I know you?" Ms. Mamie asked suspiciously.

Prick.

"Ouch."

Passion giggled.

"Oh, forgive me, Ms. Mamie. I am Elizabeth Smith, the secretary here at Graceton Elementary School."

"So very nice to meet you, Miss Smith. Good day," said Ms. Mamie as she started to walk away, not wanting to waste any more of her time.

Prick.

"Ouch."

Passion giggled again.

"Ms. Mamie, if you have a moment, I'd like to ask a huge favor of you. The first graders have a performance this Friday at 3:00, and I wonder if you could come and play the piano for us?"

She wants me to play the piano! Ms. Mamie thought to herself with a thrill. *Of course, she would play the piano for the performance Friday at 3:00.* Ms. Mamie smiled and patted Miss Smith on the arm. "I would love to play for the children. I will be there at 2:00, my dear."

Miss Smith gave her a little hug and thanked her before wishing Ms. Mamie a good day.

After taking several steps toward her home, Ms. Mamie looked back at Miss Smith with a smile and thought to herself, *What a nice young woman. I wonder what perfume she is wearing.*

Then it happened. That ugly, red heart pendant *jingled!* It sounded like a tiny bell. Moreover, it felt like a pleasant little vibration next to her heart.

"Oh!" exclaimed Ms. Mamie. That little jingle was a surprise. She liked it. She wanted more.

Both Passion and Wisdom gasped with delight and again thought how wise God was.

Over time, Ms. Mamie became acutely aware of the pricks and jingles. She most definitely did not like the pricks and wished they would stop, though she very much liked the jingles. With curiosity, Ms. Mamie began keeping a diary to note the circumstances of each prick and each jingle. With the revelation from her diary, she became more aware of her choice of conversations. The kinder, sweeter her words, the more frequent were the pleasant little vibration next to her heart. Then she remembered Daddy G and humbly said, "Thank You, Daddy G, for such a wonderful birthday surprise."

Jingle, jingle.

Daddy G gave Ms. Mamie the gift of compassion and kind words.

Chapter 8

Mica

> Let us then approach God's throne of grace with confidence so that we may receive mercy and find grace to help us in our time of need.
>
> – Hebrews 4:16

Courage and Passion watched in fear and anger as three young teenage boys gave Mica an unjust beating.

"Hit him again, Joe! Knock his head off!"

Whack!

Umph, gurgle, umph.

"Your turn, Roger. Take a whack at that stupid girlie face!"

Thud!

Gurgle, yowl, umph.

"He's all yours, Christopher. Knock his teeth out! He don't know how to use them, anyways!"

Whack!

Umph, yowl, gurgle.

The big doors of the Warehouse glided open, and Daddy G stood in the open door with His hands on his hips, looking like the jolly green giant. "What's the trouble out here?"

"Hit him again, Joe! Look at him crying."

Gurgle, umph, yowl.

"Stop!" shouted Daddy G with his commanding voice.

The fighting immediately stopped, and three red-faced boys looked up at Daddy G, surprised and a little embarrassed.

"What's the trouble out here? Joe! What's going on? This behavior is not like you, Roger. Christopher! I am ashamed of you. I am ashamed of all of you. Mica, come inside the Warehouse, please," Daddy G commanded. "*You boys go home. I will discuss this with your fathers later.*"

The three offending boys slinked away like a pack of submissive dogs with their tails between their legs.

The Warehouse door slammed shut.

Mica Burnett was the cutest little cuddly baby fifteen years ago. That's not to say he was no longer cuddly, but what teenager wants his friends to see him cuddling with his parents, even if he wants to?

Unfortunately, as Mica grew, the pallet in his mouth did not grow at the same rate as the rest of his body. So, when Mica started talking, he had the cutest little baby talk. However, now, a young teenager of fifteen, Mica did not consider his impediment cute. He was so embarrassed that he spoke softly and chose his words carefully. He did not want people to know that he could not say the "r" sound. Despite his speech impediment, Mica was brilliant. He had a keen sense of humor, had a commanding grasp of multiple interests, and made excellent grades in school. However, Mica was hesitant to interact with the other kids. All through school, Mica's speech caused him great emotional pain so that by the time he was ten years old, he had developed a severe stutter.

"Mica, my sweet, I wish I could make it better for you," his mother often said. However, there was nothing she could do. Although she took him to speech therapy and anatomy specialists, her compassion would not make Mica feel better. Finally, Mrs. Burnett made a doctor's appointment with Doctor Rich.

Wisdom, Curiosity, and Compassion accompanied Mrs. Burnett and Mica to the doctor's office, and the fairies were surprised by the visit.

"Good afternoon, Dr. Rich," Mrs. Burnett greeted the doctor.

"Good aftewnoon, Mws. Bawnett," Dr. Rich returned the greeting.

Curiosity gasped in disbelief as Dr. Rich spoke.

Mica was shocked. "H-h-he t-t-talks l-l-like m-m-me, Mom," said Mica.

Dr. Rich examined Mica's mouth, tongue, palate, and lips. Finally, Dr. Rich turned to Mica and said in all seriousness, "Well, Mica, it seems to me that you and I have something in common besides being good looking," said Dr. Rich with a wink. "Neithaw of us can pwonounce the 'aw' sound." Then, Dr. Rich turned to Mica's mother, "Ms. Bawnett, this speech impediment is called whoticism, and is quite common, and tweetable," encouraged Dr. Rich. "As for Mica's stuttewing, that, too, is tweetable. He need not live with this all his life. I choose to weveawt back to my whoticism to make my patients feel mowe comfotable."

"Oh," whispered Wisdom, "he is a wise doctor."

"That's wonderful news, Dr. Rich," exclaimed Mrs. Barnett, a bit more relaxed.

At this point, Dr. Rich began speaking with clear 'r' sounds. "Let's start Mica in speech therapy and see how he progresses," prescribed Dr. Rich. "Please understand, Mrs. Barnett, even with therapy, Mica may revert to his rhotacism, especially when he feels stressed."

Several days later, was when Daddy G rescued Mica from a beating, and it was the beginning of Mica's extraordinary life.

"Well, now, Mica, what was that altercation all about?" asked an omniscient Daddy G.

"It was not faiew," Mica replied in his quiet, timid manner, wiping the blood from his mouth.

"Is there anything I can help with?" asked an always kind Daddy G.

"I-I-I w-w-want t-to t-talk like evewy b-b-body e-e-else," cried Mica.

"Oh, Mica, My boy, I can think of a couple of or hundreds of people you would not want to talk like," quipped Daddy G.

"B-b-but e-e-evwy one m-m-makes f-f-fun of me," lamented Mica.

"That's because they have not taken the time to get to know you, and they don't understand rhotacism," Daddy G tried to comfort the teenager. *"If they took the time to know you, they would see how witty and intelligent you are."*

"W-w-what can I d-d-do, D-d-daddy G?" asked Mica. "I-I-I w-w-want to b-b-be able t-t-to t-t-talk t--to p-people. D-do Y-You h-have a j-j-job f-f-fow m-m-me at the W-w-wawehouse?"

"I think we can find you a job at the Warehouse, Mica. However, first, you need to learn to communicate with

people," said Daddy G to a disappointed Mica. "*Just a minute. I think I have just what you need."*

As Daddy G disappeared to the back of the Warehouse, Wisdom winked at Curiosity knowingly. "God the Son always has the right gift. Let's see what he has for Mica," whispered Wisdom.

When Daddy G returned, He was carrying a box wrapped in brown paper and tied with twine. "*Here, Mica. This is for you, and I think it will help answer all your questions,"* said a loving Daddy G as He handed the package to Mica. "*Let Me know what you think of it."*

"T-t-thank Y-Y-You, D-D-Daddy G."

When Mica got home, he opened the package and studied it. Because he was curious and intelligent, he kept an open mind. The package contained a book entitled *American Sign Language,* with illustrations. Mica spent weeks learning the ASL alphabet and signs, and when he felt he was ready, Mica returned to the Warehouse to show Daddy G what he had learned.

"Good morning, Daddy G. Thank You for the wonderful gift," Mica signed to Daddy G.

Curiosity gasped, and Wisdom smiled with pride at Mica's accomplishment.

"You are most welcome, Mica," Daddy G signed back. "*Do you think you are ready for a job?"*

"I would like to try," Mica signed.

"Okay, then. Here is a name and address for someone who needs a visit and encouragement," signed Daddy G, and handed the piece of paper to Mica.

Mica looked at the paper, and his mouth dropped open, and his eyes bugged. "I cannot do this," Mica signed.

"Oh, yes, you can. You converse better than most people. Give it a try," encouraged Daddy G.

"But she's a girl!" Mica signed with great feeling.

"So?" Daddy G signed back. *"She needs a friend just as much as you do."*

"Okay. But what will I talk about?" Mica signed.

"Introduce yourself with ASL. She's a girl, right? She will probably do all the talking," quipped Daddy G.

Mica and Daddy G shared a laugh before Mica turned to hurry to his assignment. All the way to the address, he kept rehearsing what he might say. When he rang the bell, Mrs. Allen answered the door.

Courage fluttered about Mica and showered the young teenager with energy from the many emeralds hidden among the burgundy of her silk organza gown.

"G-g-good a-a-aftewnoon, Maws. A-A-Allen. M-m-may I s-s-speak with T-T-Tammy?" Mica painfully stuttered.

Taken aback, Mrs. Allen demanded, "What do you want with Tammy?"

"M-m-my n-n-name is M-M-Mica B-B-Bawnett. D-D-Daddy G s-s-sent m-m-me."

"Oh, Daddy G sent you? Well, come in, Mica. I will get Tammy. Can I get you some lemonade?" offered Mrs. Allen.

"N-n-no, t-t-thank you, M-M-Ma'am," replied Mica, and he sat on the sofa as if he had a broom handle in his back. He tried to remember all the ASL he had learned, and anxious thoughts entered his head. What if she signs words I don't know? Mica thought. He did not have long to worry about it, though.

When Mrs. Allen returned to the living room, she chirped, "Mica, this is Tammy."

Dumbfounded, Mica could not even stutter. She's beautiful, he thought to himself. Her blonde hair matched his own, and her blue eyes twinkled. Finally, he composed himself enough to start the conversation. "Hello, Tammy. I'm Mica Barnett," Mica signed.

Tammy's eyes glowed brighter, and she immediately started signing. "Hi, Mica. I'm so happy to know you. Won't you have a seat? I am deaf. I can speak a little, but I sound funny."

"I sound funny, too. I stutter, and I have rhotacism. I cannot pronounce the 'r' sound."

"Jus wike me!" Tammy squealed. That's all it took.

Hope and Wisdom sat with the young teenagers and filled the room with their yellow topaz and yellow-green peridot lights. The topaz lights encouraged the young people to live life according to their own values. The yellow-green peridot gave them balance and inspired their eloquence and creativity.

Mica and Tammy signed and laughed for hours. They found they had many more things in common. They liked the same movies, the same actors and actresses, the same books, and some of the same people, although not many, and they enjoyed long walks on pretty days.

At 5:30, Mr. Allen came home from work and shouted his greeting as he walked through the door. "Honey, I'm home. Where's my baby Tammy?" Mr. Allen shouted.

Mica immediately stood and wiped his hands on his jeans when Mr. Allen entered the living room.

As if sensing a crisis, Wisdom and Courage fluttered about Mica, showering him with energy from their peridot and emerald gemstones.

"Well, who do we have here?" Mr. Allen shouted so that Tammy could hear.

"H-h-hewo, Mistaw. A-A-Allen. M-m-my name is Mica B-B-Bawnett. I-I-I came t-t-to v-v-visit T-T-Tammy," Mica said.

"If this is a joke, it's a poor one," shouted Mr. Allen in shock.

Mrs. Allen rushed into the room to intervene, "Sweetheart, Daddy G asked Mica to come visit Tammy. Mica knows ASL, and he and Tammy have been having a wonderful afternoon together."

"Does he know Tammy is deaf?" asked Mr. Allen.

"Y-Yes, I-I d- do, Mistaw A-A-Allen. D-Daddy G s-s-said T-Tammy m-might n-need a f-friend as m-m-much a-as I d-do," stammered a nervous Mica.

"Forgive me, Mica," said Mr. Allen, extending his hand. "I'm sorry I jumped to a wrong conclusion. We have had some very unkind people come to the house and telephone since we moved to Graceton."

"Th-that's okay, Mistaw A-A-Allen. I-I-I h-hope I c-can c-come a-again and t-t-talk with Tammy," asked Mica.

"Of course, you can come again," bubbled Mrs. Allen.

Mica and Tammy dated for two years, and they each felt blessed to have such a wonderful friend. They went for walks, stopped for ice cream, attended Sunday School and church services together, and signed to each other for hours.

When it was prom time, Mica asked Tammy to go with him to the prom.

"I can't, Mica," Tammy signed. "I can't dance. Besides, I can't hear the music."

Feigning displeasure, Mica signed, "That's no excuse."

Grace, adorned in lavender silk organza and amethysts, came to Tammy's rescue, showering her with positive energy.

"We can practice here at your house. Then, when we go to the prom, we can both dance a little," Mica added.

Finally, the big day came, and Mica took great pains bathing and shaving. Earlier in the week, he rented a white coat, tux, and shirt, and as he was dressing, he remembered the flowers. "Mom! Wheaw awa the flowaws?" shouted a nervous Mica.

"They are in the refrigerator, dear. I'll have them ready for you at the front door," assured Mrs. Barnett.

He must not forget the flowers, he reminded himself. Tammy had requested white carnations with a touch of blue.

When he looked in the mirror, he combed his hair back. No. That was not right. Then he combed his hair to the left. Still not right, so he combed his hair back in a pompadour. No! No! That looks stupid. So, he combed his hair to the right again and gave it a pat.

Hope and Joy fluttered around Mica and hovered about the mirror. Their yellow gemstones cast a mellow light about Mica.

When he gave himself a final check in the mirror, he was pleased and surprised. He could not believe the reflection in the mirror was his own, and he hoped Tammy would be pleased, too.

Just as Mica thought he was ready, his dad walked in. "Here, Mica," his dad said tersely. "You will need to smell good."

"B-b-but D-dad, th-his is your b-best f-f-f-fragrance," argued Mica.

"Yes, it is, and you are my best son," Mr. Barnett said before turning to hurriedly leave the room.

As promised, Mrs. Barnett had the white corsage waiting at the front door when Mica bolted down the stairs.

"Don't you look nice, sweetheart," crooned Mica's mother. "And don't you smell good. Dad, doesn't your son look wonderful?"

Mr. Barnett put down his newspaper and walked over to Mica. "Mighty handsome, my boy. Here are the car keys and a little extra money. Take good care of your lady." Then to Mica's surprise, his dad grabbed him in a great bear hug with an almost gentle pat on his back. "Before you go, Mica, I'd like to say a prayer for you and Tammy," said Mr. Barnett with an almost teary voice.

Mr. Barnet placed his arm over his son's shoulders and held his wife's hand. "Lord God Our Father, on this special night, take care of our son and Miss Tammy. Protect them from danger and harm and bring them back home safely. In Jesus' name. Amen."

It took Mica and his dad a long second to speak, hoping the tears in their eyes would not betray their masculine voices. Finally, Mica hugged his dad and said, "Th-thank you, D-Dad. I-I l-love you."

Mica arrived at Tammy's home at 6:30 carrying the box containing a beautiful white carnation corsage with dark blue tulle and ribbon. When Mr. Allen open the door, his eyes widened in surprise, and he extended his hand to Mica.

"H-h-hel-l-lo, Mistaw A-A-Allen," Mica greeted Tammy's father.

"Hello, Mica," Mr. Allen replied, shaking Mica's hand. "Looking sharp there, Mica," Mr. Allen complimented the nervous young man. "Tammy and her mother are upstairs putting on the finishing touches. They should be down soon." Both Mr. Allen and Mica were visibly nervous as they sat in the living room together.

Fortunately, Mrs. Allen came down the stairs and greeted Mica. "Good evening, Mica. My, don't you look handsome."

Mica stood and returned her greeting, "G-g-good e-e-evening, Ms. A-A-Allen."

"Mother, do you have something for Mica?" asked Mr. Allen.

"Oh my, yes," replied Mrs. Allen and turned on a dime. "Tammy will be down presently, Mica. Won't you have a seat?"

When Mrs. Allen returned, she had a white carnation boutonnière with dark blue ribbon, which she pinned to Mica's white lapel and gave it a gentle pat.

Mica took a seat and wrung his hands.

Courage sat on the back of the sofa with her silk organza gown draping gracefully about Mica's shoulders. The emeralds peeping through the organza twinkled, bathing him with soothing energy.

Despite Courage's soothing emeralds, Mica cleared his throat and shifted his weight on the sofa. He wrung his hands again and wiped them on his trousers before he caught himself. Thankfully, Mica did not have long to sit, for he heard the intriguing sound of rustling taffeta. When he stood to face the stairs, he gasped when he saw a dream.

Tammy was so beautiful. Her naturally blonde hair swooped up in French curls then cascaded through a waterfall of white silk flowers. She looked enchanting in her royal blue gown. The Chantilly lace Sabrina neckline, partially lined in matching royal blue taffeta, revealed a hint of her delicate neck and shoulders. A string of cultured pearls lay in tantalizing elegance just below her throat. Billowing waves of soft tulle ruffled over royal blue taffeta and floated in the breeze as she walked down the stairs.

For a moment, neither Mr. Allen nor Mica could speak.

"Wow!" was all Mica could say. That was all he needed to say.

"Wow," her father echoed. "You look beautiful, Tammy."

"Mica, don't you have something for Tammy?" asked Mr. Allen with a smile.

"Y-y-yes, siw, I do," said Mica and handed the box to Tammy.

With shining eyes, Tammy accepted the box and peeped inside. "Oh, Mica. Dey aw butiful, and jes the ri shad of blue." Then she turned and asked her mother to tie the corsage on her wrist.

"Tammy, you look beautiful," said Mica with a sign.

After photos and the customary curfew warnings, Tammy kissed her mother and dad. Mica shook Mr. Allen's hand and gave Mrs. Allen a peck on her cheek. Then he gave Tammy his arm.

"That's our baby," Mrs. Allen sniffed into her hankie.

"That's our beautiful young woman," beamed Mr. Allen.

The fairies Joy, Hope, and Courage fluttered about the gymnasium. Potted ficus trees decorated with little white lights offered perfect vantage points for the fairies to keep their eyes on the young couple.

The gym on prom night at Graceton High School was a gala event, decorated with thousands of balloons, tiny white lights, potted ficus trees, and white carnations. The featured band was known as The Captains, a band with a beat. They played a lot of rock-n-roll and loud.

Courage watched as Mica and Tammy arrived at the prom and saw Tammy hesitate.

"What's wrong?" Mica signed.

"I'm afraid," Tammy signed in return.

"You don't have to be afraid," signed Mica. "You are much too beautiful; just follow me."

"Mica has a surprise for Tammy," Joy whispered to Hope. "*I saw him practicing in his room yesterday."*

Hope giggled and left her spot on the tree to dance around Tammy.

As the evening progressed, both Mica and Tammy became more comfortable. Mica's friends came over to meet Tammy, and she was the center of attention, and Mica was so proud.

When the Captains started playing "Rock Around the Clock," Mica dragged Tammy to the dance floor. At first, she protested, not knowing what to do, and just stood there.

"Here it comes!" giggled Joy.

Courage and Hope watched wide-eyed.

Then, to Tammy's surprise, kneeling on one knee, still staring up at her with enchanted eyes, Mica started drumming the song's rock and roll beat on the gym floor with his hands. Tammy's eyes gleamed. She could feel the beat of the music on the floor and her smile widened! Soon she started moving her hips, and Mica continued drumming the floor, her taffeta rustled, and the ruffles billowed. Then the most remarkable thing happened. All the boys followed Mica's lead. The young men knelt on one knee in front of their dates and drummed the floor as their ladies danced around them. It was a dynamic night, one that Mica and Tammy would not soon forget.

As Tammy snuggled into her bed that night, she wrote in her diary of her dark blue taffeta dress, white carnations, Mica drumming the floor, taffeta rustling, ruffles billowing, and a sweet goodnight kiss.

The fairies, too, felt enchanted, though tired, and ready to sleep.

In the following weeks, at church, Mica really began to grow and mature physically, mentally, emotionally, and spiritually. He spent hours with Tammy reading the Bible and practicing signing Scripture, and Tammy signed hymns. Mica's favorite hymn was "He Touched Me," by the Gaither quartet.

Shackled by a heavy burden
'Neath a load of guilt and shame
Then the Hand of Jesus touched me
And now I am no longer the same.
He touched me, oh, He touched me.
And oh the joy that floods my soul!
Something happened, and now I know
He touched me, and made me whole.

"Mica," Tammy signed, "Why don't we start an ASL class?"

"Are you sure you want to do that?" Mica replied in sign.

"Yes, I'm sure," Tammy signed with conviction.

"Then, let's talk to the pastor," Mica signed.

On Wednesday night, Pastor Rob invited the young couple to meet him at his office. "Now, what is this, you two want to do?" asked Pastor Rob.

Tammy looked at Mica and nodded her head, asking him to begin.

"P-P-Pastow W-Wob, Tammy and I would like to stawt a heawing impaiwed ministwy duwing Sunday School and Chuwch sewvices," Mica said.

"Mica, did you just hear what you said?" asked Pastor Rob. "When you started your sentence, you stuttered my name, then your stuttering stopped."

"Weally?" a surprised Mica replied and signed for Tammy, who responded with shining eyes.

"Yes, indeed," replied Pastor Rob. "Now, back to your request. I think that is an excellent idea, and I can't think of two people I would rather have in this ministry. Would you like to start by signing for church services Sunday?"

Mica signed again for Tammy, and she thrilled.

"We wouwd wub to, Pastow Wob," Tammy said.

After their meeting, Mica and Tammy shook Pastor Rob's hand and hurried out.

"Come on, Tammy," Mica signed. "There's someone I want you to meet. Someone I need to thank." Hand in hand, Mica, and Tammy ran to the Warehouse.

To Mica, Daddy G gave the gift of self-confidence and communication—not to mention Tammy, his wonderful friend.

Chapter 9

Mr. Kelly

> Give, and it shall be given unto you; good measure, pressed down, and shaken together, and running over.
>
> – Luke 6:38

The fairies fluttered and hovered about Katie, flinging their gemstone energies about their little friend as she played in the Warehouse and asked a barrage of questions.

"What's in this room, Daddy G?" asked Katie. Daddy G did not have time to answer before Katie asked more questions. "Where do you keep the important gifts? What do the colors mean? Why is this blue gift over here? It should be over there."

Katie was busy with her investigation of gift boxes in every nook and cranny of the Warehouse, stopping just long enough to track a fuzzy caterpillar as it inched up a supporting post. Katie tried to follow the caterpillar to find his nest. However, the gentle insect was much too wise to lead a curious six-year-old to his safe nest.

"Daddy G, did you see the fuzzy caterpillar?" Katie asked. Where are you, Mr. Caterpillar? Where are you?" Katie sang in her happy, little girl voice.

Fortunately for the caterpillar, the familiar sound of a particular car horn interrupted Katie's concentration. It was not just any horn. This horn sounded like a bellowing bull, and only Mr. Kelly's car horn sounded like that.

"It's Mr. Kelly," squealed Katie. "Daddy G, Mr. Kelly is here!"

Katie jumped up, leaving her caterpillar behind, and ran to greet Mr. Kelly, who was just emerging from his red four-by-four pickup truck. Katie leaped into his arms and smothered him with kisses.

Mr. Kelly was tall, yet not so tall that he could not bend down to listen to her stories. He was big, but not so big that he was afraid to swoop Katie up in his large hands, roughened from years of herding cattle, mending fences, and ranch maintenance.

"Don't squeeze me so tight, Mr. Kelly," giggled Katie. "You make my tummy make funny noises."

Mr. Kelly laughed and gently put Katie down.

"Mr. Kelly, you would be a good grandpa. Grandpas are s'posed to laugh a lot," said Katie with a serious look. "Mr. Kelly, did you bring any cows with you?" Katie asked, hoping.

"No, Miss Katie, nobody wanted to come into town today. The cows wanted to stay in the field and eat grass. Besides, the bull would be lonely if the cows came to town," Mr. Kelly said with a wink.

Matthew Kelly was proud to be a fourth-generation cattleman in the Graceton area. He boasted that he was from good stock. His great-grandparents, Jake and Marsha Kelly, were some of the first pioneers who had helped build the Warehouse.

"Hematite," Faith asked, *"do you remember Jake and Marsha? They were Fred and Susan Bates' first friends and neighbors and Bible study partners. They were also God's friends and helped build God's Warehouse."*

"Yes, I remember," replied Hematite, *"and I like Matthew Kelly. He never boasts about how much land he owns, or how big his house is, or how much money he has."*

Daddy G knew Matthew Kelly well. The giant cattleman did not care about land, money, and big houses. His passion was for helping people, and he was good at it.

"Mr. Kelly, can I wear your cowboy hat?" Katie begged.

"Miss Katie, my dirty ol' hat's so big that I'm afraid you would disappear under it," Mr. Kelly teased.

"Can I feel your belt buckle, Mr. Kelly? How big is your belt buckle? I bet it's twelve inches big. Aw. Mr. Kelly, you need some new blue jeans. Yours are all torn and dirty," Katie said with genuine sympathy.

"Maybe you can find me some new jeans at the dime-store, Katie," Mr. Kelly continued to tease.

In addition to his "cowboy hat," Mr. Kelly wore a three-inch-wide brown belt to hold up the mass of blue jeans around his thick middle. His jeans were large at the waistline and smaller at the hips. To look at him, he just looked like a poor farmer with dirty jeans, dirty hands, and manure caked boots. No one would guess that he was the wealthiest man in Graceton.

"Oh, Mr. Kelly, your belt is so pretty. I like all those little flowers on it," Katie said, tracing the flowers with her dainty, bug-juice-stained finger. "What kind of flowers are they? Look! That flower has three leaves," Katie noticed aloud as she stroked the beautiful leather belt.

"I think those are dogwood flowers, Katie. Do you know the story of the dogwood blossom?"

Katie shook her head so that her tangled hair flew around her head.

Curiosity, Joy, and Hope had been fluttering about, watching Katie, and listening to her myriad of questions. Now their attention turned to Mr. Kelly's story.

Mr. Kelly took from his pocket a card with the story of the dogwood tree printed on it. "According to an old poem," Mr. Kelly began, "Jesus was crucified on the dogwood tree. The white dogwood flower symbolizes purity and innocence. Each of the four white petals has a bit of red coloring on its tip. These red spots represent Jesus's hands and feet bleeding from the cruel spikes."

"Oh," Katie purred in amazement. "I know about Jesus. Nana told me about Him." Katie paused for a second then began again, "What does that mean?" Katie asked, pointing to the enormous oval belt buckle. "Why does a buckle need horns?" Katie thought the sparkling silver buckle with an enormous steer's head protruding from the front was grand. "Mr. Kelly, your buckle is the beautifulest, wonderfulest, most awesomest buckle I ever seen. Nobody has a belt buckle like yours, Mr. Kelly," Katie said as she admired the shiny buckle. "Mr. Kelly," Katie started to ask a serious question.

"Yes, Katie?"

"Mr. Kelly, what does p-o-m-p-u-s mean?"

"Well, I don't rightly know, Katie. Does that word bother you?" asked Mr. Kelly.

"No," Katie answered with uncertainty. "I just heard some people say that word when they saw you in the dime-store."

Mr. Kelly chuckled and let it pass.

"I don't know what that word means, but I told those people that you are big and wonderful and kind, and I love you," said Katie with determination. Just as quickly as her determination burned, Katie chirped, "What do you have in your pocket, Mr. Kelly?"

Curiosity squealed, "*I want to see, too. Mr. Kelly always has wonderful things in his pockets.*"

Joy and Hope jostled with Curiosity for a position to see what grand thing the gentle giant offered.

"Well, let's see," teased Mr. Kelly as he shoved his big hand into the pocket of his blue jeans. It looked like a tight fit.

Katie knew Mr. Kelly always carried surprises in his pockets for his adult friends' boys and girls. Sometimes it was a penny flattened by the train, sometimes a stick of gum or a Tootsie Roll. Sometimes, for the boys, it was a horseshoe nail with a wonderful story. That was the best treasure.

Katie waited with anticipation shifting her weight from one foot to the other as Mr. Kelly felt his shirt pocket and the fairies flitted about in an excited frenzy.

"Well, sir, there's nothing there," Mr. Kelly teased again.

"Try the other pocket!" Katie squealed, clapping her hands and jumping up and down.

Mr. Kelly stuck his other hand deep into his jeans pocket, another tight fit, and pulled his hand out little by little. He continued to tease Katie with a gentle fist so that she had to pry his big fingers open.

Inside his gentle-giant hand was a teeny tiny bottle with a teeny tiny cork stopper.

"What is it, Mr. Kelly?" Katie whispered in awe.

"Well, sir, it's whatever you want it to be," replied a wise Mr. Kelly.

"Oh-h!" thrilled Katie.

Before handing the treasure to Katie, Mr. Kelly took off the tiny cork stopper, held the little vessel up to his lips, and blew. The teeny tiny bottle emitted a high-pitch, "Twee-e-e-et!"

"Let me try!" squealed Katie reaching for the surprise. "Let me try!"

She held the teeny tiny bottle to her little lips and blew just like Mr. Kelly. Well, almost just like him. Her breath did not return the same sound as Mr. Kelly's. Instead, it was a dull swoosh of air.

"Try again," instructed Mr. Kelly, "this time, hold the edge of the bottle just under your tight bottom lip. Then blow gently."

Katie did as Mr. Kelly instructed. "Twe-e-e-t!" Katie's eyes widened, and she giggled with glee.

"I want one," cried Curiosity with a feigned pout. Joy and Hope shoved Curiosity, and all the fairies giggled and tumbled.

"Oh, thank you, Mr. Kelly!" Katie squealed and grabbed Mr. Kelly around his leg and gave him a big "Katie hug."

At just that moment, Daddy G came out of the Warehouse onto the loading platform. Each of the two sliding platform doors was seven feet wide, seven feet tall, and three inches thick. Despite their size and weight, the two doors glided effortlessly on the original metal assembly on the top and bottom tracks and matching wheels. Each wheel measured five inches in diameter and was no small matter.

"Daddy G! Look what Mr. Kelly gave me!" chirped Katie.

"That's mighty nice. What is it?" asked a knowing Daddy G.

“Mr. Kelly said it can be whatever I want it to be. Today it’s a whistle. See,” said Katie. She blew five short tweets from the teeny tiny bottle. “See, I can toot my name: K-A-T-I-E,” Katie demonstrated.

“That’s just a fine gift,” Daddy G agreed. *“Now I will always know where you are when you blow your whistle,”* Daddy G said, winking at Mr. Kelly, then continued. *“Good afternoon, Mr. Kelly,”* Daddy G greeted the giant cattleman.

“Afternoon, Daddy G,” Mr. Kelly returned the greeting. “Can I have a word with you?”

“Certainly. Come on in out of the heat,” Daddy G invited.

Everyone in Graceton knew that Daddy G always had time to listen to anyone—anytime.

Daddy G and Mr. Kelly stepped out of the hot sun and into the surprisingly cool Warehouse, and Daddy G glided the heavy doors closed.

Katie, having little interest in grown-up stuff, skipped down the sidewalk, tooting on her new whistle: “K-A-T-I-E. K-A-T-I-E.”

Chapter 10

Ms. Savannah

Her children arise up, and call her blessed.
– Proverbs 31:28

Faith and Grace stayed at the Warehouse, anticipating Mr. Kelly's benevolence. This time, Passion came along with them.

"What's on your mind, Matthew?" asked Daddy G.

"Well sir, there's a young woman in town," Mr. Kelly began in a hesitant manner. "Ya know the one I mean. She is in terrible need, having just lost her husband, Ned, in that horrible farming accident. He didn't leave her nothin', except that broken-down trailer, four kids, and a dog."

"Yes, I know her and of her situation," Daddy G replied. *"What can we do for her?"* Daddy G continued, testing Mr. Kelly.

Mr. Kelly halted and stumbled through his next words. "Well, Sir, Ms. Savannah needs a car. She needs a big car that will hold her four young'uns and that dog. A refrigerator would be nice, one that keeps food cold and safe. Then, she needs food to put in that refrigerator. She could use a new kitchen stove, too. She has to cook on one burner, and the oven don't work."

"That's a lot of needing," agreed Daddy G then paused. *"While we're talking about needing, let's think about her trailer, too."*

"There's only one problem," hesitated Mr. Kelly. "She's awful proud and don't want no charity."

"I think I have just what she needs," Daddy G offered quietly. *"Let's go back here and have a look."*

As Mr. Kelly followed Daddy G along a cleared path, he breathed in the mysterious sensations from all the boxes. Each box had a fragrance of its own, and all together, they smelled like, well, like "glory."

Faith and Grace fluttered ahead of Mr. Kelly. They, too, breathed in this familiar sensation. This was the fragrance they always experienced in the garden when God the Father and God the Son were there.

"How's this one?" Daddy G asked, interrupting Mr. Kelly from his deep sense of tranquility. *"Grab that crowbar, and let's have a look."*

Mr. Kelly pried the side off the wooden crate Daddy G pointed out. The loosened board fell with a thud on to Mr. Kelly's boot, and he was astonished when he saw the contents. "It's a brand-new refrigerator with a freezer on the bottom," exclaimed Mr. Kelly. With greater surprise, Mr. Kelly continued, "It has an ice maker and plenty of storage for ice cream, popsicles, hamburgers, chicken nuggets, and all kinds of frozen veggies for four hungry children." Mr. Kelly retrieved his worn notebook from his shirt pocket and started writing down figures.

Daddy G's eyes beamed. *"Over here is another item,"* Daddy G said as He pointed to a smaller box.

Faith started following Daddy G and Mr. Kelly, then realized Passion had disappeared. Remembering how Passion sometimes got herself into trouble, Faith fluttered around in a circle and asked Grace, *"Where is Passion?"*

"I don't know. She was just here with us a moment ago," replied Grace. *"Oh, there she comes, and she looks a little funny."*

"Where have you been, Missy?" Faith questioned Passion.

"Oh, I've been here and there, breathing, smelling and thinking," giggled Passion.

Faith understood how Passion felt. The peace and glory as they remembered if from the garden was hypnotic.

Picking up the crowbar, and with his cattleman's muscles bulging, Mr. Kelly again deftly wielded the heavy tool to open the wooden box. "Well my stars!" exclaimed Mr. Kelly. "It's a new kitchen stove. Looky there, it has four gas burners and an oven large enough to cook a Thanksgiving turkey dinner with all the trimmings." Mr. Kelly's expression was that of astonishment. "Wonderful. Amazing!" Mr. Kelly exclaimed. Mr. Kelly licked the lead tip of his pencil and wrote down another figure. "Thank You, Daddy G," Mr. Kelly said, shaking Daddy G's hand. "This is more than I expected. Thank You," Mr. Kelly whispered, still shaking Daddy G's hand.

Mr. Kelly was a little ashamed of his reaction. Although he knew Daddy G well, why should Mr. Kelly be amazed at what

Daddy G offered? Daddy G understood. He knew that His friends were often in awe at what He did for them.

"There is one other item back here," directed Daddy G.

Mr. Kelly followed Daddy G and continued to breathe in the essence of "peace and glory."

This time Daddy G led him back to the tiny office and pointed to the bulletin board.

Mr. Kelly put on his reading glasses to read the notice. As he read, his astonishment grew bigger:

For sale at Great Sacrifice

Four-bedroom house located west on Carter Road. New roof, new carpet, new furnace, fully furnished, fenced yard. Perfect for a young family with a dog.

Call Jim

Mr. Kelly put away his reading glasses and wiped his face, giving his brain time to catch up to his surprise. "Who is Jim?" he asked Daddy G.

"You know Jim Hastings? He's your competition. He just moved to town from Dallas and bought that ranch on Carter Road, thinking he would raise cattle. Then he bought a fixer-upper sight-unseen, two miles down the road, thinking that his daughter, Beth, and her children would come live near him. He did not quite finish the remodel before Beth met a great guy in Dallas and married her *just last month. The young man is an electrician by trade and can provide a good living and a loving home for Beth and her children. So now, while Jim is happy for his daughter and her family, he's left with this*

house. Do you want to ask Ms. Savannah if she would like to move in?"

"Well Sir, all this is a great opportunity for her," agreed Mr. Kelly taking out his checkbook from his pocket. Then he paused. "How come I didn't know about that little house? I live on Carter Road," he asked into the air.

"There's only one catch," Daddy G began. *"Can you convince Ms. Savannah to come to the Warehouse on the pretense of cleaning and sweeping up?"* Daddy G asked Mr. Kelly. *"She can bring the little ones. That way we can show her the for-sale notice, and she will not think it charity."*

"I'll work on it for sure," responded a grateful Mr. Kelly.

"Matthew," Daddy G said with sincere caring in His voice, *"put away your checkbook."*

Two days later, on Monday morning, Mr. Kelly arrived at the Warehouse with the young mother and her four children.

As usual, he blew the "bellowing-bull" horn of his four-by-four pickup truck. The children squealed with delight and laughed and cried for more. Of course, Mr. Kelly blew his horn again.

As usual, Faith, Grace, and Passion were at the Warehouse playing hide-and-seek with Katie. When the friends heard Mr. Kelly's horn, they all jumped with joy.

Katie ran squealing to meet her giant friend, then stopped in her tracks, for Katie was not expecting to see a mother and four children. Katie scurried from box to box, hiding, and watching the visitors with interest. When her eyes lighted on a young red-head boy about her age, she paused.

The fairies also paused. Passion did not stop quickly enough and ran into Grace from behind.

"Be careful, Passion," warned Grace. *"You must not be too eager and obvious."*

So, Passion hid behind a big box just to watch.

As one of the big platform doors rolled open, Daddy G stepped outside and greeted his visitors. *"Good morning, Mr. Kelly."* Daddy G always called Matthew by his surname in front of children.

"'Morning, Daddy G," responded Mr. Kelly. "I think you know Ms. Savannah. I told her you have some work that needs doin'."

"Yes, I believe I do know Ms. Savannah," replied a kind Daddy G taking Ms. Savannah's hand. *"Good morning, Ms. Savannah. As a matter of fact, I do have some work to around the Warehouse, if you don't mind getting dirty."*

"I don't mind," whispered a tired and sad Ms. Savannah, "as long as I can keep the children with me. They work hard and are well behaved."

"Of course, they can stay. I can see from their restrained curiosity that they are smart and well mannered. I love little ones, so they are most welcome," replied Daddy G

Turning to Mr. Kelly, Daddy G said, *"Mr. Kelly, would you mind showing the children around while I speak with Ms. Savannah?"*

"Not at all," resounded Mr. Kelly, herding the children to the toy room, not unlike herding calves.

Of course, Faith, Grace, and Passion followed the children to the toy room, while Katie was still peeping out from behind her box.

After Daddy G showed her around, Ms. Savannah was eager to begin her work, and indeed it was dirty work: boxes needed to be moved, floors needed to be dusted, walls and windows needed a proper washing. However, Ms. Savannah was quite familiar with a mop and a broom, as were her children.

Funny thing, as soon as the work began, Mr. Kelly disappeared.

Greg, the oldest, yearning to be a teenager with a teenager's dreams, stood taller than his mother. He had young, well-trained muscles, and the thin beginnings of a red beard.

"Greg, sweetie, will you move them boxes so's I can sweep and mop?" asked his mother.

Grace watched Ms. Savannah and Greg as they worked together and admired their sweet relationship.

He moved boxes just as his mother asked. After an hour of working, sweat matted down his wavy auburn hair, and down his tanned face. Then, without his mother reminding him, he moved the boxes back to their original positions. All the time he moved the boxes, he was wondering what joys they held. However, he kept his mind on his work.

"Greg, where's yer sister, Maddie," asked his mother.

"She's over yonder, dusting," Greg answered.

"Would you go find her for me, please?"

"Yes, ma'am."

Faith was fluttering around ten-year-old Maddie who had commandeered a lemon-scented dusting spray. As she dusted, Maddie hummed a new song she had learned in her Sunday School class. "Deep and wide. Deep and wide. There's a Fountain flowing deep and wide." Faith enjoyed the child's simple faith.

"Maddie, Ma needs you," Greg said with a voice that changed octaves without warning. He spoke softly so people would not notice his changing voice.

William, Willie for short, a red-haired eight-year-old, found a large black metal dustpan in a cupboard. "Here's a dustpan, Ma," he said, lugging the pan to his mother.

"Why, thank you, Willie. Will you hold it down there so's I can sweep this dirt into it?"

"Yes, ma'am."

"Who taught you to hold a dustpan, Willie?" his mother winked. "You got that angle just right. Thank you, dear."

After Willie collected a pile of debris, he emptied the dustpan into a small metal trash can Daddy G provided. Working together, Willie and his mother made a fantastic team. Ms. Savannah complimented Willie to help him take pride in his work. In fact, she was careful to promote self-confidence in all her children.

"Ma, Greg said you needed me," said Maddie.

"Yes, dear. I can smell the wonderful lemony fragrance from the dusting spray you are usin' over yonder. When you git a chance, would you dust them boxes I jest swept under?" asked Ms. Savannah of her daughter.

"Yes, ma'am," replied Maddie as she returned to her first job.

In addition to dustpan duties, Willie was the self-appointed protector of his younger sister, Sarri. Willie kept an eagle eye on her and rushed to lend her a hand whenever he saw her struggling with a task. "Can I help you with that, Sarri?" asked Willie.

"No, thank you," replied six-year-old Sarri as she worried with a trash can. "I think I can do it."

"Okay," said Willie before he went back to the dustpan. "Just call me if you need help."

"Okay," Sarri sang out in her sweet, little-girl voice.

Sarri, the "baby," age six, going on twenty-one, worked just as hard at her task as the older children did at theirs. She always tried to keep up with her brothers and sister and made giant-sized efforts.

After Willie emptied the small metal trash can of its debris, he called to Sarri. "Sarri, when you git a minute, here's another trash can."

Daddy G watched this gallant team work together and smiled. He was pleased with Ms. Savannah's diligence and her kindness as well as the way she trained her children.

Katie watched, too. She especially watched Willie. With Grace and Passion close by her side, Passion watched Katie and Willie hoping for a friendship to blossom.

"Daddy G," Katie said, leaning close to Daddy G and cupping her hand to whisper in his ear. "I think Willie is so nice, don't you?" Katie said, without moving her eyes from Willie.

Passion giggled with delight.

When it was lunch-time, Mr. Kelly returned, followed by a small band of reinforcements, led by Ms. Mamie. She and four other women from the church rushed in, taking over the sweeping and mopping from a tired Ms. Savannah.

"Now dear," Ms. Mamie said kindly, "You have done enough. You sit here on this crate and rest your weary bones. We're taking over."

Jingle jingle.

"Oh!"

"But, but…" Ms. Savannah protested.

"No buts, my dear. You and your children have done a splendid job. Now let us help," Ms. Mamie insisted. "Betty, do you mind sweeping?" Ms. Mamie asked her friend before flitting around, organizing her band of merry cleaning ladies. "Louise dear, will you and Margaret man the dustpan and empty trashcans? Don't overdo now. I will do the mopping."

In truth, Ms. Savannah was happy to take a break. It was 2:00, and she and her children had nothing to eat that morning. As if on cue, Daddy G and Mr. Kelly came through the door of the loading dock with a rolling cart filled with sandwiches wrapped in waxed paper. There was ham and cheese, peanut butter and jelly, pimento cheese, roast beef, fruit, cookies, hot coffee, orange juice, and chocolate milk.

"Here you go, crew," called Mr. Kelly. "Ms. Mamie and her ladies thought you might need a little lunch."

With Mr. Kelly's kind words, Ms. Savannah burst into tears.

Passion left her clandestine surveillance of Katie and Willie and flew over to Ms. Savannah. Faith and Grace, as always, were close by to lend any help necessary. Ms. Mamie and Ms. Louise hurried over to hold the young mother as she cried years of stored up tears. She cried tears of joy, tears of sorrow, tears of weary mind, heart, and body, and mostly tears of relief.

"That's alright, dear. You go ahead and cry. Let those tears wash away all your hurt and sorrow," Ms. Mamie said, holding Ms. Savannah close to her heart.

Ms. Mamie's ugly little red heart-shaped locket jingled again. It was a good feeling. It felt sweet.

Ms. Mamie continued to use her gift of compassion.

Besides her new home and furnishings, Daddy G gave to Ms. Savannah the gift of precious children, a spirit of humility, and finally, joy and peace.

Chapter 11

Katie's Crisis

> Train up a child in the way he should go: and when he is old, he will not depart from it.
>
> – Proverbs 22:6

Kevin cherished each moment he spent with Katie, hard knocks and all.

Even though she never called him "daddy," he was okay with that. He told himself he would have to earn that title. He was trying. He was trying hard.

Each year, Katie grew and matured as all little people do. She had many friends in first grade, both girls and boys. They went to each other's birthday parties. They played chase with no concept of what to do when one caught another. They just wiggled and giggled, looking confused until someone else yelled, "Not it. You're it." In short, they just had fun being kids.

However, her first love was Daddy G, the Warehouse, and Kevin, in that order. She still loved playing by herself in the Warehouse, imagining, smelling, and tasting the essence of all the gifts. And she always longed for a gift of her own, although she had no idea what that gift might be.

Joy and Curiosity went to school with Katie and enjoyed new friends and activities. Curiosity, especially, took delight in this new experience, for she knew this might very well be the last time Katie and her friends would be able to see and hear her and her sister fairies.

In second grade, Katie was happy to see Kevin come to visit her teacher at school or come to her rescue anytime, anywhere.

"KEVIN!" Katie yelled with joy when she saw Kevin at school. "Did my teacher call you?"

"No. Why?" Kevin asked.

"'Cause Belinda and I got into a fight, and we had to go to the principal's office," admitted Katie.

"What was your fight about?" inquired Kevin.

"Belinda said Billy was going to give her a ring. I said that was silly and that he was too young to give a girl a ring," Katie reported. "Belinda pushed me, and I pushed her back. I tore my shirt. See. I don't like Belinda anymore."

"Well, tomorrow you can be friends again," comforted Kevin.

As Katie entered the third grade, she was a good reader. She read everything she could and soon discovered she was able to have more and exciting mind adventures. Curiosity was always by Katie's side as she read and learned new things.

"Time to go to sleep, my Katie," Kevin said as he peeped in.

"Oh, Kevin! I just can't sleep now. I'm reading about China and the Great Wall. I want to have tea with the emperor and ride with Genghis-Khan."

Kevin gently took her book and kissed Katie good night.

"Well, I think the emperor and Genghis-Khan will wait for you. Good night, my sweet Katie."

Reluctantly, Katie and Curiosity snuggled under the blanket and were soon asleep, but the next night was the same thing.

“Oh, Kevin! I just can't go to sleep now. I'm going to climb Mount Everest in Tibet in a frigid blizzard.”

On another night, she would visit Peru and hack her way through the dense jungle, or she would swim the Amazon River and wrestle a green anaconda. When she read about traveling to England and visiting the queen, she asked Kevin, “What should I wear when I visit the queen?”

“Let's see. You could wear your green dress and black patent shoes.”

“I'd rather wear my jelly shoes. They are more comfortable for traveling,” Katie said with a serious face. “What do I say to the queen? What do I call her?”

“Well,” Kevin murmured, “remember your manners, Yes, ma'am and no ma'am. And balance your biscuit plate, and your teacup and saucer, like Nana taught you.”

“I'd rather wrestle an anaconda,” said Katie in typical Katie form.

With his goodnight kiss, Kevin always crooned, “Nighty night, sleep tight, don't let the bedbugs bite. I love you, my Katie.”

“I love you, too, Kevin,” replied a sleepy Katie as she smooched Kevin's cheek.

Safe and warm in her bed, she drifted off to sleep and dreamed of exciting adventures.

Whenever Katie came by the Warehouse to play and talk to Kevin and Daddy G, she danced around while she visited with the volunteers and visitors. She was so happy there.

“Daddy G, Katie still yearns for a job at the Warehouse,” Kevin noticed aloud.

“I still don't think she's ready for a job yet, Kevin,” advised Daddy G, then added, “*In the fullness of time,*” He said.

By the fourth grade, she still had many friends, though now she had two close friends: Belinda, of course, and Abagail.

"Kevin, can I invite Belinda and Abagail for a sleepover," begged Katie. "We'll be good and go to sleep," she promised.

"Me, too, Katie," begged Curiosity.

"If Curiosity is invited, I want to be invited, too," exclaimed Passion.

"If Passion goes, I go," announced Grace.

Kevin winced, for he knew better. He thought the girls giggled at nothing. Belinda looked at Katie, who looked at Abagail, and a giggling fit erupted. They seemed to have their own little inside jokes that no one else knew. Kevin thought it silly, yet secretly, he felt a little left out. Before, Katie always laughed and giggled with him. However, he knew this was part of Katie's growing up.

"Hi, Daddy G. Hi, Kevin," Katie sang as she visited the Warehouse with a friend. "This is my new best friend, Trisha. Isn't she pretty?"

"Hello, Trisha. My, Yes. You are very pretty, Trisha," agreed Kevin. Then he turned to Daddy G and whispered, "I wonder what happened to last week's new best friend?"

"It's just part of growing up in fourth grade. Just hold on, Kevin." Daddy G advised.

Daddy G was right. In the fifth grade, Belinda was once again the best friend.

"KEVIN! Guess what?" squealed Katie.

"I have no idea. What?" Kevin said, playing along.

"We're having a dance at school!" Katie said with great excitement and theatrics. "Can you believe it? A dance! Belinda and I are making our plans. We will be in my room," Katie yelled back to Kevin as the door slammed.

"Me, too, Katie," Curiosity begged again.

"I'm coming, too," yelled Passion. "Where's *Grace?"*

Kevin was a little taken aback.

The girls spent hours in Katie's bedroom, talking and giggling. The girls experimented with hair-styles and makeup. "How do I look?" Belinda asked, holding her hair piled on top of her head. "Do I look sexier with my hair up or down and over one eye?"

There were giggles and more giggles.

"I think I'm just going to wear a ponytail," said Katie as she swung her straight, black ponytail back and forth. "I think it looks sexy."

Belinda told Katie about the "sexy" blue dress Belinda's mother bought for her. So, of course, Katie wanted a "sexy" dress, too.

"Kevin, we're going to Belinda's house to see her sexy new party dress," Katie yelled as she slammed the back door.

Wisely, Nana called Belinda's mother on the phone and chatted about the scandalous, "sexy blue dress."

The next day, Nana and Katie went on a girls-only shopping date. When they returned, an alarmed Kevin asked, "What is a 'sexy' blue dress?"

Nana smiled and whispered, "It's a sleeveless organza dress with ruffles at the neck, and it's very blue. Katie's dress is very pink."

"Oh," breathed a relieved Kevin.

On the day of the party, Kevin waited at the foot of the stairs for Katie's presentation. When she appeared, he tried to hide his amusement, though not his pride.

Grace and Passion also waited at the foot of the stairs and sighed together upon seeing Katie.

Katie slowly descended the stairs, wearing her lovely pink organza dress with puff sleeves, little ruffles around the neck, and tiny pink roses buried in layers of organza. Adorning all this beauty, she was also wearing her favorite dirty, white jelly shoes.

Of course, he took several pictures of Katie and Nana. Then Nana took pictures of Katie and Kevin. Katie delighted in the attention. However, the mood suddenly changed when it was time to go to the party.

"What am I going to talk about? What if a boy asks me to dance? I don't know how to dance!" screeched a panicked Katie.

"Where is Courage?" gasped Grace. "*She is usually here at a time like this. Passion, go find Courage! I don't think I can do this by myself."*

"Sweetie, they are the same boys you see at school," consoled Kevin. "They are probably asking their dads the same thing. If a boy asks you to dance, be kind, and say yes. He will probably compliment you on your dress, so you say something nice about his shirt or tie or his aftershave lotion."

"Oh, Kevin! Boys don't shave!" protested Katie.

"No, they probably don't, but I bet his dad will spray a little fragrance on his son's neck," said Kevin with a sly grin.

That evening, when Kevin picked up Katie at the party, she got into the car with Passion, slammed the car door, and huffed in a pout.

"Bad party?" asked Kevin.

Katie huffed again. "He didn't say anything about my dress. In fact, he did not even talk to me all night. He stayed in a huddle with his silly friends grinning at all of us girls."

"I'm sorry, my Katie. He was probably shy and uncomfortable," consoled Kevin. "You must consider how he felt. He might be home now thinking that he messed up big time."

"I don't care! Who needs boys, anyway?" pouted Katie.

Sixth grade was a little more turbulent. Kevin received several phone calls from the school, telling him that Katie had made some unwise decisions, and he had to speak with her teacher.

"Hello, Mr. Wilkins?"

"Yes."

"This is Mrs. Campbell, Katie's teacher. I don't want to alarm you. However, I thought you should know. Katie has made some rather unwise decisions as far as her friends," said Mrs. Campbell. "Would you have time to come by the classroom for a parent-teacher discussion?"

"Yes, ma'am. When would be convenient for you?" said a concerned Kevin.

"Today at 4 p.m.?" offered Mrs. Campbell.

"I'll be there," said Kevin.

Kevin spent hours teaching Katie, advising her, comforting her, and worrying about her. Kevin knew that Katie was a good daughter, and as all sixth graders must do, Katie must "learn to discern."

"Learn to discern?" pouted Katie. "What does that mean?"

Passion was there with Katie, Grace was nowhere to be found, and fortunately, Faith was not far away.

Kevin took advantage of loving and teaching moments to tell Katie, "To discern means to decide if something or some situation is harmful to you. You must stop and look at a situation or action, recognize what is happening, what the consequences might be, and then evaluate if you want to continue in that direction," said Kevin. "Do you understand, my Katie?"

As was becoming the natural response, Katie huffed and went to her room, slamming the door.

Kevin sighed, "Oh, my Katie. Even though you don't like me right now, I love you very much."

The next day at the Warehouse, Kevin confessed his concerns.

"Daddy G, being a parent of a sixth-grader is more difficult than being the parent of a fifth-grader. Teaching Katie to make good decisions is difficult."

"Imagine, Kevin, how it must feel to Katie. All this is new to her, too, and she must be confused. When you add in peer pressure, you can understand her turmoil," Daddy G advised. "*Just as I understand your turmoil now, Kevin.*"

"I love Katie, and I want only what's best for her," admitted Kevin. "though at the same time, I don't like the feeling of her pushing me away. What do I do, Daddy G?"

"Just hold on, Kevin. 'This, too, shall pass.' Just hold on," Daddy G said with an understanding heart. "*Children are like butterflies, Kevin, as they grow, you must love them and hold them gently? If you hold them too tightly, you might crush their tender little wings or, in a child's case, their tender self-esteem."*

Kevin blocked that part out of his mind. He would never intentionally hurt his Katie, for he loved her too . He also realized that his holding on was as much for himself as it was for her.

The seventh grade was a continuation of the sixth grade, just with greater intensity, and the tension tore at Kevin's heart. He tried to teach Katie to be discerning, choose the right friends, the right actions, or the right words. "My Katie, are you having a hard time in school? Socially, I mean?" asked Kevin.

"No!" sulked Katie.

"I know being in seventh grade and growing into a lady can be difficult. I just want you to make good decisions about what friends you choose," said Kevin.

"I'm fine," Katie roared.

"And I want you to be fine, Katie. I want that more than anything. But lately, I am afraid for you. I can't be with you all the time, nor would it be wise. You need to set your boundaries. I love you, Katie," said Kevin before leaving the room.

More and more, Katie came to believe she no longer needed supervision. She felt she did not need to listen to Kevin. Katie thought he was old fashioned and looked foolish to her friends. She failed to realize that her words and actions were hurting Kevin and breaking his heart.

As difficult as it seemed and against his better judgment, Kevin loosened a portion of his paternal hold. He felt lost and helpless like he was losing a part of his life again.

"Daddy G, I love her so much. I hate that she is shutting me out," Kevin cried.

"Hold on, Kevin. Not too tightly, but hold on," counseled Daddy G.

Kevin knew that Daddy G had always been right as he was now. However, this was too hard for Kevin to bear. Was he losing his little Katie? Was he losing his little daughter with the long black hair with auburn highlights blowing freely like raven's wings? In his mind and heart, he went back to the first time he saw Katie. She was the most beautiful little girl, even with mud and worm juice covering her t-shirt. He remembered how she ran to Daddy G and fell into His arms, doodlebugs, roly-polies, worm juice and all, and Kevin cried.

Faith, Courage, and Grace stayed close to Kevin, trying to comfort and encourage him. Energy from Faith's sapphires helped Kevin have greater trust in Katie, confidence in his own decisions, and greater intelligence to deal with situations.

The energy from Courage's emeralds helped Kevin make choices based on love and compassion. Energy from Grace's amethysts provided Kevin relief from his stress.

The fairies knew the truth about their gemstones, for it was God the Father and God the Son who created the gemstones and endowed them with their energies, and the fairies did not take lightly these gifts God had given them. Instead, the fairies used these gifts in ways that would please God.

In Graceton, Memorial Day was a grand day of celebration. Even the fairies looked forward to the festivities, knowing there would be children and elderly citizens to entertain and with whom to play.

"Mr. Bob, will you hang the bunting a little higher?" asked Ms. Mamie.

"Yes, ma'am," replied an amiable Mr. Bob.

"Is the bandstand ready?"

"Yes, Ms. Mamie," smiled Ms. Kendrick.

"Do we have enough flags?"

"Yes, Ms. Mamie," shouted Mr. Kelly from across the lawn.

Red-white-and-blue bunting, ribbons, and flags festooned the bandstand in the park, the pavilion at the river, and even the bigger live oak trees just as they did every year. It was a fun time for the small town, complete with traditional fried chicken, biscuits and gravy, fried okra, and a great assortment of fresh vegetables from local gardens, cabbage coleslaw, and of course, Ms. Betty's famous chocolate cake. Though Ms. Betty was no longer with the Graceton community, her great-granddaughter carried on the tradition, and the citizens of Graceton still prized this rich and light chocolate cake.

This year, Katie was a junior in high school, and she was so excited today. It was as if she met William for the first time.

Passion and, of course, Grace flitted about Katie and Nana, sprinkling the grandmother and her precious granddaughter with red rhodonite and amethyst energies.

"Nana, zip me up, please. How does my hair look? My shoes! Where are my shoes?"

As always, Nana was a bastille of strength and patience. "You look beautiful, Katie. I'm sure Willie will think so, too. When is he picking you up?"

"At eleven o'clock," replied Katie. "Oh, I'll never be ready on time."

Serenity fluttered about the room spreading her watermelon tourmaline lights to find Katie's shoes.

"I like Willie," said Nana, remembering the first time Katie had met Willie and his mother, Ms. Savannah.

While Kevin agreed with Nana about Ms. Savannah, he did not know William well. William was a nice boy, yet Kevin knew little about him or his family.

"Daddy G," Kevin started. "Do you know William well? I see Ms. Savannah with her children at church; that's all I know of them."

"I don't think you need to worry, Kevin," Daddy G advised. *"Ms. Savannah is a believer and a wonderful mother. After her husband died in a tragic farm accident, Ms. Savannah made certain that her children remembered their father and loved God. You know, Ms. Savannah worked at the Warehouse for a time. She was an excellent worker. I am very pleased with her and her children."*

"Thank you, Daddy G," said Kevin. "I want to be certain that my Katie is protected. I taught her to be discerning and to be respectful. You and Nana gave her a solid background and good training, and I will always be thankful to You. I need her to trust me and my judgment."

"That's true, Kevin," interrupted Daddy G, "*now you need to trust her.*"

"Yes. I know I do, yet it's awfully hard to let go and trust your child's judgment," lamented Kevin.

Since William couldn't wait, he came by at ten o'clock that morning in his old, used 1960 Ford pickup truck. He stopped out in front of the house and walked up to the front door. "'Mornin', Mr. Wilkins," William greeted Kevin with an outstretched hand.

"Good morning, William," greeted Kevin. "Ready for the picnic and fried chicken today?"

"Yes, sir," replied a shy William.

"I think Katie is almost ready. Nana is helping her with her dress," said a nervous Kevin.

While Kevin and William were trying to carry on a smooth conversation, Katie came bounding down the stairs. She was wearing a lovely yellow sundress with a full skirt. Her white sandals revealed perfectly manicured feet with toenails painted in "Cotton Candy" pink.

"Isn't she beautiful?" William whispered.

"Yes, she is, William. She's my only child, you know," said Kevin.

"Yes, sir. I know, and she is my only love," William said, then blushed.

Indeed, Katie was beautiful. With the deep cut "v" neckline in the back, the yellow dress accentuated her black hair, porcelain skin, and youthful figure. Katie was a lovely young lady.

"Take good care of her, William. She is still young and vulnerable," Kevin said, then hated himself for saying it.

"KEVIN! I am not vulnerable. I never have been," argued Katie. Katie would never admit that she was vulnerable, though

Kevin knew she was, for Katie had grown up almost exclusively at the Warehouse among adults who protected and loved her. Kevin knew his Katie was naïve of the new emotions that might threaten to confuse and consume her.

"Hi, Will," Katie whispered with dreamy eyes then offered her hand.

"Hi, Katie. You look swell," crooned William.

Kevin flinched. Then he asked the children to sit down. Reluctantly, they did and looked most uncomfortable, especially William.

"You're going right to the picnic? Right?" asked Kevin.

Katie let out an exasperated sigh.

"Yes, sir," replied a nervous William.

"Where do you plan to go once you get to the park?" quizzed Kevin.

Another heavy sigh emitted from Katie.

"We will look for you and Mrs. Bates; then we will look for my mother. It sure would be nice if you and my mother were in the same location," said William, trying to sound grown-up.

"What route do you plan to take to the park?" Kevin asked. He tried to stop himself when panic gripped his heart. Why was it that every time she left the house, he went to pieces?

"KEVIN!" Katie shouted in embarrassment and humiliation. "Enough of the third degree!" With that, she ran outside and slammed the door.

William stood with Kevin for a nervous moment, then William extended his hand to Katie's father. "I will take good care of Katie, Mr. Wilkins," William assured Kevin.

As Kevin walked William to the door, the anxious father said a prayer. Just then, Nana came into the room from where she had been listening from the kitchen.

"When will I get used to Katie leaving the house without a trusted adult with her?" He shrunk away when he thought of how she would roll her eyes if she knew what he was thinking.

Faith, Courage, and Grace hovered close by with their energies to aid Kevin.

As Kevin contemplated Katie going out on a date, he remembered what Daddy G said, "It's all part of growing up. *Just hold on, Kevin. Hold on*, Kevin." That phrase swirled in his head until his mind burned. He hated those words, "*Hold on, Kevin.*" How could he hold on, not knowing if she was safe until she got to the picnic? How could he hold on, not knowing if and when…. He was so deathly frightened he could not finish the thought.

It was a tense ride to the picnic for Kevin and Nana. When they arrived, Kevin made a point to seek out Ms. Savannah. "Hello, Ms. Savannah. I'm Kevin Wilkins, Katie's father."

"Oh, hello, Mr. Wilkins."

"Please, call me Kevin."

"Very well, if you call me Savannah."

"Done," Kevin said. "Savannah, William mentioned it would be nice if we could all share the picnic together," Kevin stammered.

"That would be a wonderful idea. You're worried, too?" asked Ms. Savannah.

"Does it show all that much?" Kevin asked, and they both laughed at themselves.

While Kevin and Savannah were getting to know each other, Nana set out their picnic food on a quilt. She thought it best if she kept busy; that way, she would not think so much about the "what-ifs."

Finally, from a distance, Kevin heard William's old red pickup even before Kevin saw it. The old truck was all William could afford. Despite its spitting and choking and spewing, the red truck was reliable transportation. Katie was in the middle of the front seat next to him.

"Thank You, Lord," Kevin whispered.

"You're *welcome, Kevin*," replied God the Father. "*Did you forget that I am always here?*"

"Amen," agreed Savannah.

Nana said nothing, though secretly said her quiet prayer of thanks.

As the day continued, everyone at the picnic felt festive and began having fun. Relay games were a central part of the Memorial Day celebration, and even the older adults got involved in modified games. The mayor made the introduction of town council members, local politicians and honored all U.S. veterans of foreign and domestic wars. By far, Mr. Whitman was the oldest veteran, having served in the US Army during the Spanish American war.

"Daddy G," squealed Katie. "There's Lawrence!"

When the Mayor introduced the WWI veterans, Lawrence stood at attention to pay his respects. Lawrence's old wounds, now healed, gave him the strength of conviction and purpose in life, and he remained faithful to his earlier commitment to God.

Katie waved to Lawrence, who was still at attention, and he winked at her.

The microphone squealed, demanding the crowd's attention, and The Mayor announced, "Will all of the pastors and spiritual leaders of Graceton, please come forward."

Just like the volunteers at the Warehouse, Graceton spiritual leaders also enjoyed a kindred spirit. From the first day, Leo and

Susan Bates had met Jake and Marsha Kelly, Graceton had been a close community.

"Rabbi Rachman, Mica Barnett, and Tammy Allen, will you come forward please?" called the Mayor. When all assembled on the platform, the Mayor continued, "Rabbi Rachman, as our most senior spiritual leader, will you offer a blessing on our celebration and bless the food? Mica and Tammy, will you sign as Rabbi Rachman prays?"

The honorable rabbi cleared his aged throat and said, "Let us pray."

The crowd became quiet. With hats in hand and heads bowed, Graceton paid respect and gave thanks for another safe year and the bounty on the tables before them.

Rabbi Rachman prayed, and Mica and Tammy thrilled in their hearts as they signed for the hearing-impaired in the crowd. "Blessed are You, O Lord, our God, and King of this universe. Thank You for life and for this food. Bless this celebration and keep us safe."

Everyone said, "Amen." Then the feast began. It was like a frenzy of bees or a swarm of locusts. Not a crumb remained, and everyone settled back for a quick nap before the games began.

Among the high school students registering for the swimming competition was Greg and his brother, William. Both Greg and William were strong, experienced swimmers, and Katie, of course, was nearby to cheer for William.

When the game judge picked up the microphone, the loudspeaker squealed, disrupting the tranquility.

"Will all swimmers please take their marks?"

When the swimmers were at the mark, the judge called, "Ready. Set. Go." The gun fired, and the swimmers hit the river, creating a frenzy of splashing water. The first swimmer to swim out to a buoy and return to the starting line, the judge proclaimed the winner. In case of a tie, the swimmer exiting the water first, won the winner's title.

"Swim, William!" cheered Katie, jumping up and down and clapping her hands. "Swim fast."

William did swim fast, but he was not fast enough to catch up with his older brother, Greg. William came in second place. Katie, Kevin, Nana, and Savannah met the tired brothers in the shallow water with towels and hugs. Greg congratulated William with an older-brother bear hug and a pat on the back.

When the last swimmer came in, the crowd settled back down to naps, games of checkers, and arm wrestling, while the ladies talked.

William and Katie also settled down on a quilt with Kevin and Nana. William was winded as was Katie, though not for the same reason. She had almost lost her voice, cheering for William.

It was a wonderful day.

Suddenly, from a distance, came a faint call for help. The dreamy, content picnickers almost did not hear. The call came again. This time, Greg and William both heard the cry and sprang from their places of rest as startled picnickers searched for information.

What's wrong? Who is it? What happened?

"It's young Mrs. Tinny calling for help. Her baby, Tommy, was out in the river, and he was struggling," Katie said.

"Was he trying to emulate the older boys swimming to the buoy?" asked Nana.

Simultaneously, Greg and William dove into the water and sprinted out to the drowning tot. When Greg grasped Tommy, he tried to comfort the boy, "You're okay, Tommy. You're okay. Just relax," Greg said, trying to calm the little one. "We're almost to the shore."

As soon as Greg walked out of the water carrying Tommy, the crowd cheered. Mrs. Tinny raced over and scooped her baby into her arms. “Thank you, Greg. Oh, thank you,” she said over and over. Greg was the hero of the day.

However, the adulation died down as Katie looked around for Wil. “William?” called Katie. “Willie? Where is Willie? Greg, where is William?” Katie was becoming more desperate, and by now, Ms. Savannah and her other two youngest children were at the river's edge.

Ms. Savannah was wringing her hands and crying, “William, my Willie.”

The other ladies in the crowd tried to console Ms. Savannah. As she cried, her work-worn body shook with grief, and she wrung her apron.

Trying to console Katie, Belinda could no longer hold her desperate friend. Katie broke loose and ran into the river, and her lovely yellow sundress became saturated and clung to her youthful body. From the sandy beach, Belinda called, “Katie! No, Katie! Don't go into the water!”

Kevin realized what was happening and ran after his daughter, calling, “Katie! Katie! Don't go!” In unmeasurable fear, he, too, dove into the water and swam after his daughter.

Katie was not a strong swimmer like William. Nevertheless, she was desperate to find him. She swam in circles choking as she called, “William! William! Where are you, William?” Finally, Katie called out one last time before giving in to exhaustion.

Just before Kevin reached his daughter, he watched in horror as his sweet Katie sank into the tannin-browned water and disappeared. The whole scene was like a nightmare as Kevin dove under the water, again and again trying to find his Katie and William, coming up empty-handed each time.

Upon losing strength, Kevin wailed, “Daddy G! Have I lost my baby again?”

After what seemed like hours, picnickers gathered at the river's edge to assist Kevin out of the water. He was in shock and so exhausted that his rescuers had to carry him the final few gut-wrenching steps.

“Mr. Wilkins, I'm Deputy Sheriff, Sam Perry. An ambulance is on the way. Is there anything you can tell me about what happened?”

Kevin could not answer. He just stared.

The stunned, shocked crowd reluctantly began to disperse and return to their homes.

“Those of you who want to join us in prayer, the First Baptist church will be open. Rabbi Rachman, Father Brown, will you join us?” invited Pastor Rob. “Mica and Tammy, will you come, too?” As everyone joined in prayer, the church was overflowing with concerned citizens. Pastor Rob did not expect such a turnout.

Mr. Bob drove Kevin, Nana, and Ms. Savannah to Ms. Mamie's house.

Ms. Mamie tucked Nana and Ms. Savannah into the twin beds in the pink guest room. Mr. Bob stayed with Kevin in the blue room. The family doctor arrived to check out the two shocked parents and Nana and gave them sedatives.

Ms. Mamie rocked and prayed, and her red valentine locket jingled, but she did not notice.

As night engulfed Graceton, emergency services set up lights.

“James, set up two sets of lights. Put one here and the other fifty yards downriver,” the town maintenance supervisor called. “Make sure the divers have plenty of light.”

As a diver surfaced, Sheriff Putnam asked, “Anything?”

“Still, nothing. No bodies. No survivors,” responded the exhausted diver.

“It's been six hours. Might as well shut down,” lamented the Sheriff.

“Are you sure you want to come back to work, Kevin?” asked Daddy G.

“Yes. I need to occupy my mind,” replied Kevin. Throughout the long day, he tried to inventory gifts and remember all the gifts Daddy G gave and to whom. Kevin tried to remember all the lives Daddy G touched. That gave him little consolation, yet he continued to organize gifts and categorize them, though his mind would not cooperate. All this distraught dad thought about was his sweet Katie. In his mind, he remembered Katie running with hair blowing, Katie playing in and out of the Warehouse, Katie, yearning for her own gift. Then he tried to imagine what kind of gift she would have received. That was even less comfort. He missed her so. He not only missed her, he feared for his Katie. Truly, that was the worst.

Then the phone rang, and Kevin jumped.

“Mr. Wilkins,” the sheriff began. “We found the children.”

Kevin sat down, steeling himself. He could not breathe, feeling light-headed and sick to his stomach.

“We found the young man six miles downriver. He washed up on the riverbank. We can only guess that he developed a cramp and could not fight the current.”

“Katie?” whispered Kevin, dreading the answer.

"Apparently, she lost consciousness and floated a while. She came to rest in a wooded area at the river's bend. She is dehydrated and eaten up by mosquitoes and ants, but she is alive. She is in hospital room 203."

"Alive! My Katie is alive!" Kevin dropped the phone and rushed out with Nana at his side.

Little Katie found herself walking down a road as usual, yet this road did not lead to the Warehouse. Although the surrounding houses and trees looked familiar, the road looked strange. The warm dirt felt good between her toes, and the sun was warm on her six-year-old neck. Little beads of sweat moistened her long black hair, which by now was beginning to mat around her face.

Ahead of her, she saw two girls about her age, and Katie called out to them. "Hi, there! Hi! Wait for me. Can I play with you?"

The girls were each wearing yellow cotton dresses, no shoes, and carried brown paper bags crumpled at the top. When Katie caught up with the girls, she did not recognize them. "Hi. I'm Katie. What's your names? Where are you going? Can I go with you?"

The girls in the yellow cotton dresses said nothing. They just kept walking. Katie thought that was strange, although she continued walking with the girls.

A little farther down the road, there were four other people, also unfamiliar to Katie. The pebbles in the road became bigger, looser, more jagged as the road narrowed. The stones hurt Katie's feet and caused her to stumble. She fell. When Katie got up and brushed herself off, she noticed there were twenty more people. As the crowd grew, Katie realized she did not know any of them, which was very curious. Still, she followed the girls, who continued to glance back at her with steely eyes, and sinister giggles.

"Don't you want to be my friends?" asked Katie, becoming a little disturbed.

No answer.

It was getting late in the afternoon, and Katie felt her stomach squirm. Looking at the brown paper bags the girls in the yellow cotton dresses carried, Katie asked, "Do you have anything to eat?"

No answer. The girls remained in an ominous silence.

"I sure would like some chocolate milk and cookies," Katie announced.

No answer.

The crowd kept getting bigger and bigger, moving closer and closer, faster, and faster. By now, the growing crowd of people with dead eyes engulfed Katie, pushing her, shoving her in the direction the crowd was moving. Forward, always forward; never stopping; never a break to rest. Just forward.

"Where are we going?" cried a fearful Katie.

No answer. The girls pulled at Katie's arms. Now the girls had sinister grins that made Katie even more uncomfortable. They pulled still. It hurt her arms, and she tried to pull away.

"Ouch!" Katie cried. "Ouch! You're hurting me. Where are we going?" Katie's pleas became more frantic as she tried to twist free.

No answer, just sinister stares.

"This is not the way to the Warehouse. I do not want to play anymore," cried Katie. "I don't want to go that way!"

The people in the crowd seemed oblivious to her presence. Their unseeing eyes just stared ahead. They kept pushing, shoving, walking, shoving. The crowd restrained Katie from turning around to escape. Instead, they continued pushing, shoving, enslaving her in dizzying circles. The aimless crowd walked and pushed, moving her further away from home, their dead eyes never seeing her. She knew she did not want to go in that direction.

"No! No! No! I don't want to go that way!" Katie cried now in a panic. Still, the little girls in the yellow cotton dresses and sinister grins kept pulling at her and hurting her. "You're pulling my hair! It hurts!" shouted Katie. "You're ripping my dress. Don't pull my dress. You're hurting my arm. Let me go! Let me go!" Katie screamed, wrenching her arm as she tried to get free. "Let me go!" she pulled, unable to escape from their grasps. "Why don't you let me go?"

Again, no answer.

The now faceless crowd grew and pushed and shoved. Daylight began to turn to gray-purple dusk. "It's time for me to go home," cried a frightened and melancholy Katie. "Let me go home." Still, she was being pushed, pushed, not knowing where she was going. Pushed and disoriented, unaware how long or how far the feckless crowd moved her away from home.

"Please, let me go!" screamed Katie.

The little girls in the yellow cotton dresses and sinister grins paid no attention. Instead, they laughed nightmarish, scraping laughs.

Katie was beginning to tire. Her feet stumbled in the dirt and stones, yet no one helped her. The little girls just kept pulling, their grasp getting tighter and tighter. Katie felt more helpless. Her fear became more and more intense.

The strange crowd of faceless people grew and closed in. Even with so many bodies pressing around her, Katie felt a chill run through her blood. Growing fear and darkness strangled her. Suddenly, Katie thought she saw familiar silhouettes against a darkening sky. She squinted. But the crowd was relentless. The evil girl's countenance changed from sinister to callous, then to angry, and now they were menacing and gruesome. Katie felt their grasps continue to tighten on her arm and now around her neck, and her entire body. They continued to pull Katie farther, farther away from home. Away from the safety of her home so that the safety of the Warehouse dimmed.

"Let me go!" she screamed and then began to cry. "Let me go!" Still, the callous, forceful girls tightened their grasps.

At the moment she felt weakest, Katie looked up, exhausted and numb with fear. She thought she saw someone traveling in the opposite direction. Yes! Yes, it was a woman wearing a periwinkle-colored blouse. Katie thought she knew the woman. Yes, it was Ms. Mamie. "Ms. Mamie! Ms. Mamie, help me! Ms. Mamie!" The woman walked freely and sang as she walked. No one pushed her! No one pulled her against her will!

Again, Katie tried in vain to break free of the crowd. The gruesome-looking girls in the yellow cotton dresses still restrained her, dragging her along, bruising Katie's wrists with their grips.

In desperation, holding her arm out, Katie looked back toward the woman, reaching and pleading for help. She wanted to make her way to the woman moving in the opposite direction. In the direction of home. In the direction of the Warehouse where Daddy G and Kevin waited.

Although Katie struggled to call and plead, no sound came from her lips. "Please! Someone help me!" Katie screamed a silent scream. "Oh, why won't someone hear me?" Fear and panic tightened their hold on little Katie.

Two men soon joined the woman in the periwinkle blouse. Katie knew those men. These men did not have gruesome-looking faces like those of the pushing crowd. These men had sweet, happy faces. One man was small and had a happy, pleasant smile. He was walking a dog. His companion was a big man who had a big belly and wore a big cowboy hat. A large belt held up his enormous khaki pants, and the belt had a silver steer for a buckle. She knew these men. They were happy men. Instinctively, Katie cried out, "Help me! Help me, Mr. Kelly! Help me, Mr. Bob!" She tripped and fell and hit her head on a stone. Now, her head ached down to her toes, and she tasted dirt and something warm seeping into her mouth. Blood! Her blood!

"Is this a dream? If it's a dream, why can't I wake up? I must wake up!" Katie cried. "Wake up! Wake up!" Her mouth was filled with blood and dirt so that no matter how hard she tried, no scream came from her mouth.

Through the pushing crowd, Katie saw two more men going in the opposite direction. They were old men riding horses. Even though Katie did not recognize these men, she cried out, "Help me! Help me!" Katie cried out. "Help me!"

The two older men were laughing and talking, then they stopped.

"Did you hear me?" Katie tried to scream. "You did hear me," Katie shouted, wanting to feel hopeful as she tried to reach out for help. All the while, the crowd continued to push and devour her. "I'm Katie! Katie Wilkins! I want to go to the Warehouse!"

"Well, my sakes. Looky there. It's little Katie Wilkins," one of the old men said to the other.

"Who are you?" Katie called through labored breath and still reaching back for help.

"I'm John. John Wilkins from Missouri. This here's Leo Bates."

From the relentless, pushing, muffling crowd, Katie called, hoping the old men could help her, “Do you know the way to the Warehouse? Can you take me home?”.

“Well, I think we do.” John chuckled and exhaled a blue puff of smoke from his pipe. “Do you 'member the way, Leo?”

“Yep.”

“Let's mosey over an' see if we kin help this little lady.”

Katie was unsure how they did it, but the two older men crossed the chasm that separated them from Katie and the angry crowd.

“Move away! Move away, I say!” shouted Leo Bates, as the faceless crowd divided, letting him pass.

“You're not afraid?” Katie asked.

“No sir, we ain't. We done been through aplenty of hard times, and we know what to do,” replied Leo.

“Up you go.” The older man named John reached down and swooped Katie up to the back of his horse. “Come on, Biddie, we got to git this little lady home.”

Biddie nickered and blinked back at John.

“What you doin' out here, Katie?” asked Leo.

“I don't know,” replied Katie. “I'm must have wandered off. I must be lost.”

“Well, just rest yerself,” said John. “I'd say the Lord has a mighty great thing for you to do? What do you think, Leo?”

“Yep, a mighty great thing fer you to do,” agreed Leo.

As John and Leo rode on, Katie fell asleep, resting on John's back.

As they neared the Warehouse, John whispered, “Okay, Miss Katie. Do you feel safe now?”

“Yes, sir. I do,” replied a sleepy Katie.

“Head on over that'a way. That there's the way to the Warehouse,” encouraged Leo.

"Thank you, John. Thank you, Leo. I will never forget you," whispered a tired and grateful Katie.

"Off you go, Katie girl," said John. "And say hello to Daddy G for us, and tell Him John, and Leo says thanks for everythin' He done."

John and Leo moseyed off and out of sight through a cloud of blue tobacco smoke.

When Katie turned around, she thought she could see a light. "It's the Warehouse!" she thought to herself. "Daddy G!" She felt a warmth penetrate her weary body, and she fell. The tall man with the big belly and a big cowboy hat picked her up with rough hands covered with white hair and gently carried her the rest of the way home.

Beep. Beep. Beep.

As Katie regained consciousness, she heard strange beeping sounds; however, she was no longer afraid. She heard soft, sweet voices and cried, burying her face in the man's thick burly neck, crying tears of joy and great relief. From the safety of the burly man's gentle arms, Katie looked toward home. She saw Daddy G coming, running and His face reflected joy as He ran to meet her. Following Daddy G was Kevin, weeping, reaching out for Katie. Last, she saw Nana, and Katie fainted.

"Hang on, Katie. Hang on, my Katie."

It was Kevin. Nana was with him, and Daddy G was standing in the corner with His giant arms folded, not in anger, but peace.

"I thought you hated those words, Kevin," Daddy G said, trying to lighten Kevin's spirit.

"I did. Yet now those words seem natural, being for my Katie," Kevin whispered. "Hang on, my Katie. Dad is here."

The beeping of monitors in the hospital's intensive care unit was constant but soothing. However, all Kevin wanted to hear was soft in and out of Katie's breathing. He touched the head bandage that covered her stitches and kissed her forehead, and then with subdued excitement said, "She's breathing, Daddy G. She's breathing," said a relieved Kevin.

Daddy G left the intensive care unit to give the news to those friends in the emergency waiting room. Ms. Mamie clenched her fingers in earnest prayer. Mr. Kelly and Mr. Bob knelt beside their chairs and prayed and waited. Even Sweetums, sporting her new bright yellow service vest, was lying quietly next to Mr. Bob. When Daddy G came into the waiting room, Mr. Bob was the first to stand, followed by Ms. Mamie and Mr. Kelly.

"She's breathing on her own," shared Daddy G.

With that, the friends from Graceton dropped on their knees in thanksgiving. Then Daddy G went back to join Kevin in the intensive care unit.

Katie's left leg was in traction, and her right arm was in a cast. The deputy sheriff's report indicated: "While swimming, Katie was the victim of a naturally occurring springs cortex. She was pulled down into a deep, rocky hole in the river and sustained a broken leg, a fractured arm, and a concussion. The only thing that kept her breathing and saved her life was a mysterious air bubble."

When Katie opened one eye, the eye that was not swollen shut, she saw Daddy G standing in the corner of the room with his arms folded and one leg crossed over the other. He looked pleased.

"Daddy G. You came," Katie forced out through chapped lips and a raw throat. "You came for me."

"Of course, I came for you, Katie dear," Daddy G whispered, then continued. "*Someone else came, too. It's your dad.*"

"My dad?" Katie whispered quizzically through her pain. Then she saw him. "Kevin? My dad?" Katie breathed.

At that moment, the intensive care nurse came in to gently let them know their fifteen minutes was up.

Reluctantly, Kevin again kissed Katie through the thick adhesive bandages on her forehead. Then he led Nana out, holding her shoulders. Nana stopped beside Katie's bed and kissed her "baby."

"My Katie. My Baby Katie. Welcome back," whispered Nana through her tears.

As Kevin and Nana were leaving the intensive are area, Katie called, Dad. I love you.

Epilogue

Through the years, Daddy G distributed many gifts to residents of the small, insignificant town of Graceton.

To Katie, He gave the gift of wisdom and discernment. She went to college to study elementary education, and when she returned to Graceton, she received her heart's desire, a job at the Warehouse. She also received her special gift, teaching little ones. She taught Sunday School at her church, and she also started a day-care in the Warehouse.

To Mr. Bob, He gave the joy of helping Mrs. Rheinheart. Even though she died many years ago, Mr. Bob continued helping others in need with Sweetums by his side and Dog always in his heart.

To Mr. Kelly, already a loving and giving man, Daddy G continued to provide him with financial means and a loving heart.

To Ms. Mamie, He gave the gift of compassion, love, and sweet conversation. Ms. Mamie established scholarships for anyone wishing to study piano.

And, by the way, she continued to wear that ugly plastic heart-shaped locket.

To Ms. Savannah, He gave many gifts, albeit at a high cost. She received the gift of humility in receiving a new house for her family. Through receiving, she learned to give without expecting anything in return. She also received Graceton's

"Brave Mother" award for enduring the loss of her beloved William. After which, she was always ready to stand beside a grieving mother, wife, or daughter and offer her arms of love.

To Kevin? Kevin received the gifts of joy, faith, perseverance, a job at the Warehouse, a home for Nana, and a daughter. He received his daughter twice.

Although Daddy G distributed many gifts from His bounty in the Warehouse, He still has gifts for anyone who asks for them. Can you smell their fragrances? Do they smell like hope? Faith? Do they bathe you with a sense of peace? Are they your heart's desire? With so many gifts still in the Warehouse, one may be yours. All you need do is reach out and claim it and say, "Thank You, God."

> "And the peace of God, which surpasses all understanding, will guard your hearts and your minds in Christ Jesus."
>
> Philippians 4:7

To God Be The Glory

God's Gifts

There are different gifts, but the same Spirit gives His gifts.

To one, He gives the gift of wisdom; to another, He gives the gift of knowledge.

To another, He gives the gift of Faith, and to another, healing.

He gives the ability to work miracles; or to prophecy; to another the ability to judge spirits; to still another, He gives the ability to speak in different languages, and to another the ability to interpret those languages.

All these gifts are given by the same Spirit according to His will.

> As each of our bodies is one, but has many members, so we are all members of that one Body, the Body of Christ our Lord.

1 Corinthians 12:4, 8-12

TO MY READERS

If you have enjoyed this book, please leave a review on Amazon
https://www.amazon.com/Warehouse-Joyce-Crawford/dp/1733897720
Thank you
Joyce Crawford

www.ingramcontent.com/pod-product-compliance
Lightning Source LLC
Chambersburg PA
CBHW030352310726
48979CB00001B/272
* 9 7 8 1 7 3 3 8 9 7 7 0 9 *